"*Arthur, King* is an intriguing blend of history, fantasy, and intrigue, a clever intermingling of two of Britain's darkest—and finest—hours. It ties the recent and distant past together in fascinating ways—and in exciting knots! Characters both real and legendary are lively and convincing. I recommend it without reservation."

—Harry Turtledove,
author of *Prince of the North*

STRANGER FROM THE SKIES

"You must have bailed out just in time. You say your name is King. You got a first name?"

"Men call me Arthur."

"I'll bet your friends at school kidded the pants off you," the airman said, laughing. "Arthur King. Where's Merlin?"

"Have you seen him?" Arthur asked hopefully.

"Right. At least you still got a sense of humor after losing your Spitfire. Now let's see if we can hitch a ride back to the air base."

ARTHUR,

KING

Dennis Lee Anderson

HarperPrism
An Imprint of HarperPaperbacks

HarperPaperbacks   *A Division of* HarperCollins*Publishers*
                   10 East 53rd Street, New York, N.Y. 10022

Copyright © 1995 by Dennis Lee Anderson
All rights reserved. No part of this book may be used or
reproduced in any manner whatsoever without written
permission of the publisher, except in the case of brief
quotations embodied in critical articles and reviews. For
information address HarperCollins*Publishers,*
10 East 53rd Street, New York, N.Y. 10022.

Cover illustration by Joe Burleson

First HarperPrism printing: January 1995

Printed in the United States of America

HarperPrism is an imprint of HarperPaperbacks.
HarperPaperbacks, HarperPrism, and colophon are
trademarks of HarperCollins*Publishers*

❖ 10 9 8 7 6 5 4 3 2 1

Many friends helped me find the way to this tale. Foremost is my screenwriting partner, Mark Lee, whose fevered imagination is my alter ego, critic and lively muse. What a grand friend. I want to thank Hollywood's most energetic and tireless film agent Jon Klane, who encouraged telling Arthur's story as a novel and whose eye for story gleams with a gemlike fire.

I want to thank my soul of patience agent Clyde Taylor who found terrific editors like John Silbersack and Christopher Schelling. I am grateful to them, in turn, for finding Nancy Hanger, the world's most caring copy editor. My teacher, Tony Arthur, and my friends, Bob Amstrup, Tony Russell and Tom Rosquin, helped find rare Arthurian lore and Spitfire arcana. My kind, wise colleague Bill Wu gave critique and comfort.

I want to thank my beautiful, loving wife, Marie, and our wonderful children, Becky, Garrett, Michael and Grace. I wish also to thank Averill Raymond, my brave generous aunt and Phil my intrepid brother. This story was written for all of them.

Finally, this tall tale is dedicated to "The Few" who fought and won the Battle of Britain, the young men who helped save the world we inherited, the one we must all try to save, treasure and improve.

1

Jenny Hamilton and Edith Mullins pulled their nursing capes from the coatrack and elbowed their way through the sea of blue uniforms that crowded Merlin's Pub. A tipsy lieutenant from Bomber Command swayed gallantly and swung the door open for the women.

"Stay, please," the lieutenant implored, licking a trace of John Courage from his sudsy mustache and hoisting his pint glass. "Two lovely ladies like you leaving, and the night's still so young. It's a waste and a shame."

Edith gave the bombardier a playful shove and a peck on the cheek, leaving a lipstick mark. "Close the door and mind the blackout, ducks. We'll be back," she promised. The door swung shut, locking the cloud of tobacco and beer smell behind the taped and curtained windows.

A wind from the Thames blew the wooden pub sign

with the picture of Merlin on it. The chains creaked in the breeze and Jenny pulled up the collar of her navy-style cape against the chill from the mist that coated the wet streets. Jenny looked up to see a full moon rising above the river, throwing its pale light on the surface chop and illuminating the boil from the wake of a barge that chugged along under Waterloo Bridge.

"We can still get something at Holborn's before the play," she said.

Her friend patted her on the arm in familiar fashion. "Oh, Jenny, let's just go straight to the theater. A registry nurse like me wouldn't know what fork to hold. Some of us aren't doctors with titles, you know."

"Nonsense, dear. I'm famished. We'll find a cab." Jenny strode briskly along the Victoria Embankment, marching like a trooper, making Edith hurry to catch up.

No cabs appeared on the blackout-darkened causeway. "We'll do better on the Tube," Edith suggested hopefully. "Charing Cross Station is close."

The moon moved with them along the riverfront. Even with the lights of the great city shuttered by nearly a year of war, the lunar glow showered the ancient stone of London, making the embankment glisten. Shivering slightly, Jenny stuck her hands in her cape pockets and sped up. Her copper hair streamed behind her like the train of her cape.

"I want to get out of the night," she said urgently, almost in a whisper. "I hate being out in the open."

"Jenny, the night's beautiful. I do so love a full moon. So romantic."

"The lads at hospital call it the bomber's moon. They say it'll guide the Germans in."

Edith put her arm round her friend's shoulder and gave it a squeeze as she walked with her. "Jenny, the Huns haven't touched London. Maybe they'll leave us alone."

"They're going to invade us," Jenny said bleakly.

"We'd better hurry." And she walked even faster. Her ears pricked up. In the silvered distance, she heard a faint drone. First, a low hum chorused. Then the hum swelled like a huge swarm of bees droning in from the estuary. Jenny gripped Edith.

"They've come," she said. "We've got to run."

Both women looked up and saw the black wings crossing the moon. Edith stood paralyzed, like a rabbit in the road. She saw the black crosses of the Dorniers and Heinkels block out the moon. Now their engines roared, joined by the whistle of the first bombs, screaming down toward the river and the docks. The darkness suddenly turned bright with white-hot light and flame. Jenny grabbed Edith's arm, pulling her along. The street filled with the slap of running feet and the faraway groan of Civil Defense sirens.

"Come on, Edith!" Jenny cried. "We've got to get underground." Her friend only whimpered, but Jenny yanked her along, joining the crowd swelling at the entrance to the Underground.

The high explosive shook the earth and the Luftwaffe's bombers growled their way across the vast expanse of London, guided in by the light from the bomber's moon. One stray bomb blasted the block that housed Merlin's Pub, knocking the sign loose so it creaked on a single chain. The picture of Merlin hung, with the old man gripping his staff as if he were defying the strike from the sky.

The bomber fleet moved on, vanishing like a dark shadow, but promising to return with the night and the moon.

The pale moon moved, stately between the gray thunderheads. Arthur Pendragon, king of the Britons, could not move at all. The king lay in the cold mud of Cornwall, his head stunned and bloody. He commanded himself to rise, and the soldier in him tried to obey. But the elbow of his sword arm gave way and he slumped back, like an upended beetle, armored but helpless.

Gazing skyward, he watched lowering clouds sail by him like the dragon ships that raided the coast at Tintagel. The clouds lowered and whirled, a roiling curtain of black sky filled with thunder and mist. Salt spray from the seaborne storm stung Arthur's cracked lip where the blood had caked. A red spray clouded his vision. His good eye blinked. The other, deviled by the red mist, closed shut.

A low moan and the sight of a lifeless hand gripping a pike told him what he already knew in the depths of his reeling mind. The dead and dying surrounded him on the bloody plain. In great mounds, in stacks, in piles. Arms, legs, cast off gauntlets, battered helmets. Entrails, spilt brains, viscera. The stench of death invaded his nostrils, his very being.

He felt numb nothingness beneath his leather jerkin. The legs. Gone? No feeling to the toes, not even a hot stab of pain or a dull, cold ache. Above the waist, injury howled. Beneath the steel breastplate and gorget, the cracked ribs poked into his skin. Dread filled Arthur. He feared he was stove in, but alive enough to watch himself die.

The black sky lowered until he felt himself passing out into a dark vortex. The calloused fingers of his sword hand clutched and grabbed and grasped, trying to close around the haft of the dragon-hilted sword. But he remembered. Excalibur was gone. Merlin, too, had vanished in the fray. He lay wounded without defense or protector.

Excalibur, pride of the House Pendragon, the sword forged from the steely scales of a dragon that breathed fire from the earth's core. Excalibur, the claim to the kingdom. Lost. Arthur's mind wandered, dulled by pain and loss of blood. Consciousness fled him and he dreamed. Floating free above his broken body, he cried out as the storm rushed around and about and through him. He flew like a spirit and shouted "Excalibur!" into the howl of the empty wind.

Then he cried out for the old man and the darkness took him.

His bruised eyes cracked open and the dark, blooded mist was gone. Arthur's tongue explored his lip. He licked cautiously and tasted dried blood. A wind kicked up, blowing his hair beneath a dressing that wrapped his eggshell-tender skull. Still weak, he turned his head and the helmet caught his eye. Slung from the branch of the blasted ash, the helmet stared down at him in silent reproach. The sightless helm hung empty as a boneyard skull. Yet the steel dragon rampant, welded fast above the visor, appeared as unbowed as Arthur himself just before the storming of Coventry.

Still groggy, he muttered his own name. Arthur, son of Uther, the Dragon, and king of all the Britons. Father of Mordred. Now, where was Mordred? That son of a bitch. The window in the church at Coventry came to mind and the memory dropped in, unpleasant as a carrion bird.

The king's hand slapped leather, reaching for the scabbard. The sword, still gone. It wasn't a dream. Its loss was real pain. The king uttered an animallike moan of despair. A shadow fluttered over him, dark but solid. The night creature's black wings cut the edge of the wind, whistling. The shadow laughed. Then it rasped, and croaked and lighted on the helmet. The raven blinked its odd, silvered eyes at Arthur and peered at the king down the length of its probing beak.

The raven cocked its head, inspecting the stricken king as he might an after-dinner bug. Perched atop the steel dragon, the raven's wings rustled. It dropped to the ground and strutted in a wide circle. The king followed the bird's trail with his eyes until his neck popped and his sword arm separated at the shoulder. The king felt a great throb of pain, ground his teeth and swore.

The bird vanished behind Arthur's back. A leathery old man with oddly metallic eyes stood next to the shattered branch, leaning on an ash-wood staff. His silvered head was tonsured like a priest, and he wore the leather armor of a mercenary. The ancient seated himself on the gnarled stump of the lightning-blasted tree and waited, his starlit eyes blinking, birdlike. The old man peered down at Arthur. Finally, the ancient leaned forward and tapped the dressing on Arthur's forehead with a talon-shaped fingernail.

"The lizard's poultice worked," he remarked. "You look more a lizard than a dragon at the moment. Where is the book?"

"Where is Mordred?"

The ancient shook his head. Carefully, he gripped Arthur's leg, straightening it from the knee until the king yelped. The ancient let go and Arthur could move his legs.

"You'll walk. And the poultice will soothe the head wound. Before you can say 'Bob's your uncle,' it'll heal smooth as a virgin's bottom."

"Who is Bob?" the king demanded. "I have no such uncle."

"You kings take everything so literal," the ancient said. "Just an expression. You've no Uncle Bob, so far as I know. And I know most of it."

"Then tell me where my men are gone to, Merlin. My troops, my knights. And where am I?"

"What's the word we like, from kings and commoners?"

"Please, Merlin."

"Just so. You're in the cradle of Stonehenge, two days ride from court. My home, or what's left of it."

The shadow fell suddenly across Arthur's dragon-crested breastplate, then swept across his face. Like a series of church windows opening round him, the fading light of day's end flowed in, through and around him. The play of interlocking light and shadow turned round him like a miller's wheel.

Merlin drew a dagger and raised it to the dropping sun, so that it flashed like his eyes. "Stonehenge, Arthur, is where I hold court." The old man pointed to the stone menhirs rising in somber grace. "These stones are a few old things I brought from across the sea."

"Bloody hell," Arthur swore. "This is the druid's lair."

"How many druids have you known to curse them so quickly?" the ancient snapped. "The druids were my teachers and my kinsmen."

"I never knew it."

The ancient smiled gently. "The things you don't know still would fill a History of the Kings of Britain, Arthur Pendragon."

The sun dropped from sight behind the crags that made the storied wheel of Stonehenge. The wounded warrior king lay in the center at the hub.

"My men, Merlin."

"Gone like the green leaves of summer. Like a door. Like your vanished queen. You are alone now, Arthur, with the wolves circling."

"My men abandoned their king? How could they? It's treason."

Merlin leaned forward and his strange eyes flashed. He reached forward. For the first time, Arthur saw a blue druid's spot painted on Merlin's forehead. A drop of red lay in the center of the spot so it formed a circle within a circle. With the talon fingernail, Merlin tapped Arthur's forehead.

"We're living in treacherous times, my king. You tell me where they went. You already know. It's all in your mind."

The king groaned, and then let the world unfold beneath his eyelids. Even with his eyes closed, he knew the ancient could see his thoughts and read his soul. For Merlin, the king's memory was as open to him as the wizard's own sacred book.

Arthur remembered. To his practiced warrior's eye, the victory at Coventry seemed assured. The town surrounding the sacred chapel yielded easily, with the common folk scattering and the rebels giving ground. Mordred's faithless knights had fled, leaving him only the rump guard of Hun mercenaries. They would fight to save their skins, but no siege would be necessary to bring down the rebellion. There were too few of the enemy.

Ram and catapult rolled through the outer gate of the outpost, pushed by a determined legion of Arthur's followers. When the king's outriders reached the chapel, a shadow swept the field. Ill omens appeared. The hanged man, swinging from his heels with his viscera and eyes plucked out. The black crows circled aimlessly. Arthur's men looked to him anxiously. The king felt black rage and hot blood rising to his face.

Mordred was in the chapel that dominated the town that rose from the old Roman stones. "Break the door," Arthur ordered, and it was done.

The king's men streamed into the nave. The enemy's horned helmets could be seen lurking in the chapel between the half-built columns, with Huns hiding behind rows of sharpened stakes.

Arthur's men vaulted the stakes and fell on the Huns. Short and bloody work was done on the chapel stones. Arthur moved among the fighting and the dying, swinging the two-handed Excalibur like a scythe. Mordred's minions sold their lives dearly. The Huns fought with characteristic savagery. The Britons hated the yellow-haired invaders from across the sea. Too many Camelot men lost wives and kin to the raiders, killed outright or held in slavery. Arthur's legions hacked away as if they were killing plague dogs.

The Camelot men fought their way, hand-to-hand, deeper into the half-built sanctuary. King Arthur's sacred chapel rang with the song of the blade. But the sight that greeted the attackers was worse than the carnage of combat. In the nave, a goat lay disemboweled. The beast's blood formed a dripping five-pointed star, painted crudely on the stones laid out before the sacristy.

"Desecration!" Gawain the green knight shouted. "Find the king!"

The page Malory ran and searched out the arm that held Excalibur's flashing blade. "King Arthur!" the youth cried. "We've found Mordred's sign! The mark of the beast! Come see."

Arthur lumbered through the crush of fighters like a natural force, as if his swinging blade were a great wave spilling onto the shore, scattering streamers of bloody foam before him. The king halted only to stare at the bloody, inverted star. He looked up to see the iron-hinged doors that blocked the entry to the tower.

"Bring in the ram," he ordered calmly. The innards of the chapel fell quiet, a sudden calm broken only by the moans of the dying.

Coventry chapel's tower door was five inches thick, but the ram split the door like kindling. Arthur crossed the passageway, then fell on his hindside. His men halted and dropped the ram, transfixed by what they saw in the base of the tower. Arthur tried to pick himself up, and he slipped again, for the blood ran like quicksilver in a puddle on the chapel stones. The king rose slowly and choked at the sight of the maiden bound and spread upon the altar of straw. She lay burst like a half-bloomed rose, her sightless eyes filled with unspeakable horror.

Arthur searched the darkness recoiling up into the stone spiral of the tower stairs. The red eyes blinked at him from the shadows. Mordred grinned and spoke, his words rasping in his throat, raw from the taste of blood.

"Don't begrudge me, Father," the man in the dark said. "She was the only virgin in Britain, so far as I could tell."

"Mordred!" Arthur shouted. The king tossed his helmet aside to see better into the shadowed tower. Mordred balanced against the railing, near the top of the steps that led up to the rose window. His cloak rustled, and an alabaster hand flashed in the darkness. The red eyes blinked pitilessly.

"The girl amused me, Father. So did you, when you slipped on your arse, sliding about on my pretty one's juices. You can be so clumsy."

"Cover the maiden!" Arthur ordered as he rushed up the tower steps. "Yield, Mordred, and repent the foul thing you've become."

"I am what I am," Mordred rejoined. "Better than a hypocrite."

The long blade of Excalibur swept ahead of the climbing king. Mordred's black gauntlet shot out from the shadow. Mordred met Arthur's steel blade with an iron torch. The metal clashed and the flames singed Arthur's beard. The king slapped down the flames and gritted his teeth against the pain.

"How's the old queen, Arthur?" Mordred asked, his tone solicitous as he tried to poke the king in the throat. "Weren't you married here?"

"Bastard!"

"You're the one who knows that best, Father."

The sword cut through the air, knocking the torch from Mordred's hands. The red-eyed man dropped from the shadows, onto his knees. There, in the light, his eyes transformed from the gleaming red they radiated in darkness to the pitiless green of a beautiful serpent's orb. His pale, handsome face and ruby lips radiated the beauty of an angel. He kneeled on the stone steps and clasped his hands as if in prayer. "Mercy, Father! I beg quarter."

The powerful figure of the king towered over the alabaster youth. In an instant's lapse, Arthur saw some semblance of the creature as kin. Where the father was lean and tanned by life out of doors, the boy's features were fine and his full lips pouted, concealing sharp animal-like teeth. Mordred's hair was flaxen, like the Huns. The only feature he'd taken from his mother, Morgan Le Fay, was the arresting green that made his eyes twin emeralds.

Mordred raised his hands, palms up, in entreaty, his voice pitched to a high octave, nearly that of a youth in song. "Mercy, my king. You've beaten me. I submit." He lowered his head. Tears flowed from the young man's strange eyes. "Let me live, my liege, and I'll do penance." He wrung his hands and his words held a pleasing, soothing lilt. Arthur listened, prepared to relent, then looked over his shoulder at the body in the tower.

"Penance? For that?" Arthur pointed Excalibur's blade at the splayed form of the girl. Sir Gawain had retrieved a bishop's cape and covered her. Gawain closed her still-staring eyes and looked up sadly at his king.

"You've never tried to see what good there might be in me, Father," Mordred pleaded. "Neither have I, but perhaps there's still time before I'm as old as you."

"What you've done only God can forgive, Mordred," Arthur said gravely. "But yield and I'll consider your suit for penance."

"Oh, I yield, Father. I yield."

"You've divided the kingdom, slaughtered the innocent and worshiped the unholy."

"It's my nature. Sorry."

Arthur kept his sword leveled at Mordred's chest. He surveyed the ruin below him. His men busied themselves binding the Huns, who glared at their captors from beneath their blue-painted faces. The chapel carried the odor of the slaughterhouse. Arthur glanced up at the rose window, seeking comfort in the radiance of its tracery. In the window, the hand-cut figure of the king and queen clasped hands and gazed up at a perfect rose, unfolding into bloom, the bride and groom's signet of courtly love.

"Father! Look out!"

Mordred's hand shot forward and Arthur felt a sting at the throat. As he swayed and his vision blurred, he saw the dagger that struck him like an adder. He clutched at the dragon breastplate that adorned his chest. He fell to his knees and down the steps, dropping Excalibur. The king felt the weight of the sword lift from his hand as he staggered, strength flowing from him like a burst wineskin. He smelled Mordred's breath, hot and sour. The youth whispered in the king's ear, "Tell your ancient friend I've got his book. I'll see you in hell, Father."

The king's men bolted up the steps and reached for Mordred, but grasped hold of an empty black cloak. Before he passed out, Arthur heard the window shatter and felt the shards of glass from the perfect rose flying into his face. The sound cut him to the quick, and he plunged into the abyss.

Arthur came to with a tap from Merlin's taloned finger. The mists that whirled round Stonehenge broke into patches, revealing spangles of stars. A full moon broke through the mist, showering silver light from the ancient rocks. Arthur rubbed his head. His skull ached and he felt poisoned. Merlin leaned forward, his raw, scarred knuckles grasping the strong, oaken quarterstaff he wielded in battle and magic. His silver eyes blazed with hard fire.

"The last that he said, Arthur." The ancient's voice held an unaccustomed urgency. "The book."

"He said he'd got it."

The ancient rested on his haunches and rubbed his silvered fringe. He shook his head slowly from side to side, sadly, and groaned as if he had watched treasure melt into sand. Quietly, he muttered, "He's got the book."

"Which book, old man? You have so many."

"So many, and they all matter," Merlin muttered. "But this one matters most. It carried forward my time remembered to chapter the twentieth, in the riddle of counted days and things to come."

"What things?"

"Mordred has stolen the path to the future. It's a kind of code to the future of your kingdom. Or, the end of it. When I returned from my travels, I knew that it must have been Mordred rummaging in my goods, if only from the foul smell in the cavern."

"Then he's taken two things dear between us. My blade, and your book."

"More than dear, Arthur. Precious. And, in his hands, dangerous to all. If Mordred discerns the use of the book, he will usher in an unthinkable reign."

"I'll hunt him down, old man. But I need my men."

Merlin shook his head abruptly. "They're gone."

The king gripped the ancient's arm. "Where, old man?"

"Lost and wandering, Arthur," the ancient said. "As you were after Mordred's dagger touched your throat." The ancient sighed. "When your followers saw you stricken and disarmed, the Huns gained the day."

Arthur reached for the empty scabbard. "What are we to do?"

"Reclaim the kingdom, Arthur, if it can be done. It's more difficult to put something back together than it is to break it apart."

"Mordred's got the sword," Arthur muttered. "How could that be?"

"Probably thought it was his to begin with. Usurpers feel a strong sense of entitlement, as do unloved children."

The wounded king winced, hating to be reminded of his blood tie to Mordred. He tried to shift and each move brought him pain. "Where is he?"

"Somewhere far, and yet near, and still in the company of Huns. Chapter the twentieth charted the furthest distance of my travels, and opened Britain to its darkest hour. The kingdom stands alone, with the enemy at the gate."

"You're speaking beyond me, old man."

Merlin nodded. "It's the curse of my second sight, to see and sometimes speak beyond my fellows." He tugged at the stubble of his salt-and-pepper beard. "Could you fight on without Excalibur, I wonder?"

"What choice have I?"

"There are always choices," Merlin mused. He pursed his lips and stared at the ground. "You could return to your humble origin. Where your father hid you as a stableboy. Mordred might let you live out your days, if you hide."

"The king of the Britons does not hide."

"Then it's win, or die."

"Life has been ever so, for me."

"But to prevail, you must face Mordred. Unlike your changling son, you will be unaided by magic. I will not be there for you. To move through the window of the ages is as for a dragon to pass through the eye of a needle. You are a mortal. Your son is half a witch."

"Yes, I remember," Arthur said bitterly. "A night's dalliance and I pay for it forever!"

"Mordred has powers of enchantment. He has the blade, and the book. Armed with such instruments, he could lay Britain at his feet, or leave it in ruins."

"Merlin. I must try to stop him."

"You are wounded and weak."

"What would you suggest then, old man? Surrender?"

Merlin straightened himself one joint at a time. He hefted the stick. It was oak, sturdy and plain. No one would have seen it as other than a walking staff with an ornate half-moon burned into the wood near the knob.

"Mordred's gone to a place of evil. A war zone, they call it. You would find the place strange. The soldiers there wouldn't recognize you, or obey you. You'd be just another serving officer for a distant king."

"I was born in battle. I can fight anywhere, Merlin."

"True enough, my liege," Merlin said, nodding. "But the weapons they wield there would be unknown to you. Perhaps beyond your reckoning. Still, a keen wit is always the best weapon. I think it's a good thing I taught you to read."

"What good will reading do me in battle?"

"You'll see. I can help you only a little. My most potent spell runs the span of three moons. The conjure of it will tire me greatly. In that cycle of time and tide, you must complete your quest. The poison Mordred touched you with is slow, but deadly. You must find Mordred, or lose your mortal life."

Arthur's sword hand reached for his throat. He felt the fleshy part where Mordred's dagger struck. It throbbed with a dull pain. Merlin gazed at the sky and watched the clouds cover the moon. It passed out of sight and a meteor flashed its trail beyond Diana the huntress. The ancient proferred the stick to Arthur. The king reached for it.

"Take this, Arthur Pendragon. May it serve you as well as the sword you seek. And remember, you must find the book. Only in that way can the page be turned back and Camelot reclaimed."

In his weakened state, Arthur felt a surge of healing warmth flow into him. The king rose, holding the staff for balance and gaining his feet as the mists of Stonehenge enshrouded him. He stepped forward, moving sightlessly in the fog.

2

The mist broke and Merlin's stick rose up from the floor of the steel box that imprisoned the king. Arthur let go of the stick as if it were a serpent. His feet pumped a pair of pedals, not unlike those from the weaver's trade, and the steel box plunged like hot lead from a battlement.

A roar like the Abyssinian lion growled in Arthur's ears. He felt mad terror as the steel box plummeted straight down toward the green earth and the granite wheel of Stonehenge. He saw strange wheels shaped like sundials whirling before his fingertips. It was devil's machinery. He heard the wind howl, and the metal shriek, and he felt his guts rise up to his throat.

Arthur banged his fists at the blue sky that surrounded him from his shoulders up. He found himself trapped in a hard, crystal bubble the shape of Merlin's prophecy ball. The king tried to tear free, finding himself bound to the box by dungeon restraints. "Sorcery! Madness!"

The king grabbed the stick, and his steel cage soared. He looked through the crystal, seeing a snout protrude from the bubble. It was a flying ship, a winged war canoe. The canoe had wings, with red-and-blue druid's spots marking the tips. The green earth vanished and Arthur's bubble burst through a white cotton mass of cloud into brilliant sunshine, pressing the king hard into the chair that bound him. His head felt as if it were weighted with stones, but he'd never seen a sight so beautiful as the hard, blue sky that expanded endlessly above him.

Suddenly, the roaring ceased, and Arthur heard only the howl of the empty wind. The blood rushed from his head and he felt his skin pressed hard against his face, his shoulders and legs heavy. He held the stick and it pulled back and the cage tumbled backward. He plummeted, twisting. He became dizzy and banged his fists against the enchanted bubble. He grabbed a lever. It didn't move. He pushed it and the thousand-headed lion sputtered, then roared to life again.

Arthur found himself flying upside down in a corridor of blue tunnel that hurtled by him. "Merlin! Merlin! Please get me out of this!"

Arthur grabbed another handle and the bubble dropped away from the cage. The king fell from the steel canoe into an empty, frozen sky. He howled like a blue-painted Pict as he fell free from the demon machine that shuddered and swooped away from him like a dragon speared in flight.

Arthur yanked at the straps and belts. He tumbled, legs over head and spun through the freezing wind. Falling, he felt a steel ring hitting his face. He sailed over onto his back and reached for the ring and pulled.

His shoulders jerked and he stretched like a dungeon wretch on the rack. He heard a great snapping, like battle standards whipping in the wind. Arthur looked up and found himself dangling under a great, white silken cloud.

"Gods and devils," the king shouted. His jittery laughter echoed inside the strange leather helmet strapped to his chin.

The harness that suspended Arthur rose up from his shoulders in dozens of strings, tight as a lyre's. He drifted in the wind. The floating sensation was pleasant. The breeze caressed Arthur's windburnt face.

The parachute canopy twisted slightly. Arthur craned his neck to see everything he could, remembering the time Merlin made him a hawk. Frightened as he was by the unnatural circumstance, Arthur loved the white cloud's drifting flight. The king twisted under the harp strings to try and see all the green world below him. He gloried to find himself blown like a dandelion. He floated past a stately puff of cumulus cloud.

As he dangled, he heard a dragonfly buzz in the distance. The buzzing grew in intensity, until it droned and filled his ears and made them hurt. Two dragon machines burst out of the clouds. They roared by, inside of longbow range. Their snouts spit fire and chattered unnervingly.

One beast bore the druid's mark on its hind quarters. The other one displayed a black cross on each of its stubby wings. A long snap of the dragon's fire darted from its snout and the roaring druid beast burst into a ball of flame. Arthur choked down his fear. The orange blast scorched Arthur's face and buffeted him, swinging him like a pendulum. He inhaled the odor of burning hair and flesh. He batted at his fire-scorched beard and shrieked.

The heat singed his hands and he looked down to see the earth rushing up at his feet with the speed of a boar.

3

The biggest man in the Third Reich after Hitler rose up heavily from beneath his silk sheets in his personal railroad car. Reichsmarshall Hermann Goering patted slumber from the pouches of his dreamy eyes. The Iron Man then reached for the coffee on the silver tray. Next, Goering grabbed the bottle of paracodeine pills to calm his pink, quivering hands. He chomped a couple of pills, the first of forty for the day. Today was Adler Tag. Eagle Day. August 13, 1940. Prelude to Operation Sea Lion, the planned invasion of Britain.

The armored train Goering dubbed Asia carried him from Occupied Paris to his bomber squadrons in the splendor afforded a Manchu prince. It chugged to a stop near the coast at Pas de Calais. Mobile eighty-eight millimeter flak guns formed an iron ring around the train and paratroopers of the Hermann Goering division stood steely-eyed guard. Goering's paratroops sported broken noses, jagged scars and rugged chins that jutted beneath bullet-shaped helmets.

Robert the valet draped a wine-colored robe on his chief and shaved the Alte with a straight razor. He powdered Goering's baby-smooth face so one could barely see the purpled veins that burst like rouge on the Alte's cheeks. Robert poured more coffee and served strawberries, Black Forest cake, eggs Florentine, potatoes from Poland, ham from Denmark and cheese from Holland. Fresh bread from the French countryside. Now that Goering had devoured the Continent for breakfast, he prepared to gobble up the English.

After breakfast, the valet helped Goering fasten the dozen gold buttons of the sky blue tunic and hooked the silver, braided belt. The crowning touch hung from Goering's ample chin, the enameled cross of the Blue Max, the German Empire's highest decoration. The valet lowered the bulletproof window of Goering's coach and the chief leaned out to inhale the salt air.

Goering could see the Channel beyond the hedgerows. Its gray churning whipped in a stiff wind. Mist shrouded the English coast, then thinned, revealing Dover's cliffs, white as fresh bread.

"Today," he said. He turned and smiled. "Consider, Robert, what it is like to possess virtually everything that you see. Can you imagine that?"

"Imagination on such scale eludes me, Herr Reichsmarshall."

"So," Goering said, chuckling. "If I presented you Churchill's frock coat for a trophy, you'd examine the crease to see if it needed a press."

"My honor is in service," Robert replied, inclining his gray cropped head. Robert handed his chief the jewel-encrusted baton that signaled Goering's rank.

"Your service is honor itself, Robert," Goering said. "If my young eagles serve half so well as you, we will win this unfortunate war."

"Unfortunate, Herr Reichsmarshall?"

"Who wants to humiliate the English? They are good people, the Anglo-Saxons. Very Aryan. Bad leadership is their curse. Their drunkard king."

"King George, a drunkard?"

"He's no king. Just a tailor's dummy. It's that drunkard Churchill. He wants to be king, or führer. Get rid of that ambitious old fool and we'll have a new order. Glorious peace, guaranteed by my eagles. A steel roof over the Continent."

"Peace is a fine thing, Herr Reichsmarshall."

"We Germans are done asking for it. If Churchill's hardheads don't give us peace, we will take it. We will beat it into them with the mailed fist of my Luftwaffe."

"Then they should be reasonable."

"They will be, or they will be crushed."

A group of blue-liveried Luftwaffe officers gathered at the railroad car. Eagles carrying swastikas in their talons adorned the officers' fashionable peaked caps. Young, blond and superior in bearing, the Luftwaffe men flocked to Goering, his knights of the new order. Goering stepped from the rail car, regal as a caesar, accepting their salutes with a wave of his jeweled baton.

Within minutes, the caravan of Luftwaffe staff cars rolled up to the windy, sugared sweep of beach that hugged the Channel coast. The blue knights slammed the steel doors of their vehicles and tumbled onto the sand, slapping each other like schoolboys on holiday. Together, they gazed across the twenty miles of gray sea that separated them from England. The young men smiled, sure the Luftwaffe would deliver the victory. All smiled except for two.

The pessimists were Adolf Galland, commanding general of fighters for Luftflotte Three, and General Anton Kleist who commanded the bombers for Three

Group, the Germans' largest air fleet poised to attack the British.

Both fliers wore leather jackets, black boots and the cold scowls of realists. Galland, with his Clark Gable mustache and Knight's Cross, could have been a film star and was the darling of the Reich's maidens, but Hitler said he looked too much like a Jew.

Kleist was pure Aryan, but a gauntness in his face and a hollowing behind his pale blue eyes suggested he felt more haunted than haughty. Like Galland, he had ridden to victory in Spain with the Condor Legion. Kleist and Galland remained the only flying generals who dared give Goering unpleasant news. Galland tossed his cigar and crushed it in the sand with his heel as Goering stepped delicately onto the beach from the Duesenberg coach.

"He looks like a Renaissance prince," Galland observed sourly. "Or the Faery Queen."

"Men vanish for saying such things," Kleist said. "The SS is everywhere. The black knights."

"I won't vanish," Galland replied carelessly. "I'm going to be killed in the air. Until then, the Third Reich needs me."

Goering, all medals and flashing jewelry, approached the pair and smiled with narcotic euphoria. The baton rose and the generals saluted.

"How goes the war on my Eagle Day?" Goering demanded jovially. "How are my eagles doing?"

Galland loosened the jaunty scarf that was stuffed into his leather jacket and lit a fresh cigar. "It's too soon to declare victory, Herr Reichsmarshall."

Goering's jolly manner faded and he scowled. "What do you mean?"

"The weather is bad already today, and we are losing too many planes."

"Galland is right, Reichsmarshall," Kleist said. "We can't replace them quickly enough at this rate."

"Nonsense!" Goering turned his back on his generals and shook a handful of pills from the bottle. The men heard his teeth gnash as he ground the pills with his strong teeth. "We beat the French in six weeks. The English are outnumbered and their training is inferior."

"The English are more stubborn than the French, Reichsmarshall ," General Kleist observed. "And our fighters have to fly much farther to get at them. They have fuel only sufficient to fly for twenty minutes over Britain. Then they must return, or go down in the sea."

Goering glared. "Then they must make their minutes count! I expect nothing less than superhuman effort from my troops. The pride of the Luftwaffe is at stake. Understand?"

The generals nodded, knowing Goering's rage equaled his appetite. Goering gazed across the sweep of sandy beach to watch his other hunting hawks, the young, flaxen-haired officers who carried bombs to England. His bloodshot eyes twinkled. And he smiled. "There," he said. "Spur the lads on and wish them luck for me."

"They'll need more than luck," Galland said, drawing on his cigar and blowing a ring of smoke into the quickening breeze.

Goering's round face swelled up and his puffy eyes widened with surprise. When he spoke next, his tone was curt. "Tell me, General Galland, what will win the war, since you are the expert?"

"We could use a squadron of Spitfires."

Goering's face purpled. "Such impudence."

Galland and Kleist stared at the ground. It was Kleist who looked up first. Kleist's eyes burned like pale, blue coals. His face was tan and his skin still raw from the recent fighting in Norway. He spoke softly.

"For once, General Galland is right, Herr Reichsmarshall. Unless we commit all available forces, we could lose the Battle of Britain."

"I will not hear such treasonous talk," Goering said. "The Luftwaffe has been given everything it asked for. The best equipment. The best wines and cheeses and women. Now, I expect the piper to be paid."

The Luftwaffe chief stumped off and waved his baton carelessly at the staff officers, who followed him to his Duesenberg like a line of ducks.

"That Pied Piper has no sense of reality," Kleist said. "The window of time to defeat Britain is closing."

"It's we who will pay," Galland said grimly. "Unless we solve the fuel problems and knock out the Spitfires quickly, we will need help from the devil himself."

Anton Kleist nodded. "You may have something there, Galland. I have a young man named Major Morgan coming to see me. His cables indicate he is full of plans for a new kind of bombing offensive."

"I don't know any officer named Morgan. Was he in Spain?"

"He's been in Africa helping the Duce subdue the inhumans. Now, he wants to help me. His request for transfer was urgent."

Absently, the general traced a design in the sand with his boot. It was an inverted star. It was odd. The star-shaped symbol had invaded his subconscious in recent days. He found himself doodling the star, or tracing it in the ground. Galland looked up, hearing the drone of the Luftwaffe fleets returning.

The sky filled with the dark wings of bombers, groaning their way home from England. One was on fire. It plunged and burned in a field of hay just beyond the beach. A Messerschmitt ran short of fuel just before it reached the coast and fell into the sea. Galland stared at the Dover cliffs.

"Those cliffs look like bleached bones," he muttered. "Or grave markers."

Kleist traced the inverted pentagram with his boot again. He clapped Galland on the shoulder in a gesture of comradeship.

"Take heart, Galland. It's we who command the air, not the *verdammt* English. We are the Reich's winged warriors. We may yet prevail."

Galland chewed his cigar and grimaced. Kleist turned and marched away, whistling a tune that Galland hated, and Goering loved: "Off to Bomb England."

4

When Mordred smashed his body into the king's window at Coventry, the shards of crystal unfolded like the blooming of a giant, glassine flower. Mordred tumbled from the tower and the sun blinded him. He felt the wind rush in his ears. He blinked and saw the flashing blade of Excalibur flying toward his neck like the headman's ax. Mordred twisted to escape the freefalling blade. He turned his body facedown and shouted the incantation from Merlin's book:

"Ad inexplorata!"

Mordred felt the leather slipcase of the book slip from his cloak and he grasped for it. His hand closed on it as he gasped, watching some pages fly free. He screamed the incantation twice more and plummeted, the stones of the courtyard rushing up at him. Then he saw the sword race past him. Something told him to reach for it, his bloodied knuckles closing on the dragon-scaled hilt, and he watched his hand flash a brilliant blue. He could see the bones in each finger. The flagstones of Coventry chapel's yard melted away beneath him.

Mordred heard a noise like the ocean pounding against chalk-white cliffs. The knave fell into the bowels of the earth. The air rushed round him, and falling farther still the kaleidoscope of his memory unfolded before him.

Mordred remembered the king tossing him the shovel. The boy immediately flung it on the stable floor. He looked around, eyeing resentfully each tail that whisked on each beast's behind. The chamber smelled of oats and straw and dung. Except for the absence of fresh rushes, it smelt a good deal like court.

"What am I doing here?" the boy demanded. He rubbed at the small, star-shaped scar on his forehead. "This won't do."

"You are here because if you can't live peaceably in the castle, you will work in the stable," Arthur said, keeping his voice level.

"I didn't do anything!" the boy retorted, his emerald eyes flashing.

"You bit a lady in waiting, and she's taken ill."

"You don't care if I bit that sow," Mordred sneered. "You're angry because I called you Father."

"It is not permitted. You are not acknowledged."

"Aren't you my father?"

The king's face purpled and he tightened his grip on the dragon-scaled hilt of Excalibur. "I am your king. That's enough. Now pick up the shovel. As of now, you're the prince of spades."

Mordred stared at the shovel and the flies on the dung heap. With sly quickness he snatched a fly from the dung and held it. The creature struggled, its single free wing buzzing until the boy popped it in his mouth. The boy smiled, his white teeth somehow all too perfect, almost serpentlike.

"Perhaps I can amuse myself here after all, Daddy."

"Are you of this earth, boy?"

"You should know, Father. Did you love Lady Morgan?" The boy giggled. Handsome, almost beautiful like his mother, yet repellent. He could not open his mouth without infuriating the man who sired him. Then, as fury rose in him, the sight of Mordred's sharp, animal-like teeth would fill the king with dread.

"Pick up the shovel," Arthur said.

Mordred knelt. He picked up the shovel slowly and filled it with dung. Then he flung the spade full of dung full force at the king. Arthur was on him in an instant, in a rage, hitting him, hard, in the face and smiting his half-royal, half-bewitched bottom.

Some days later, the lady who had been bitten died. As the life fled from her gray face, the name Mordred crossed her lips.

Major Ludwig Franz Morgan woke from an uncomfortable sleep as the Junkers-52 transport buffeted through the cold drafts that swept the Italian Alps. A natural flier, he was not prone to airsickness, but the bumpy flight in the hard bucket seat of the corrugated metal transport would disorder the stomach of the hardiest fighter pilot. Still, the queasiness he felt couldn't be ascribed to flying. Ludwig Franz Morgan felt anxiety bordering on dread.

He scratched the sleep from his eyes and opened the reports from his briefcase. The information was all so dry, put down on paper. He felt far away from the sleek Macchi fighter that he flew to strafe the dark-skinned North Africans. All the subhumans that fled before the raking fire of the fascist air forces excited Morgan. But the thrill of such attacks could not be communicated in paperwork; the rush of excitement from bombing a village to dust and watching multitudes flee in terror like a mortal wave.

He tried to scribble some notes, but the aircraft hit a downdraft and his hand scrawled across the page. Compulsively, he scratched the design that had been occupying his mind. It was the star. The inverted star. Something like the runes that the SS cherished. Morgan wondered what it meant, and why it so obsessed him.

The major dozed, his lank blond hair falling across his forehead, so deeply tanned from the North African sun. He fell into deep sleep and the dream occurred again. The dream of the blood red sky and the winged man. The man with the red eyes who waited for him in the darkness of the tower. The gargoyle, the demon, approaching. Coming closer. An updraft hit the aircraft and Morgan pitched forward, waking in a sweat. He felt a hand on his shoulder and screamed.

"Major! Wake up," the buxom flight attendant said, massaging his neck and shoulders. "You were having a nightmare." She was a flaxen-haired former Lufthansa maiden, and she knew how to calm a panicky passenger. She stroked the handsome major's hair. "There, there," she soothed. "The war. It's frightening to think of sometimes, *ja*?"

Major Morgan shook like a leaf. His eyes were wild. "We've got to bomb them!" he said, gripping the young woman's arm so that it hurt. "We've got to bomb them all!"

"Who must we bomb, Major?" the flight attendant asked, stroking his trembling cheek.

"All of them! All the English. Every one."

The young woman smiled comfortingly. "They will surrender soon, Major. The Führer has promised us. Who told you we must bomb them?"

"The demon," Morgan whispered. He reached for his papers. The flight attendant's eyes widened. An inverted star was scrawled in a continuous pattern across the borders of all the major's papers.

Excalibur sailed from Mordred's hands and the vortex ceased its whirl. The ocean roar subsided and his body became buoyant, as if he were prince of the air, floating. The cold darkness transformed to mist, becoming a wet fog whose moist droplets encased Mordred's body. He looked below and saw the ocean churning. He propelled himself forward, as one swimming. The fog broke into luminous patches, and above him, he saw the yellow orb of a full moon.

The waves crashed, rolling onto the sweep of broadswept, powder white coast. Mordred's feet touched earth and he looked up to see an enormous stone fortress, with two iron tubes jutting from it like siege machinery.

"Have really I done it?" he asked himself. He bit his lip until he tasted the salt of his own blood. Real enough.

He got up and dusted the sand from his breeches. He looked down to see that his feet were encased in a pair of fine, black leather boots, much improved from the roughhewn leather the Britons used. Instead of chain mail and jerkin, he patted his arms to find them encased in snug-fitting wool. Badges that meant nothing to him decorated his tunic. Mordred gazed up at the fortress and saw a searchlight beam sweep majestically, illuminating a red flag with a twisted cross.

"A rune," he murmured. "A Hun rune." He heard a

guard shout, and he understood the challenge. Same old Huns.

Mordred heard a rustling. He saw the book lying at his feet, the leatherbound manuscript spread on wet sand that glistened from phosphorus particles left by the fleeing tide. A few pages blew loose and were carried away on the wind. A panic filled Mordred and he knelt quickly to gather the volume. He pressed the book to his breast and panted like a wild animal. "The sword!" he whispered, and cast his eyes wildly about.

He spotted the dragon-scaled hilt, with its knob of gold, gleaming dully in the moonlight, nearly the color of burnished sand. Mordred scrambled over to it. He could barely lift the hilt. The sword hefted heavily, like lead, more than a man's weight.

"It's no good to me," Mordred muttered, straining against its weight. "I do not divine its magic, yet." He panted, then promised himself, "But Mordred will learn the arts of the king's sword." He scanned the beach, searching for prying eyes. Finding none, he spotted a cave at the cliff base.

Mordred dragged the sword Excalibur into the cave and lodged it between a large stone and the cavern's wall. It sank deeply into the wet sand. "There," he grunted. "Good for now. Until I read further in the book and discern its use."

Mordred emerged from the cave, hugging the book. He strode onto the beach, intending to give the Hun fortress a wide berth until he could gain his bearings. He found a footpath leading away from the fort but winding up the cliff face. He scrambled up the rocky, moonlit path, each step as foreign to him as if he had set foot on the lunar surface.

A winged shadow, accompanied by a deafening roar, passed over him. Mordred clung, terrified, to the cliff face. Another and another passed over. It was as if they were a family of dragons returning to their aerie. He shuddered at the sight and remained hidden in the rocks until he was sure they had gone. Then, he renewed his ascent.

Major Ludwig Franz Morgan made his way nimbly along the clifftop. He had left his new quarters early, before even reporting in, because he had to see the sight he'd waited so long for. Dover at dawn, the English target. The valise he carried bristled with plans, manuals and maps. Up from two years exile as the Duce's air attache in Africa, he had much to share with his Luftwaffe comrades. Morgan was startled by the sight of another observer.

As the man approached, Morgan's heart filled with anxiety, unease and ultimately an unnameable sense of dread. The moon shimmered among the clouds and faded into the approach of coming daylight. The stranger was upon him, grinning oddly. The man could have been his twin, except for the strange star-shaped scar on his forehead, and his eyes, the curious serpentine green.

"Guten morgen, Major," Morgan said uneasily, raising his hand in salute.

Mordred's hand shot out and gripped Morgan by the throat, crushing the major's windpipe with unnatural strength. The German officer felt the power flee his legs and his knees turn to jelly. He struggled helplessly, gasped and thrashed like a fish on the gaff, until he sank lifeless to the stone that capped the bluff. As the breath of life fled his lips, Mordred kissed him.

"With your life, warrior, I gather unto myself your strength, your spirit, your knowledge," Mordred whispered over the major's fresh corpse.

He bit Morgan's tongue off and swallowed it. He wiped his lips with his fingers. Mordred tore at the major's tunic, troubling himself little with the buttons. He made his way through the pockets with the ease of an expert in pillage. He found the major's paybook and paged through it quizzically. He smiled at the major's resemblance to his own image, captured in a perfect, small picture attached next to the man's name. The issue date was 1938.

"Morgan," he muttered. "Morgan, L. F. Like mother. How thoughtful." He looked about and picked up Morgan's valise. He stuffed Merlin's volume into it. Then he tossed Morgan's body over the cliff to the waves that crashed below.

Armed with his new identity, Mordred strode confidently into the new age.

5

Winston Churchill descended into the underground control center of RAF Fighter Command at Bentley Priory. On his way down the spiral steps, he cursed the English damp. Once inside the brightly lit concrete warren, the old man cheered up. He raised two fingers in his "V" for victory signal and chomped down on his cigar, flashing a grin fit for the newsreels.

"Well, Air Chief Marshal," he said, rubbing his pink hands together, "this looks like the nerve center."

Air Chief Marshal Dowding nodded and sniffed. Dowding, a nonsmoker and vegetarian, wanted to tell the prime minister to extinguish the cigar, but thought better.

"You see before you, sir, the place where we will know victory or defeat is at hand five minutes before it occurs."

"We don't use words like defeat, Air Marshal,"

Churchill grumped. "Our faith in victory rests with your people, few as they are."

An RAF captain whose smile melted permanently to his face during a fiery cockpit escape ran up to Dowding. He preferred a flimsy.

"See to your job and don't mind me, Dowding," Churchill instructed the Fighter Command leader. "My sightseeing can wait."

Some saluted, but most wearing the sea of blue uniforms that filled the underground complex called Camelot went about their business.

The inside of Fighter Command hummed with the activity of a well-directed hive. Dowding and Churchill stood on the upper deck, looking down at the crisp-looking women who staffed the plotting board. Each WAAF with her own set of headphones and pointer waited for the call from the officers on the upper deck. The officers, in turn, waited by the telephones for the spot reports of incoming Luftwaffe formations.

The phones jangled constantly and the pointers started scraping across the plotting board that detailed the map of southern England and the Channel coast. The upper deck of Fighter Command's HQ soon reverberated with bells as the early warning calls flooded in. They came from the Observer Corps spotters who watched the coastal skies with their binoculars, and from the Chain Home radar stations whose existence remained a closely guarded secret. The WAAFs moved their pointers across the plotting boards as swiftly as croupiers, each stick representing RAF or enemy movement.

"There's a good deal more of Jerry out there than usual, sir," the rubber-faced major informed Dowding. "It looks as if there are at least five formations. More than three hundred aircraft. Heavy stuff. Heinkels and Junker Eighty-Eights."

Churchill let his cigar go dead. "Well, Dowding?"

"Chain Home tells us the Hun is sending hundreds over the Channel. They've been building up for it. They've moved their forward air fields up to Calais. It explains the calm in most sectors the past weeks."

"What's it all mean?"

"They'll hit the airfields again. Try for the munitions and fuel depots. With this many of their *fliegerkorps* airborne, they may also try for the docks in the Thames Estuary to burn the supply convoys."

The bells never ceased. Fighter Command alerted all its sectors, according to Dowding's plan. Within minutes, lads in the Hurricane and Spitfire squadrons answered their scramble bells. Engines revving, the slender planes of the Greater London Defense Area roared into the sky, emptying Eleven Group's fields at Hornchurch, East Church, Biggin Hill, Tangmere, and Middle Wallop coming in to support Ten Group in the south.

The spot reports accelerated. Bomb damage at Biggin Hill and Duxford. Runway cratered at RAF Croydon. One of the enormous radio towers of a Chain Home station set afire at Detling, but one radar tower still functioning.

The pointers moved. The chalk scraped the boards, totting up reports of enemy kills against sightings of RAF planes downed. Churchill watched, his eyes narrowing to slits. He dabbed his forehead with a handkerchief. The cigar disintegrated to a green cud caught between his grinding teeth. He lit another and a cloud of smoke drifted into Dowding's pained face. The air marshal had greater worries than his chief's cigar. Too many chalk marks reflected Hurricanes and Spitfires shot down or missing.

"The lads simply have to shoot down more than they lose," Dowding said. "If the current loss rate continues without effective replacement, Fighter Command will cease to exist within six days."

Ravenlike, Churchill croaked, "After that, we can only expect that landings will be imminent on the coast and from the sky."

"Just so. The mathematics of invasion."

Churchill cleared his throat. "I've charged Lord Beaverbrook with aircraft production. We'll take it up with him. You'll get your planes, Dowding."

"If Britain is to remain in the war, I must."

The pointers moving rapidly across the plotting table moved the little swastika flags toward London, indicating that Goering had indeed finished his continental breakfast and intended to chew up England for the next course.

The silken daisy collapsed and Arthur hit the lake feet first. The fur-lined boots pulled him down like twin anchors. As the water closed over him, the king reached for lily pads that frogs leaped from in terror. As the king's body sank, water invaded his lungs. The straps and buckles of his harness might as well have been chain mail. The lake was a green shimmer of fronds and reeds and sunlight penetrating the depths.

Arthur sank like a sword anchored by a stone. He thrashed and choked and sank deeper yet until he saw the lady in the lake.

The woman floated among the reeds, moving toward the sinking king demurely as a lady at court. Arthur could see she wore nothing but a smile. Her scarlet tresses floated above her pale, pink skin. Her emerald eyes flashed and her ruby lips pouted. Her naked breasts bobbed. The king choked back his terror of the apparition. Water filled his nose, his throat and lungs, yet he did not feel himself drowning. The woman was comely, bewitching.

She held her hands out, beckoning. He felt strength flowing from his chest. She was elusive, a mer creature, but as she floated before him, she became all any drowning man could want as his last sight. With that, her bare legs scissored above him and she was swimming fast toward the light and the shadows filtered between the lilies on the surface of the lake. Arthur raised his arms and his body lifted gently from the muddy bottom. He followed the lady and, gaining strength, began to swim toward the light.

The sun flashed in the rearview mirror atop the Spitfire cockpit, blinding Bill Cooper momentarily. The flash of sunlight quickly became an attacking Messerschmitt's yellow nose, firing a 20-millimeter cannon in staccato at Cooper's tail. The radio in the cockpit crackled.

"Break right Red Two! A Hun from the sun."

"I see it! So help me, Hawley!"

"Listen, you bloody Yank," the liquid voice of Gilbert Hawley scolded. "I don't care a fig if he buggers you, but don't lose the plane."

"Thanks, pal," Cooper shouted as he tried to twist his crate away from the Hun's cannon.

His starboard wing and control surfaces shredded by 20-millimeter fire, Cooper's plane started shaking uncontrollably. The Spitfire turned over and Yank popped the cockpit bubble open. He released his harness and dropped headfirst into the wild blue nothing.

The American tumbled, his helmet and goggles flying away from him.

He jerked the ripcord and the slipstream from the canopy sucked the tears of rage from his eyelids. The chute popped, jerking Yank like a marionette in the sudden silence. Furiously, he bicycled with his legs, his eyes scanning the horizon for the Hun. He spotted the Me109. It was drawing a lazy circle, turn-ing, then quickly bearing down on Yank's canopy.

The Hun plane passed so close that the prop wash rippled Yank's cheeks. He could count the red-and-blue RAF roundels painted beneath the Messerschmitt's cof-fin-shaped cockpit. An ace. Yank tensed up in dread of being shot out from under his parachute. The plane passed by like a shark and Yank could see the face in the cockpit. The German saluted crisply and his air-plane roared away. Damned if he hadn't painted a Mickey Mouse on his tail.

Bill Cooper swung helplessly under the silk and realized he had wet his pants.

He watched the Messerschmitt become a black dot, then disappear. Cooper's breath came in short, urgent puffs. He looked around, and the sky filled with the roar of another aircraft engine. Daimler Benz. Not a Merlin. Another Hun, straight out of the sun.

Cooper watched in horror and felt as if he were out of his body, floating above it. It was as though he were watching someone else's death. The tracers pierced his canopy, setting it ablaze.

The second Hun, a twin-engine Me110 sped by, its fuselage a blur except for the black cross and a scar-let five-pointed star on the nose. Yank's canopy became a twist of flame, like a Roman candle's balls of fire on the Fourth of July back in Connecticut. Yank Cooper fell free from the melted suspension lines and passed out, never seeing the black water of the lake rushing up at him.

Arthur burst through the surface of the water, his lungs nearly exploding. He coughed and flailed and looked wildly about. Floating on the surface, he spied the sodden silk daisy that dropped him from the dragon machine. Next he saw a gloved hand shoot up from the lake. His feet freed from the heavy flight boots, the king began swimming in ragged strokes toward the hand. Arthur crawled onto the muddy bank, pulling the half-drowned man along with him like a fisherman hauling a net. Exhausted, Arthur pulled the man into the reeds that lined the shore.

"You're a heavy bastard," the king said, panting.

An emblem on the young man's sodden tunic caught Arthur's eye: embroidered silver wings with the letters "RAF" woven beneath a crown. The king patted his own drenched jacket, realizing he too wore the same winged crest. He loosened the young knight's scarf and opened the youth's eye with thumb and forefinger to look for signs of life. The youth spewed a full flagon of pond water into his face.

Bill Cooper coughed water from his lungs until he choked, then he coughed some more. Arthur slapped the youth and grabbed him by the lapels of the drenched blue jacket.

"Do that again and I'll knock you down," Cooper gasped as he shook water from his close-cropped brown curls. With an effort, he pushed himself up to a sitting position.

"What place is this?" Arthur repeated, giving the drenched man a fresh shake.

The flier grabbed the lapels of Arthur's tunic. He leaned up close into Arthur's face. "Hauling a guy out of the drink doesn't give you the right to slap him," Cooper said. He pushed Arthur back. "Gimme some air."

Arthur let go of his companion and looked up at the sun streaming through the leaves of a large, gnarled oak. A raven sat atop a twisted branch. It peered down at the king and its oddly metallic eyes blinked at him.

"Merlin? I'm lost."

"You're northwest of London, chum," the American said. "Unless we drowned in that duck pond and the sky gods are having a laugh on us."

Arthur tried to stand. His legs buckled and he sat against the stone. He looked up at the raven in the tree. The raven's wings flapped by Arthur's head and the bird soared away. Arthur looked down at his companion, then noticed the blood soaked into the blue material of the pants leg above his own knee. He sat back heavily, fumbling with buttons and zipper, confounded by both. He finally gave up.

"You must've caught some shrapnel, or cockpit trash," Cooper observed. "Let me have a look at it." Yank ran his fingers over the area of Arthur's leg where the blood stained his trousers. "You'll live, but it needs tending. The pants are goners, though."

Arthur leaned painfully against the rock and saw the oaken staff with the silver half-moon burned in the grip floating in the reeds. He plucked it from the water and felt stronger the instant his hand closed on it. He leaned on it, rose and tested the leg.

"I can walk," he said. "This is Britain, then?"

"Somerset," Cooper said, nodding. "But it's a long walk home."

"Surely."

"Fighter Command probably knows our approximate position. Gimme a hand."

Arthur leaned against the staff and extended his free hand. Cooper pulled himself up painfully, one joint at a time. Like Arthur, he was well knit and sturdy, neither tall nor short. He had a boy's ruddy cheeks and short hair that crinkled like one of the king's hunting terriers. In age and grace, he looked as if he stood on the brink of advancing from squire to knight. He took a few bandy-legged steps and stretched his arms wide to test for breaks.

"They'll probably have someone lookin' for us. Say, what's your name, brother?"

"King," Arthur murmured. "King."

Cooper pumped the sovereign's hand. "Well, King, thanks for pullin' me from the drink. You got a first name? Some of you limeys got two first names."

"Men call me Arthur."

"What do women call you?" Cooper said, laughing. "I bet your friends at school kidded the pants off you. Arthur King. Where's Merlin?"

"Have you seen him?" Arthur asked hopefully.

"Right. At least you got a sense of humor after losin' your ship."

Arthur looked off in the distance, then turned his gaze back to Yank. "Tell me, what's your name, sir?"

"Forget the sir stuff. I'm American as apple pie. Name's Bill Cooper, but all your lot calls me the Yank."

"Where do you hail from, Yank?"

"Connecticut, chum. The new world."

"I don't know the new world, or any Connecticut chum."

"Feels like I've been fightin' the Huns long enough, I hardly recall it myself."

"The Huns? Have you seen Mordred? Is he with them?"

"Jeez, King. I don't know any by name, except for Hitler, and Goering maybe. It's not all that personal. We're RAF. They're the Huns, and we kill each other. You know the score."

Yank looked up at the sun dropping beneath the tree. The long shadow of afternoon descended. He scanned the skies for planes, and seeing none, he walked a few more feet, climbing to the top of a copse where he could see into the oat-colored fields that lay beyond the lake and the stand of oaks.

"Wait a moment," the American said. "Look. Over there. That must be your plane. Mine got blown to hell."

"That's too bad," the king said quietly.

"You bailed out too, right? I mean you weren't just swimming in the lake for your health, were you?"

"I was in the lake. And now, I'm on the ground."

"Right. You catch on quick," Cooper said. "You must be pretty banged up. Maybe the crash shook a few marbles loose. C'mon. Let's go have a look at your machine."

Arthur leaned on Merlin's staff. It felt right in his hand. Like a sturdy walking stick. King Arthur hobbled after Yank. Arthur's Spitfire had skidded in on its belly. One wing was torn free and rested a dozen yards away from the fuselage. The propeller blades had snapped, but the fuselage was largely intact. It was, Arthur noted, about the size of a dragon. A small one.

"This was my machine," Arthur said slowly. "I recognize it."

The American climbed up onto the crumpled wing and peered into the cockpit. "Any landing you walk away from is a good one."

"Yes."

Cooper climbed down off the wing. He ran his hand, almost lovingly, along the fuselage, then gave the wreckage a pained grimace. "Just so much more scrap iron. The old man's gonna kill me soon's he finds out I lost another Spitfire."

Yank sat down on the wing and studied the palms of his hands. They were raw and red, calloused and covered with the scars of endless hours spent on engines. His hands carried the small marks and smooth spots of burns from the welder's torch and pinches from the wrench. Yank Cooper sighed and fished a pack of Lucky Strikes from his pocket. He examined the sodden pack and pitched it in frustration.

Arthur peered at the pack and shook his head. "Lucky Strikes," he murmured. "Look, Yank, if this old man tries to kill you, I'll defend you," Arthur said softly. "Many men lose their steeds in combat. It's no shame."

"That's decent, Lieutenant King. But I've gotta be able to fight my own battles in the squadron. And up there," he said, jerking his thumb toward the sky, "I just haven't been winning many lately."

"I sympathize."

"What squadron are you from, chum?"

"I beg your pardon?"

"What's your outfit? Your group?"

"My group is a long way from here," Arthur said. "I'm afraid for the moment they're lost."

"I get it." The flier got up and walked the length of the fuselage. Behind the red-and-blue RAF roundel, he carefully examined the numbers and letters. He moved his lips as he read. He slapped his hand to his forehead and turned away.

"Sorry, King."

"What is it?"

"You came from 601 Squadron. Eastchurch."

"Yes, that must be right."

"Well, they got wiped out this morning, almost down to a man. The Huns flew in with 109s and 110s dropping incendiaries and iron bombs. They strafed the field. Burned it. Caught everyone napping. You may be all that's left."

"All that's left of my group? Are we nothing more than numbers?"

"I know how you feel. Sherman was right. War is hell."

"What was his group?"

"He fought with my grandfather in the Civil War. Burned Atlanta and a path to the sea."

"He must have been very fierce."

"He was. We could use him now against the Hun. Hell, we could use Joe Louis. We need all the bloody fighters we can get, way this war's going."

"The war goes badly, then?"

"You ought to know. You need a new Spitfire, too. We better start back to my squadron, seeing as yours is out of commission."

Arthur heard the rush of wings. The raven dived, took wing and flew away. It was near dusk and Arthur heard an unearthly trumpet that sounded like a jester's horn. Yank began waving furiously and running down the little hill toward the road. A lorry with a Whitbread Ale sign painted on its side rumbled down the road.

"That's our transport," Yank shouted. "C'mon, King. We may not have our Spitfires, but we'll ride to the Royal Air Force in style."

"Royal Air Force," Arthur murmured, hobbling after the American. The lorry rumbled to a stop and Arthur eyed it as suspiciously as if it were a griffin. The driver, an apple-cheeked man with a nose cold, gave the pair a salute.

"'Ello guvs," the driver said, blowing his nose and snorting, as if he had sampled his wares. "P'raps you gallants can direct me. Winston tore down all the road signs to confuse the Hun, and all he did was end up confusing old Harry."

Yank hoisted Arthur up into the half-open cab. "I guess we're all lost, Harry," the American said. Arthur looked at everything, the steering wheel, the gear shift and the gauges with their needles and incomprehensible marks. It was like the inside of the dragon machine, approximately.

"Got anything to drink?" Arthur asked. "I've never been more thirsty."

"That's the spirit," Harry said, proffering a flask. Yank took a nip and winced. Arthur accepted the flask and took a long pull. He smacked his lips and the driver engaged gears. As dusk fell, the lorry rumbled generally in the direction of London and the airfield at RAF Hornchurch.

Chief Air Marshal Dowding maintained a small office at Bentley Priory that was as Spartan as his own habits. He neither drank nor smoked, earning him the nickname "Stuffy." The room deep inside Fighter Command owned only a few sticks of government furniture, a few worn maps and Beaverbrook's vital production charts from the aircraft factories that speckled the industrial Midlands from Birmingham to Coventry. Though the air marshal was not jolly, still he possessed a lean majesty. His blue RAF uniform hung from his gaunt frame and his blue eyes brimmed with the sad knowledge of all the young men he had sent to flaming deaths.

Over his half-specs, Churchill looked up from the production charts on Dowding's desk. Failing to find ashtray or spitoon, Churchill tapped the long Havana untidily on the linoleum. Dowding sighed. The prime minister looked up from the mass of paper. The man who led England was half Buddha, half bull terrier concealed behind a cloud of mysterious yellow smoke.

"Well, Dowding. Who won the day?"

"We are scraping by, sir. Barely."

"What's the future percentage?"

"We know the Jerry barges are traveling all the way down the Rhine to embarkation points on the Channel coast. Some ciphers indicate they would mount Operation Sea Lion by September, if they have air superiority."

"What do Beaverbrook's charts tell you?"

"The factories are working round the clock, but we are losing trained pilots faster than we can replace them. If Goering keeps hitting the airfields, we shall be in a bad way."

Churchill examined the Strength and Staffing Memo. Nearly seven hundred planes, Hurricanes and Spitfires, on ready status. As for crew, five hundred and forty-five pilots. The odds remained about three to one.

"If we'd started our buildup a year earlier, we shouldn't be facing this mess," Churchill grumbled. "It was a lonely time. Few listened. But you know that," Churchill said, grinning. "You're a gadfly yourself, Stuffy."

"Just persistent, sir." The air marshal grimaced at the nickname.

"If you hadn't told me to hold back the squadrons from France, we should have squandered them before Dunkirk. You were right and I was wrong."

"France was the preliminary, sir. We're in the main event, RAF versus Luftwaffe."

"It's up to your lads, Stuffy. Herr Hitler wants a new dark age. I mean to deny him."

Suddenly, the prime minister's shoulders sagged. The bull terrier left him. His jowls hung and he looked old. "Think of the children, Dowding. In Poland. Czechoslovakia. In France and the Low Countries. Think of our own children, huddling beneath the bombs in the Underground."

"We shall do our best."

Churchill gave the charts a last look. He sighed and blew a puff of stale-smelling smoke. "God save England. God save the world."

The air chief marshal held the door for the prime minister and followed him up the iron stairs that led to the surface and transit back to Government Quarters in London. They mounted the stairs slowly, as if each bore a great weight.

Arthur and Yank climbed down from Harry's truck a bit unsteadily. As they motored the back roads of Essex searching for a road sign that hadn't been torn down to confuse Nazi paratroopers, the trio toasted Churchill, good King George, the RAF and all Yanks. Arthur quickly comprehended that the Yanks knew nothing of cricket. Neither did Arthur, but he listened to Harry's minute explanation of the game with polite interest.

The king regretted the journey's end and leaving the good Harry. Arthur looked at the barbed wire fence that surrounded RAF Hornchurch. There was that druid's mark again, painted on the sign above the gate. The fence was strange to Arthur. As a siege-work, it didn't look as though it would hold against even the smallest battering ram. Arrows would pass through. Still, it wouldn't do the horses any good.

"Good luck, lads," Harry said, offering his hand. "You keep the Hun at bay and pray I find me way to London before the keg runs dry."

"Maybe you ought to take a nap, Harry," Yank suggested.

"Bollocks," Harry declared. "I've many a mile to go before my day is done. Be sure to save the country for God, Harry and England." With that he mashed the gears and weaved down the country lane, honking in salute.

"Excellent fellow," Arthur remarked.

"A swell guy," Yank agreed.

The HQ office for Dragon Squadron at RAF Hornchurch was little more than a tarpaper shack with windows cut from it like a child's drawing. Like most of Air Marshal Dowding's newly formed squadrons, Dragon operated from cramped quarters erected hastily on grass fields. Flight Leader Gilbert Hawley totted up the day's score with a soft pencil.

"Balls," he muttered. Lieutenant Hawley detested paperwork, but Squadron Leader Richardson made it clear that not a drop would cross the lips of any flight leader before the report was done.

Hawley glared at Tommy Stubbs, the other flight leader. Stubbs, who resembled a beer barrel with a mustache, pitched darts at a photo of Hitler. It irritated Hawley that Stubbs, a reservist, could get his paperwork done so quickly. "Bull's-eye," Stubbs said jubilantly.

"Hang it, Tommy! Will you cease your nattering?" Hawley snarled. "I can't get any bloody work done while you're having fun."

"I'm owed a bit of fun, Hawley," Stubbs said, flinging a dart dead center in the Führer's toothbrush mustache. "I'm releasing tension."

"Well, I'm bloody tense. I just want to be done with this bleeding report so I can get a decent drink."

"Let me help," Stubbs said cheerfully, tugging at the drooping mustache that he wore in the style of the Bomber Command chaps. Stubbs pulled up a chair next to Hawley.

"Bloody forms," Hawley swore, pushing the paper stack away with his slender hands. Tommy Stubbs's hands were raw and pink. In his sausage fingers, the soft pencil fairly flew over the report, filling all the right checks and lines that indicated aircraft readiness and pilot availability, kills probable and kills confirmed.

"Didn't they teach you to write at Eton, Gil?" Stubbs asked airily.

"They kicked me out," Hawley snapped. "Failed my sums."

"Cambridge, then?"

"Got the sack there, too. Latin."

Stubbs chuckled. "How did the earl take that?"

"The less said about my father, the better. Where did you learn to write, the London Zoo?"

Stubbs grinned and waggled his mustache. "Me father's pub. The account books. Nothing fancy.

Account books organize just like an after-action report. Thought you'd have got that at Cranwell."

"We learned how to fly at Cranwell. Not like you hobbyists in the reserve. Don't forget to carry the American missing," Hawley said. He tapped a cigarette against a gold monogrammed case. "Hope they send a replacement that can tell a Spitfire from a Messerschmitt."

"Too bad about the Yank," Stubbs remarked, presenting the completed form to Hawley for his signature. The flight leader signed it with a gold pen.

"Damn the Yank," Hawley retorted. "He was knocking down more Spitfires than the Germans."

"He was a good fellow."

"He was a real swell guy," Hawley sneered, mimicking an American accent. "He just couldn't kill Huns or save himself."

"Have a care there, Hawley. He's coming through the door."

Arthur followed Yank Cooper as carefully as a blind man holding fast to a guide. Yet the king's eyes remained wide open to every new thing he saw. In the gathering dusk, the airfield at Hornchurch bore faint resemblance to military encampments. The king recognized men-at-arms who must be sentries. They carried quarterstaffs with knives poking from the end and wore helmets that looked like soup pans. In the distance, he saw the shadowy forms of Spitfires. They were being attended to by squires.

There were tents, as if the company were encamped for a tourney. There was no castle. Arthur pricked his finger on a wire fence and licked his fingertip, tasting his own blood to ensure the reality of his surroundings. A bell clanged, and Yank took him by the arm.

"C'mon. Squadron briefing."

Arthur nodded and hobbled after the Yank. They mounted crude wooden steps into a lodge tent. The bright electric bulbs made Arthur blink. He searched the tent vainly for an open flame, but found only the faces of young pilots staring at him and a stern-faced monkish man who stood behind a lectern and in front of a coat of arms, a winged dragon.

"That's Squadron Leader Richardson," Yank whispered, pushing Arthur into a folding chair at the rear of the tent. "Don't get him mad."

The Hornchurch briefing tent with its rows of wooden chairs reminded Arthur of chapel pews. Richardson's chalk scraped the board, sending shivers down Arthur's spine as he saw the date marked: AUGUST 14, 1940.

The men with the Spitfire machines called themselves Dragon Squadron. It was Arthur's symbol from the House of Pendragon. Could they know? He decided to say nothing, so they wouldn't brand him a madman or warlock. Under the heading marked "Losses," the chalk board displayed druid dots and black crosses.

"You heard Winston on the wireless, lads," Squadron Leader Richardson said. "If the British Empire should last for a thousand years, this shall be our finest hour."

"A thousand years," Arthur whispered.

The fliers groaned and swore under their breath. The anger filled the tent. "What's this?" Richardson demanded. "What's the row?"

"Row, sir?" Tommy Stubbs piped up. "It ain't a thousand years we're worried about. It's today, with the Huns cutting us down like barley hops."

"No one knows that better than me, Stubbs," Richardson replied quietly. "Every plane, every pilot is as precious as gold."

"We lost three golden planes today," Stubbs persisted. "And two pilots. It's just luck we got the Yank back."

"Well, our Yank is precious, isn't he?" Hawley said, his thin lips forming a sneer. Several pilots snickered. Arthur, sitting next to the Yank, watched Cooper's open face turn scarlet.

"That's enough," Richardson said. "Flying Officer Cooper got back to fly another day. Survival matters."

Yank glanced up at the squadron commander. Arthur had seen his expression in the faces of young knights. Afraid. Eager to please. Terrified of failure. The king knew such quality could make men carry the day in battle, or paralyze them.

"Certainly," Hawley pressed. "But will our precious Yank ever bring his plane home, or better yet, notch a Hun? I just want to be sure that so long as there are so few of us, that each man pulls his weight."

"Save it for the roundtable, Hawley," Richardson said abruptly. "We remain grateful to our American friend who has come so far to help us."

"Right," Stubbs put in. "Yank even found us a fresh pilot."

Richardson stared at Arthur in the back row. The king's sunburnt, battle-scarred face contrasted in sharp relief to the near youths who made up Dragon Squadron. Arthur appeared a wolf among cubs.

"You there," Richardson said. "What's your name?"

Arthur rose slowly and leaned on Merlin's stick. Slowly, he said, "Lieutenant Arthur King, at your service. From Eastchurch, sir."

"That's 601 Squadron. Sorry, King. Well, I don't care if you're Jack the Ripper. You can fly with us until your papers catch up."

"Papers, sir?"

"Until they get the record sorted out at Fighter Command, you're officially missing and I can use you. Want to fly with Dragon Squadron?"

"Fly?"

"You're a Spitfire pilot, aren't you?"

"I flew a Spitfire. Yes, sir."

An insistent ringing flowed into the tent from just outside the blackout curtain. Before Arthur could turn, the pilots were crowding out of the tent. Cooper was pulling his harness on. Arthur grabbed his arm.

"Alert bell, King. Come on. We've gotta run like hell."

Arthur followed Yank. The men of Dragon Squadron flowed out of the tent like yeomen answering the call of trumpets. Arthur felt a hand on his shoulder. It was Richardson. Arthur could see each bead of sweat on the balding squadron leader's pate.

"King, take the Hurricane, the last machine on the field," Richardson said. "It's not much, but it's all we've got."

"I can't fly tonight, sir," Arthur stammered. The king's legs buckled. He leaned on Merlin's staff. Richardson gave Arthur a cold stare.

"Can't fly? Or won't?"

Cooper ran up, his parachute harness buckled. "It's his leg, sir," Yank said. "He was pretty banged up."

"You're the one, Yank," Richardson scolded. "Lose my Spitfires and bring me a pilot with a game leg."

"I'll be better tomorrow, sir," Arthur said. He winced, knowing he sounded fainthearted. "I'm sure of it."

The bell's clanging was joined by the wail of sirens. The first bombs plowed into the far end of the field. The crump vibrated and cracked Arthur's eardrums. The briefing tent collapsed on top of Richardson and Arthur. Arthur pitched facedown through the blackout curtain into the mud. He looked up to see a wall of flame rolling toward him.

* * *

The twin-engine Messerschmitt Zerstörers came in fast and low at fifty feet off the deck. They arrived barely before the sergeant major could ring the bell. The roar of the twin Daimler Benz engines on the raiding planes drowned out the bell. Tracer fire from the 20-millimeter cannon and the 7.9-millimeter machine guns lit the night sky so the RAF ground crews could see the shark teeth painted on the Messerschmitt snouts. And the five-pointed stars.

Twin five-hundred pounders skipped onto the edge of the airfield, hitting the fuel trucks. A fireball erupted, turning the night a golden yellow. The fighter-bomber, buffeted by shock wave and heat, zoomed just above the cloud of exploding oil.

The lead attack plane swooped into a banking turn, wagging his wings in signal for the other three planes to follow him in. Below them, the Spitfires burned in their hangars. The Zerstörer leader dropped the plane down so low that the ground rushed by like the tunnel of time itself.

The fuel truck ignited and knocked Arthur and Yank off their feet. The fireball singed their eyebrows. The king watched a man jump from the fuel lorry and run, a column of flame propelled along by two burning legs. The air filled with the driver's screams. Ground crew tossed blankets on the man and wrestled him to the ground, rolling him over as he swallowed his tongue and died.

The flying machines roared over the king's head, so low Arthur could make out the black crosses on their gray bellies. He watched the cylinders drop, expecting splashes of flaming oil or lead. Instead, the ensuing explosion bounced the king's body like a straw doll. He was sure he would die, but the explosions mounted like thunderheads, deafening him first.

The men on the ground cried out in agony all around Arthur. Suddenly, he realized he had indeed come home and this around him must be the battle foretold by Merlin. The king looked up from the tarmac, pushed himself to his feet. Leaning on Merlin's staff he began hobbling across the burning field. He spied a small fort that bristled with a demon machine that spit fire into the night sky. It was a BREN gun. A sergeant major gave orders in the gun pit.

"Turn left thirty degrees and elevate, you silly buggers! They're coming round for the second pass. Lead them and elevate the gun, you bastards!"

The two-man crew cranked the gun as high as they could and turned. The corporal's right eye dissolved and his face turned to jelly as incendiary shreds showered the gun pit. The private screamed at the sight of his burning friend until Arthur dropped into the pit and punched him unconscious.

"Help me!" the sergeant major shouted as he pushed the incinerated corporal from the gunner's seat. "Elevate, you bastard! Elevate!"

"I don't know what you mean," Arthur cried out.

"Turn the bleeding crank, or we're dead men, sir!"

Arthur turned the crank and the sergeant major pointed the quartet of .30-caliber gun barrels at the diving enemy planes. Arthur watched the bullet strikes pocking the airfield and heard the scream of diving engines just above his head.

The BREN gun jammed. "Pull back the receiver group," the sergeant major shouted. Arthur shook his head in total befuddlement. The non-com gave the receiver group a slap with the flat of his hand. "Pull that, you sod!"

Arthur pulled the receiver until it snapped and the

gun cleared, spitting a blast of exploding tracer fire into the night sky. One plane passed low overhead and strafed the tarmac. The second got caught on the wing and hurtled into the airfield, bursting into a shower of flaming metal and burning fuel.

"Bloody hell," Arthur gasped.

"That's right, Lieutenant," the sergeant major growled. "It's bloody hell." He let fly another burst, but the fighter-bomber had zoomed out of range.

Cautiously, Arthur peeped over the rim of the sandbag pit. It was chaos on the airfield. He saw Spitfires burning brightly. A firecracker snap of the ammunition cooking off in the wreckage made the field a killing ground. Streams of water from the fire engines poured ineffectually onto the flames that consumed the tents, trucks, hangars and planes.

Squadron Leader Richardson strode onto the field, his eyes filled with tears of rage, and the king saw that command weighed heavily on the monkish man. Suddenly, the pierce of a whistle cut through the night sky. Arthur heard a by now familiar engine's roar. Only this one was much louder.

"Stuka!" the sergeant major shouted. "Dive bomber!"

Richardson looked up from the field to see bullet strikes peppering the ground around him, trapping him where he stood. In an instant, Arthur was out of the pit and hobbling toward the squadron leader. The German dive bomber's wings whistled death as it plunged toward Richardson, its wheels suspended like talons beneath its bent wings.

The squadron leader fired a Webley revolver at the Stuka, as though he were David slinging stones at Goliath. Arthur stepped between the hail of bullets. By the time he reached Richardson, the squadron leader was on his knees. Arthur moved forward stolidly, heedless of the steel rain.

"Grab hold," Arthur ordered, extending Merlin's

staff to the wounded commander. "Do it, or die, Squadron Leader."

The commander grabbed hold of the staff. Arthur, by now on his knees, dragged Richardson to a ditch. They tumbled in as the Stuka dropped its bombs and pulled up, winging away into the dark like a giant bird of prey. Arthur and Richardson were buried beneath a shower of exploding earth.

The king blinked his eyes. A bare bulb shone down on him like the sun. He closed his eyes and turned his head, seeing stars burst beneath his eyelids. He opened them again and looked around the little room. The room looked like a monk's quarters, only it was made of canvas sail material, wood and black tar. The walls were papered nearly solid with pictures of the flying machines and women in scant clothing.

The medic passed the salts under Arthur's nose again and the king shook his head. "Much better, sir," the medic said. "You'll be all right, you will. Can ye sit up?"

Yank sat a few inches away from Arthur on a steel bunk. He looked anxious. "What about it, Arthur? Ya gonna pull through?"

"Where are we?"

"Richardson gave you my wingman's bunk."

"I beg your pardon?"

"The bed, Arthur. I think you've been taking too many bumps to the head. You got my bunkmate's bed, because he's dead, see?"

"The Huns killed him?"

"Like they're killin' everyone," Yank said. "They nearly got you, chum. At least you saw the action," Yank lamented. "The tent came down on me and I never saw daylight till it was daylight. At least no one else got their plane's off the ground."

"And that's good?"

"Hell, no! It's terrible. But I don't have to make excuses why I couldn't get my crate up. We're gonna be down for at least a week until the squadron gets refitted and more planes come in from Coventry."

"Coventry?"

The medic dabbed a tincture of iodine on Arthur's skull, and the king flinched. He grabbed the medic by his gas mask bag. "Are you trying to poison me, knave?" Arthur demanded.

"'Ere now," the orderly gasped, trying to tear free from the king's grip. "You're an officer an' a gentleman, sir. I'm fixin' your bleedin' skull."

"Let him go, Arthur. He's just puttin' the iodine on so your scalp wound heals." Arthur freed the medic, who backed away from him, his eyes wide.

The medic backed out the the flimsy wooden door, massaging his wrist. Richardson popped his bald head through the door. "How are we?" he asked.

Arthur pushed himself up on the cot and said, "I'm all right." Arthur watched Yank salute the squadron leader. It was the same with knights meeting in the heath or meadow, raising an open hand to show they intended no harm.

"You look all right for a man who was buried alive," Richardson said. "We nearly bought the farm."

"Which farm?" Arthur inquired politely. Yank and the squadron leader laughed.

"Right," Richardson said, grinning. "But you saved my bacon, King."

"We all need our bacon," the king said, agreeably, making Richardson laugh again.

"I wish everyone had that attitude," Richardson said, glancing briefly at Cooper. "I had my doubts about you, King. I thought that old stick of yours was an act. We actually have had a few lads who shirked."

"Sir?"

"When the Blitz came and the Hun rolled us out of France, some lost heart. And some never had it. I've had to send two boys to mine coal in Wales for LMF." He looked again at Yank.

"LMF, sir?" Arthur said.

"Lack of moral fiber. So we send 'em to mine coal. I'll be glad to see you in a Spitfire, King. I need all the fighter pilots I can get. Cooper, look after him. King's in your charge, now."

"Yes, sir."

"Get him to hospital first thing. I want to make sure he's in shape by the time we get the new planes."

Richardson picked up Arthur's staff and inspected it. The hard wood was scorched and mottled from lightning strikes. The squadron leader looked at the half-moon carved into the crest just below the knob. "What interesting work," the squadron leader observed quietly. "Where did you get this, King?"

"I got it from my old man."

"Ah, family heirloom, then. Where do your people hail from?"

"We held territory near Tintagel, sir."

Richardson nodded. "How quaint. Well, get some rest, both of you."

As Richardson left, Arthur rose painfully from the cot. Leaning on Merlin's staff, he hobbled over to the window. Masking tape held the glass fast against bomb strikes. The blackout curtain was tacked to the sill. Curious as a bird, Arthur turned the knob and pulled the shutter.

"Arthur! That's against the rules."

"Whose rule?"

"Military regulation, dummy. You open that curtain while it's still dark and you light the way for the Hun. I've got to kill the light."

"I wouldn't want to make you kill something just because I opened a window, Sir Yank."

"You talk funny, even for a limey, Arthur." Yank turned the switch on the bare bulb and the little room plunged into darkness. "There."

"Military regulation," Arthur whispered. It was like a foreign language: familiar, yet just beyond the twist of his tongue.

Arthur's breath quickened. The room was black as a tomb. The American opened the window and the damp air rushed into the stuffy quarters. Arthur leaned on the windowsill and watched a silver tail of cloud, attached to a sliver of new moon.

"It's the new moon," Arthur said. "The first of three."

"The more moonlight we get, the easier it is for the Hun to send the night bombers. The real heavy stuff."

"Night bombers?"

"The Heinkel-111s. The Junker 88s. All the twin-engine jobs that carry the big bombs. When those birds drop their eggs, you won't want to be there. Well, let's turn in and get forty winks."

"Your pardon, sir?"

"They all say I talk funny. Hey, get some sleep. Then we'll get you to the flight surgeon. He'll get you fixed up."

"Surgeon!" Arthur said, his voice rising in alarm. "Are there leeches?"

"Take it easy, chum. They might stick you with a needle. You want leeches, get a lawyer. I don't mind doctors. It's like a holiday."

"I need to know more about this flying business."

"Don't we all," Yank said. "Say, let's turn in. I'm bushed." He closed the blackout window as the first streaks of cold dawn poked through the cracks.

Arthur rested his head on the foam rubber pillow.

Its soft strength confounded him. The bed also was too soft. He found his gaze held by an instrument on a side table between the bunks. It had a pair of luminous needles and numbers in a circle of twelve. A third small needle moved in steady progress around the circle.

"Yank," Arthur said.

Bill Cooper, turning on his bunk, replied drowsily, "Yeah?"

"This instrument on the table. What do you call it in the new world?"

Yank turned over, his expression puzzled. "Same thing we call it here, pal. An alarm clock from Sears Roebuck. To tell me when it's time to hit the bricks."

Arthur nodded. "Its purpose then is the telling of time?"

Yank rolled over, pulling his thin military blanket up to his ears. "You're a kidder, Arthur. Its purpose is to roll my ass out of bed if the batman doesn't do it first. Which is in about forty minutes."

"Oh. Yes. Well, thanks."

The men sank back on their cots. They both immediately fell into a deep sleep as the cold dawn rose from the scorched earth of RAF Hornchurch. Arthur exhaled a kingly snore. The king of the Britons sounded like a warthog rutting in the bog, but with his beard singed from his leathered cheeks, he looked curiously childlike in the dawn of the new age.

6

General Anton Kleist pulled off his leather flying helmet. He felt gritty and exhausted, the adrenaline drained from him after the cross-Channel mission. The odors of cordite, sweat and aviation fuel permeated his flight suit. He wanted brandy. Kleist clumped up the stone spiral stairway to his quarters, his rooms high in the castle tower reserved for one of the most powerful men in Europe, the commander of Bombing Group Three.

He turned the iron key in the ancient lock and let himself in. The flight suit fell from his shoulders. He climbed out of the coverall, and in his boots and breeches, he stepped over to the basin to wash his face and hands. Standing stripped to the waist, he imagined the heat from the bath, soothing his aching muscles after the fatigue of night combat.

He looked up to see his falcon, Nietzsche, twitch and shuffle unnaturally on its perch. Even in Kleist's exhausted state, he sensed the slightness of movement, the hooded hunting bird perking itself oddly. General Kleist looked into the mirror and saw the green, serpentlike eyes, ringed with their fringe of red. The man in the mirror smiled.

"Hello, General," Mordred said. He sat in a camp chair, his legs crossed. His slender white hands were folded on his knees, holding a thick book the size of a hymnal. "I let myself in. There was no key."

The general's hair prickled at the base of his skull. He tried to avert his eyes from the green-eyed man's gaze. But he could not do it. Haltingly, he said, "You are a junior officer. Your presence in my quarters is forbidden."

Mordred rose from the camp chair. One golden eyebrow arched, moving the star-shaped scar up on his smooth, broad forehead. "I am many things, General," Mordred said. "But junior officer isn't one of them."

Kleist inexplicably discovered his hand, so sure on the bomb run, to be trembling. He gathered his faltering courage. "You are in my command. You serve the Führer, and me. I order you to leave, Major."

Mordred chuckled. He placed the book on Kleist's bed. It was a copy of *Mein Kampf.* "I've been reading your leader's book. What a lot of ideas he has." Mordred's eyes flashed and the Luftwaffe general felt his knees buckle from an unseen force in the room. The bird rustled its feathers and shrieked. Mordred nodded abruptly and the bird fluttered unerringly to his shoulder, though its eyes remained hooded by the cowl.

"Hear me, you bloody Hun," Mordred said. His voice held the timbre of hollow thunder. His teeth flashed. He looked like an animal, feral and wild, in human form. "Listen to me and mark my words well, as your life depends on obedience."

The German general fell down on one knee. He held his head as if it might drop from his shoulders.

"You belong to me, body and soul." Mordred's eyes glittered, holding the general in their thrall. "I've come to kill a king, and you will help." The green eyes flashed, like the basilisk. "Any questions?"

Kleist stared at Mordred, paralyzed, attempting to resist, but the German nearly drowned in the twin pools of fire that formed the demon's gaze. Within the orbit of Mordred's eyes, Kleist could see faraway mountaintops and winged creatures. He could see the ocean and watch the pounding of his own heart. He became lost in the moment and felt born again and dead all at once. He held out no thought to flee. Anton Kleist was consumed in the green fire. He wanted to die, but only at the hands of this man. And in his service, he felt a compelling craving for lust and slaughter beyond what war could offer. His eyes were like the Führer's.

It took three minutes for Mordred to take possession of General Kleist's soul.

Mordred's task completed, he smiled almost tenderly. "There are things I require you to teach me, Hun. Things about this time and place, words peculiar to the age. And things about your machines. Particularly your siege engines and such. Do these for me, and you may live to serve my pleasure. *Verstehen sie?*"

"I understand," General Kleist croaked, his voice of command transformed to a raw, hoarse whisper.

"Kneel for us."

The general dropped to his knee and kissed the ring on Mordred's finger, the ring with the stone cut in the shape of his scar, the five-pointed, inverted star.

*   *   *

The white stones of the castle, Chateau D'Eauville, glinted hard as diamonds in the summer sun. The shrubberies of the maze concealed the flak guns that protected HQ for Luftflotte Three, the largest of Goering's striking fleets. Mark IV Panzers lurked in the orchard, and the half-tracks waited patient as armored lizards in the vineyards.

Goering's armored Duesenberg rolled into the courtyard of the chateau and the Alte peered out the bulletproof windows, surveying his surroundings with the pleasure of a man who knew any castle in Europe was his personal plaything. Goering loved castles now even more than when he was a boy playing with lead soldiers.

His surprisingly small feet stepped delicately from the staff car. Goering gathered his greatcoat round his massive shoulders like a cape. He gazed up at the turrets, each flying a red swastika banner like some medieval battlement at Nuremburg. The Alte's paratroopers gave the stiff-armed salute and Goering waved his baton at them jauntily.

"A small castle, but it will do in a pinch," he clucked. The great one was happy and alert, his mood elevated by the little pills he chewed.

"Perhaps if we achieve our goal, the Reichsmarshall can return to Carinhall for a well-deserved rest," his aide-de-camp said.

"I will not rest until the British lion eats crow, Major," Goering vowed.

Their boots crunched on the white stones of the chateau as if they were grinding the bones of Europe. They walked briskly across the courtyard and descended the stairs into the cellar that retained its musty aroma of cork and oak. The fine Bordeaux and Beaujolais were emptied out, booty sent to Carinhall, Goering's palatial estate. Now, the wine cellar held the operations room for Luftflotte Three, General

Anton Kleist's command and the largest bomber fleet on the French coast.

In the underground chamber, the radios crackled, their signals filling the dry air with static electricity. The Luftwaffe technicians staffed the arrays of radios that linked Goering's Luftwaffe legions from Norway to Cherbourg. Goering himself believed in neither radio nor radar. He called them cheap magic tricks. All Goering cared about was warplanes. Frightful planes with iron crosses and iron bombs on the wings. Better than lead soldiers.

The Alte marched imperiously past the technicians, breezily acknowledging salutes until he arrived at the plotting table, where blond, busty young women stuffed into crisply pressed Luftwaffe jackets moved pointer sticks on the giant map of England. The Luftwaffe staff officers waited anxiously like gamblers at a roulette table. As one, they brought their heels together and saluted the Reichsmarshall. He waved at them, smiled, and they relaxed, except for the dour and intense General Kleist, looking more sober than usual. Next to him stood the insolent General Galland. And a young officer in Kleist's shadow, a crafty-looking boy with a scar.

"Still want a Spitfire, Galland? Or do you think your lads might yet make do with Messerschmitts?" Goering inquired acidly.

Galland puffed on his cigar and shrugged. "The Messerschmitt's not magic, but it's a fine machine. Actually, I prefer it."

"Good of you to say so," Goering said coldly. "Well, you don't get a Knight's Cross for being a coward. How goes the battle with the English?"

Galland shrugged. "We kill them, but they keep coming at us. We would do better to finish off their airfields and fighters. Then you could put your paratroops in the courtyard at Buckingham Palace."

"It's the radar, Herr Reichsmarshall," General Kleist said. "They see us coming."

"Radar," Goering sniffed. "A box with wires. A toy."

"Radar is magic, Herr Reichsmarshall," Galland declared. "Electronic magic. They know when we are coming, and they can choose where to join battle."

"What of it?" Goering demanded. "We have more planes."

"The warning from the radar means we must use fighters to protect bombers, instead of finishing off Fighter Command on the ground. A battle of attrition wastes planes. Not to mention pilots," Galland said sourly.

Goering peered at Kleist. The general looked as if he hadn't slept in days. Too many missions, perhaps, Goering concluded. Too bad, but war was hell. The Alte returned to Galland.

"The pilots, Galland," Goering said darkly, "are paid on my chit book. Can you beat the English, or are you cowards?"

Galland shrugged and puffed his cigar as if he didn't give a damn about the Reichsmarshall's opinions. Goering's face turned scarlet and he turned to Kleist. "General Kleist! What do you have to say?"

Kleist cleared his throat and spoke slowly. He inclined his head as if listening, as if another whispered words in his ear. He turned to Goering. The Reichsmarshall recoiled, finding the general's pallor ghastly.

"My aide has a plan, Herr Reichsmarshall ," Kleist said, his voice jerky and machinelike. "You should hear from him. He is full of ideas."

"General," Goering said solicitously, "it appears you are not well. Do you require medical leave?"

Kleist shook his head automatically. "I would not leave the battle. Not at this historic moment when the British are to be beaten."

Goering nodded solemnly. "Your aide, then. What does the boy say?"

Mordred brushed a wisp of flaxen hair from his high forehead. He clicked his heels and smiled, his lips stretched to cover the fine points of his teeth. "I am Major Morgan, Herr Reichsmarshall. Lately with the Romans in Africa."

The Reichsmarshall stroked his ponderous chin. "I thought I knew all the lads. Were you with the Condor Legion?"

"No, Reichsmarshall. I've been traveling," Mordred said, his manner courtly.

"So, youngster, what is your accumulated wisdom at such a green age?"

"How old were you when you led the Red Baron's squadron?"

"Twenty-two," Goering replied, beaming broadly. "But when I led them, it was my squadron." Still, his smile broadened. The quickest route to the mighty one's heart, after his stomach, was his ego. He stroked the Blue Max medal that choked his ample collar. "Tell me how you would tame the English lion."

Mordred unrolled some of the papers taken from the slain Major Morgan's briefcase. Some officers leaned forward, peering at the strange scribbled stars that bordered the page.

"I give you Operation Camelot," Mordred said confidently. "My plan to beat Britain." Mordred gazed round the table until his green eyes held each officer's attention.

"To tame the lion, you kill the lion's cubs," Mordred said. "As many as you can, as quick as you can. Turn away from the airfields and bomb the people, and their wives and young. When enough English mothers highborn and low are weeping, or slain, the nobility will yield. They are rotten."

"There are rules of war, you know, Major," Galland objected.

Mordred's eyes shimmered as he gazed around the table. He ignored Galland.

"Nobody asks the winner if he played by the rules," Mordred declared. Some of the officers shifted uneasily, watching the Alte for his opinion. "When the Norse raiders sacked the coast of Britain, they held to no rules. They took what they wanted. Are we not descended of the line of those same blond raiders? Are we not the gods of war?"

"These are not the Dark Ages," Galland insisted. Goering stared intently at the green-eyed officer.

"Really?" Mordred asked, half amused. "They should be as dark as we can make them." His eyes flashed. "For our enemies, this should be the darkest hour of the darkest age." Mordred met the eyes of each man at the plotting board and spoke deliberately, his words filling the room, the ring of them rising in a musically mesmerizing lilt. "Why spare Britain? Do you care for British children more than for Poles?" He rolled up his papers and smacked the plotting table with them.

"I've read the reports!" Mordred hissed. "You must do what you did in Warsaw. Flatten Britain as you did Rotterdam. Make them bleed and you'll take the jewel in the crown. London!" As he spoke, his slim hands moved little flags across the board, all converging on the Thames Estuary. The only sound in the room was the crackle of radio static.

"Operation Camelot! The subjugation of Britain from the air. Forget tactics and think of conquest."

Goering frowned thoughtfully. He stroked the blue medallion on his chest, and a warm smile slowly enveloped his cherubic face. He nodded at Kleist. "Anton, this boy is dangerous."

Kleist's face was bathed in shadow. His splayed

fingers rested on the rim of the table. The German general bowed as if he were under a great weight, and he spoke each word carefully. "I know that, Herr Reichsmarshall."

Mordred bowed with a flourish. "Then, I take it my plan will be considered, Reichsmarshall?"

"I like officers with imagination, Morgan. You will go far."

Mordred nodded and smiled. "Thank you, Reichsmarshall. You have no idea how hard I worked to be here at this moment in time."

Goering saluted with his baton. "Operation Camelot, then." Mordred returned the salute snappily.

The RAF Hospital lay midway between RAF Hornchurch and Churchill's country house at Chartwell. Bill Cooper drove the open MG sportster and Arthur fell in love with the Machine Age as the wind blew his hair. A horseless chariot. Could even Merlin have foreseen such wonders? Arthur gaped at the gauges, fascinated. Arthur kept a keen vigil, watching Yank move his hand easily between the steering wheel and the gear shift. Yank turned into a side road and motored down a shady lane. The king understood steering quickly, not unlike the wheel of a ship. He remained mystified by propulsion.

"What makes it go?" he shouted above the wind.

"The engine? Less than a hundred horses, but she gets the job done."

"This engine is a female horse?"

"Just like Spitfires. Temperamental." Yank laughed and slapped the king on the shoulder. "You think you get 'em under control, and any time they want, they toss ya."

"How many kinds of engines are there, do you suppose?" Arthur asked blandly.

"The only one I need to know about is the Merlin that makes my Spitfire go."

"Merlin makes the Spitfire fly." Arthur stated the question as a fact.

"You know the drill, chum. Twelve-cylinder Merlin. Rolls Royce. The best engine there ever was. Till they invent the next one."

Yank wheeled around a bend, sending the road gravel flying. A horse cart pulling a hay wagon appeared. Yank hit the brakes and skidded wide of it, pitching Arthur sideways. Arthur watched Yank's foot depress the pedal as the MG raced away from the hay driver.

"Get a car, you old hayseed," Yank shouted at the top of his lungs. "No one tells these old codgers it's the twentieth century."

"Perhaps we should go back and tell him," Arthur shouted.

"Forget it."

"Your foot makes it go and stop," Arthur declared flatly, as though he had discovered the earth was round. "It's magical."

"You bet. You get the wind in your face on a hairpin curve, that's magic," Yank said absently, as he wheeled up to the iron gateway to the RAF Hospital for Kent and Essex.

Arthur looked up at the twin Union Jack flags that waved in the breeze from the stone gate posts. A pair of stone lions rampant, bearing scepters, stood guard at the gate along with the Tommies who brandished Enfield rifles. Arthur admired the bayonets, but he wondered that there should be such a long wooden club with so little a sharp point attached to the end.

"Identify yourselves," the corporal ordered.

"Duke and duchess of Windsor," Yank rejoined, flashing a pass signed by Richardson.

"Clear to enter, sir," the corporal barked in best parade ground bellow. "Open the gate, Private."

The MG rumbled past the gate. The corporal muttered, "Cheeky Yank."

A circular gravel driveway led to the hospital, an estate donated by Lord Beaverbrook, the press lord in charge of aircraft production. Since the fall of France, it had been transformed from a weekend retreat for lawn parties into the RAF's best-equipped hospital.

Bill Cooper parked next to a row of ambulances, converted lorries that still bore Bovril and Lipton advertising beneath their hastily painted Red Cross markings. Arthur heard the groans of wounded men being carried on stretchers up the steps. The king started, seeing some of the stretcher bearers were women wearing impossibly short gowns.

One woman stood giving instruction to a small group on how to don a hideous mask. She would pull the mask on and shout "Gas!" Arthur noticed none of the soldiers wore armor. Even the mask, which looked knightly, was sewn from roughhewn canvas.

"You couldn't fend off a small blow with a helmet like that," Arthur remarked as he and Yank passed by the stretcher bearers.

"Yeah, but a mask might save you from the gas," Cooper said, slapping his own gas mask pouch. "Say, where's yours?"

"Lost it," Arthur said quickly. "I need it, of course. To guard against the gas. Which gas, exactly?"

"The trouble with poison gas," Yank said darkly, "is it could come at any time, right out of the sky. My old man got gassed in the first war."

Arthur looked up, alarmed, as though the clouds might drop on his head. Warily, he stared at Yank. "From the sky?"

"Where would you think it'd come from, Arthur? The Huns ferrying it across in their bombers, right?"

"Right," the king said. "And we meet them in battle with our Spitfires."

Yank clapped Arthur on the shoulders. "Right, but let's find the flight surgeon first."

"Everyone here is gravely hurt, except for us."

"You did your share. Let's get your leg looked at. Richardson's orders."

They walked through the entryway. Arthur leaned against Merlin's staff and watched Bill Cooper sign the register, and watched the whirl of doctor and nurse, gurneys and stretcher bearers. Then he signed his own name with a featherless quill that bled ink from a sharp point. Arthur King. Yank looked at the ornate letters and whistled. "Some fancy hand you've got."

Arthur waited in the white room by himself and trembled. Strange odors permeated his nostrils and he felt trapped. A plump woman entered. Her raven hair fell from her forehead in strangely bobbed ringlets and her lips were painted a ruby red. She wore a white, pleated gown, cut severely at the knees.

"Here, ducks," the woman said. "Be a good fellow and undress."

"I beg your pardon, maiden."

"I've been called a lot of things, luv, but maiden is new to me," she said, patting his shoulder. "Now, do what I said, fresh, and get out of your clothes."

"You'll not see me naked, I assure you, good lady."

She put her hands on her hips and said sternly, "I'm Nurse Mullins, not your nanny, so I'm not going to undress you. You'll have to do it."

"I'll not undress," Arthur said stubbornly. "It's unseemly."

Nurse Mullins gave him a dark look. "Off with the trousers, luv. Your pants, silly boy. Unhook 'em. That's an order."

"You're giving me an order?" Arthur said incredulously.

"Do what I say or I'll call my bodyguards."

Arthur shook his head and laughed. "Well, if you hold such lofty command, I suppose I'd better obey."

He looked about uncomfortably. He tugged at his tunic. He'd fumbled with the buttons half the morning and dreaded doing it again. Exasperated, Nurse Mullins shook her head and unbuttoned his tunic.

"Fighter pilots," she clucked. "Big men in the sky. You're all little boys, really."

"What are these?" the king murmured as she removed the jacket.

"What, buttons? Say, did you get a bump on the head?"

"Yes," Arthur said quickly. He thumbed away at the buttons, marveling at their efficiency. "Good idea, buttons," he murmured.

Slapping his back, Nurse Mullins said, "Now, drop your knickers while I fetch the doctor."

"The doctor. I was told there will be no leeches."

Nurse Mullins looked at King thoughtfully. "You did get hit on the head."

Arthur's face became childlike, the steel gray eyes lost, his strong forehead creased with worry. "Sometimes I don't know where I am," he said.

Quietly, Nurse Mullins walked over to Arthur. She pulled a dressing gown down from a peg and handed it to him.

"Don't worry, ducks," she said. And she was out of the room like the white rabbit. Arthur looked about wildly, as though he'd been dropped from the moon. He looked out the window and saw the rolling green countryside. It hadn't changed much, except for the wheeled machines that belched smoke. He felt his bladder pressing. He gritted his teeth and gripped the windowsill as he looked about. He found the bedpan, thanked Merlin and relieved himself.

Arthur shifted uncomfortably in the gown. He hadn't worn such garb since he cleaned stables in sackcloth as a boy. This gown had no hind side. His rump felt the cool breeze that blew through the open window.

Another lady entered, this one holding a board that she wrote on. She wore a white coat and her ginger-colored hair was tied back tightly. She smelled good, like the dried flowers spread in the king's chambers by the ladies of court. Arthur's throat constricted as he watched the woman.

He'd never seen a woman write.

"Where is the physician?" Arthur asked. "I've already talked to a woman."

"Well, you're going to talk to another one," the ginger-haired lady said. "I'm the doctor. Jenny Hamilton, military surgeon."

She walked briskly to the window and pulled the curtain wide to allow in more light. The daylight brought up the roses in her cheeks. Arthur shook his head. "I don't understand."

She turned and faced him directly, her eyes a startling green, like the Irish Sea. "You're not going to be a bother, are you, Lieutenant? I might be the first lady doctor you've met, but the world is changing fast."

"That fast?"

"Be a good fellow and climb up on the table. Don't make trouble for me, and I won't make trouble for you."

"Who rules here, please? Nurse Mullins said she must be obeyed."

The ginger-haired doctor laughed. "She must, indeed. But so must I. This is my domain, even more than Edith's. Come along, we haven't got time for fooling. There're lads who are seriously hurt."

Awkwardly, the king mounted the examining table. His royal ass settled on the cushion and his feet dangled like a boy's. The doctor began a series of professional pokes and prods. He reared back from her. "You're not going to bleed me, are you?"

"Take blood? No, Lieutenant. We're looking at the leg."

She checked the dressing. The king felt himself aroused. He hugged his arms to his chest and bent over, and he stared away. But still, his gown rebelled and he was mortified. The doctor looked up, staring straight into the steel gray eyes of the king.

"Don't be embarrassed, Lieutenant. It happens all the time. Be glad you're not hurt a little higher."

"Yes," he rasped.

She cut open the field dressing with a pair of surgical scissors. Each motion was precise, and as she traced the periphery of his leg wound, her fingers worked gently, strong and surely.

"You've got some bits of shrapnel in the leg, Lieutenant, but they're in the fleshy parts of the muscle. I wouldn't want to bother a surgeon with this. They'll work their way out over a few weeks. I'll give you some pills for pain."

"Pain doesn't bother me."

"Oh, don't be such a pilot," she said, exasperated. "You can still fly. These are little more than aspirin." Jenny placed the pillbox in Arthur's tunic. "Well, now that we're here, let's have a look at your heart." She raised her stethoscope and placed the contact piece lightly on his chest. The king's chest swelled slightly at the ginger-haired lady's touch. "You've got a nice, strong heart, Lieutenant."

"Are you a queen?" The words leaped out. Jenny Hamilton reared back.

"I beg your pardon?"

"This is your domain. Are you a queen, then?"

Flustered, the doctor laughed. She dropped the stethoscope and cupped her chin in her hands. "I've helped a lot of boys from Fighter Command," she said. "I've never heard that line."

"You look like a queen," Arthur persisted.

The doctor shook her head and smiled. "That's good to know." She patted him on the cheek. "Your heart, and your libido, are in the right place, King. You can fly in a week. Now, I've got to get back to the real world."

"I've got to see you again," Arthur said. "Jenny."

She shook her head. "Sorry, King. It's not possible. I don't date much, particularly fighter pilots."

She turned and strode out of the room. He slipped off the table and stood on the cold linoleum, the wind flapping the backside of the gown. Yank Cooper stepped in, caught sight of Arthur in the gown and sank to the floor, giggling like a fool.

"You're going to have to tell me where to get a robe like that, Arthur. It's definitely you."

"I've got to see that woman."

"Hospitals full of 'em. They all go for fighter pilots."

"I want the one I just saw."

"I'll see what I can do, Arthur. I'm something of an expert with the ladies."

"Really?"

"Nah. They're trickier than Spitfires. C'mon. Pull up your fly and let's get some ale. I'm thirsty."

"What's a fly?"

Cooper rolled his eyes. "Okay, pal. I'll wait in the car."

"And what's a date?"

"You're gonna have to tell me all about what your people do on Saturday nights, Arthur. We got some serious drinking ahead."

The fog slowed their drive to London, but Arthur paid little attention to the road or the demon machine. The fog he was seeing wore a cloud of ginger hair and possessed eyes like the Irish Sea.

7

The streets of London in the blackout appeared like caverns of doom to Arthur. The little car rumbled forward, its snout throwing out a faint light from dimmed headlamps, lest the pair light the way for bombers. As they rolled forward in the fog, an occasional sentry could be sighted, a soldier with the helmet and sharp stick. The little roadster passed by tumbled mounds of stone that looked like the rubble of castles that fell under siege. But there were too many to count, and Arthur became benumbed by fear and awe at the sheer size of a possibly enchanted city. "Where does it end?" he murmured darkly.

"What, London? We're barely in town."

"Nothing like Tintagel. My country was different."

"You must've come from the rube towns, country boy. Richardson says, when you're tired of London, you're tired of life."

"It's too big. How many people abide here?"

"Abide? Lots of 'em left town when old Hitler set loose the dogs of war. Women and kids, they sent 'em out to the country. But mostly, they've come back. There's got to be a million, at least."

"What's a million?"

"Hell, Arthur. A million here and a million there, it adds up."

"Too many to count, then," Arthur said quietly. "And they're all in danger from this Hitler?"

"You ought to know it, pal. My old man saw Hitler coming."

"Hitler, then, was in the new world?"

"Not Hitler. My old man. He flew in the Great War. Said if the Hun ever came back, we'd have to beat him all over again."

"These Huns have always been a lot of trouble. Did you fly with your father in the Great War?"

"Geez, Arthur, I'm younger than you. This is enough war for me. I crossed the border to Canada and signed with the RAF. Next thing I knew, I was on the boat. Three weeks later, I was in a Hurricane. Then they gave us the Spitfires."

"Will the Hun be coming in boats, do you suppose? Or will they come in their air machines?"

"What's this? Quiz the Yank?" The American shook his head. "Okay, I'll play along. If we don't stop 'em in the air, we're gonna have to fight on the beaches, and in the hills and the streets. That's the way Churchill sees it."

"Churchill is one of your seers, then?"

"My old man—and he's another Yankee, remember—he said Churchill was one of the most far-sighted men England ever raised."

"You love your father, then?"

"I wish to God he was still alive. His ticker gave out last year. Said he hoped he never lived to see another war. He didn't."

"The Great War, then, was some other great war."

"The war to end all wars? Yeah, Bill Cooper, Sr., flew with Rickenbacker, the ace of aces. Then he flew mail until his heart gave out."

"Chain mail?"

"Against the law where I come from, Arthur. A chain letter violates U.S. postal rules. Nope. We were flying air mail by the sack till the airlines got the job. Then I dusted crops. Country fairs. Air races. A little of this and a little of that."

Arthur shook his head. He found himself dizzier than when he was trying to fly the Spitfire. It was like trying to understand a familiar language, but knowing only half the words. "Where is Merlin, now, I wonder?"

"Right here, pal. He's up there." He chugged to a stop and pointed at the sign.

A sudden gust of wind cut a slash through the fog and Arthur heard a chain creaking. He looked up to see a pub sign of an old man with a long, white beard holding a stick that looked just like Arthur's. This old man looked slightly comical with white beard and pointed cap. The sign announced Merlin's Pub in ornate, gold letters.

"That Merlin is not familiar," Arthur said. "That one's a joke."

"Guess there could be more than one. Let's go in and get pissed, Arthur."

"I'm glad there's a place for it," Arthur said. "I've been meaning to have a go since hospital."

"That's the spirit."

As Yank opened the blackout-curtained door to the pub, Arthur felt a sudden rush of air over his head, the flapping of a great raven's wings. He watched the bird fly swiftly down the fog-enshrouded street, cawing out a raspy refrain of what passed for laughter, if birds could indeed laugh.

The men stepped into a smokey, noisy pub. Since his arrival in the twentieth century, Arthur had wondered at the sticks that smoked. Everyone seemed to dangle them from their lips. Yank produced a packet of Churchman's No. 3 and offered one to Arthur. The king accepted it, holding the paper cylinder between thumb and forefinger as he'd seen. He watched Yank put the cigarette between his lips. Then he watched the American flier strike a sulfur match with his thumb. The king's nostrils flared and he resisted the impulse to run from this fresh deviltry.

Yank exhaled puffs of dragon smoke from his nostrils. Yank held the match up and lit Arthur's cigarette. The king coughed and felt the fumes of hell searing his nostrils and throat. He threw the cigarette down and stomped on it as though it were a poisonous reptile.

"Not your brand, huh?" Yank said. "I could use a Lucky Strike myself."

"Why would anybody use those things?" the king demanded, outraged.

"Everybody's doin' it."

"What a vile proposal," the king sputtered. "Thank you, Sir Yank. I'll not need another of those."

"Well, you do drink an ale, don't ya, Arthur?"

"Do they have ale here?"

"Stout and bitter. The best."

"Well, then, let's have the best."

They crossed into the crowd of blue uniforms. A tinny phonograph played Tommy Dorsey, competing with a badly out-of-tune standup piano where the lads leaned in each other's faces and bawled a chorus of "Pack Up Your Troubles in Your Old Kit Bag." Arthur recognized the place immediately.

This was the main hall where the warriors gathered to feast and drink and tell their tales. The women wore preposterous suits. But they smiled and laughed and consorted like the women of old. Arthur looked round Merlin's Pub, taking it all in with the hawklike apprehension for detail that Merlin the magician had endowed him with. There was so much to see. The walls were painted with flowers, and he could not tell why. There were coats of arms adorning the smoke-stained walls, and there were trophies.

Behind the long oaken bar there was a looking glass, the largest Arthur had even seen. Looking into, he could see all of Merlin's Pub behind him, and it stood out in relief, like an enormous tapestry of the hunt. He saw the men singing at the big box that made music. He saw women dancing with the men, crowded so their shoulders bumped each other, not at all like the graceful dances of court. More like the peasant revels on market day.

Arthur saw men throwing darts. Yes, he recognized that. There was a circular target, and in the center of the target there was a likeness of a man with a comical mustache. One of the darts hit home.

"Right in Hitler's eye!"

Arthur looked up above the bar and saw two framed likenesses. They were the most sharply rendered paintings he had ever seen, in tones of black and white. One was titled "King George," the other was "The Honorable Winston Churchill."

"Churchill, then, is wizard to the king," Arthur said.

"He'll have to do a wizard job if we're going to beat Hitler," the one-eyed barman said, leaning forward to make himself heard above the din. "What are you drinking?"

"Two pints of Best," Yank Cooper yelled across the bar. "And Arthur doesn't pay. He pulled me out of the drink."

"The Channel?" the barman inquired.

"Nope. Some farmer's duck pond, but I'd have been just as drowned."

"Two pints," the barman declared, pulling the stick. Arthur delighted in watching the amber foam roll into a pair of glass mugs. The publican handed the mugs across the bar.

Bill Cooper raised his pint in toast. "To the king."

Arthur nodded gravely. "To the king."

The barman had drawn himself a draught. "And to Mr. Winston Churchill. May he send Adolf Hitler to hell where he belongs, the devil."

A chorus of "Here, here," rumbled up and down along the bar. Arthur stared straight in the mirror and started. It was his own face he took in. Barely all he recognized were the steel gray eyes. No armor, nor buckler, nor kingly locks dropping from his shoulders. He was a new man, and a strange one. He saw the blue suit, the strange knot drawn around his throat and the wings on his broad chest. And he looked down at his uniform pocket and traced the letters inscribed between the pilot's wings. "R," he whispered. "RAF."

"And here's to the RAF!" the barman cheered.

All along the long bar they huzzahed and all arms were lifted. Six pints later, Arthur felt a sense of warmth and well being. Then he looked in the mirror and saw the woman.

Her white coat was gone. She wore a green, broad-shouldered jacket that matched her eyes. Arthur recognized the ginger hair, braided atop her pleasingly angled face. Her lips were red, of course. That startling red. Trailing the woman with green eyes was Nurse Mullins, who wore a gaudy dress and laughed like a bawd.

"Jenny!" a voice cried out across the crowded floor. "A dance, Jenny. They're playing 'In the Mood.'"

"Well, I'm not. Thanks ever so," Jenny called out, laughing. Arthur stood transfixed, watching her make her way through the madding crowd to a corner table that somehow stood, magically, ready for her and her lady-in-waiting.

"I've got to talk to that woman," Arthur said.

"What woman? There's lots of 'em," Yank said, eyeing the row of empty pint mugs that the pink-faced publican swept from Arthur's spot at the bar.

"That woman," Arthur said, pointing her out. He moved toward the woman in green as sure as if he were storming a castle. Where fliers or their dates failed to yield, he'd smile and give them a light tap on the shin with Merlin's stick, then they moved. Yank followed, unsteadily, moving his lips as he counted the four pints he had downed to Arthur's seven. "Jeez, that guy can hold it."

Arthur approached the table and Edith Mullins smacked her lips together to even her lipstick. She beamed at Arthur. "Why, Jenny, dear! Look! It's the lieutenant that didn't want to drop his trousers. And he's brought a pal."

"Would you honor us with your company?" Arthur asked.

"Now, that's a posh way to put it," Edith said happily. "Come on, luv. Have a sit."

Arthur inclined his leonine head toward Jenny Hamilton. "Then, it's all right?" he asked. His throat felt raw. His voice was husky from the room full of smoke or something else that made the words catch in his throat.

"Sit, if you wish, Lieutenant," Jenny said, meeting the gaze of his steel gray eyes evenly. "There's no one here to stop you."

Yank slid onto the bench next to Arthur, earning a pinch from Edith.

"How's the leg, Lieutenant?" Jenny asked politely.

"King, Jenny," Edith piped. "His name was Arthur King and he didn't want to drop his knickers. I never heard of such a thing. Who's your friend?"

"Bill Cooper," Arthur said quickly. "He's from Connecticut."

"Oh, a Yank, then!" Edith said radiantly. "I've never met a real Yank. Any relation to Gary Cooper? You're shorter than he is, aren't you?"

Bill Cooper blushed, then covered a belch. "I'm considered above average in my parts." Edith squealed immediately and squeezed Yank's shoulder.

"Well, I'd love to see your parts, William Cooper," Edith said coyly. "I've never been to America."

"Connecticut," Arthur corrected her, and Cooper nodded gravely. "It's the new world."

Jenny covered her mouth to hide a laugh. Edith, she knew, was impossible. "You were telling me about the leg, Lieutenant. Are you taking your pills?"

"I don't mind pain."

"Yes, you said so," Jenny said. "I've found that men who say that quite often are hiding something. You can try to ignore pain, but you shouldn't."

"'Shouldn't I?"

"Be man enough to admit you're in pain, then the healing can begin. Don't you see?"

"What a strange notion. Pain is to be overcome, not moaned about."

Jenny Hamilton turned her nose up and gazed round the pub. Her sea green eyes took in the whirl of dancers, and she stared into the smoke and confusion as if she were herself looking out to sea.

Arthur watched the bend of her neck and the soft down on her chin as she looked up at the cornices above the bar. Her gaze fixed on the torn tail section with its black swastika and red background hanging from the wall like a wound. The tail section formed the center of a display of machine guns and bits of propeller wrenched from Messerschmitts and Heinkels.

"Those trophies, up there on the wall. Did you take any of them in the fighting?"

"Nothing up there belongs to me," Arthur said. "I don't even know what they are."

Jenny smiled, her lips parting the slightest bit so that Arthur could enjoy her smile, warm and open. He started as she put her hand on his cheek. "That was a nice answer, Arthur King," she said. "I don't like war trophies."

"I see," the king said. She let one warm hand fall into his and the king felt the blood rush from his head. With her other hand, she stroked his cheek.

"I don't like war trophies, Lieutenant," she said. "And I don't mean to be one. Do you understand me?" The king nodded.

"I would not have you on a wall. You would live in my heart."

Her eyes widened with surprise. She shook her head as though she were a bit dizzy. It could have been the smoke, the drink and the music. "How strangely you talk," she said. "Are you from somewhere else? From India?"

"I don't know India," Arthur replied. "I know some places on the coast and in the high hills. I hail from Tintagel."

Jenny Hamilton sighed. "You sound like a romantic," she said. "Are you a poet, Arthur?"

"Someone must protect the realm. Poets do more important work. They interpret the heart."

Jenny nodded. Quietly, she said, "So sad that someone must always do the fighting and protect the realm. We need more poets, Arthur."

A shadow fell across the table. Edith leaned heavily against Yank and smacked her lipstick loudly on his cheek. Arthur looked up to see the largest man he'd ever seen in Britain, in any century. The corporal wore the green beret of a Royal Marine. He possessed hands the size of prize hams. One ham held a pint, the other turned, palm up in courtly fashion.

"Like to ask the lady for a dance," the corporal said in a basso timbre deep as the Channel. "If that's all right, sir," he said in a tone laced with mockery.

A brace of Marines stood behind the corporal. Their large arms were crossed expectantly. "Shall we dance, my fine lady?" The corporal's eyes, gone pink around the blue irises, revealed that he must have been very drunk, yet he held steady on his feet.

"No, thank you," Jenny replied.

"Come on," the towering corporal insisted. "Here's your chance to be with the real men, the Royal Marines."

Edith piped pleasantly, "We're all here to have a nice time. No fusses, now." She patted the arm of one of the Marines standing behind the corporal.

"We'll all have a nice time," the corporal said. "As soon as the lady shares a dance with Corporal Thomas Ives. Better than the RAF riff-raff."

"Corporal Ives, the lady said no," Arthur said quietly. "A knightly courtier understands 'no' from a lady."

"Well, you may be a gentleman, sir," the corporal sneered, "but I never saw you gentlemen in your Spitfires protecting my lads on the beach at Dunkirk. You were in the wrong place then. It may be you're in the wrong place now."

"I don't know about Dunkirk, Corporal," Arthur said evenly, "but it's plain for all here to see that you don't know your place."

"Arthur, please," Jenny said.

The corporal squinted at his pint, then slowly poured it onto Arthur's RAF wings. "Sorry. Sir. Clumsy of me. Not at all knightly."

As the stain spread on Arthur's uniform jacket, he rose from the table. "You are a clumsy fellow," Arthur said, upending the table so that it fell square on the corporal's commando boot.

As the table shifted, the corporal grabbed it and

tossed it over his head and threw it aside as if it were kindling. He grinned. "I'm so glad you did that, sir."

Arthur nodded appreciatively. "Clumsy. And strong."

The corporal's haymaker punch landed square on Arthur's jaw. The king saw all the stars that Merlin had taught him, and a few new ones. He dropped to his knees, gripping Merlin's staff.

"You'll have to do better than that, sir," the corporal said. "You're fighting the boxing champion of Six Commando now."

"Then let's fight," Arthur said, thrusting the staff up into Corporal Ives's ribcage. He heard Ives grunt and feared he'd hit an oak tree with legs.

Ives's second punch cleared Arthur's head and he heard the corporal's friends shout, "No fair! Give Ives a weapon!"

Then the king heard a metallic click and looked straight into the cold steel of a dagger.

Arthur wielded Merlin's stick like a quarterstaff and smashed it down on the corporal's wrist. Hearing the knife drop to the floor, he rammed the stick at Ives's middle. The other Marines piled onto Arthur. Somewhere in the back of the room amid the shrieks and screams and cheers that whirled around the fight, the wail of Artie Shaw's clarinet mixed with the wail of an air raid siren.

The room shook and the mirror over the bar shattered. Arthur, suffocating beneath the weight of his assailants, heard Yank shout, "Arthur, air raid!"

Arthur gripped the stick and rammed it as hard as he could, hearing a moan. It might have been Ives. The pile of bodies gave way as the lights in the pub blinked out.

"Yank! What gives?" Arthur shouted. He felt a hand pulling the stick.

"Come, Arthur, we gotta blow," Yank said. "The bombs are heading this way."

The Yank pulled the king along in the darkness. They pushed toward the door along with the others, crowding together like sheep. Arthur sensed panic. Then, from above, Arthur heard the barrel-chested baritone of Corporal Ives.

"Calm down, everyone!" the corporal ordered. "Don't press, and don't push! Orderly exit, everyone! Just like Dunkirk!"

The crowd stopped pushing, and Arthur could feel a hundred or so people listen, holding calm for just an instant in the blackness. Outside, he heard the groan of aircraft engines in the air. It terrified him. In the distance, the streets vibrated as if pounded by elephants' feet.

Then there was Ives's commanding voice. "Everybody to the shelters, single file through the door to Oxford Street Station. Observe order, and we shall survive. Remember, we're Britons!"

The door swung open into the darkened streets of the blacked-out city, and the pub crowd moved out in ones and twos, just as the second wave of bombs began to hit a few city blocks away.

"Come on, Arthur," Yank whispered. "It's our turn." The quick flashes of the incendiaries lit the sky some ways across London at the Thames. The fires reflected off the low clouds over the river.

"They're hitting the docks," Yank said, pulling Arthur along down the darkened street. The bomb flashes looked like Jupiter striking his anvil.

Arthur held on to the Yank as the American moved forward in the darkness. "Where's Jenny?" the king demanded. "I've got to find her."

"Arthur, she's gone to the shelters. We've got to get there, too."

"What shelter?" Suddenly, a wavering groan filled their ears.

"Heinkel! Get down!" Yank jerked Arthur down

onto the cobblestones. The street began to rumble and collapse before them, like a gargantuan domino falling. The king's lungs filled with dust and an explosion transformed night into day. Arthur coughed, choked and felt blind panic. Yank lifted him up.

"C'mon. The shelter's just down the street."

They held on to each other as the fires from the incendiaries raised a hellish, orange light all around them. Arthur watched great red trucks rumble down the street, with men in armor jumping from them. Suddenly, great streams of water issued forth from gigantic snakes that looked like the Loch Ness worm. Yank pulled the trembling Arthur past the spitting snakes.

"We're almost there," Yank said. "There's the gate to the Underground."

"Do we descend into hell itself?"

"It's hell up here, Arthur. Come on."

Yank jerked Arthur down the steps and the king inhaled the odor of crowded humanity, the smell of sweat, and fear and soiled clothing. But there were also ragged choruses of song breaking out to give courage in the dark.

"If you say it's safety, Yank, then I believe you," Arthur said.

Bill Cooper guided the king down the steps of Oxford Street Station. Bombs fell on the street above. The king looked behind him at the tunnel entrance to see a fireman running. A flaming timber crushed him like a stone dropped on a beetle. Yank pulled Arthur down the steps.

As they descended the stairway, the air grew thick and stale. The Underground was sweltering with human heat. In the dimness, Arthur could make out great arches towering above him. The steps were filled with people, like the catacombs. But all these were alive. Huddled, frightened and alive.

"Is this what you call shelter, Bill?"

"It's the Oxford Street Tube Station. It's where the Underground comes through. You never seen a subway before?"

"Not this one. Is it a catacomb?"

"All I know is people can stay safe from the bombs here."

An electric torch flashed in their faces. The beam of light fixed on their chests, illuminating their pilot's wings. The man holding the flashlight stepped forward, a plump, elderly man with an Air Warden helmet.

"RAF, is it? Why aren't you boys upstairs?" the Air Raid Warden inquired politely.

"Spot of leave," Cooper said.

"Come along, then. I'll get you a spot of tea. Mind the step. Don't tread on the ladies."

Arthur followed the flashlight's beam down to his feet, where he found innumerable bundles, women and children wrapped in their blankets. Ignoring the rumble above, they slept. The king stepped lightly between them. The three threaded their way among the thousands that crowded the main platform at Oxford Street Station, and then passed through a curtain held by the warden.

Inside the curtain, there was a door with a sign that said "Officials Only." They entered an office crowded with khaki-clad workers.

"I've brought me a pair of knights of the air," the warden announced happily. "Two of the gallant few."

Everyone came to their feet, applauding. Arthur was bewildered. The warden thrust a steel cup from a Thermos flask into Arthur's hand. "Sit out tonight's raid, and you'll be back up in the air soon enough."

"What do you folks do here?" Yank asked.

"We've got more than a hundred thousand people sheltering in the Underground," the warden said. "Even a few from the colonies, like you, sir."

"You protect all these people, then," Arthur said.

"Right you are," the warden said proudly. "We keep order, though people are mostly good. We also make sure that the ones who don't behave aren't a bother to those that do mind the rules. We administer sanitation and good order through the night."

"The bombs drop until morning, then," Arthur said.

"Ordinarily. It's gone on like this for a week now," the warden said. "It feels like the Hun's got every bomb in the world. There was a thousand souls killed in Stepney night before last."

"A thousand," Arthur murmured. "In one night."

A woman in khaki refilled Arthur's teacup. He held it with both hands and stared at it earnestly. He watched others sip their tea and did likewise.

"There would have been a good deal more killed if not for you lads," the woman serving tea said earnestly. "We thank God every night for the RAF."

"Thanks," Bill Cooper said, sipping noisily. He sat on a bench next to a table with a shortwave radio.

Arthur sipped the tea, finding its flavor pleasing. At first, he thought it might be hot mead. He watched the warden seat himself next to the large box with the knobs and fiddled with it.

"Let's find the American fellow on the wireless," the warden said. "In honor of our visitor from the new world."

Arthur looked to Yank. The box with the knobs squawked. Arthur watched apprehensively. Every moment held a new wonder, bursting with bombs or horseless chariots, metal-winged dragons with Merlin motors or coals that dropped from the mouth. But the box talked, and Arthur sat, hushed.

"I'm Edward R. Murrow for the Columbia Broadcasting System," the box declared. "And this, is London."

The king's tea splashed his knees as he dropped his cup. The khaki woman dabbed at him with a towel, but Arthur paid her no mind. He had eyes only for the demon box.

"As I speak, the bombs are falling on London," Murrow announced solemnly as the high-pitched scream of five-hundred pounders whistled around him. "The bombs are falling in the West End and the East End, and all along the River Thames tonight. But no one here is talking surrender.

"Winston Churchill, the leader of all the British peoples, has declared that London can take it, and London is proving him right," Murrow continued. "Every night for a week now, the bombs have fallen, killing women, killing children, chasing this island people into their train stations deep in the London Underground.

"Their answer has been to fight the dark power of Hitler during the hours of darkness. To answer his hatred with good cheer and quiet courage. The Battle of Britain is on in full earnest. Only providence knows when or how it will end, but all Londoners and English peoples everywhere are pinning their hopes on the Royal Air Force, those knights of the air who are dueling with the enemy even now in their Spitfires and Hurricanes."

The thick air of the office filled with static. The warden twisted the knob and the box fell silent. "Not bad, that Murrow chap," he said. "Of course, he's no Winston Churchill, but for an American, he's right eloquent." The warden winked at Arthur. "Don't you think so, sir?"

"I'm sorry," Arthur said.

"The fellow speaking on the wireless. Edward R. Murrow. Grand, isn't he?"

"Grand, yes."

"Sounds like he's right here, don't he? That's the

shortwave for you. Even in the Underground. Radio, miracle of the age. Always told the missus so."

"So that was Murrow," Arthur said slowly. "In the box."

"Oh, yes. Mr. Murrow's broadcasting from somewhere nearby. He's probably not further than a block from Downing Street and the offices of Winston Churchill himself."

Arthur shook his head and turned to Yank. "I must meet with Winston Churchill. This can't go on, the killing of women and children."

"Meet Churchill? Come on, Arthur. He's got enough to worry about."

"You don't understand, Yank," Arthur said urgently. "It's important."

"I don't understand you a lot of the time, Arthur. But I know we'd better worry about holding up our little end of the war."

"What about meeting the king?"

Yank knitted his brow. "I imagine the king's pretty busy, too. Wouldn't you be, if you were in his shoes?"

Arthur had to agree. Twentieth century, or not, the man was a monarch, even if he had a minister named Churchill to help him. Every age had its Merlin.

"You just stay close to me, Arthur," Yank said. "I'll get us home."

The sirens began wailing the melancholy cry of the All Clear. Clerks in the auxiliary office began pushing pins into maps that other clerks just as quickly removed. The air raid warden tapped Arthur lightly on the shoulder. "You'll have to go along now, gentlemen," he said. "Our work is just beginning. We're going to have to begin the cleanup."

"Thanks for the tea," Yank said.

"Thanks for coming all the way from America to defend our island," the warden said. "You're a good lot, you Yanks."

"He's from Connecticut," Arthur corrected.

Yank led Arthur out through the office door and into the multitude that trudged toward the steps leading to the surface. As they mounted the stairs, Arthur's nostrils filled with the odor of sulfur, burned timber and charred flesh. "This is Mordred's work," Arthur muttered.

"Come on, Arthur. Let's find the car and see if we've still got a squadron."

"I've got to find Jenny."

"She's a doctor, Arthur. If she's all right, she'll be working. We've got to get back to the squadron."

They ascended the Tube station steps into the light of a charcoal dawn filled with the reek of wet timber and ash. The gray light revealed that several blocks surrounding the Oxford Street Station had been particularly badly hit. Arthur saw a child's hand reaching from beneath a pile of bricks. Arthur fell to his knees, staring at the small hand.

Overhead, through the grayness, everyone looked up, listening to the washing machine drone of Junkers engines. They looked up, along with hundreds of others scurrying to their homes and offices. Suddenly, ack-ack guns cracked away.

"Must be a stray!" Yank shouted.

Some ran toward the shelter, but Arthur and Yank joined dozens who raced in the direction of the guns, adrenaline conquering fear. They ran down a lane where a burst gas main belched fire into the street. They ran around the flame jet and mounted a pile of rubble. Arthur and Yank clambered down the bricks and darted into Hyde Park. Arthur saw gargantuan harp strings rising into the fog. The barrage balloon crew turned their cranks furiously. Suddenly, the wires pulled taut and snapped.

An explosive burst blasted a fiery hydrogen cloud through the fog and Arthur felt heat that could melt flesh. He plunged his face into the wet grass. Another explosion followed, accompanied by the scream of twisted metal. The ground shook. Arthur looked up to see the crew running from the gun pit.

Arthur leaned on Merlin's staff and steadied Yank as they watched the flames. "Let's have a look," the king said.

They stumbled ahead and ventured into the trees on the fog-shrouded green. A stand of oaks looked as though an enormous tent had fallen upon it. The fabric flapped from the tree like a silken cloud.

"Barrage balloon," Yank said. "Wonder whether the gun crew bagged the Heinkel, or the balloon."

They made their way beneath the trees that snagged the balloon remnant and stepped onto the common. There lay the charred wreckage of the twin-engine bomber. It lay smoldering like a metal dragon. A pair of hands, still encased in flesh, clung to the control yoke in the shattered glass nose. The charred skull of the pilot grinned like a death's head.

Arthur inspected the wreckage. Something caught his eye. He kneeled down and picked up a piece of torn fuselage. It bore the mark of the pentagram.

Mordred caught his first sight of London from between his knees at fifteen thousand feet. The gunner's seat of the Me110 afforded an excellent view. The fires burned across the great metropolis. The stars winked through the bullet-resistant glass and the new moon flashed as the twin-engine bomber roared through the night. Mordred gripped the MG-15 machine gun. Kleist had demonstrated the weapon. It was no more demanding than a catapult. Pull a trigger and unleash hell's fire. Mordred peered over, watching the spot fires lighting up the London docks.

"This is grand," he said. "You must teach me to fly this machine."

"A bomber is a complex system, intolerant of error," Kleist's disembodied voice replied on the pilot intercom. "You must use the gun when the enemy attacks, as I showed you. We must work as a team."

Kleist's hands trembled on the controls. Even with the demon seated behind him, his voice, his words, his very presence made the general's head throb. "The gun is yours. Use it well, or we may die."

"Just so," Mordred replied. Through the luminous gunsight ring, Mordred scanned the starlit sky that sped by. His eyes were drawn back to the fires below. "How fast are we going?"

"We've got a tail wind tonight, the devil's own."

Mordred gasped at the sight of the firelit darkness unfolding beneath him. "Has London become so great? It spans many territories."

"It is, indeed, London you see beneath us. The Thames River estuary. Our bombsight point is the Isle of Dogs," Kleist replied. "I am dropping bombs."

The entire aircraft vibrated as the Junkers engines growled. Kleist pulled a lever and his tonnage plummeted toward the London docks.

"Bombs away," the Luftwaffe general announced. Mordred craned his neck and waited, sweat popping from his forehead and misting his goggles. He tore them aside and opened his eyes as wide as he could. Seconds later, the incendiaries burst like roses blooming in flame.

"What a sight," Mordred said. "A siege from the air."

"We wanted to build even bigger bombers," Kleist said. "But Goering said no. He wanted to please Hitler and build more of these."

Mordred's ears popped as a staccato burst of machine-gun fire opened up. "Heads up!" Kleist shouted into the intercom. "Night fighter."

A shadow roared by, darkening the gun sight. Mordred's hands froze on the machine gun. He failed to hear the shrieking in his earphones. "*Schiessen!* Shoot!" Kleist shouted as the dark wing vanished like Leviathan in the deep.

Kleist jerked the control yoke and the bomber turned heavily. Mordred could see only his black leather gloves. Sweat streamed from his forehead and he felt bile rise in his chest. His breathing quickened as he saw first the firefly pops, then the skyrocket arc of tracer ammunition streaming straight at him. He pressed the trigger and the machine gun bucked wildly.

Mordred's own tracers streamed out of the gun. Night burst like exploding stars as the tracers met. His knees turned to jelly, his stomach buckled and the bomber dropped beneath the flaming debris.

As the Zerstörer plane twisted and fell, the fiery docks rose up at him and his mortal stomach pit floated queasily toward his throat. The Messerschmitts nosed up at the last instant and Mordred was pressed heavily back into the metal seat. The Junkers engines cried havoc as the bomber swooped away from the Thames. Tossed and torn in his straps, Mordred retched into his oxygen mask and he tore it off, terrified of choking in his own spit. As quickly as it began, the pitching and rolling ceased and the aircraft stabilized.

"Are we finished?" Mordred cried.

"We're alive," Kleist shouted. "That's what matters." For the seconds of the plunge, the general had felt himself free of the grip of Mordred's power. For an instant, he felt his soul let loose again and free to fly the plane. But as the aircraft regained altitude, the sway of Mordred's will overcame him like the lowering of a great headache across his skull.

"We've dropped a thousand kilos of bombs. If we make it back across the Channel, we'll live to do it again," Kleist said. "Then they can try to kill us again."

Mordred hung on to the machine gun like a drowning man holding on to the rim of a boat. He felt the urge to vomit, but he also felt the red coal of victory burning in his chest.

Fifteen minutes later, as pink streaks of dawn creased the gray-lit skies, the bomber bumped its wheels onto the grass field near the castle of Chateau D'Eauville. The Luftwaffe crew chief waving the flags signaled them to turn left, opening the taxiway for the other bullet-nosed bombers that drifted in through the morning mists, some crashing to earth like meteors, others feathering their propellers like giant birds of prey.

Mordred and Kleist dropped through the belly hatch of the bomber, their boots hitting solid ground. Mordred shook the rubber out of his knees and strode with Kleist toward the control tower. A warrant officer ran up to Kleist and saluted.

"General Galland wants a word with you, Herr General."

"What can that bastard want?" Kleist muttered.

Kleist shook a cigarette loose from his pack and offered it to Mordred. Mordred had discovered that he liked cigarettes nearly as much as he liked explosives.

General Galland leaned against the control tower, puffing on a cigar. There would be no mistaking Galland for a bomber man. His black leather jacket, white scarf and slightly insolent expression marked him forever as a fighter pilot. He saluted carelessly. "Kleist," he said.

"We are tired, General Galland."

"My lads are tired of getting cut to pieces on fool's errands."

"You're wasting my time. We're already planning tomorrow's raid."

Galland fell in beside Kleist and Mordred as they crossed onto the bridge that spanned the castle moat. "Kleist, your methods are unchivalrous and endanger my men and machines recklessly."

"When did you become cautious, General Galland? Resting on your laurels now that you've got your Knight's Cross?"

Galland took the general by the shoulder and looked him in the eye. He could not help but notice that the bomber general's eyes looked vacant, haunted. "What possesses you, Kleist? We are wasting bombs on targets of no strategic value while my pilots are getting chopped up on bomber escort by the Spitfires and Hurricanes."

Mordred cleared his throat. "General Galland, I can hardly believe your fighter pilots are afraid to take on the outnumbered Royal Air Force. What would Goering say? Operation Camelot has his complete support."

Galland crushed his cigar beneath his heel. "Operation Camelot," he said contemptuously. "We're wasting a first-class air force to kill a lot of women and kids."

"Haven't you heard there's a war, General Galland?" Mordred smiled and he rubbed the star-shaped scar on his forehead. "Come, General. War in this age is the death of chivalry. Keep up with the times."

"We will not beat the British by slaughtering civilians," Galland retorted. "And we're losing planes that will be needed for the invasion."

"Civilians? The word is strange to me. You mean common folk, rabble? Do you give them a moment's thought? I'm amazed."

Kleist groaned and grabbed at his head as if he felt a sharp pain. Again, Galland noticed the jerkiness of his colleague's movements and his pallor.

"My aide disagrees with you, Galland," Kleist said hollowly. "The attack on London was proposed at the staff meeting, and Goering agreed. Camelot proceeds."

Mordred smirked and ran his tongue over the fine points of his teeth. "The Führer is committed to absolute ruthlessness. You are not in disagreement with Hitler, are you, Galland? Haven't you read your own leader's book?"

The fighter officer looked over his shoulder. He saw the red slash of the Reich's Battle Flag waving from the castle parapet. He saw an open car rush by, carrying a pair of cold-eyed SS men in black uniforms. They were everywhere like a plague these days. The Führer's watchdogs.

"No one wins an argument with the Führer," Galland said carefully. "I just believe there is a better way of winning the war."

Mordred shook his head slowly as if addressing a child who was slow. As he spoke, his green eyes glittered and Galland was caught by their deep-set emerald color, beautiful eyes, but emotionless as a stone.

"Every Englishman, every English woman and child is an enemy. Every woman slain will never assemble a bomb. Every child killed is one less to bear arms against us one day. One less mouth to feed when we conquer Britain."

Galland looked at Mordred. "You make it sound very personal, Major."

Mordred snapped a match with his thumb and lit his cigarette. "You are right, General. Even if you are dropping bombs from a great height, I find war is damned personal. I take victory as personally, and enjoy it." He exhaled a puff of smoke through his nostrils.

Galland shook his head and gripped Kleist's hand. It was cold to the touch and Galland recoiled.

"Your aide is one of the new breed, Anton," Galland said. "You should keep an eye on him. And get some sleep, or check in with the medics. You look like shit."

Galland turned about-face and marched away. He knew that the green-eyed major was watching him. He could feel the hairs prickle on the back of his neck as he hurried back across the bridge. Galland had met Hitler and did not fear him. The sight of the major filled him with a wave of nausea.

*   *   *

Kleist lay on his bunk, weakened and benumbed. It was not the fatigue of combat. He felt ill, but not feverish. In fact, he shivered as if he were at high altitude in his aircraft, or as if his blood circulation were failing.

The green-eyed man sat across the room, hunched over the general's field desk. The room was thick with yellow smoke from Mordred's chain smoking. The Gauloises were noxious, but Mordred enjoyed them more than the German military issue cigarettes. Kleist's nerves were frayed from Mordred's ceaseless gramophone playing. Everytime the needle floated to the end of the platter, the stranger returned it to the beginning of the song, "That Old Devil Moon." It was maddening.

While the clarinet shrieked, the stranger pored over an ancient volume. The falcon Nietzsche flew in aimless circles above his head. The green-eyed man would run a finger over the yellowed pages, and Kleist could only watch. The general lay suspended, helpless, as if floating in time, so tired that he could not get up, his energy drained from him.

The stranger looked enough like a man, but there were subtle differences. The ends of his fingertips were pointed. And his teeth were sharp, ratlike. Yet, when the green-eyed man smiled and talked to Kleist's comrades, it was as if he were the most charming officer they had ever met. Couldn't they see he was not one of them? Not real? Or, too real. Kleist shivered. Mordred turned a page and cursed in a tongue that was strange to Kleist, but he took it to be a variant of the English he learned in school.

"Who are you?" Kleist croaked, alarmed at the harsh sound of his own voice. "Are you a spy, an enemy?"

Mordred turned to Kleist, annoyed at the interruption, and placed the sharpened talon to his lips. "No Hun has need for fear of me," the stranger whispered, his lips curling round the yellowed incisors. "But anyone in my personal service must dread me."

"What are you?"

Mordred's eyes gleamed in the dark. "Need you ask, General? I've come from a place beyond death. Just be glad that I need you."

Mordred returned his gaze to Merlin's pages, ignoring Kleist as if he were a hunting hound by the fire. Merlin's writing confounded Mordred. The frontispiece to the text was a variant of the characters that illuminated the *Book of Kells,* yet more elusive and obscure. Much of the meaning eluded Mordred until his taloned finger crossed the first reference to his father: Arthur Rex Pendragon. There, the language shifted to the words hidden away in the monasteries, the hated Latin verbs.

"At Britain's darkest hour, the king will return," Mordred murmured. He looked up at the falcon that flew circles inside the castle chamber. "Will he, little friend? Will he come? Will we finish our contest, then?"

Mordred remembered his father's futile attempts to persuade the monks from the monastery to teach him the language of God. The lessons made him nauseous. *Amas, amat. Deus in excelsis.* The words stung him. On the day of a particularly long lesson, he killed a cat, merely for spite, just by looking at him. He could wilt flowers with his gaze, also. He'd learned that trick from Mother.

The monks quickly comprehended that the language of God was obscene to Mordred. If they smote his hand with birches, he would gaze at them with his deep green eyes. His stare would make them feel faint and swoon. Soon after Mordred arrived at court, the animals began to vanish. Small ones at first. Some weeks later, the king's hunting hound was found on the fen at Glastonbury Tor, its heart torn from its chest. The blood was drained from the corpse. Mordred's name was whispered, but none dared carry it to the king without proof.

The priests, including the learned Geoffrey of Monmouth, urged Arthur to banish the halfling child. But Merlin, the chief adviser, urged patience.

"Everyone at court feared Mordred's gaze," the halfling murmured as he turned the pages forward. They were wonderfully illustrated with inventions of the age, including the flying machines.

There were pages devoted to the rise of the Huns, their leader, and his crusade against Britain. Mordred recognized the sorcery in the Hun leader's dark, piercing eyes that floated spiritlike above the comic mustache. Mordred knew immediately why the Hun chieftain had armies to command. He had the power of the eyes. He, too, must have been hated as a child, Mordred mused. Everyone loathed Mordred. Except for Mother, and she was far across the emerald sea, in the dark tower. And even she had kicked him out. Was it ambition, desire or jealously? Mordred wondered.

Morgan Le Fey knew her son well, his appetites and capacities. During his early childhood, she would lavish her love, or deny it if it suited her pleasure to torture him. And it often did suit her to torture him by ignoring or taunting him. She never let him forget that he was half-human. If he excelled at a charm or a spell, she gave him a golden apple. If he failed, a blue bolt from her sorceress' eye would make the headache roar until his young skull might explode.

Thus, she taught him the appreciation of her arts, and her particular form of affection.

She banished him from the dark tower in Eire while he was still a raw boy. He begged, kneeled and begged, to be let back in. A look from her pitiless eyes informed him that it was useless to ask. He beheld the blue fire in her eyes and knew he would be left in the cold.

"Of course you may return," the dark lady said, a bloodred smile warming her ruby lips with voluptuous promise. She was pale, so pale. And so beautiful in her dark, emerald cape that enfolded her body like a shroud.

"When you possess your father's isle, you are welcome in my chambers, halfling. Only then will Mordred and Morgan be whole."

The child kneeled and keened. He cried into the wild wind and whined, "Why me, Mother? You vanquish him! It was you who slept with him." A blue bolt for reward of Mordred's suggestion.

He kneeled for her, the sharp stones of the castle entry cutting his knees, the cold wind cutting through his patchwork rags.

"It's said in Merlin's book that only a male child can take the kingdom. Bring the crown of Arthur to me. Bring me his sword, and we will be happy."

The door to the tower swung shut. So, the boy Mordred turned and walked into the wild wind, knowing there was no home for him in Morgan's tower until he ruled in his father's domain.

The stones of the tower at Camelot shone in the sun. The pennants flew fine colors. Mordred hated it. Arthur, he quickly decided, was a fool. The king welcomed him, promising to make him a page, and finally, a knight.

Alone among those at court, Arthur seemed oblivious to the child's nature. He was not unnerved by the boy's teeth or withering gaze. Finally, it was only behavior that divided father from the as yet unacknowledged child.

Mordred's time at Camelot moved by degrees from

mischief to cruelty. Finally, even the king came to
dread Mordred's appearance at court. The furtive
looks, the shiftiness, the eyes. And he came to fear
there was no cure or hope of improvement for the
son of a witch. Mordred made friends among the
lesser knights and squires jealous for advancement.
He divided the court until it became a chamber of
whispers, with courtiers moving like pieces on a
board.

"Mordred was Mordred," the changling mused as
he pored over Merlin's text. "How could he love me,
who would dine on his flesh and call for ale to wash
it down?"

Mordred's exile came with the death of the first
girl. Banished, he found his friends in the wilderness
among the Huns who had moved inland from their
coastal raids. First, they took him hostage. Then, he
took them by main force of his blazing green eyes.
The same eyes that had withered life from the king's
prize hound could bend any Hun's mind to
Mordred's purpose.

His mother had given him that much, anyway.
That legacy would have to do until he could deliver
his father's domain to the power of the dark tower,
where Morgan waited to return his love in exchange
for power over men.

Kleist tried to rise from the bed and found he could
not. Too weak.

"Why did you come for me?"

Mordred stared at Kleist. The eyes were horrible.
In a lightning motion, he replaced the needle at the
beginning of the record and the clarinet grated at the
edge of Kleist's soul. "That Old Devil Moon."

"You are useful to me," Mordred said, his tone
matter-of-fact. "You will advance my cause. I mean

to present your leader the king of Britain's head on a pike."

Kleist felt his head aching, the unnatural pressure building so it felt as if it might come off and roll on the floor. He groaned. "What in hell's name are you?"

Mordred turned away as if he were ignoring an insect in his path and the pressure eased on Kleist's head. "You should hope that I never give you the true answer, General."

Mordred returned to the pages of his ancient book. He ran his fingers across each line of text, some of it formed from runes. Mordred's body swayed in rhythm to the scratchy gramophone music. The record ended and the falcon ceased its circling, dropping onto Mordred's shoulder. Mordred whispered a few words of endearment to the predator. He nuzzled it onto his arm and lifted the hood gently.

"Do you care for the bird, General?"

Kleist nodded weakly. "I trained it."

Mordred caught the bird's eyes and stared intently. The falcon fell dead from his forearm in a heap of feathers on the stones.

"Lest you think to betray me," Mordred said. He swung his boots under the desk and returned to his studies, oblivious to Kleist.

9

Dragon Squadron's pilots shifted about in the stiff-backed wooden chairs of the briefing tent. Some plainly were bored by the latest installation of the "Know Your Enemy" film series. Not Arthur King. He watched the German armies march across the wide gray screen and roll into France with the rapt fascination of someone enchanted. Moving pictures. Pictures that talked. Merlin's magic sometimes seemed simple by comparison.

When the lights came up, Squadron Leader Richardson marked the blackboard, the chalk sending a shiver down Arthur's back. Richardson finished sketching the inverted five-pointed star and turned to the squadron. His brow furrowed as he examined his briar pipe.

Gilbert Hawley's arm shot up first. "What's that, Squadron Leader, some hashed up swastika?"

"It's the insignia of a special, new Luftwaffe formation, Hawley."

"Same old Huns. Different mark," Hawley retorted.

"Air Ministry don't think so," Richardson said patiently. "They think a new fleet has been formed, one with a new mission."

"Usual Air Ministry rubbish," Hawley retorted.

Tommy Stubbs cleared his throat. "Quit interrupting, Gil. I thought you wealthy chaps had better manners."

Hawley turned to Stubbs and inspected him as though he were milk gone bad. His eyebrow arched. "I beg your pardon, Tommy, but I don't need some Cockney reservist to tell me manners."

Stubbs grinned, flashing a gold tooth. "You don't know your betters, or your manners, Gil. Some Cockney's are aces, and some chaps with titles are not."

"That's enough," Richardson said tersely. "This is a briefing, not a row. I want to talk about this insignia." He tapped his pipe stem lightly on the star.

"All right," Hawley said, folding his arms and rolling his eyes. "We shall hear tales of Hitler's terrible new order."

Yank whispered to Arthur, "Hawley's a know-it-all." Arthur nodded solemnly, and he started when Richardson called out his name.

"King here can tell us a bit about this new discovery," Richardson said. "Step up to the lectern, Lieutenant King. We have a roundtable forum here in Dragon Squadron."

"I beg your pardon, sir?" Arthur said, mystified. The pilots shifted their chairs into a half-circle, facing the lectern.

"Roundtable time, King. Every pilot gives his view to the others. We speak our minds and share our knowledge. We do it in the round, so none is accorded more weight than the other. Even Hawley's views are taken into account." The squadron laughed and Hawley folded his arms resentfully.

"Yes, sir. Jolly good."

Arthur looked about cautiously. He found every pilot in the squadron was staring at him. Young, earnest eyes, clear, focused and curious. Even exhausted from combat, the fliers had fresh faces. The flower of knighthood. Arthur recognized them. They looked like his best men from the ancient age. He rose and leaned upon Merlin's stick. He stepped forward gingerly. Arthur approached the lectern and Richardson removed a drape covering the metal fragment Arthur retrieved from the bomber wreckage in Hyde Park.

"I've already sent the report along," Richardson said. "This fragment will go to Air Intelligence. Now, Lieutenant King, tell my lads what you told me." Richardson spoke gravely to the squadron in a confidential tone, "Lieutenant King is something of a medievalist, a Cambridge man."

Sweat streamed down Arthur's neck. How could he speak to these new men without informing them he was mad? He stared at the fuselage fragment, and then at the chalk sketch of the inverted star.

"What I found this morning on the wreckage of the machine is a special sign," Arthur said haltingly. "We know that across time, this sign has stood for a particular sort of evil."

"Different from your everyday Nazi evil?" Hawley said derisively. "Leave that for the propaganda boys that lie to the simpletons cowering beneath ground in London. These Huns just want to win the war."

Arthur shook his head. "I beg your pardon, Hawley. I think it goes beyond that." Arthur held up the fuselage fragment so every man in Dragon Squadron could see it clearly.

"We know that across many years any who love this emblem worship darkness. Why else would they destroy the innocent? That's not war. It's merely hatred. Murder, vile. Hitler must be in league with them."

"What's it got to do with us?" Hawley asked. The flight leader slumped in his chair and closed his eyes.

"More than one thousand people died in Stepney night before last," Arthur said quietly. "Does that mean anything to you, Hawley?"

Hawley yawned. "It means Jerry has the good sense to drop his load on the lower classes where it'll do some good."

"I've known men like you," Arthur said quietly. "You're a good warrior, aren't you?" He could feel the men watching him, listening to him. He wanted so to say the right words. "You're a real killer, aren't you, Hawley?"

"Killing the enemy's just my job. Whether the Hun wears a swastika or a gingham frock is someone else's problem."

"Your sort, Hawley," Arthur continued, "likes fighting well. But the people we are charged to protect don't matter much to you, do they? Do you lack chivalry?"

Hawley's lips pulled tight, his clipped mustache turning up in an imitation of a grin. "Are those little people sitting in a Spitfire cockpit, King? For that matter, are you? I haven't seen you do any flying yet."

"That's enough, Hawley," Richardson said. "We're getting pretty far afield. You can take a seat, King."

Richardson retrieved the fuselage fragment from Arthur, who returned to his seat next to the Yank. About half the men grinned at Hawley. The others watched Arthur. Richardson tapped his briar pipe on the lectern.

"King retrieved this insignia from a Heinkel that bought it over London. We think it's from a new fleet, tasked specifically to kill civilians."

"Good," Hawley said. "Maybe it'll take pressure off the airfields."

"Who can say?" Richardson said. "But if there's a civilian panic, Parliament could give Churchill the boot. Then you'd better practice your German, because we'll all be speaking like Huns."

Hawley sniffed. Tommy Stubbs raised his hand. "What does that star thing mean, anyway, Arthur? It looks like it's bottoms up." The king rose from his chair. Again, he felt the men watching.

"It's the mark of the devil," Arthur said. "Whoever wears it does Satan's bidding. That's the ancient tale."

Stubbs lit a Players Export. "That follows, doesn't it?" he said. "I suppose that puts us on the side of the angels, right?"

"Briefing is ended, gentlemen," Richardson said. "You may smoke."

Every flier in Dragon Squadron lit up, and Arthur was amazed that they all so craved the little sticks with smoke coming from the end.

Arthur and Yank trudged across the muddy field. The mechanics were fitting the Spitfires with new, variable pitch propellers. Other ground crew were fitting extra body armor behind the leather seats, per instructions from Air Ministry. The squadron remained on fifteen-minute alert. Arthur remained dependent on Merlin's stick.

"You must teach me to fly those machines, Bill," Arthur said, pointing the stick at one of the Spitfires.

"Hell, Arthur, I got shot down same as you. You could probably teach me a thing or two."

"I doubt it."

"Aw, gee. We all have stuff that we learn from each other, the good ones, anyway. Tommy Stubbs is one of the best natural fliers I've seen. You take Hawley—he's good, but he doesn't want to share anything. Says he's scared he'll have to fly with a rotter and that'll be the end of it."

Arthur grabbed Bill Cooper's arm. They stood on the edge of the field behind a petrol truck. His fingers closed around Cooper's sleeve. "You're not listening to me, Bill. I'm telling you I've got to learn how to fly. Mordred's up there, somewhere, and I have to fight him."

Yank tore his arm loose and he stared at Arthur quizzically. "What is this with this Mordred character? I've never heard one limey so fixed in his mind on one Hun. Sometimes I think you're a little loony, Arthur."

"I don't know what loony means, Bill Cooper, but I am a desperate man and I have to learn how to fly. It's important for all of England that Mordred is met and beaten."

Yank shook his head. "You can fly. I've seen you."

"I crashed, my friend," Arthur said. "You couldn't really call that flying."

The Yank removed his forage cap and scratched his head. He squinted at Arthur. "You really can't fly."

"That's right."

"But you were in a Spitfire."

"That's also true."

"So, you must have had permission to get in the cockpit. You've gotta be RAF to get onto an airfield."

"Yes."

"What is it that I'm missing about this picture, Arthur? You've got me very confused."

"I am, as well, my friend. But I have my orders to follow. And they come from a very high place."

Yank whistled. He looked about and no one was close by. A dispatch rider rattled off the field on a BSA motorcycle, carrying Arthur's piece of fuselage off to the intelligence section at Air Ministry. The wind blew in Yank's hair and he shook his head. "You're on a secret mission, right?"

"That's as good a way of putting it as I can think of, Bill."

Yank shook himself a Churchman and snapped a match with his thumb. The gesture still made Arthur jump. "You must be from Air Ministry, come down here to check us out on our efficiency, or our security or something."

Arthur wondered what in blazes Air Ministry was, but it seemed that everyone was talking about it. He nodded his head solemnly. "Breathe a word of that around Dragon Squadron and there will be hell to pay, Yank Cooper."

Yank beamed and he blew a smoke ring. That amazed Arthur. The American's face glowed with the childlike pleasure of being let in on a great confidence.

"Your secret's safe with me, Lieutenant King. I bet you picked me out cause I'm an American and those limeys want to know if I'll squeal." Yank shook his head knowingly. "They could torture me and I wouldn't tell. I'm no security risk. And you can take that back to ministry. I'm quiet as the sphinx."

"No need for that, Yank," Arthur said. "You've got to teach me how to fly."

Yank clapped Arthur on the shoulder. "Right, old man. First lesson's tomorrow. Dawn patrol, just like Errol Flynn. I can play as long as you do."

"Remember," Arthur said confidentially, "I'm not supposed to be flying yet. The leg."

Yank gave an exaggerated nod. "The leg, Arthur. Right, the leg."

"There's one more thing."

"Anything for our friends among the higher-ups, Lieutenant. What'll it be?"

"You've got to help me find that woman. Doctor Jenny."

"That's a cinch. Glad to see you got you're priorities straight, Lieutenant. Learn to fly first, then grab the girl. Yeah, you picked the right guy, all right. I'm stickin' to you like glue."

Arthur cocked his head, puzzled. "I beg your pardon?"

"Enough," Yank said, putting his arm around Arthur's shoulder. "Let's go get your kit sorted out. Richardson let me have some duffle from a guy who was going to sleep in my quarters."

"Where is he? I wouldn't take another man's kit."

"He's dead. He didn't know how to fly either."

Yank laughed as he jumped across a mud puddle and onto the planking that led to the mess tent. Briefings made him hungry. Even for powdered eggs.

First light at Hornchurch formed salmon-colored streaks painted through mottled cloud formations. The cloud cover broke up into a vaporous herring-bone pattern. Arthur sighted a pale, slender slice of the new moon fading into the sky at dawn. The king followed Yank Cooper across the field that led to the hangars. Arthur watched the dew clinging to dandelions on the grassy field, and his breath, small puffy clouds sailing into the icy air.

They came to the last hangar where a ground crew worked away, ministering to a sleek Spitfire. The armorers, known among themselves as "the plumbers," carried chain belts of .303 ammunition to be fed into the aircraft's eight guns. The petrol truck rumbled off to the next hangar. Yank walked up to the Spitfire. Casually, he returned the salutes of crewmen, who grunted "sir" deferentially.

Arthur put his hand on the nose of the aircraft as gently as if he were patting the muzzle of a favorite war horse. "It's beautiful," he said.

"Yep," Yank replied. "Simply wizard."

"So, it's got magical powers, then."

"The Mark-Two Spitfire can out turn any Messerschmitt the Hun sends up after it," Yank said. "That's how come I'm still alive. Magic enough for me."

"What makes it go so?" the king asked casually.

Yank stared at Arthur, the American's brow furowing with just a trace of Yankee skepticism, as if he were the young man at the fair. "You know as well as I do, Arthur. It's the Merlin engine, right?"

"Merlin's engine. Right."

Yank shook his head. He chinned himself onto the wing and swung his leg across it like a gymnast. He nodded at one of the crew, who stepped aside and allowed him to climb onto the nose. Bill Cooper unhooked the engine cowling so that the engineering symmetry of the twelve-cylinder engine was revealed to Arthur.

The engine looked like an anvil, complicated by tubing and fixtures that the king could not begin to understand, except that he gleaned there must be great power contained in it. For the creature that the engine rested inside of was, indeed, beautiful and threatening.

"Twelve-cylinder Rolls Royce," Yank said solemnly. "We've come a long way since Kitty Hawk and the Wright Brothers."

"Yes," Arthur said, utterly bewildered. Yank

closed the cowling and hopped to the ground. He looked up at the propeller and exhausts, admiration warming his apple of a face. The armorers jumped off and Yank was alone with his plane, the sleek Supermarine racer with its graceful camouflage wings.

"One thousand, one hundred and seventy-five horses all packed into the nose of that aircraft," Cooper said, his tone hushed. "No wonder they call it a Merlin."

"The power of a thousand horses," Arthur said. "And it's Merlin's doing. When do we fly the machine? And how?"

Yank stared at the Englishman. Yank Cooper felt ready to take a dare, or to be let in on the secret. But Arthur merely stared back, his steel gray eyes unblinking.

"You really don't know how to fly, do you, Arthur?"

"I told you the truth, Yank. I need your help."

Yank shook his head sorrowfully. "I wish I knew why they gave me the short straw," he said. He looked up at Arthur. "If you're on the level, pal, I think you're going to die."

"If I do, it's in a mighty cause," Arthur said. "And if I live, you, Bill Cooper, will have helped all of England."

"You're a strange duck, Arthur King."

"Help me fly, Bill."

Yank sighed and ran his fingers through his close-cropped brown curls. "Let's get started, Lieutenant." He marched toward the hangar door.

"Don't we have to get in the airplane, Yank?" Arthur called after him.

Yank turned and grinned. "If I'm gonna kill you, Arthur, I'm going to do it carefully. We won't be starting our lesson in that airplane. It's a widow-maker."

Arthur cocked his head. In a puzzled tone, he said,

"Isn't that the machine we use to fight the Hun? That's the machine I've got to learn."

Yank nodded. "Maybe you will. But we need something a little more basic. C'mon."

Arthur followed Yank from the hangar. Some ground mist clung to the ground, and the pair watched a Spitfire taking off from the far end of the field. The plane bumped along, fitfully at first, then gaining speed and smoothing out as it accelerated. The propeller spun and sung like a hummingbird, pulling the slender plane away from the earth in a graceful climb. The landing gear folded like a nun's hands. Arthur's breath caught in his throat as the plane lifted into the morning light and the sun glinted on its wings.

"Like a falcon," he murmured. "Like my hunting bird." The king turned to Yank and said, "What plane will we fly today? I'm ready for anything."

"You better be, King."

They walked behind the hangar where an aged biplane, a Hawker Hart, rested on two tires that looked like overstuffed cushions. The wires held the twin wings together and the propeller looked forlorn. Arthur looked at Yank, his expression puzzled and his gray eyes anxious.

"This is a flying machine?"

"Basic model," Yank said, grinning. "We crawl before we walk. We walk before we run. We run before we fly."

Arthur walked around the open cockpit. He gazed at the foot stirrup that hung below the bottom wing. He plucked the aileron wire and turned to Yank.

"Perhaps I am going to die."

Yank nodded vigorous agreement. "If you're on the level, it's entirely possible, Arthur."

"Let's get on with it," Arthur declared. He put his foot in the stirrup and swung his leg over the leather cockpit rim. It was about the exact height and dimension of the saddle for Battle, his favorite steed. But Battle lived and breathed and champed at the bit. The Hawker sank under his weight like an aged swayback and the aircraft squeaked as he sat in the leather basket seat.

Arthur loved flying. Yank nudged the open cockpit aircraft up into the cold, blue sky at about five thousand feet and the king felt his face cut raw with a cold, glorious, wind-whipped sting. Arthur felt wholly alive and exhilarated. Yank put the Hart into a gentle, banking turn and they could see below them the rich, green and brown patchwork of English earth.

When Merlin transformed Arthur into a hawk, he could see all below and about him. But somehow, this was grander. As a hawk, he flapped his wings like a bird. But this experience of motored flight was somehow outside of him. He felt intensely the humming of the wires strung taut between the wings. He reveled in the cold blast in the face. The scarf protected his throat like a gorget and the leather jacket became his breastplate. The engine vibrated and roared with its own discrete life.

The engine, he finally understood, was that powerful thing that pulled them along and made the propeller knife through the air like a spinning dagger. And he knew that the wings, just like the hawk's, provided lift.

Arthur longed to fly with the grace of his own falcon, never far from his heavy-gloved hand, even coming with him to vespers at Conventry. He finally understood the falcon's flight, and its joy.

Arthur watched the control column stick move with a life of its own as Yank manipulated the controls from the instructor-pilot's seat behind him. He was too caught up in the moment to be the serious student. Ecstasy owned him.

The plane banked sharply and the king felt his stomach rise toward his throat as Yank Cooper put the biplane into a dive. Arthur looked straight down to see the ground rushing at him. Suddenly, he feared the tempest.

"Pull up!" Arthur cried into the microphone.

"You pull up!" Yank replied. "Pull the stick back. It's your move, King!"

Arthur grabbed for Merlin's stick, which he had carried into the cockpit with him. Nothing happened and the aircraft continued to plunge. "The control stick!" Yank yelled. "Between your legs, dummy!"

At the last possible instant, Arthur grabbed the control column and yanked it back. Instantly, he saw the nose of the Hawker buck up in front of him and he was looking up at blue sky and cottony clouds.

The aircraft stalled and began to twist. The king felt panicked, stampeded, utterly out of control. The nose leveled, then began to dive again. The engine backfired and started, and once again, the control column moved between Arthur's legs with a life of its own.

"You could have killed us," Yank said into the microphone. "There's no doubt about it, my friend. You really don't know how to fly."

Arthur felt the shame warm his cheeks. It felt like the first time his brother Kay knocked him from a hobby horse and stood above him shaking his head. The king gingerly closed his hands round the control column. Reluctantly, he choked out the words, "Please, sir. Let me try again."

"Okay," Yank said easily. "I'll give her the throttle and you pull the stick back. But take her easy, just like you was riding a prize pony."

The king thought about a horse, then he thought about the bucking craft that jiggled and vibrated beneath his feet. He pulled the stick back in an easy motion and he felt the nose rising again, this time smoothly. And suddenly the plane transformed into a chariot that was lifting gracefully toward the sun.

"That's better," Yank said. "Now push your stick forward and level her out."

Arthur complied. He heard the roar of the reciprocating engine and felt the pedals moving gently beneath his feet. He felt suddenly as though Merlin and the Yank had given him a magic carpet.

"How high are we, Yank?"

"About five thousand feet. Low enough so we could get down fast if we had to."

"Five thousand feet," the king whispered. "God in heaven. And me, too."

Yank pushed the stick forward and put the nose down gently, turning toward the grass field. As they descended toward the field, Arthur watched the needles fluctuating on the simple panel before him. He saw that as the plane dropped in altitude, the center needle also inclined toward the left.

Alternating between watching the needles and the ground looming, Arthur gloried in the speed. On one gauge, he read the words, "air speed" and saw the needle jiggling around the 100 mph mark. The aircraft nosed up gently and the rubber wheels bumped against the grassy field, bringing the biplane to a gently shuddering stop. Arthur twisted his neck round so that he could look at Yank, who grinned at him, his face insectlike behind the oversize goggles.

"Now, you try it, Arthur," Yank said. "Don't worry. I'll tell you exactly what to do."

The king swallowed, his throat parched. His pulse

quickened and excitement gained over fear. Mastering difficult steeds had been his life's challenge. He clenched his fist and pushed his thumb up. He breathed deeply and nodded that he was ready to go.

10

Deep in the cellars of Chateau D'Eauville, there was a closed room where the castle's stocks of wine had been stored. After the Occupation, Kleist emptied the cellar and shipped the wine to Goering's estate at Carinhall. Goering accepted the vintages as tribute and sent the general a note, thanking Kleist as a loyal knight of the Luftwaffe.

Now, a different knight occupied the cellar. The list of tasks Mordred presented to Kleist was nearly complete. Lead ingots, three, smelted and cast from stocks of ammunition. A single gold ingot melted from the chalice that had been the pride of the chateau. That much had been kept from Goering's clutches, but now belonged to Mordred, who waited in the shadows.

The blacksmith, a corporal named Rudi of Bavaria, had obediently placed the lead ingots and the gold into the smelters retrieved from the village. Rudi, called "Little Rudi" by his comrades, squeezed the bellows like a toy, turning the coals a bright red just as he did in his home village of Bad Tolz. The ingots melted into liquid pools and hung suspended in the smelter. Wordlessly, Rudi turned to his next task. In the Goering Grenadiers, orders were not questioned.

Kleist stood nearby, holding a torch that burned low while the bare-chested smith finished his work. The granite chips flew like small splinters and arrowheads as the burly smith pounded the hammer and chisel, making the metal and stone sing in the darkness. After an hour passed, he had finished his work, and the blacksmith stepped back from the boulder. He stood emotionless as a stone himself, his chest bathed in sweat from his work. Rudi waited for a sign of approval, or an order from his commander. But General Kleist remained where he was, holding the torch, almost like a statue. Even in the torchlight, Rudi noticed his commander was as pale as a ghost. The smith felt a cold breeze and Mordred stepped from the shadow.

The blond major patted the massive shoulder of the blacksmith, almost as if he were patting the flanks of prized stock from the stable. "You have done well, Little Rudi," Mordred said. "General Kleist was correct. You are truly the strongest man in the garrison."

The smith bowed his shaven head, his chin receding into a neck as thick as a bull's. "Thank you, Herr Major. *Meine Ehre ist treue.* My honor is loyalty."

"Good," Mordred said. "I doubt that another man in the regiment could have lifted that sword as you did."

Rudi cast his eyes at the two-handed broadsword that rested on the flagstones of the cellar. Slowly, he shook his head. "No. No one else could, Major. I am sure of it. It was all I could do to drag it into the truck. It was nearly lost in the surf."

Mordred nodded. "Yes, but you didn't lose it. You brought it here, to me."

"For the general, Herr Major," the corporal corrected him. "It was his order."

Mordred's eyes flashed. "Yes, of course. And if you were ordered, you would lift the sword again, wouldn't you?"

"Of course, Herr Major."

"Well then, do it." The corporal turned to General Kleist. The general nodded his head and the blacksmith bent over to pick up the sword. Mordred watched the man's muscles straining against the weight, each sinew of his broad back and shoulders tightening like cords stretched to their limit. It took him a full minute to lift the blade by its hilt.

"It is heavier by the instant, Herr Major," the blacksmith grunted.

"Place it in the stone, please," Mordred said, his voice dropping down in pitch to a whisper of desire. The sword fell into the crevice Rudi had cut in the stone as if into a sheath. Rudi fell onto the cellar floor and lay on his back, panting from exhaustion.

As Rudi lay on the floor, resting, Mordred poured an iron ladle of hot lead into the crevice that Excalibur rested in, to seal it in place. To crown the work, he ladled the ingot of gold, so that the hot, precious metal solidified around the edge of the blade and the dragon-scaled hilt. He returned to the smelter.

Moving quickly toward the blacksmith, Mordred poured the remaining ladle of lead onto the Bavarian's eyes. The blacksmith screamed in agony and writhed on the stones. As he kicked and thrashed, Mordred stepped back. Then he dropped on his knees and grabbed the smith by his thick bull's neck, crushing the windpipe. As the death rattle caught in the Bavarian's throat, Mordred's lips met the smith's and he sucked the life from the corporal's lungs. When Mordred turned and looked up at Kleist, his lips dripped saliva, and he panted with the animal strength of the Bavarian, whose crumpled body lay lifeless on the floor and empty as a husk.

"I needed his strength," Mordred said. He wiped his lips. "Now, I've got it."

The torchlight flickered, bathing Mordred's face in shadow and light. The general trembled, but he did not move. His eyes were caught in Mordred's stony-eyed gaze. The general knew he beheld the basilisk.

The obsolete biplane turned into the wind and the gauge told Yank they were losing airspeed. Still, Yank didn't talk on the microphone. In the front cockpit seat, the king handled the stick heavily, but with a certain aptitude. Yank suspected the strange lieutenant from Air Ministry had flown before. The air at six thousand feet carried the bite of a harvest apple. The king banked slightly, pulling the stick to starboard while tentatively pressing the rudder pedals. Arthur felt pleased and full of himself, until the first shots rattled the aircraft.

The biplane quivered. Another series of blasts shook the plane from nose to stern. Arthur heard Yank laugh. "Ease up on the stick, Arthur," Yank advised. "Don't clutch when the guns are firing. You'll put us into a spin."

"What guns?"

"Lewis guns, Lieutenant. Twin caliber three-oh-threes, mounted over the wing for gunnery training. You don't think I'd take us up unarmed? This crate may be a box kite with wings, but we're still in a war."

"Those were our guns, then," Arthur called into the microphone. "Not some Hun?"

"I fired a short burst. Try it yourself."

"I don't know how to fire a gun."

"Pull the bar in front of you. Pull smooth, don't tug. About three seconds, then let up."

Arthur held one hand taut on the control column. Leaning forward, with his head looming over the open cockpit, he reached and pulled the gun control. The nose of the aircraft bucked as another burst of gunfire rattled. He suddenly realized that he had transformed the plane from a box kite into a weapon. "That's good," Yank called out. "Let 'er rip."

Arthur watched the tracers arc into a cloud, and he felt a surge of personal power. He felt at one with the aircraft. Lift, propulsion and firepower. Immediately, they were one to him. He dropped his gloved hand from the gun control so that it brushed Merlin's staff, which rested at his feet in the cockpit. The staff seemed to leap into his hand. It could have been aircraft vibration, but Arthur felt the wizard's stick pulse.

"Hey, Arthur! Pay attention! Put the nose up."

The king looked to see that he'd let the plane drop into a gentle dive. But the biplane was gaining speed and the quilt of England was rushing up toward them. He pulled the control column back and the nose rose again. He let go of Merlin's staff.

"That's it," Yank said. "Better." A pair of black wings flapped in front of the propeller chop. The raven swooped, cawing as it flapped its noisy feathers. "Put the nose down, Arthur!" Yank yelled. The king obeyed and the biplane dived.

"You want to keep the hell away from birds, Arthur. One flies into your propeller and we're finished."

"I think I knew that bird," Arthur called back into the microphone.

"Not too well, I hope. That was too close for comfort."

The biplane dropped to five thousand feet, passing below the cloud where Arthur fired the clearing burst. The dark-winged bird dropped from the cloud and it filled Arthur's gunsights. But it wasn't a bird. The raven had vanished and a Messerschmitt 109 took its place.

Before Arthur could move, the plane's sharklike snout dived past the ring of his metal gunsight. All he could make out was the large black cross behind the cockpit. The prop wash from the enemy fighter buffeted his face.

"We've gotta run for it," Yank declared, and Arthur felt the stick go lifeless, the controls taken away from him. The biplane dived.

"Why don't we fight?" Arthur shouted. "We've got guns!"

Yank nosed the biplane into a steep dive, the wings shuddering as if they might tear free from the slender fuselage. Dozens of pellets stung Arthur's face beneath his goggles as the aircraft plunged into a cloud bank a bare three thousand feet above the earth. The moisture soaked Arthur's face and the sting of the droplets inside the cloud eased as the plane leveled out.

"Where's the Hun?" Arthur cried.

"Better hope we lost him, King," Yank responded.

"Why didn't we shoot?"

"Hell, Arthur? Why didn't you shoot?"

"It happened too fast."

"You're damn right." They flew blind, enshrouded by the cloud. "We can't stay in here forever."

Yank cautiously nosed the biplane down again.

Arthur watched the altimeter needle drop, and the cloud opened like a curtain, then hung heavily above them like a blanket. The king turned as far about as he could, the silk scarf chafing his neck. He saw Yank, pale and worried behind the goggles. The king looked at the sky beyond and felt dread as his ears filled with the powerful drone of the Messerschmitt.

Arthur reached for the gun control bar and depressed it, but nothing happened. A jam. The biplane dived and Arthur could see the tracers from the Messerschmitt sail toward them. The enemy plane's yellow nose grew large as a boar's snout in full charge. Yank dived and Arthur could feel the tear of raw air against the wing roots.

The plane leveled and Arthur could see they were flying even, in parallel with a stand of oak trees that lined a road a dozen feet below them. Arthur looked over his shoulder and saw the German fighter's belly, black crosses on gray wings. He watched in horror as the nose cannon erupted. The 20-millimeter shells drilled spumes of dust in the road and Yank nudged up to treetop level.

Suddenly, the Messerschmitt wagged its wings as though the machine changed its mind and broke off the attack. It turned and climbed until it became a black mote vanishing into the cloud-dappled morning sky.

Just as it was about to disappear, Arthur sighted the glint of wings in the sun. From high above, Arthur saw the distinctive swallow wings of a Spitfire dropping from the sun. Its wings crackled, spitting fire at the fleeing German. A flower petal explosion bloomed, filling the high air with gasoline and debris as the Spitfire hit the Luftwaffe pilot's fuel tank.

Arthur turned to see that sweat streamed from Bill Cooper's goggles, and he was shaking, as if palsied. "Let's get home," Yank said, turning the biplane back on a heading to Hornchurch, the joy of flying fled from his face.

The biplane bumped onto the field at the far end of Hornchurch Aerodrome. Arthur listened to the engine shudder as the propeller feathered. Yank steered it, furtively, behind a maintenance hangar.

The king hoisted himself from the front cockpit and carefully placed his foot in the metal stirrup so he wouldn't put his boot through the wing fabric, the way Yank showed him. Bill Cooper dropped to the ground and began to walk away. Arthur clapped his gloved hand on Yank's shoulder.

"Thank you, Bill. I shall do better next time. I'm sure I can."

Yank stopped. He stared at Arthur as though he were looking straight through him. "I don't know who you are, King, and I don't care. But I won't be going up with you again. Not for all the tea in China."

"Tea? China? What do you mean?"

Yank pulled off his leather helmet and threw it on the ground. "It's crazy. I must've been crazy. We almost got killed for no good reason. I took you up for a barn hop in a war zone. Who was I kidding?"

"Are you bothered about the Hun machine? Isn't that part of it? It gave chase, then one of your comrades vanquished it. That's combat."

Arthur looked at Yank. He could see all color had drained from his face and the young flier's hands were shaking.

"We almost bought the farm, Arthur," Yank said angrily. "I won't do that on a lark. Not for you. Not for some Air Ministry experiment. Get another tour guide."

"I need you, Yank. You're the only one in whom I have confidence."

"I don't want your confidence, Lieutenant. I just want to live."

Arthur watched Cooper stump away. The king gripped Merlin's stick and swore. Overhead, he heard the now familiar roar of a Spitfire's powerful Merlin engine. But it was spotting and stopping, as though it would fail. Arthur looked up and saw the aircraft sideslipping toward the field with black smoke and yellow flames snicking from the engine cowling.

Yank began running toward the far end of the field where a crowd gathered. Arthur grabbed Merlin's staff and hobbled after him. The fire engine sirens cranked up. As Arthur hobbled, he heard the ambulance bell. The crash equipment rolled out and the king ran raggedly until his chest pounded.

Only one of the fighter's landing gear had dropped beneath the fuselage, so it dragged onto the airfield like a wounded crane. The landing gear snapped and the Spitfire skidded on its belly, throwing debris. The aircraft tumbled nose down, curling the propeller like a bent dinner fork. The machine's hind quarters rolled tail up like a grave marker.

Firefighters launched water streams that dumped clouds of steam on the cowling. Rescue workers in heavy suits rushed forward. The cockpit was locked open as if the pilot had attempted to bail out but failed. He hung limp as a rag doll, still harnessed in the cockpit. Arthur saw blue sparks on the instrument panel and heard the snap of flames. A firefighter fumbled with the half-conscious pilot's safety straps.

Arthur's leg throbbed as he hobbled past the firefighters. The king could smell fuel. He jammed Merlin's stick beneath the pilot's straps as the control panel caught fire. With the straps pulled an inch away from the pilot's chest, the firefighter's gloved hands closed on the safety buckles and the airman fell free of the cockpit. Two rescue workers pulled him across the grass and the firefighter tackled

Arthur. A low *whump* and the cockpit ignited. The Spitfire exploded in flame.

The pilot's pale blue eyes popped open. His sandy hair hung in limp hanks. His hands trembled. The rescue crew elevated his legs.

"He's going," Tommy Stubbs said, chewing his mustache. "Sure but we'll lose him. The shock will kill him."

A stretcher crew pushed through the crowd, and Arthur saw Jenny wearing her white doctor's coat. Jenny rushed to the pilot and grasped the youth's wrist.

"Get him to the ambulance. We'll need blood." She worked the scarf loose from his Irvin jacket and inspected the metal tag on his neck chain. "A-positive, and lots of it."

"We're losing him, miss," a firefighter said. The stretcher men lofted the pilot toward the field ambulance.

"I won't lose him," Jenny said. "Not yet."

The ambulance doors snapped shut and the vehicle rattled down the muddy field. The king walked after the retreating ambulance as if in a trance. He bumped into Gilbert Hawley. The leader of Dragon Squadron's Red Flight promptly punched Arthur in the jaw, knocking the king to the ground.

"You were the sod in the two-seater, weren't you?" Hawley demanded.

"What?" Arthur replied, rubbing his chin. "Yes."

Hawley kicked Arthur in the shin of his good leg. "You've as good as killed my wingman."

Yank ran and helped Arthur up from the ground. "What are you talking about, Gil?"

"The Scot was flying 'tail-end' Charlie for me, and I left him when I saw the 109 bounce you boys in that antique. The Hun got the Scot whilst I was wasting time saving your worthless lives."

Tommy Stubbs walked up. He scratched his head and looked at Yank. "What exactly were you lot doing up there?"

"Arthur needed some gunnery practice."

"So, you take him up without authorization and I lose my wingman," Hawley said. "I'll have you up on charges. There'll be an inquiry."

Tommy Stubbs leaned close to Yank's ear. He tugged at his mustache and spoke quietly, nearly in a whisper. "Look, Yank," he said. "Hawley's a shit, but he's got a point. Suppose we go to the old man first."

Arthur saw from Yank's face that the day had gone very wrong. The field smelt of burnt rubber, scorched metal and flesh. The air hung thickly, as if life had gone out of it.

"Have King wait in quarters," Stubbs urged. "Come along now, Bill. We'll try to get the old man to see your side of it."

Hawley was already marching in the direction of the squadron leader's billet. Stubbs took Yank by the arm, almost as if he were a prisoner. The American went with Stubbs, his expression that of a sleepwalker.

Without Yank Cooper to fill up the room with his energy, his quarters seemed even smaller than they really were. About the size of a monk's cloister. The little room of stretched canvas and wood bracing had a single window, taped over for air raids. Pull back the blackout curtain and the window commanded a view of the grass field at Hornchurch. Across the field, Arthur could see the pilot's ready room, the camouflage netting and the anti-blast revetments, large piles of earth designed to protect the fighter planes on readiness.

At strategic points, there were fortified sandbag pits with the ack-ack guns of the sort Arthur fired his first night in squadron. Hornchurch was a castle without walls. At the moment, Arthur longed for his own castle. He heard Camelot calling, like a silent siren. He felt loss and dread.

Absently, Arthur examined Yank Cooper's personal belongings, searching restlessly for clues to the age he'd been transported to. On the small wooden field table, there was one of the extraordinary pictures that the king had admired for their keen realism and detail. He'd never seen such pictures in the monks' illuminated manuscripts of his time. Yank called them photographs, and he said they came from a black box he carried with him everywhere. He called the black box a "Kodak" and never said why.

That pictures should emerge from a black box seemed like necromancy to Arthur. Arthur understood necromancy, and sometimes welcomed its intervention. Merlin's magic had made him king, but where was Merlin now?

Arthur picked up the photograph. There were two men in the picture, both pilots like Yank. Smiling, they leaned against a double-winged aircraft similar to the one that had carried Yank and Arthur in their adventure that morning. An ink scrawl formed a signature at the bottom of the photograph.

It said simply, "Big Bill Cooper & Eddie Rickenbacker. Hat in the Ring Squadron. France, 1918."

The man in the picture could have been Yank himself except for slight changes in fashion. Longer scarves wrapped each man's neck, and each wore a long leather coat that dropped past the knee. They sported knee-high boots. But the men were the same cut as Arthur knew from the ready room at Hornchurch and his own troops. The men in the photograph were warriors.

The second line of the faded ink caption read, "Knights of the Air. Forever Faithful."

There were books piled on Yank's table, unlike any the king had seen. Instead of calfskin and parchment, they were constructed of the flimsiest pulp. The pages were splashed with bold colors. No gold in them, no rich ochres or deep green and scarlet textures.

And no scenes of religion or the hunt, changing them entirely from books of Arthur's day. Yank called them comic books, and it was plain to see he loved them.

Arthur applied himself to the flimsy pages of *Smilin' Jack.* He looked at Jack's airplane turning snap rolls and diving. The comic book pilot made it look easy, and if his own airplane were shot with a "rat-tat-tat," the figure called Jack effortlessly popped out of the plane under a parachute.

Another book, *Aces,* depicted aerial warfare with the double-winged planes shooting each other. Arthur recognized the red- and blue-colored roundels on the wings of the English airplanes, and the black crosses that belonged to the enemy. Moving his lips as he struggled to form words on the page, Arthur discerned one that he recognized: "Hun."

The Huns wore exaggerated mustaches and spiked helmets. "Well, that hasn't changed," Arthur murmured. "They always were an odd-looking lot."

He pulled *Aces* from the stack and was startled by the next title.

The book was cloth-bound, frayed and well-thumbed, as though a boy had read it many times. The title was *King Arthur and the Knights of the Round Table.*

"Round Table," Arthur murmured. "I know of no such table." He began to thumb through the book, pausing to see illustrations. A few things were right. Much was wrong, but it was a story about Arthur, king of England, sure enough. Suddenly, a cold wind chilled Arthur's neck. He turned to the window, but it was shut. He found Merlin sitting on Yank Cooper's bunk, wearing the blue jacket and trousers of an RAF group captain.

"You'll never learn how to fly by reading the Yank's books, Arthur," Merlin said. "They're for children, really."

Arthur hastily pushed the book of the Round Table beneath the others. He knew the man sitting on the bed to be Merlin. This was the old man he knew, but his scratchy salt-and-pepper beard was missing. His mustache was silver, and it was as neat and clipped as Squadron Leader Richardson's. Still, his eyes shined slightly, metallic at the edge, like ball bearings in a Spitfire.

"I see you've still got my stick," Merlin remarked. "Has it helped?"

"I got hit in the leg with some shards of metal, Merlin," Arthur replied. "A new war injury. I use the stick to help me walk. It eases the pain."

"Nothing I ever taught you was about easing the pain," Merlin said sharply. "It's pain that makes us alert. It's an alarm. The stick was meant to help you fly. Can you fly?"

Arthur shook his head. "The Yank is teaching me. He's trying, anyway. But he's having trouble with it. Or with me. Why in the devil's name can't I find you when I need you, old man?"

"You're certainly having trouble finding things, Arthur. Have you found your sword? Have you found Mordred? The book?"

"Merlin," Arthur growled, "I'm lost in the fog of these strange times. I have trouble finding my own way through each day. What do you want of me?"

Merlin shook his head gravely. "It's not what I want, Arthur. It's what you've got to do. You've got to save England. It's that or else."

"Or else what? Why am I here? What's the good of it?"

"You didn't mind travel to far-off places when you were winning easy victories," Merlin observed. "You've got to do your job as protector of the realm, or there will be no realm to protect. Mordred will win. Magic runs in his veins. You have only your natural talents, and what help I can give you."

The king leaned against the taped window that opened to the field. His shoulders sagged. "The weapons of this century defeat me, old man."

He felt a hand on his shoulder. "Perhaps you need some talisman," the elder said. "Take this." He presented Arthur with a knife in a sheath. It was a double-edged commando dagger. The king withdrew it from the sheath. The maker's mark beneath the crosspiece was stamped 1940. But on the flat of the blade, "Excalibur" was engraved in ornate letters.

"Until you find the real one," Merlin said gently, "this may help you."

Arthur seated himself on Yank's bunk and stared at the blade. The king's leonine head dropped. He sighed heavily. "Thank you for the gift, old teacher. It's something I understand. But flying a machine. God. It's far too complicated."

Merlin nodded. "Flying always was difficult. Most people are afraid to soar. They remain bound to the earth by their blindness to see any higher purpose. But is flying really more demanding than the learning of Latin and sums, or the names of the stars? You learned all those things at my knee, Arthur Pendragon. Whether there will be a future, or a present, depends on your willingness and ability to learn many things quickly."

Merlin got up from the bunk. He walked over to Yank's field table and sorted through the books. He picked up the book about King Arthur and chuckled.

"Don't pay too much attention to this," he said. "It's a fairy tale. Most of it wrong. It lacks reference to Mordred. The Round Table idea has some merit." Merlin clucked his tongue. "Legend is so untrustworthy." He continued to rummage through the stack.

Beneath the comics and pulp books, Merlin found a plain yellow folder bound by three metal rings. It was titled *Pilot's Manual for the Supermarine Spitfire*. Merlin presented the book to Arthur.

"Now, here's magic, liege. Read this well and learn its contents. If you're going to joust, you've got to ride the steed."

The king accepted the manual. He looked up at Merlin with the trust of a child. He opened the book and gazed at the dizzying array of dials, gauges and needles that adorned the first page. A long tear fell from one gray eye and he shook his head, then hit it with the flat of his hand.

"Can't be done, Merlin," he whispered.

"Read," the wizard commanded. "You passed from ignorance as a boy. Now, you've got to be a man. A man can conquer anything he sets his mind to. Even the air."

Arthur looked about helplessly. He could not see out the window of Yank's billet. A deep fog had descended on the airfield, enshrouding all of Hornchurch. He looked up and the old man was gone.

Time passed and the fog did not lift. Arthur sat on the bunk with the manual at his feet on the wooden floor. He began to read carefully. The section on pilot's controls and equipment began to make sense to him. They made no less sense than the complicated code of chivalry, which had to be committed to memory, or the complexity of the components of a knight's armor. Arthur became entranced with the words, which finally took on meaning, context and, as with all realms of knowledge, finally assumed the rhythm of inner music.

When he looked up, the old man had reappeared, a trace of a smile haunting the edges of his clipped silver mustache. The wizard pointed to the enchanted stick and the dagger. Arthur picked them up.

"You are sitting in the cockpit of a Spitfire, Mark Four model, I believe," Merlin said. "They are all pretty much the same."

In one hand, the king grasped the oaken staff. In the other, he held the commando dagger, still encased in its boot sheath. Holding the sheathed knife in his closed fist he edged it forward gently.

"There," Merlin said in an encouraging tone. "If you let the engine throttle open up too quickly, your machine will jump the field and you'll be nose down in the hay."

Arthur nodded vigorously. "And the rudder trim?" he asked.

"If the engine is torquing and pulling your aircraft to port side, keep the rudder hard to starboard. You don't want to lose your center of gravity."

"Gravity." The king repeated the unfamiliar word. "If I should lose it?"

"Buttocks over teapot, again. Nose into the mud."

"Right," the king said. "Can this thing really be done? Do you suppose I could fly these machines after all?"

"You never asked such questions when you pulled the sword from the stone before the multitude gathered at London town, Arthur."

"That was magic. And I was very young. I had confidence."

"You're smarter now, and you have experience. And the place where magic and machinery meets is really one and the same, if you think about it. Tell me the difference between enchantment and the radio."

"I couldn't begin to."

"Exactly. Now, are you ready, Arthur?"

"Ready for what?"

The wizard took the king's hand and pulled him up from the bunk. They opened the flimsy door to Yank's quarters and walked into the fog. The gray shroud that blanketed Hornchurch crept through the blades of grass and rose from the earth like smoke. Arthur trailed Merlin through the mists, following him with the same faith he knew as a boy.

The squadron maintenance officer approached Merlin and saluted. Merlin returned the salute with the formality of a general staff officer.

"Come down from Air Ministry, have you, sir?" the maintenance officer said. "If there's anything you want to see, just ask one of the sergeants. No one will be flying today. Not in this muck."

Merlin nodded agreeably and said, "Carry on." The maintenance officer hurried away like a white rabbit. It seemed, if possible, that the fog thickened and deepened to become an impenetrable ground-level cloud as the pair made their way to the hangars. The mist yielded little to the muddy yellow lights of a hangar where the ground crew worked.

Arthur leaned over to Merlin. "What the devil is Air Ministry?"

Merlin grinned sagely. "Higher authority, Arthur. A kind of war council. If you salute smartly enough, everyone thinks you represent higher authority."

A sergeant approached Merlin. "Number seven is fueled, armed and prepared for takeoff, sir. All it waits on is the weather."

Arthur looked at the machine, sleek and lethal in appearance. He watched the ground crew finish their work. They looked like his squires in Camelot, preparing his war horse, Battle, for combat.

The Spitfire, poised on its slender landing gear like

an unsheathed dagger, looked like a thing meant to
fly. The graceful nose, the swallow-shaped wings and
tail. The eight recessed ports for the Browning guns,
spaced like talons along the wings' leading edge. The
three-bladed propeller, dominating the nose like a
trio of short swords. Arthur shivered, whether from
the cold fog or sight of the aircraft, he could not tell.

Now, except for Arthur and Merlin, the hangar
was empty. The wizard walked across the hangar
floor. He opened a locker and returned with
parachute, leather helmet, oxygen mask and life vest.
Absent his ragged warrior's beard, the ancient looked
ageless. His skin was youthful. He held out the flight
kit to Arthur.

"Put it on, my king," Merlin commanded. "Today, I
am your teacher, but also your squire."

Arthur looked out beyond the hangar. The fog
hung like a wall of mud. The king shifted uncomfortably in his boots. "We can't expect to fly in this soup,
Merlin," Arthur said. "All the pilots say this kind of
fog is deadly."

"You must have some faith in an old man, Arthur.
Have I ever killed you before?"

Arthur grimaced. He looked around, as if searching for an exit. Finally, he shrugged his shoulders and
began to don the flight gear.

"I'll sit in the cockpit, at least," he said. "I'll famil-
iarize myself."

Arthur climbed onto the wing. He seated himself
inside the cockpit, putting his head back on the
leather-cushioned headrest. The array of the cockpit
panel made him dizzy. He looked up to see Merlin on
the wing. The wizard handed Arthur his staff. The
king accepted it like a scepter. Like pieces of a puzzle
prepared for amazement at court, the cockpit panel
began to fall into place before Arthur. He went by
the book and called off the names.

Fuel gauges. Oil pressure. Oil temperature, magnetic compass, turn-and-bank indicator, airspeed indicator, artificial horizon, rate-of-climb indicator. He identified each one with a touch of his finger and received a nod of approval or a cluck of reproach from Merlin as he called them out correctly or made a mistake. He repeated the procedure until he had named each dial and gauge correctly. The magician grinned and jumped down from the wing, lithe as a youth.

"Time for a spot of drink at the mess, then," Arthur called out from his perch in the cockpit. Merlin answered him with laughter that rebounded eerily from the hangar walls. When the laughter ended, the sage spoke.

"No strong drink until after you start your engine, Arthur," Merlin ordered.

With that, Arthur's mentor grasped one of the propeller blades and turned it. He repeated the procedure a half dozen times, and the king felt a jump of life beneath the Spitfire cowling. Each time the propeller turned, it made a gulping sound. "Merlin," Arthur called out, his voice rising an octave. "What are you doing?"

"Turn your ignition switch," the magician commanded.

The king's gloved hand reached and he turned the switch "On." He let go of Merlin's staff and it seated neatly beside his leg. He pushed the starter switch to "Energize." The engine fired. A small explosion and smoke belched from the manifold. Arthur watched the rpm needle jump. A roar. His fingers, his hands, his arms tingled. His entire body vibrated with the revs of the Merlin engine. It roared like liquid thunder. The needle climbed past 1,000 rpms and Arthur felt as though he had been grafted to a living thing. Suddenly, Merlin was on the wing.

"Remember," Merlin called out above the steady

rumble of the twelve cylinders, "open the throttle gradually, just as if you were bringing your steed at tourney from a trot to a canter. Don't gallop until you feel it."

"This is madness!" the king cried over the sound and fury of the Rolls Royce engine.

Merlin frowned. "Arthur, you've come a thousand years. You might at least see if you can go a thousand feet." Patiently, like a parent buttoning a child's coat, Merlin connected the radio leads to Arthur's helmet.

Merlin pulled the cockpit shut, so the bubble dome encased the king. Arthur looked up the long nose of the Supermarine craft and sighed mightily. He closed his eyes, then opened them and closed his hand on the throttle. At his touch, the aircraft began to roll ponderously into the fog that enveloped the field. Arthur felt blind panic as the aircraft advanced into the mist.

Suddenly, the king's radio crackled to life. "Dragon King, this is Dragon Wizard," Merlin announced. "Follow my lead, over."

His heart pounding, Arthur responded haltingly, "Dragon Wizard, this is Dragon King. Acknowledged, over." His throat was completely dry.

Unable to see beyond the fighter plane's nose, and moving into a gray cloud that wrapped the cockpit bubble, Arthur pushed the throttle forward. Arthur felt each bump of the grass field beneath him. He felt everything, his senses supercharged. As the speed indicator jumped, the fog grew thicker. The wheels rolled rapidly and the needle bolted toward 100 mph. He felt a jump in his stomach and a lift as though the palm of a great hand raised the aircraft. The king trembled, and remembered the manual. The gloved hand left the throttle only long enough to retract the landing gear and adjust trim.

"Pay attention and have faith," Merlin's said, each syllable enunciated with bell-tone clarity in Arthur's earphones. "You're airborne, King Arthur."

Flying blind, on faith, the radio and Merlin's guidance, Arthur soared aloft into the gray heavens.

12

12

At eleven thousand feet, Arthur's Spitfire burst through the cumulus. Sunlight showered across the wings of the fighter and the king was dazzled by the blue-white brilliance of the sun reflected from the tops of the clouds. Rising up into the bright blue sky, he felt transformed from mortal to high-flying silvery wraith. He inhaled the oxygen in his mask. It burned at his lungs and upper throat. He felt immortal.

"You are flying solo," Merlin's ancient voice rasped through the radio static. "The French would say solitaire, derived from the Latin. Being as one, or the fact of being alone, solitary."

Arthur nudged his control column to starboard, banking the Spitfire and staring at the pageantry of the cumulus sea that swept by beneath him.

"I would ask to be alone for a moment, Merlin. I need solitude."

"So be it, Dragon King. Call if you need me," The radio fell silent.

Arthur leveled the aircraft, then opened the throttle and pulled the stick back into a steep ascent. Like Icarus, the king climbed toward the sun. The needles inched upward, the rate of climb indicator tilted and the ball of the artificial horizon rolled back like a miniature globe. The minutes ticked away as he climbed and Arthur's Spitfire finally soared above twenty-five thousand feet.

The king felt the weight of his skull against the leather headrest. He felt the edge of faintness as the blood was pulled from his head into the lower regions of his body. In this royal moment, on a course toward the sun, the king knew he could go no higher, or he would never return to earth. He had reached maximum ceiling. The Spitfire's altimeter needle ticked somewhere above thirty-two thousand feet.

"Merlin," the king called out into the microphone. "Birds would perish, but here am I!"

The disembodied voice of the ancient crackled, breaking the radio silence that separated wizard from king during Arthur's long ascent. "The men have mastered the machines that will send them flying high above the world."

"Yes," Arthur replied. "We are, indeed, capable of much."

"But still, you have not mastered yourselves," the ancient continued. "Far below, on the ground, in the mud, the laws of slaughter still prevail, as if there had been no advance from your embattled day to this threatened hour."

"Yes," Arthur said, nodding beneath the visor of his cold leather helmet. "Where is the golden rule?" Arthur asked, watching the sun flash on the wings. "Why do we do unto each other, instead of for each other, Merlin?"

"Man's condition mystifies me, Arthur," the ancient replied. "I can see the future, but quite often I do not comprehend it. If there were a cure for cruelty, it would be worth almost any price."

The engine noise of the twelve-cylinder Merlin was now a quiet, steady hum. The three blades of the Rotol propeller spun like a silent, silver fan, pulling the Spitfire along, high and over above the rolling banks of clouds.

"Change your radio frequency to three-zero-zero, Dragon King," Merlin commanded. "Acknowledge, over."

"Dragon King acknowledges," Arthur responded. He loved the language of the radio. Also, he felt a fierce kinship with his own radio call sign. It held the same meaning as his father's name, Uther Pendragon, who sired him to become king of the Britons. Arthur's gloved fingers shot forward and he changed the radio frequency knob.

"This is Camelot calling," the radio dispatcher said. It was the crisp, cool tones of Control back at Fighter Command. "Stand by for a special transmission from the BBC."

Another familiar voice issued forth from the cockpit radio.

Arthur had heard the sonorous voice before in the pub and in the officer's mess back at Hornchurch. He knew it to be the voice of the man in the picture that hung above the mirror in the pub and the mess and many other places he visited with Yank. It was the minister they called Churchill. The scratchiness and static that filled the radio spectrum fell away. Arthur flew level, cruising at 250 miles an hour. The engine hum receded and Churchill's voice held him spellbound.

"The Battle of Britain is underway," the prime minister announced gravely. "Very soon the whole fury and might of the enemy must be turned upon us.

Hitler knows that he will have to break us in this island or lose the war."

"Right," Arthur whispered. The oxygen seared his lungs, but his breathing quickened with excitement as he listened.

The prime minister continued: "If we fail, then the whole world, including all that we have known and cared for, will sink into the abyss of a new Dark Age made more sinister, and perhaps more protracted, by the lights of perverted science."

"Yes," Arthur whispered.

"Let us therefore brace ourselves to our duties and so bear ourselves that, if the British Empire and its Commonwealth last for a thousand years, men will still say, 'This was their finest hour.'"

Arthur turned his head. From the corner of his eye, he saw the black spot. He blinked furiously, but still it was there: a raven, resting on the wing of his racing Supermarine fighter. The raven spread its wings, soared aloft and flew parallel to the Spitfire. Arthur watched, transfixed. He heard the metallic clicking of the radio knob changing back by itself.

"Now that you can fly, Arthur, you must fight. And you must find the blade and book within the two moons left to you. Or all this before you will have been as a dream seen through a glass darkly."

"Riddles, Merlin. What is it you mean?"

"When Mordred took the book, he stole a look into Britain's possible future. In possession of the book and sword, he can do much harm. He means to be crowned king, using Excalibur as his proof of claim. If that should come to pass, the new Dark Age that Churchill speaks of will, indeed, unfold. It will be a new order, with tyranny triumphant."

"I'll find Churchill. He must be warned."

"It would do you no good. He'd think you mad. It is Mordred who holds the key. It is Mordred who must be defeated before he grows so strong that he takes charge of his Hun allies. You must find Mordred and vanquish him. Only then can you return the sword Excalibur to its proper time and return to meet your destiny."

"And what if I should fail?"

"Another future will unfold. One of the many possible. And under Mordred's dread heel, none of them would be good."

"But Mordred must be as lost in this time as me. How can he lead a host of enemies while I'm still learning where the buttons are on my pants?"

The bird croaked, and Merlin spoke again. "Yours are different cases, Arthur. You are here under what protection I can give you. But you are mortal. The milky blood of an enchantress flows in Mordred's veins, as well you know."

"No one knows better than me," Arthur sputtered. "She enchanted me. I was a rude boy. What did I know of women, or witches?"

"His circumstance of birth is unimportant. It's the power he wields that matters. You have two moons to find Mordred and deal with him. Otherwise, he will steal as many lives as he needs to add to his own strength. Before long, he will be too strong to be defeated."

Arthur strained his eyes, trying to keep sight of the black bird dancing above the clouds at altitudes undreamed for any creature not lifted by enchantment. He thought he caught sight of the raven swooping far below, then he saw it was a bomber. One of hundreds. The dark-winged planes broke out of the puffy clouds below Arthur, assembled in echelons of vee-formations.

The twin-engine aircraft droned toward the Thames and London. Arthur realized they were Heinkels, Junkers and Dorniers, like the "Know Your

Enemy" drawings posted at Hornchurch. So many poured from the clouds, they turned the sky dark as a locust plague. The radio was crackling with activity. Cool, steady voices of Fighter Command began assigning vectors for interception. It was a jumble to Arthur. He moved his control column forward, pushing the Spitfire into a steep dive.

The king's stomach floated toward his chest as his plane plunged through six thousand feet of ice blue sky toward the bomber swarm. His eight .303-caliber machine guns crackled as he sailed through the top of the formation, hurtling like a boulder dropped from a parapet. Rushing by, he saw the black crosses on the wings. A wing tore loose from a JU88, with the aircraft exploding in a great ball of fire, showering Arthur's plane like flaming hail.

His aircraft was buffeted and he pulled the control column back, attempting to break the dive. There were black and brown spots everywhere, in front of him and filling his peripheral vision, like when he was a trout in Merlin's pond. On the edge of blackout, the king sensed the spots must be planes. His plane pitched and yawed, and Arthur felt sick as he rolled upside down. The Spit rolled crazily, its control cables snapped. The king's hood slid back and he pushed the release button for his harness. The parachute cracked open and the shock tore away one of Arthur's boots, sending it flying into space.

The king's parachute drifted perilously beneath a ceiling of black crosses and drumming engines. A giant, twin-engine Junkers fell past Arthur, burning like a magnesium flare, its bombardier trapped in the nose bubble screaming silently as the stricken bomber hurtled by.

The king hung suspended, watching the cloud of enemy aircraft rumble on toward London. As the cloud receded, he watched the mottled green dots of

RAF fighters pounce, darting and diving into the enemy formation. There were so many Huns that the RAF looked like hornets buzzing at a stag.

"There're too many, Merlin!" he shouted, his throat raw in the windstream. Hot tears welled up in his eyes as he watched the black cloud move on. Suddenly, the air surrounding him was cold and quiet and he could feel the wind freezing his cheeks.

The king scanned the horizon and the treeline as the canopy dropped him to earth. Arthur's feet hit the wet ground and he tumbled facedown into the mud. His injured leg shot with fresh pain. It felt like being thrown from a horse a second time. Swearing, Arthur reached for the commando knife. It was sheathed in his remaining boot. He began cutting himself free from the suspension lines. Rising from his knees, he spotted Merlin's stick in the mud. He kicked it and howled as his big toe throbbed.

The stick sailed through the air, falling at the edge of a wood obscured by mist. The king hobbled toward where the stick fell, and he heard the rustle of movement in the wood. Instinctively, he gripped the dagger.

Strange, helmeted figures emerged from the wood. Stepping furtively between the trees, they formed a half-circle round Arthur. The king could make out the sharp points of pikes, and the gnarled knobs of war clubs. The men who moved out of the mist were white-haired, old men. Some were bearded. One had a milky eye. Each was armed, many with weapons familiar to Arthur's day. Each pointed his weapon at Arthur. A stick. A sword. A few wielded pitchforks.

"Sit down, you. And put your hands above your head," a stout old man with a walrus mustache commanded. He wore a soup pan helmet and a woolen sweater with three stripes on it. "*Sit-en-zie, Fritz. Verstehen sie?*"

Arthur dropped the dagger and raised his hands.

"Wait, Horace," a gaunt pikeman called out. He stepped forward and picked up the knife. The pikeman's Adam's apple bobbed like a cork as he spoke. "Look at the lad's jacket, Horace. Look here, RAF wings."

Horace advanced suspiciously, his pike pointed directly at Arthur's chest. "Who do you fight for?" he demanded.

"For the king," Arthur replied. "Whom do you fight for?"

"We're the king's men, alright," the sergeant replied. "Home Guard, Essex."

"This lad probably shot down that lot we took in the woods, Horace," the gaunt pikeman said. The half-circle of men kept their weapons at the ready.

"Britain still has need of pikemen, then," Arthur said quietly.

"There's not enough guns, and you can tell that to Churchill," Horace said. "Your lot in the Regulars left too many Lewis guns on the beach at Dunkirk. We make do with what we've got."

Arthur looked up at the sky. It was silent, the bombers and fighters long gone. He squinted at the sergeant in the soup pan helmet. "You'd fight the Huns with pikes and sticks, then? And swords?"

"We'll hunt 'em down and stone 'em with rocks," the pikeman said, his Adam's apple bobbing. "We'll beat 'em like we did in the last show."

The sergeant called Horace sighed. "Poor child. He listens to the wireless too much. Churchill. All he talks about is you gallant few."

Arthur grinned. "What do you think of this Churchill?"

"He's all right," Horace said. "As good as the king, if you ask me. Created the Home Guard." The sergeant grinned. He placed two fingers between his lips and whistled. More pikemen stepped forward from the woods. "We took these, didn't we?" the sergeant said proudly.

Arthur looked past the guardsman to see a pair of disheveled German airmen. They were boys in blue coveralls. Their hair was dank, blond and dirty. Their blue eyes were wary. A guardsman offered the airmen each a cigarette. They accepted, their hands shaking.

"*Danke,*" one said.

"There, see," Horace said, walking over and inspecting them as though they were a pair of shoats at market. "They're not ten feet tall. We can beat them and their paper-hanging Führer, too, I should think."

"Yes," Arthur said. "If all Britain stands like your company, we may yet beat them."

"Here now," Horace shouted, his voice rising. "Form up. Ranks of two."

The pikemen assembled, six men in front and six men behind the Luftwaffe crewmen. The men smartly moved their pitchforks and pikes to port arms, so they pointed toward the cold, charcoal-colored sky. The clouds were closing rapidly. Maybe the clouds would protect England.

"You come with us, Lieutenant. We'll arrange transport," Horace said. "Compliments of the Home Guard."

The gaunt pikeman handed Arthur his dagger. The king grinned and placed the knife in the sheath of his remaining boot. He regarded his bare foot ruefully. Another guardsman stepped forward. In his hands, the old man held the boot that had flown from Arthur's foot during his rapid descent.

"It must be yours," the old man said.

"Thank you," Arthur said, rubbing his bare foot. "I was unshod. Better to march in boots."

The king sat in the mud and pulled on the boot. His foot was swollen and the fit was snug. He nodded thankfully, then he picked up Merlin's stick. Strength flowed into Arthur's arm from it. The king hobbled the long mile to the village in the company of the guardsmen and the captured crew. The Essex men bought him a few pints at the King's Head Pub and gave tea to the Germans. The guardsmen sent Arthur back to Hornchurch in the fastest available transport, a haywagon pulled by tractor.

13

An enormous fire blazed in the great hall at Chateau D'Eauville. A boar turned on a spit. The serving staff wore livery of black and silver thread and shoes with enormous silver buckles on them of Reichsmarshall Goering's personal design. The hunting tapestries were gone, sent to Carinhall by Goering's art experts. In their place hung the Luftwaffe's heraldry.

As the smartly tailored officers drifted into the torchlit hall, Mordred strolled along the great stone archways inspecting banners of the bomb groups and fighter squadrons. The stranger smiled, recognizing a banner of the red griffin rampant. From another pillar of stone hung a banner of a diving eagle, then a flag with a steel gauntlet and mace. One group's insignia displayed a Viking, fearsome as those who raided Tintagel. Another familiar symbol, the death's head. A banner with an inverted pentagram hung, suspended between the others. Kleist had ordered it sewn on instruction from Mordred.

All the planes in Kleist's armada now bore the sign of the pentagram. Under Major Morgan's orders, the ground crews couldn't paint the inverted stars on the aircraft fast enough.

"This looks like my father's palace," Mordred remarked to Kleist. "It's overbearing. He would call it gracious." Mordred accepted a panatela from Kleist.

"Your father? What nature of man was he?" Kleist asked, clipping the cigar for Mordred, then lighting it. The general had accustomed himself to acting as manservant to Mordred. It was the only way to control the grinding headaches. The quicker he served, the lesser the pain.

But Mordred was subtle. On their forays from Kleist's quarters, it was he who played the part of the attentive aide. Kleist hoped for rescue, that his own staff would recognize this impertinent major for an impostor. In fact, for a monster in human form. But the underlings never recognized the spirit of the man who held Kleist captive. And if Kleist tried to stray, the headaches returned. And all the time, every waking minute, Mordred's demands increased.

Information, training, history. He read books with the speed of a code-breaking machine, and if a term puzzled him, Kleist had better be awake to clarify it. The only thing the monster could not do was operate an aircraft. He seemed content to leave the flying to Kleist. In the air, at the controls, the general felt a moment's peace. The rest of his life in the monster's company formed a nightmare from which there was no waking.

Mordred snorted a puff of yellow-stained smoke and rolled the cigar between thumb and forefinger. "These are good. Find me a box, will you? My father was a boor. All he wanted to do was to slay dragons and feed widows."

"He wanted to do good, then," Kleist said. The general held out hopes that if he learned about his captor's origins, he might achieve the means of escape. He must ask his own questions. "Your father was a good man?"

"My father was a holy fool. He defied me, and I left him for dead." Mordred let the words sink in. "That was a long time ago."

Kleist's features, already shrunken, registered little surprise. He rubbed his head. The aching resumed. Mordred looked up at a banner hanging from the stone arch adjacent to the great table. The banner depicted a comic mouse in short pants fastened by two large buttons. The grinning mouse wielded a bloody axe.

"That's a rat, isn't it?" Mordred asked.

"Oh," Kleist said. "Mickey Mouse is Adolf Galland's emblem. He got it from the movies. Maybe the movies is where Galland belongs."

"What's a movie?" Mordred asked.

Kleist shrugged. "You don't know the cinema?"

Mordred gazed at Kleist and the headache became nearly unbearable. The general buckled at the knees as though he were about to faint.

"I'll ask the questions," Mordred said simply. The pair walked into the feast, with Mordred supporting the general by his arm as if he were helping him along the way.

The staff was whispering that General Kleist did not seem well, but they dared not mention it in his presence. Not while he held Goering's favor. He had been elevated recently to commander of the entire bombing effort against Britain. There was word also of a promotion for his aide.

Goering held court at the center of the main table in the great hall. The servants filled the Alte's jeweled goblet, and he smiled dreamily like Bacchus, his cherubic face blooming with narcotic euphoria. Goering was less a general than an event. On this evening at the great table, he wore a leather hunting tunic and silk shirt with puffed sleeves. He cuffed his lion cub, Caesar, affectionately.

The huge man tore meat from the bone with the gusto of a confirmed carnivore. Then, dainty as a lady, he would pick fresh blueberries from a bowl of cream and pop them in his mouth. Furtively, he would shake pills from a bottle. He passed the cream pitcher under the table to the delight of the cub.

The fliers seated by Goering ate noisily and downed tankards of beer. They laughed and flew mock dogfights with their hands. But now and then, the laughter registered an octave too high.

"Your knights look worried, General Kleist," Mordred remarked. "Why is that?"

Kleist, for once, returned the stranger's stare dead on. "If there is fearfulness, your strategy is the cause, Major, whoever you are. There's more food at the table because there are fewer fliers. But the Führer wants still more daylight raids on London."

"Good. He approves of my plan."

Kleist's voice was hollow and ragged. His eyes were ringed with dark circles and his skin held a faint yellow tinge only masked by the firelight.

"Code Camelot? Your plan for murder? Yes, he likes it well enough, but still we are losing too many men to make it work." The general hung his head. He nudged his chin up from his chest and continued. "The leader wants to punish London, but the RAF is mightier than we suspected. They have more fighters than we knew. And they are brave. Galland's prophecy was correct."

One pilot downed a tankard in a single gulp to great applause. He stood and bowed, spreading his arms wide. More applause and laughter. Then, the room became still as the fliers watched the young ace pee in his sky blue breeches, the stain slowly spreading. Goering's eyes narrowed and the pilot looked round helplessly. His comrades hustled him from the hall.

As they carried him away, the flier craned his neck in Goering's direction, and yelled, "Iron Knight, why are you sacrificing us?"

The fighter pilots shifted their gazes uneasily. Goering leaned forward over his cutlery, his eyes slightly aglaze. Each wondered what he had heard and what the words meant to him.

Mordred was on his feet, running to the Reichsmarshall's place at the head of the table. He lifted a bottle of Chardonnay and poured a splash into Goering's goblet. Mordred bowed deeply as if at court, then downed a goblet of wine himself in a single gulp, like the hysterical flier of a moment before.

"Our comrade is anxious about invading Britain," Mordred quipped. "Here's a toast to the Reichsmarshall , the man who will conquer England!"

The fliers rose to their feet and cheered. Goering waved to the band and the musicians hurriedly struck up "Off to Bomb England." The Luftwaffe chieftain gathered his girth and rose tipsily. He drew his dagger from its golden sheath and tapped Mordred lightly on both shoulders.

"You are a knight of the Luftwaffe," Goering entoned ceremoniously. "I announce forthwith your promotion to colonel. Congratulations, Oberst Morgan, architect of Operation Camelot."

Goering nodded in General Kleist's direction. "And congratulations to the general who saw such talent." Kleist returned the nod bleakly. "And to your continued good health, General," Goering said, raising his goblet.

The meal continued. Goering ate ravenously. Mordred strolled back to his place next to Kleist. He spooned an enormous serving of jellied currants onto a piece of bread and devoured it.

"So, you are promoted," Kleist murmured. "Soon, you will have my job."

"Warlords can't resist flattery," Mordred said, licking the jam from his fingers.

"I'll remember that." He drank a sip of wine and winked at Mordred. "What would happen to you if I were to die?" The general's face contorted into a twisted smile. "You must need me, or I wouldn't live, eh, Oberst Morgan? Who would fly your plane?"

"With the devil's luck, by the time you're dead, I'll rule Britain."

"You, rule Britain? Isn't the devil busy enough in Berlin?"

"It's what I've come to do, General. And I'll not be denied. The blood of kings runs in me. And I'll spill anyone's blood to get what I want."

"You wish to rule the English?"

"Nothing so small. I want complete dominion over all their lands and territories. And I want them to serve me, as you serve me. Your Führer understands. Enslavement is the ultimate aphrodisiac."

A wave of applause mounted as Goering ascended the flagstone steps to the fireplace behind the great table. One by one, the young pilots mounted the steps. Around the neck of each flier, Goering draped a ribbon from which hung a large iron cross.

"By order of the Führer, each of you is invested in the Order of the Knight's Cross," Goering declared. "Now, vanquish the *verdammt* British."

Kleist whispered hollowly, "When medals multiply so quickly, it is a sign that war does not go well."

"But they do so love their shiny decorations," Mordred said, relighting his cigar. "How reassuring to know men will still throw themselves to their death for a twist of ribbon."

The company whistled and booed as a flier drew a velvet curtain aside and unveiled a large oil portrait of Winston Churchill, a painting abandoned when the British army fled France.

"Who is that?" Mordred asked. "Some English chieftain? He's as fat as your boss. Are all chieftains fat now?"

"He may be fat, but he's a hard man. He's like a magician," Kleist said gloomily. "The English seem to worship him. Even more than the king."

"More than the king? Then he must die, too," Mordred declared. He rose suddenly and hurled a dagger at the oil portrait. It struck right center of Churchill's heart and quivered.

Mordred leaned forward on the table, staring at the dagger in Churchill's heart, his eyes blazing. "We will kill the king and his court magician. And then Mordred will rule."

The Luftwaffe men cheered wildly. Drunken fliers piled over the table and hoisted Mordred up on their shoulders. Mordred's cheeks flushed with pleasure at being the hero of the night. Goering had fallen asleep, his cherubic face dozing next to his soup.

14

Arthur sat at the armorer's bench examining the moving parts of the gun and comparing them to the diagrams in the manual. He pulled on the receiver group of the Browning, fascinated by the tensile strength of the spring on the .303-caliber machine gun. The receiver slammed home with a satisfactory snap and Arthur clicked his tongue. He'd got it.

The king read from the Browning manual and shook his head. It sometimes hurt his brain to have to think so much on mechanical matters. But he felt a quiet pride that he had mastered the gun. "I finally realize now why you took such pains to teach me how to read, Merlin," he muttered to the shadows of the maintenance hangar. "Thank you."

The armorer's room was lit dimly by the low-wattage bulbs suspended from tin lamps. Arthur pushed the technical manual aside. He turned the light switch off and on repeatedly, watching the filament glow inside the bulb.

"I'd like one of these for my chambers," he murmured. "Light so fine and steady that I could read all night if I wished."

Tommy Stubbs entered the room quietly. He stared at Arthur quizzically. Finally, he spoke. "Somebody sees that light flash behind the blackout curtain, they'll think you're a Nazi spy, King. Positively Fifth Column."

"Forgive me," the king said. "It was flickering. I was testing it."

"You're a strange one," Stubbs observed, picking up the manual. "We don't have a single officer in squadron who'd bother with book learning after duty hours. It ain't natural."

King smiled. "I want to learn about everything you've got here. Do you know that with three hundred rounds carried in the aircraft wing, we can only fire these guns for fifteen seconds? That's not very long, is it?"

Arthur smoothed his hand on the rifled barrel. "The manual says the projectile fires at two thousand, six hundred and sixty feet per second. Can you imagine an arrow doing that?"

Stubbs shrugged. "Give Jerry a shot in the arse, and if you're lucky you go home," he said gruffly. "Squadron Leader Richardson would like it more if you learned how to bring home an aircraft. There'll be an inquiry for taking that Spit up without authorization. You broke all the rules."

"I know," Arthur said. "Do you suppose I'll face court-martial?"

"They're killing too many of us for all those formalities. They'll take your pay instead. Cheer up, King. Air Ministry credits you a kill."

"What?"

"Hurricane chap from Biggin Hill claimed a Junkers bomber, but his gun film showed you got the Hun. You were the only Spitfire in the sector."

"That's good, then?"

"Jolly good. If you're going to bail out of your ship, taking a bomber with you is the way to do it. Bagging Huns is our job."

"Our job," Arthur said, brightening. "Yes, it is. Isn't it?"

"Now leave these dreary books and let's have a drink."

"Thanks, but I'm going to study."

"Not so, King. Every serving officer shall attend Lord Beaverbrook's dance. Richardson's orders. They're even letting the Yank out for the night."

"The Yank?"

"He's a good lad," Stubbs said, clapping Arthur on the shoulder. "Not a lot of sense. But that's Yanks for you. Too many Western movies."

"Western movies."

"Right. Cowboys and gangsters. Barbaric country, America. Come along. We'll drench ourselves with aftershave and have a pint."

"Aftershave."

"Right. Some sweet-smelling stuff for the birds."

"Birds," Arthur said helplessly.

Tommy Stubbs embraced the air and hummed as he danced a rhumba with an imaginary brunette. "You know, King. Birds. Soft and lovely. Voices higher than ours. Lips ruby red. The lights are low, the gin is strong, and there you are, dancing cheek to cheek with an auxiliary or bouncy nurse."

Stubbs emerged from his reverie and slapped the king on the back. "Right. Now, let's get to it." With finality, the flight leader snapped the Browning manual shut and ushered King Arthur out of the armory.

*   *   *

A tobacco cloud issued from the Georgian doors of
Lord Beaverbrook's manor. The minister for aircraft
production maintained a sprawling estate that offered
occasional rest for the Royal Air Force. Stubbs and
King elbowed their way into a sea of blue uniforms
and bobbed hair. By the time the king entered the
main hall, he found his cheeks streaked with Coty
from fresh nurses and WAAFs. Arthur rubbed his
face and looked at the red smudge and called out to
Stubbs in alarm. "I've been bit," he cried over the
din.

"Nonsense," Stubbs said, hugging a WAAF and
giving her a pat on the bottom. "You were only
nicked. Close combat ahead. Bandits, twelve o'clock
high."

The dancers jitterbugged around Arthur. Their
motions defied any resemblance to the king's notion
of dance. They clapped their hands and lindy hopped
high in the air. The band belted out a Dorsey medley.

"They're playing 'In the Mood,'" Stubbs shouted
above the din.

The revelers whirled like pagans. "What do you
call this?" Arthur cried helplessly.

"Opportunity," Stubbs replied, handing Arthur a
pair of foaming pints from the bar. "Keep my beer
warm, will you, King?"

Stubbs elbowed his way onto the dance floor and
cut in. He stomped his shoe to the beat of the bass
drum as a WAAF brunette started chewing her gum
in time to his insistent step. Stubbs spun her by the
waist and lifted her high above his head. The trumpet
blared.

"Sounds like a call to arms," Arthur murmured.
The king downed both pints. He felt someone take
his arm. It was Nurse Edith. Her cheeks were heavily

rouged and her lips formed a smooch to smooth her lipstick.

"Fancy, if it isn't the lad who won't take off his knickers," she cooed. "Want to cut a rug?"

Arthur felt dizzy. The room was filled to the rafters with gray smoke and human heat. He looked up to see thousands of balloons dropping dreamlike from the ceiling. "Thanks, but no," he said. "I need some air."

"Too bad, luv. Just don't forget I saw you first. Even before Jenny." The king started in surprise as Edith goosed him. Then the words sunk in and he grabbed her arm.

"Is Jenny here?"

"Somewhere," Edith said vaguely, scanning the crowded room. "Who's that lifting the girl on the dance floor? He looks strong."

Arthur moved away from Edith and tried to keep from being pulled into the dancers' tide. He caught a glimpse of Yank far across the room. "Bill!" the king cried out. But Cooper vanished.

Arthur plunged into another wave of merrymakers, their laughter high-strung, their movements exaggerated. He pressed on, pushing through the mob like a swimmer. The crowd pushed him along into a corridor replete with trophies of the hunt where the young people smoked and drank and pressed against each other.

Arthur stumbled through a doorway into a study. He drew a breath and stared up at a row of oil paintings. Each portrait depicted a different age of the manor, with lords and ladies draped in sequins and lace, leather, and boots, or armor of their proper time. A portrait of Churchill hung above a fireplace. Arthur wondered how a man in such clumsy dress could command respect. He stared long at the man's bulldog face staring back at him.

He was still staring as Jenny Hamilton walked up behind him.

"It's all in the eyes, isn't it?" Jenny said. "You can see that he's serious," she continued. "Those eyes tell the world that he means what he says."

Arthur turned, delighted. "He does, indeed, look determined," the king said. "Have you ever met him?"

"No, Lieutenant. I've only heard him on the wireless, like everyone."

"Yes, that's how I know him." He could not take his eyes from her. His throat felt raw. "From the wireless."

"You ought to be dancing, Lieutenant. This is a party."

"It looked more like a battle."

"I agree," she said, laughing. Her ginger hair shook on her shoulders. She wore a dark cape with a small white patch embroidered with a red cross above the breastline. She wore a fragrance that hinted of thyme.

Arthur found himself watching the graceful curve of her neck. He felt goosebumps and cleared his throat. "So, my lady, why aren't you at the party?"

"I hate crowds. Everywhere is crowded now. The hospital. The Underground. Everyone huddles to escape the bombs. I only came tonight because of Edith."

"I saw her."

"She's a dear. I thought I'd escape the mob and see some of the old things kept here."

"What old things?"

"Everything in this house is ancient and lovely. I must see it all before I have to return to the hospital."

"Would you show me?"

"I can't imagine a fighter pilot would be interested in antiquity."

"Sometimes I feel lost in this time," Arthur said quietly.

"Really? I thought all of you RAF lads just love your planes and flying. And that's about it."

"Not a one of the lads here is spending the night with their plane," Arthur said.

Jenny laughed again. "That's true, Lieutenant. But they certainly didn't come to see tapestries."

"Perhaps," Arthur said. He found himself memorizing her face. "Actually, I came hoping to see you."

She smiled. "That sounds like a line, Arthur King."

"What's a line?"

"Don't play the fool," she said cheerfully. "I'll give you the tour. Don't try to give me the business."

She gathered the cape round her shoulders. Away from the dancers, a chill intruded, curling up from the floor and seeping through the cracks in the walls. Jenny led Arthur down the hall, turning at the music room. "Oh, dear," she said, stepping back quickly. Arthur peeked over her shoulder to find Tommy Stubbs atop a harpsichord and astride Nurse Edith. One couldn't tell where Stubbs' shirttail ended and Edith's skirts and stockings began.

"For God's sakes, King," Stubbs growled. "The poor girl passed out in all that heat."

"Forgive me," Arthur stammered.

"Can't you see I'm trying to revive her?"

Arthur pulled Jenny from the doorway, held her by the shoulders and stared at her quizzically. "Is that a line?" he said.

She giggled. The giggle turned to laughter and soon her ginger tresses were shaking from her shoulders. The king laughed, and together they leaned against the walnut paneling. "It was a line, wasn't it?" the king persisted. The king's lips found Jenny's and she drew away.

"I'm sorry," she said.

"What about?"

"I don't mean to lead you on, King."

"I want you to lead me, Jenny. And I will follow."

She patted him lightly on the cheek. "You do have a smooth line. And a nice face."

She got up and began to walk away. Arthur rushed after her. "Please," he said, taking her arm. "I don't understand. Have I offended you?"

The woman turned to him and smiled sadly. "You're lovely, really," she said, touching his cheek, this time letting her fingers linger. "I simply don't get along with fighter pilots. Too many of them die in my care."

Arthur bowed. "Then, tonight, I shall not be a fighter pilot. I shall be as peaceable as the lion with the lamb."

"You really are quite different. Almost courtly."

"My foes say I am ruthless," the king replied. "But I truly am a peaceable sort. Show me the manor. I want to learn about everything you find beautiful."

"Come along," Jenny said, taking his hand.

They left the music room portal, hearing a crash of keys and a slight cry of surprise. "Oh," Edith cried, her voice pitched high. The king and Jenny strolled together in the dimly lit hallway until they saw the warm, orange light emanating from the library. The library formed the east wing of the house. It was nearly the size of Arthur's castle solarium in Camelot.

"So many books," the king said. He turned to Jenny. "How many monks does your lord have in his employ?"

"I beg your pardon?"

"The books. How could Lord Beaverbrook come by so many?"

"He buys them like any other man," Jenny said, slightly puzzled.

"The English are a nation of readers. Is it different in your end of the country?"

Walking quickly along the library wall, Arthur ran his fingers along the leather spines. He touched the titles. "This is marvelous," he declared.

"I quite agree," Jenny said. "I'd love a library like this. I suppose I'll have to content myself with bookshops."

She walked to the great stone fireplace and kneeled, warming her hands by the blaze. Her long hair glowed a golden orange in the firelight. Arthur's eyes left the books and found Jenny's eyes. "I feel as if I know you," he said, approaching her.

She settled herself and folded his hand in hers. "Let's sit awhile."

"Yes," he whispered. She nestled in the crook of his arm. She touched his cheek again. "What is that?" she said, sniffing.

"It's aftershave," he said proudly. "I'm drenched with it."

"I know," she said. "Still, you're very nice, King."

"I saw you with the boy who crashlanded the Spitfire yesterday. You looked like an angel."

"The death angel, I fear," she said, a trace of bitterness entering her voice. "We lost him. He was just the latest. I'm sick of it. Crash and bang. They die. Your gods of war gobble them like nuts and spit back the shells."

"I'm sorry."

"Why sorry, Arthur? It's not your fault, is it?" The king shook his head and watched her like time. Slowly, Jenny rose to her feet. She stood to examine an enormous two-handed broadsword suspended above the fireplace. She placed her fingers on the flat of the blade engraved with the date 1066.

"Maybe killing is in our blood," she said. "Maybe we can't stop it. Thousands of years of battle. A thousand alone since this sword was forged for the sweet purpose of cleaving a man in half."

"Fighting was different then," Arthur said.

"I doubt that."

"Men rode to battle on a field of honor and fought in single combat. Now, they load machines with a rain of fire that falls on man, woman and child alike. There's no honor in it. No just goal. Just murderousness."

"You sound as if you knew that time."

Arthur lifted a mace from the wall. He hefted it with professional ease in order to check the balance. He grinned ruefully. "Some great power should take our weapons away from us, Jenny." He replaced the mace. "Disarm us until we know might from right."

"Do you really mean that?"

"Yes," he said, averting his eyes. "Please. Show me some more old things."

Her hand touched his cheek. "You're not like the others, are you?" The king shook his head and smiled. She took his hand and moved with him quietly among the antiquities. He gazed appreciatively at the Turner watercolor and his smile deepened at the Tang vase. When he saw the display of armor, he moved straight toward it like a general inspecting troops.

With a professional's ease, he inspected each suit, probing with his fingers for the weak spots and the chinks and grunting appreciatively at the advances in breastplates, jointed armor and metallurgy. At the end of the line stood an ancient suit of chain mail and leather. Emblazoned on the breastplate was the crude, engraved image of a dragon rampant. Arthur touched it, then his fingers recoiled as if he'd put them on a hot stove.

It was his own, personal armor. A brass plate at the base said simply, "Found, monastery in Cornwall. Origin unknown."

"Merlin," Arthur whispered. He felt the hair prickle on the nape of his neck. "Where are you?" The crack of a billiard ball failed to shake Arthur from his reverie. He placed his palm on the breastplate as if in communion with it and closed his eyes.

"Someone's playing in the next room," Jenny said. She opened the door to the billiard room. "Oh, dear," she said. Two older men in dinner jackets emerged from the billiard room, each chalking his cue. A cigar jutted like a cannon from the shorter man. And the eyes in the painting glimmered from the man. "Mr. Churchill," Jenny gasped. "We didn't mean to interrupt."

"Nonsense, young lady," he replied. "It's we who are interrupting you. Have you met your host?" Lord Beaverbrook, a rumpled man with a tuft of white hair like a monk's tonsure, took Jenny's hand and kissed it. He turned and walked to Arthur, who ignored the men and continued to stare at the armor.

The aircraft lord joined Arthur. He patted the breastplate. "It's one of my favorite pieces," Beaverbrook said. He smiled proudly, his expression that of possession. "It's my pride and joy. The breastplate was found in Cornwall. I have not confirmed the lineage of it, but I believe it to be authentic. Do you know the legend?"

Arthur's eyes never left the breastplate. "It's the House of Pendragon."

"You do know it!" Beaverbrook said, surprised. "It's said that when Arthur's armor and sword are found, the king may yet return. I learned that tale as a boy. I always hoped, somehow, that it might be true."

"I'd know this symbol anywhere."

"Well, it was more than a lucky find. Got it in a shop in Wales from a strange old chap." Beaverbrook furrowed his brow, and looked at Arthur with keen interest. "He had starlight in his eyes, it seemed."

"I come from that end of the country. We have people there who are like that."

"Yes," Beaverbrook said, dabbing his bald pate with a kerchief. Again, he regarded Arthur. "Is there anything else in my humble manor that interests you?"

Arthur turned. Urgently, he said, "Have you got a sword? A jeweled dragon forms the hilt."

"Oh, that," the lord said. Beaverbrook's brow furrowed. He squinted as if deep in thought and replied, "I have a Rolls Royce motorcar. It's called the Excalibur. But no, I have no sword by that name. I'd pay dearly for it. A king's ransom."

"You believe it exists, then?"

"It must," Beaverbrook replied. "I've been waiting all my life to see such a thing. Any Briton loves the myth of Arthur. If there's a legend, there's a history to it. If there is history, there's truth, Lieutenant."

Churchill walked over, his brandy glass full. "What does the RAF tell us about their view of the war tonight, Beaverbrook?"

"The lieutenant knows his armor. He appreciates antiquity."

"I hope he appreciates the armor you're putting in the Spitfires. Newer stuff."

As the king bowed, he stole a glance at Jenny. "How fares the Battle of Britain?" Arthur asked. "It is quite confusing from my personal vantage, sir."

"That's honest of you, Lieutenant," Churchill responded, blowing a large puff of smoke that drifted into the darkness beyond the firelight. "Whether we stand or fall depends largely on you."

"I know," the king replied. He looked up. "Do you know Mordred?"

Churchill turned to Beaverbrook, his glance questioning. "What's a Mordred? Some new kind of Messerschmitt?" He clapped Arthur on the shoulder.

"You just keep shooting them down, young man. You've earned our gratitude."

"Not yet, sir," Arthur replied.

Churchill grinned approvingly and knocked back his brandy. "Just so. What I'd expect from one of the gallant few."

"We wouldn't mind more company," Arthur said, his expression and voice even. "Some of the few tell me they are getting lonely, sir."

Churchill grunted. "We're doing our best, Lieutenant. The sentiment is appreciated. Beaverbrook is making Merlin engines, and Britain is training pilots as fast as it can."

"And I think the Spitfire needs a heavier gun, sir," Arthur continued.

Churchill looked at the pilot, interested. "Really? What's your name, young man?"

"King, sir. Lieutenant King. I've read all the books on the Browning, sir. And the latest material on the Hun fighters. The Germans are using cannon. They tear great holes in the wings, sir."

Churchill nodded. The aircraft lord put his arm round the king's shoulder. "The lieutenant speaks like a man who knows his weapons," Beaverbrook said, brandishing his cue. "You are welcome to come back and discuss your knowledge of ancient armor or the armament of the Spitfire."

"Take a note, Beaverbrook," Churchill said gruffly. "Study cannon. Now let's leave these young people to their evening."

Beaverbrook smiled at Jenny. "And are you also from King's part of the country, my dear?"

"I'm from the RAF Hospital, my lord," Jenny replied. "I should love to escape it to see all of your library sometime."

"Well, then, we must arrange a tour. Meanwhile, may we bring you some refreshments?"

"How kind, my lord," Jenny replied. "We fled from the noise."

"A little music of a quieter kind, then," the industrialist said. He winked. Then placed a record on a Victrola. He dropped the needle and rejoined Churchill in the billiard room.

Arthur looked at Jenny. She appeared faint and he placed his arms around her waist and shoulders. The scent of her hair intoxicated him. "Are you all right?"

"Arthur! That was Churchill. Aren't you excited?"

"Yes," Arthur said simply. Then he frowned. He shook his head and muttered. "The Yank said he wouldn't understand about Mordred. He was right."

"Arthur, what are you talking about?"

The king gathered Jenny's caped shoulders in his arms and walked her to his suit of ancient armor. He stood staring at the breastplate and iron collar with the dragon signet on it while faint strains of Glenn Miller emanated from the Victrola.

"There's some strange magic in this night, Jenny," Arthur said quietly. "That music is beautiful."

"It's 'Moonlight Serenade.' Very popular."

Jenny looked up at Arthur and raised his arm. She began to lead and the king followed, his feet shuffling in a gentle sway to the phonograph music. She moved confidently, and the king smiled.

"This is more like the sort of dance I know," Arthur said. He held Jenny tightly and looked past her shoulder to the window. A blackout curtain covered it, nearly to the ceiling, but through the leaded panes near the top, he saw a moon, growing in fullness.

"The moon is racing," he said, "like time itself. We don't have enough time, Jenny."

Jenny nestled in Arthur's embrace. "That's not a line?" she whispered haltingly.

"No," he replied. "There's no time for that."

"There's never enough time," Jenny said softly as

they swayed to the music. The needle skipped. Both looked at each other, slightly bewildered, and Edith blundered into the room, still adjusting her skirt. She carried a flask and placed it on the table next to Arthur's armored display.

"Jenny. The hospital lorry's waiting," she said, swaying slightly. "It's past midnight." She smiled dreamily. "I've been a bad girl, I'm afraid."

Jenny hugged Arthur, almost involuntarily. She broke free of the king and said breathlessly, "I must run. It's late."

"I have to see you again." He kissed her, deeply, until the room seemed to vanish around them. Jenny held on to the king's arms and the king's kiss.

"Oh, well," Edith said. Jenny finally broke free. Hurriedly, she kissed Arthur's cheek.

She gathered the cape round her shoulders and darted into the hallway. Arthur rushed after her, down the darkened hall and out the door. A truck was already grinding its gears. The women hidden in the shadow of the lorry's canvas bellowed a tipsy version of "We'll Meet Again."

Before Arthur could call out, Jenny vanished down the midnight highway. The king stared up at the racing moon and shivered, his blood racing, his mind a blur, his heart in Jenny Hamilton's caress. He found Edith's flask in his hand and he took a long swig. The liquor was smoky and hot, but did him no good. His mind was filled with thoughts of Jenny, but something else bothered him. He remembered the armor and marched back through the moonlit corridors of the manor.

As he unclipped the steely-scaled collar piece from the dragon breastplate, the king muttered penance. It wasn't theft, really. The armor was his. He was merely reclaiming some of it for luck. He was a king, not a burglar, after all. He made his way back through the hallway, into the fresh air, feeling like a thief in the night.

Standing on the gravel path, the king stared at the sky. The moon sailed like a ship, and there was a lady in the ship beckoning to Arthur. Was she the milk white Lady of the Lake, the one who proferred Excalibur? Was Jenny that lady? Gone from him so suddenly, she filled his heart with dreams and desire. He yearned for her. Arthur thought about her in white silks in a field of daisies. He felt her so close he could sense her scent, a departing trace of lavender in the crisp air.

Arthur stared up at the moon, wondering at the pale beauty and the gathering danger that its fullness held. He turned to walk inside and saw the shadow moving toward him, then the pale fist. He reeled at the punch to the jaw, and kneeled from the force of the blow to the side of the head. The king fell to the ground.

"There you are, you bloody thief," his attacker said, kicking Arthur in the shin.

"Don't kick him while he's down," another man yelled in drunken glee. "Wait until he gets up. Then give it to him."

Arthur rose, searching in the darkness for his enemies, who surrounded him like wolves. Suddenly, the night turned inky black and the king gasped for air. They'd thrown a horse blanket on him. His feet were swept from under him again. "There," the first assailant shouted. "Now kick the cheeky bastard."

A rain of kicks and punches fell on the king. He was kicked in the back and kidneys, but luckily, the blanket shielded the force of the blows. He struggled to tear his arms free from the blanket. He gasped for air. Arthur got one arm free and grabbed hold of something alive. It was an ankle. He pulled his enemy to the ground and rolled on to him. The blanket fell free and he felt his assailant's hot, whiskey breath in his face. It was Gilbert Hawley.

The others fled and Hawley's eyes bulged in fury as Arthur held him to the ground. "Next time we'll finish the job, King. You won't fly in this squadron."

Arthur rolled the blanket so it covered Hawley's chest. Then the king pinned the flier's arms to the ground with his knees.

"There is no 'next time' in combat, Hawley," Arthur said, grasping the flight leader's ears and pulling them back painfully, as if Hawley were a horse and he were inspecting its teeth.

"I've done nothing to you. Why attack me?"

"You're a Yank lover, you shit," Hawley said. "Drop in from nowhere and lose me my wingman, then take my plane. You bet I'll get you next time. I don't care if you're King George's bastard nephew."

"I don't know what you're talking about," Arthur said. Hawley struggled and Arthur held him fast to the ground.

"Big mystery pilot," Hawley sneered. "The man with no records. He cozies up to the do-nothing Yank and does whatever he pleases. I'll find you out, and then I'll kick your ass right out of the RAF, or my name isn't Gilbert Hawley."

"What do you mean, the 'do-nothing' Yank?"

"He's done nothing since he got here, except fall out of the sky and waste airplanes. And men. I wouldn't have lost my number two if not for your amateur flying. You Air Ministry clods want the Americans in the war? What for?"

Arthur gripped Hawley by the lapels of his Irvin jacket. "You're slandering my friend," he said. "Take back your lies."

Hawley chuckled. "What kind of an inbred ass are you? Do you really talk that shit at the palace, or are you some sort of unique fool?"

"We'll see who's the fool," Arthur said. Gradually, he eased the pressure on Hawley's shoulders and stood up.

"Get up and find a weapon, Gilbert Hawley."

Arthur reached for his boot and slowly withdrew the commando dagger. Hawley grinned and produced a clasp knife that he carried in his pocket. He snapped it open and the blade shimmered in the moonlight.

"Imagine, two gentlemen at sword's point," Hawley said. "You're not all bad. I'm going to hate to cut out your liver."

"Stop it, Arthur!" Bill Cooper yelled. He stepped out from the shadows. "Cut him and they'll bring you up on charges at a court-martial for sure."

Hawley laughed. "Well, if it isn't your lost lamb, King. Where were you hiding, little Yank? Behind the stairs like a child at Christmas?"

"Shut up, Gil," Cooper said.

Arthur called out, "How long have you been here?"

"Long enough to see you were doing something stupid, Arthur."

Hawley chuckled. "Never a truer word was spoke." He folded his knife shut and put it in his pocket. "Lover's quarrel. I'll leave you to it. Maybe your Yank will tell you some flying stories."

Hawley sauntered away, laughing. The laughter sounded oddly familiar to Arthur. Hawley sounded like Mordred. "How long were you hiding there, Yank?" Arthur asked.

"Long enough."

"Why didn't you help?"

"What kind of a crack is that? I stopped the fight."

"So you did. Why didn't you fight the Messerschmitt?"

"Don't you know when we're outmatched?"

The American gave Arthur a wounded look. "I thought we were friends."

"I thought you'd come to my aid."

"I couldn't see in the dark," Cooper said. "I was just being cautious."

Arthur looked up at the moon. He looked at Yank. "I see."

Yank tore at his tie. He kicked the ground so hard he yelped in pain. "What do you know about air combat, Arthur? You can't even fly."

"I know that if you don't rush to aid your comrades, battles are lost."

"Hawley's right," Cooper said bitterly. "You don't know shit. The Huns have killed a hundred squadron leaders and flight leaders since May. For some of us, it's hard enough just to get the wheels up. You know so much, you go fly the goddamned Spitfire."

"I did, Yank," Arthur said quietly. Cooper looked at him in disbelief.

"Bullshit."

"Got a kill. A Junkers bomber, Stubbs tells me."

Yank sat down slowly. He poked his fingers in the gravel and let it shake loosely in his hand. He looked up at the moon. Arthur could see a tear on Cooper's face, moving slowly, like a stream in tributary to the sea.

"Why can't I do it, Arthur?" He looked up at the king. "Flying combat is my job. Why can't I do my job?"

The king sat down next to the American. He shook Edith's flask. The king took a swig and let the pleasant, smoky taste wash round in his mouth. He offered the flask to Yank. "A long time ago, before my first battle, I was afraid that I would die. So I spent the night trembling. I was, in fact, sick. A strong, ill-humored feeling."

"Did you go for sick call?"

"We didn't have such things."

"Okay, Arthur. So they gave you a Victoria Cross."

"I don't know what you mean. I was ill, and I didn't want to fight. One stubborn old man found me shaking in my tent."

"Who was he?"

"The old bastard who taught me all the tricks."

"I'd like to learn a trick about not being scared shitless every time I scramble."

"The old man didn't give me any tricks that night. Just some good advice."

Yank took a swig of whiskey and handed the flask back to the king. "So what was your old man's secret?"

"He told me to concentrate on what to do, not on what might happen. That's fatal. Live each moment's problem and get on to the next moment. At the end of the battle, I was among the living."

Yank sighed. He took the flask and finished its contents. He coughed like a balky engine.

"First time I soloed in a Spitfire, I knew it was something I was born for, Arthur. I felt like I was part of the machine, and it was part of me. When they gave me my wings, I believed I was a hero."

"And?"

"My first patrol, I found out the wings are just a piece of cloth."

"If you do give up, Yank, you'll never learn about the man wearing the wings. Except that he quit when his friends needed him."

"All I know right now is that I feel incredibly alone."

"We're together in that anyway," Arthur said. He watched the moon fade and a line of purple turn to gray in the eastern sky. It was nearly dawn, and the sky seemed to shimmer with the promise of day as the stars faded and blinked.

"Get up, you frauds," Hawley shouted as he ran down the stone manor steps. "Squadron's on five-minute readiness."

Cooper rose unsteadily. "What's the deal?"

"Hun bombers to London," Tommy Stubbs yelled, staggering after Hawley and stuffing his shirttail beneath his uniform jacket. "Hundreds of 'em.

Goering's whole fleet." He stared at King slightly cross-eyed. "You've got my flask."

A lorry pulled up. A guard with a steel helmet cranked a siren while the fliers from Dragon Squadron piled into the back. Some held their heads. Others puked over the lorry's safety rope. Arthur dodged one pilot's mess and climbed in.

"Did I ever teach you how to land?" Yank asked Arthur in the hot, canvas-covered darkness of the lorry.

"Never got to it," Arthur replied.

"So, after the Junkers?"

"I fell out of the plane."

Yank shook his head. "There's got to be a better way."

"Quite agree, Bill."

The lorry rumbled down the road, heading toward the streaks of pink crossing the eastern horizon. Arthur ached for a whiff of oxygen drawn from the mask to clear his head of the whiskey and Jenny. Furtively, he unbuttoned his large tunic pocket. The iron collar of the dragon's gorget was in his possession. Something in him felt apologetic toward Lord Beaverbrook. But Arthur reasoned, the armor was really his own. He was merely reclaiming it.

The gorget was not Excalibur, but it was a start. Rolling toward the call of battle, he ran his fingers across the scaled steel of the collar piece. It was a piece of his armor. It was a piece of himself. Immediately, he felt more at home in the unknown age he had dropped into.

15

ordred concentrated on the chessboard that
rested atop an ammunition crate in the ready
tent. He smoked a pipe taken from Kleist's stand,
a meerschaum carved in the shape of a death's head.
Mordred was studying how to take Kleist's rook when
Adolf Galland stormed into the tent and hurled a
crumpled wad of paper. Mordred, absorbed in the
game, ignored Galland.

"Oberst Morgan!" Galland snarled.

Mordred gazed up tranquilly. "Not enough
schnapps last night, Galland? Or too much?"

Galland picked up the crumpled paper and
unfolded it slowly. "These aren't operations orders
that bear your signature, Colonel. They're death war-
rants," the fighter general said. "Our escort planes
are ordered to fly so close to the bombers that they're
nothing but target practice for the Spitfires."

"Still, those are the orders, Galland," Mordred said

calmly. "I've read your record. When you flew with the Condor Legion, you were brave."

Galland turned to Kleist. "Have you abdicated your command, General? Tell me why we've stopped attacking real targets. Why hospitals and town centers instead of radar stations? One of your squadrons hit a children's home last week. The BBC had a field day."

Mordred blew a lazy ring of smoke from the yellowed pipe. "Since when, General Galland, is war supposed to be sane?" Mordred snatched one of Kleist's knights. "Is not war calculated insanity?"

Galland swept the chess pieces from the board. "My men are not pawns."

"No?" Mordred's face twisted into a smile and he rubbed the star-shaped scar on his forehead. "Even a pawn can take the king under the right circumstances."

Outside the tent, the frantic shouts of service crews pulling bomb trolleys was drowned by the roar of Junkers engines. The ground shook as bombers rolled forward into the takeoff pattern. The engines screamed as the propellers rotated and black smoke snorted from the exhaust manifolds. Galland pulled the tent flap open and shook his head mournfully as the first wave of bombers soared aloft like laden birds of prey.

"Is this the battle we wanted?" he asked. He turned to Kleist. "You are turning the world's greatest air force into a pack of jackals. The English propagandists call us murderers, and the world listens."

"What do you care what we are called so long as we win?" Mordred said simply. "War is murder. Until one side yields."

Mordred packed the meerschaum and lit the death's head bowl with a match he snapped with his thumb. He inhaled the mixture of latakia and sulfur, then winked at Galland.

"The second bomber wave is taking off," Mordred said. He rose from his cot and began donning a fur-lined jacket. "Must get ready for the show, General. Get your fighters airborne for Channel rendezvous."

Mordred attempted to restore the pieces to their original positions on the board. "The Third Reich doesn't have time for weaklings," he murmured. "And neither do we."

"These missions contravene the Geneva Convention," Galland said. "There's international law against the deliberate killing of civilians."

Mordred puffed his pipe. He tamped the hot coal with his thumb and puffed again. "That sounds like something my father made up. How damnably silly."

"And who was your father?"

"A dead fool," Mordred answered. "As dead as England will be when we are through."

"Just hope that England doesn't become the Luftwaffe's graveyard," Galland said. He stomped out of the tent and Kleist stuffed his trouser cuffs into his boots.

A klaxon sounded and the crewmen assigned to the second wave began trotting out to their waiting aircraft. Kleist and Mordred lifted the tent flap and watched the young men in bulky coveralls jog toward the Heinkels. By now, the airfield buzzed like an enormous beehive, the air filled with the noise of windmilling propellers. Mordred chuckled approvingly as a five-hundred-pound bomb was wheeled by with "Churchill's cigar" painted on it in gothic letters. Mordred picked up the white king from the chessboard.

"The pity is that Galland is right," Kleist muttered, watching the scramble. "We're not getting anywhere with these terror raids." He looked at Mordred. "You said it would be easy. Are you a liar, luring us all to our deaths like a siren?"

Mordred shrugged. He held up the king piece and examined it thoughtfully. "Where does the king of England keep himself these days? Does he lead his men into battle?"

"Hardly," Kleist said. "Kings are obsolete. We got rid of most of them in the last war."

"How novel. Who took their place?"

"The strong men. Hitler is a leader. King George is just a waxworks dummy, hidden away deep in Buckingham Palace. His people see him only in newsreels. Those are the moving pictures."

"The shadow pictures," Mordred murmured. He replaced the king on the board. "Still, he is the king and symbols are important. What if we could make the king disappear?"

"The English would be enraged," Kleist said. "They would fight harder."

Mordred picked up one of the white bishops and examined it. "What about the warlord Churchill? Is he one of your strong men? If he were removed from the field, would England fight on?"

"Churchill matters," Kleist replied. "His loss could demoralize them. He's more than a dictator. He gives them the will to fight."

Mordred's lip curled slightly at the edges, betraying an impish smile. He pushed a black bishop across the board so that it knocked over the remaining white bishop, threatening the white king.

"What if we got rid of them both?"

Kleist zipped his fur-lined jacket. He looked at his captor with genuine curiosity. "How?"

Mordred lifted the white bishop. "Kings love churches, don't they? At least, my father did. What if we were to bomb the greatest church in England? Would the king come out to comfort his flocks? Would Churchill join them?"

Kleist stroked his chin and nodded. "They might.

They've made propaganda visits to the bomb victims in the East End of London. But it would be impossible to find them there. They're like rabbits in a warren."

"But a large cathedral is a target we could hit. *Nein?*"

"Easily," Kleist said. "We could saturate it. Nothing would be left."

"In my day, the grandest cathedral was my father's church at Coventry."

"Coventry stands," Kleist offered. "It's the most beloved church in England, full of sacred treasure and grand design. Like Cologne."

"If I were king," Mordred mused, "I wouldn't be a figurehead." He studied the chessboard and his slender face darkened. "Nobody loves Mordred, except Mordred. That will have to do."

"If you were king?" Kleist murmured. "What sort of thing are you?"

"You begin to amuse me, General. When I am king, perhaps I'll keep you for my pleasure. Like a pet."

Mordred picked up a black knight and made a sweeping gesture. He knocked over the white bishop, putting the king in double check. Kleist picked up the king and tried to move it. He shrugged his shoulders. It was no use. Mordred pushed the black bishop and knocked over the king.

16

Arthur's Spitfire burst through the ceiling of cumulus at fifteen thousand feet. In nearly vertical battle climb, the blood drained from his face. Gravity pressed him deep into the cockpit. His arms felt like lead, but his hand on the control column felt sure. The gloved hand on the throttle gave the Merlin engine a steady stream of fuel and he could see the blue flames jetting off the exhaust manifold. The cockpit felt as cold as Wales in winter, but the chill didn't bother the king. He loved flying.

Arthur followed Stubbs and the Yank in a vic formation. Arthur listened to the strange universe that enveloped him, the world of tweaks and squeaks and metal groaning at high stress. He listened to the drone of the Rolls Royce engine as its twelve pistons pulled it up toward the sun. His own breath flowed and ebbed like the tide inside the oxygen mask. Sunlight showered in through the perspex canopy.

The radio, with its faraway chatter and static, formed a chorus to the fighter group's ascent.

Through the din of crackle and buzz he identified a gaggle of foreign voices and knew immediately they were Huns. The enemy chattered away in open frequency, concealed by the clouds.

Gradually, the guttural Hun grunts grew louder, ever closer to the Channel coast. Arthur strained to see the black crosses. At the same time he tried to remember everything he ever read about his marvelous flying machine.

A hundred memorized instructions crowded Arthur's mind. How to operate landing gear controls, and how to manage the task of landing the Mark II Spitfire. Nose up. Three points down, dragging the tail nicely. But not now. Landing would come much later. After the fight. After the Hun closed for battle.

Arthur mentally recited the muzzle velocity and rate of fire of the Browning machine guns. With a round fired at three thousand feet per second, arrows and catapults couldn't touch the speed of .303 bullets. They were simply murderous. He whistled into the oxygen mask.

A memory of Arthur's ancient armor resting in Beaverbrook's library flashed through the king's mind. Reflexively, he reached for his throat and pulled at his scarf. Suddenly, he felt himself a primitive. Then, he remembered the bombs dropped on London and he searched the skies for the new primitives that flew for Goering.

"The abyss of a new, dark age," he murmured. The Merlin engine hiccuped and Arthur shook himself from his reverie. "Concentrate," the king admonished himself.

The manual said to harmonize target interception for the Spitfire's eight guns at four hundred yards. Stubbs told them they'd chucked the manual back in

France. Two hundred yards was the ticket. Get up on Jerry's arse and give it to him from behind. Stubbs's advice was reliably blunt. The Spitfire's ammunition, ten pounds of steel delivered in a two-second burst. The manual said that would bring down a Hun bomber. Stubbs said the manual was full of shit. Too many Hun fighters got away unless they were hit in a vital spot like a fuel tank or cockpit. Just like a chink in the armor.

The king watched the cockpit gauges. Oil pressure. Fuel pressure. Artificial horizon. Altimeter. They had become his new kingdom. New and barely comprehensible to him, but still, he commanded and the aircraft obeyed. Merlin had been a hard taskmaster, but Arthur knew how to learn by watching and listening. And most of all, by reading. What he wanted most dearly was to land the crate. No more bailing out. It was becoming unseemly. The radio crackled and a polite, liquid voice relayed an urgent warning from the ops room at Bentley Priory.

"Chalice, this is Camelot calling. You've got a large formation, inbound at Dover. Bandits. At least one hundred. Staggered formations at angels ten." The controller's voice sounded as if he were announcing arrival of an overdue train.

"Chalice Leader acknowledges," Stubbs replied. "Looking for trade."

As Blue Flight approached the Channel coast, the cloud cover broke, revealing a phalanx of Nazi bombers flying in loose gull-winged formations more than a mile below the Spitfires of Dragon Squadron. Messerschmitt 109s and twin-engine 110s flew top cover a thousand feet above the Heinkels and JU88 bombers.

The line of 109s and 110s flew in *schwarm* formation, spreading diagonally across the sky like an oil slick. "Jesus," Yank said in the clear. "Goering must have sent 'em all."

"Blue Leader to Blue Flight, tally ho," Stubbs said tersely. "Go. Go. Go. Go!"

Stubbs's Spitfire did a half roll and plunged toward the wave of bombers. Arthur dived in trail, the momentum filling the pit of his stomach as the Spitfire plummeted earthward. He watched his gun sight fill with the sturgeon shape of a Heinkel. He pressed the firing button and watched the tracers drop lazily toward the black cross midway down the fuselage. Arthur narrowly avoided collision with the fishbowl nose of the bomber as he leveled out and flew past, the inverted star on the fuselage flashing at him. He pressed his firing button, loosing a quick squirt.

The sun flashed in the king's rearview mirror. He felt the control surfaces shudder as he watched bullets stitch a line across his right wing. It unfolded for him like a slow dance. He felt paralyzed as if watching a serpent. He sucked his breath in and wrenched the stick as his feet worked the pedals. He dropped quickly from under the flash of the sun in his mirror, but the blinding light was quickly replaced by the bright flash of Hun guns. The canopy shattered. A mix of glycol, glass and oil sprayed Arthur's goggles.

Mordred wrenched the pistol grip of the MK-15 machine gun and kept the firing button depressed so long the barrel nearly melted. His hands vibrated. Adrenaline fired through his bloodstream as bullets streamed out of the JU88's nose. "Right!" Kleist shouted from the pilot seat. "Now, the coup de grace!"

The tracer spray arced past the Spitfire, then the British plane sailed into the ring of Mordred's gunsight and he stitched the wing in a deflection shot as his quarry tried to roll away. The roundel symbol shredded. Mordred's heart pounded in his chest, thundering as if it would burst free of the harness straps that held him fast to the cockpit.

"We'll follow him down to verify the kill," Kleist said. He jerked heavily on the control yoke and the aircraft turned heavily, obeying his command. The only freedom that Kleist felt from the stranger's mental dominion when was his hands were distracted by the gun controls and Kleist commanded the aircraft. "Confirm the kill and you have a trophy shot. Then we'll fly on to drop our eggs on London town."

Blood poured from Arthur's right shoulder where the shard of steel from the shattered cockpit pierced his coveralls. He heard the snapping spark of electrical wiring. It was a short. A smell of burning rubber added to the glycol stench. He couldn't let go of the stick and he couldn't pull the canopy back. The horizon ball bobbed and the altimeter needle read "zero." He'd lost power and the aircraft dropped like a rock. He pulled back on the stick and watched the trees rush by as the aircraft's nose reared up like a stallion.

The Spitfire's prop snapped and the intake ploughed a furrow in the field. The earth shook as the two-ton aircraft raked across the field. The king's eyes bulged as a row of oaks hurtled toward him. The aircraft lost momentum as the wings' spars tore free. Still the fuselage plowed forward another hundred feet, the world unfolding for Arthur like a kaleidoscope.

Sitting in shocked sudden silence, Arthur was overpowered by the odor of hundred-octane fuel. His trousers soaked through as the fuel gushed on to his knees. He used his good hand to unbuckle the harness. He pulled his bleeding arm free and rammed the canopy to the rear with his good shoulder. He clambered out and tumbled on to the field. He sensed movement to his right, then heard the low, twin-engine drone of an approaching aircraft. He looked over his shoulder to see the Junkers bomber making a banking turn. Groggy and faint from loss of blood, he stumbled and ran.

Arthur saw the plane dropping low and watched the spray of dirt from the bullets tearing a line that raced past his boots. He saw the bridge and the black water and tried to leap the last few feet to the stream, but lost his footing. Holding his good hand over his head, he cringed as the bullets tore around him. He looked up to see the dark cross of the aircraft's belly dropping toward him.

He clenched his fist and pulled it across the sky, giving his enemy a last defiant gesture, the battle salute of the House of Pendragon.

Mordred sighted in on the scrambling figure of the man. At the last possible instant, he saw the grounded flier making the strange clenched-fist, cross-armed gesture. Then he saw the intense, leonine face with his hard, gray eyes staring straight into his gun sight.

"Father!" Mordred cried.

The plane zoomed low. Mordred's hands loosened on the machine gun's pistol grip. The intercom crackled fiercely.

"Why didn't you shoot?" Kleist shouted.

Mordred watched the crumpled figure on the ground dive into a stream and shuttle crabwise under a stone footbridge. "Father," he whispered.

"We're getting low on fuel," Kleist said. "Too low for London. We're turning round."

"How did you do it, Father?" Mordred muttered. "Are you to follow me everywhere? Will I see you in hell?"

Their fuel was down nearly to the reserve tanks. Just enough to get them back across the Channel as long as they didn't get jumped. Mordred cleared his gun and cursed Merlin under his breath.

"What did you say?"

"That plane should have exploded."

Kleist turned the plane's bullet-shaped nose back toward the base in France. The radio was filled with the chatter of bombs and battle, but Mordred heard none of it. It was as if the battle happened in a far-away land, while his father came close enough to touch him.

"He lives," Mordred whispered. The bomber raced across the Channel. Mordred looked down at the waves and saw the water had the same hard, gray, coal color as the shade of his father's eyes.

The king lay on his back in the stream. The icy chill of the water revived him. He watched the dark cross of the Junkers bomber vanish. With an effort, he reached with his good arm and grabbed hold of an oak root that snaked off a boulder into the rushing stream. He pulled himself heavily on to the damp stone.

Arthur heard the flutter of wings overhead and he looked up to see a raven descending in the last instant before he passed out.

The king regained consciousness in the surgery ward. The odor of iodine and salts brought him around. He rose bolt upright on the gurney, straining against the straps that held him. The shoulder wound weighed down like a bucket of lead dropped from a castle bailey.

"It's him, Jenny! It's Arthur King, big as life," Edith called out. "You'd better hurry. He's gone pale as a ghost. He's nearly out of blood."

Arthur's head swayed about and the room, a whirl of light and mirrors. The room was white. White light. White cloths and sheets. Eyes peeped at him, mummylike raisins perched above white masks. He inhaled the vial of salts passed beneath his nose and he swayed violently.

"Grave clothes!" the king shouted, tearing at his hospital gown. "These are grave clothes. You'll not have me! I'm not dead!"

Edith fell across the gurney, pinning the king with the strength of a wrestler. He saw her lips as ruby slashes and her rouged face was grotesque.

"Here, now," she soothed. "You've got to settle back, old thing."

Arthur, panicked, butted Nurse Edith, bruising her lip.

"Oooh. You!" she yelled. "Get him a sedative. He's still strong as a bull!"

Suddenly, Arthur inhaled the scent of lavender soap. Jenny's ginger hair fell across his face. He grabbed the surgeon by the arm of her white coat.

"Let go of me, Arthur," Jenny said firmly. "You've lost too much blood. You need a transfusion."

"I need you," the king gasped. He tightened his grip. "Don't leave me."

"You're in a crisis, Arthur," she said urgently. "We've got to operate."

"Stay with me," Arthur said. He groaned with pain that made his eyes roll up in his head. "I command you."

He felt her breath on his face. Its sweetness made his eyelids flutter. His lips tightened across his teeth. "Hold me down," he said.

"Edith!" Jenny shouted. "Get me help! I'm losing him."

"Hold me," the king repeated. "I command you." He swayed back, his head hitting the gurney. Jenny found herself lying across his chest.

"Arthur, stop," she cried. "Why won't you lie back? Any man would!"

"That's it," the king whispered fiercely. "Hold me just like that."

Slowly his good hand found its way to his right shoulder. His strong fingers poked and probed. The king's breath came in gasps, like a great cat. Jenny heard a wet smack and a piece of metal the size of a shilling flew from Arthur's bloody shoulder. It landed on the linoleum with a plink.

"There," Arthur groaned. "Better. Now, cobwebs. On the wound."

"Edith!" Jenny shouted. "Come help!"

"Right. Bless the wound. Cobwebs and mud from holy ground." Arthur's eyes rolled full tilt behind the eyelids and his breathing eased. Edith ran into the ward, carrying a sponge that oozed chloroform. It wasn't needed. Arthur was out cold. He slept like a child.

17

Jenny slept in a wicker chair outside Arthur's room. Sorley, the ward surgeon, watched Jenny draw even, shallow breaths that blew a wisp of ginger hair across her cheek like a slight spring breeze. Even exhausted, she was beautiful. Sorley clucked over the circles beneath her eyes. She scrunched one hand beneath her chin and the other hung limply from the chair.

"Jenny," Edith urged, joining Sorley. "Doctor Jenny, you've got to wake up. It's time for rounds."

Jenny nodded vaguely, but remained in deep sleep. Sorley was a big, balding internist who had lost his wife in the opening round of the Blitz. Still in the grip of grief, he could not avoid the longing he felt when he saw Jenny. Any man would, he knew. Sorley pricked some ear wax from his stethoscope with a fingernail and shifted on his big, padding feet. He wanted nurse to do the waking.

"Jenny!" Edith said, shaking her shoulder. "It's nearly midnight. You're on duty, luv."

Jenny nodded, but the sandman still claimed her. Shaking her head and tapping her foot, Edith said somewhat petulantly, "This isn't getting us anywhere, Doctor Sorley."

Sorley replaced the stethoscope round his neck and tapped Edith on the shoulder. "That'll do, Nurse. I'll take Doctor Hamilton's round."

Edith huffed. Duty wakeup was one of her principal areas of authority. "It won't make her favor you, Doctor," she said, sniffing. "She's simply mad about that lieutenant with the shoulder wound."

"That's enough, Nurse," Sorley said. He smoothed his lab coat and slicked a strand of thin hair across his pate. "Jenny's worth three surgeons. We can take her place tonight. She's taken countless rounds for others."

"Don't I know it, sir," Edith said primly. "And she's near wrecked herself caring for that big Welshman. I've never seen her like that."

Sorley lit a cigarette and shrugged. "She's a good physician," he said. "But she's a young woman, too. It's only normal, I suppose."

Edith sighed, her ample bosoms puffing like a turtledove's. "They are heroes, aren't they? The lads."

"We've no shortage of mangled heroes," Sorley said tersely. The doctor tossed his cigarette and scuffed it into the linoleum. He marched off to the sound of sirens from ambulances bringing in fresh casualties from the night bombing raids. Every night now, it seemed that there were more raids, and with the raids came more victims.

Yank drew the curtain behind him in the darkness and leaned over Arthur's bed. He worked the chewing gum in his jaw methodically and removed a small hand mirror from the pocket of his Irvin jacket. Moonlight streamed in through the French windows and Yank could see that the little mirror steamed up with Arthur's breath, which came in steady, even pulls. Yank loosened his tie and slumped into a chair next to the bed to wait until Arthur came round.

Jenny flung the curtain open. "Who are you? What are you doing here?" She wielded a scalpel like a dagger. The stainless steel flashed in the moonlight. Yank raised his hands in surrender.

"Easy! I'm a friend. You the ward nurse?"

"I'm the doctor!"

"You're the one," Yank said, his hands held high. "You're Jenny."

"And you're his American." She lowered the surgeon's knife.

"Right, I'm Arthur's friend." He never took his eyes from the scalpel. "His very good friend. Bill Cooper. From Connecticut."

"He doesn't need a friend now. He needs rest."

"You can put that cutter away, miss," Cooper said. "I'm on your side, see?"

"I'll harm anyone who endangers his recovery. He's my patient." She placed the scalpel in her kit and dropped it in an oversize pocket.

"He's crazy about you."

"Is he?" Her voice rose. She shivered. She leaned on the bed, watching the king, and considered Yank's words. "Crazy," she murmured. "Crazy about me? How lovely."

Arthur stirred. His good arm swept across his chest, flailing at the glucose bottle anchored to his arm. Jenny replaced the arm gently and straightened the stiff, white sheets. She leaned over him with her stethoscope and listened to his heart. Satisfied, she turned and took Yank by the wrist.

"Lieutenant King is fine for the moment," she said. "Now, allow him his rest."

They stepped into the hallway. Cooper offered her a Lucky Strike, which she declined. He lit one for himself and just as quickly offered her a stick of gum.

"Are all Americans as free with everything they have?" The question was curious, not hostile. "Do you share everything?"

"There's a girl sends me stuff from home. Smokes. Candy. Gum. That kind of thing."

"How thoughtful. She must like you."

"She's a pip."

"Do you like her?"

"Sure. She's my kid sister."

"I'll bet she's got your photograph on her mantle. That with all your news clippings. She probably boasts over you to all her pretty friends. I imagine you're the neighborhood hero somewhere in America."

"Hartford," Cooper mumbled. He sunk into the wicker chair and examined the burning tip of his cigarette. "I'm no hero."

"All of you lads are heroes to us, you know," Jenny said gently. "It must be very frightening up there."

"Some are more scared than others."

"Like yourself?"

Yank nodded.

"I'd say that's manfully honest."

Yank grinned weakly. "Yup. I crossed the Atlantic to find out I'm an honest coward."

"You fly against the Hun every day. What coward could do that?"

"I fly, all right," Cooper said. He fiddled with a gum wrapper. His hands shook. "I don't fight. I just sort of fishtail around until it's time to come home."

"Doesn't everybody?"

"Some fight. That man in there," Cooper said, pointing at Arthur's room. "He's the real thing."

"Because he kills the enemy better than you? That makes him better?"

Yank shook his head. "Naw. There's some that can do that, and they're real shits. He's just a remarkable guy. A couple of weeks ago, he couldn't fly. That didn't stop him. I've been flying for years. Why can't I do what he does?"

"Perhaps he's been fighting much longer. He's experienced in war."

Yank chewed his gum so hard it popped. "Perhaps."

"His body is covered with scars," Jenny remarked.

"He's come down the hard way twice, just since I knew him. That'll put scars on you."

"Not the kind of marks I've seen," she said. "Old scars, in odd places. He's got scars from scalds, from burns, from knives. He's got scars from flogging, for God's sake. Was he in India?"

Yank looked up at her, interested. "Damned if I know. I really don't know much about Arthur. But I feel like I do, somehow."

"I feel that way, too, Yank."

"Bravest sonofagun I ever met. Sorry. But he's also the first one of your people that treated me decent."

"He is decent, isn't he?"

"And he packs a hell of a right cross." They heard a crash in Arthur's room that sounded like a giant oak smashing into the floor. They got up and rushed into the room.

The king staggered under his own weight, trying to pull himself up from the tiles. He reached for the bed's iron railing and gripped one of the bars. He pulled himself up and swayed, turning to see Yank and Jenny. His eyes were wild and an arm thrashed as if he were fending off a blow from a club.

"Leave me be!" He groaned and swayed, barely maintaining his balance. "We need solitude." His eyes rolled up in his head.

Jenny rushed to him and thrust herself under his good shoulder. She staggered beneath his weight. "Help me!" she ordered Yank. "He's delirious." Her knees buckled. Yank rushed forward and tried to press his head beneath Arthur's other shoulder. Arthur roared in agony. The king pitched forward, falling face first on the floor.

"God," Jenny exclaimed, jumping free. "He's heavy as a horse. We'll never get him up."

Arthur had passed out. The full weight of his body pressed Yank, who lay flattened against the floor like dough beneath a rolling pin. Yank wheezed, trying to regain his wind. The American grunted. Then, like Atlas, he began to lift Arthur, supporting the big man's weight on his shoulders. Slowly, by inches, Yank succeeded in pushing Arthur up from the floor.

Yank finally held Arthur in his arms, his knees bent as if he were hefting giant barbells. Cooper panted as if ready to give birth.

"Can I help?" Jenny asked anxiously. Yank shook his head and slowly pushed Arthur's weight up on to the mattress. By getting his arms angled beneath Arthur's back, he succeeded in rolling the king on to the bed as if he were an enormous log. Yank collapsed, gasping, on the cold hospital floor.

"That's amazing," Jenny said. "How did you do that?"

Yank shook his head sadly. "You should have seen my old man when he was dead drunk in the street. He was one heavy sonofabitch."

Yank patted Arthur on his good shoulder. He took the end of the sheet and dabbed some of the sweat from the king's brow. The gesture was tender. The American looked at Jenny, who watched him, her smile tender and open.

"Take care of him, huh?"

Jenny nodded and Yank Cooper made his way out quietly.

*   *   *

A cold breeze woke Jenny. After ushering Yank out, she had fallen asleep in the chair next to Arthur's bed. She suddenly felt an emptiness, and she looked about wildly. The icy wind chilled Jenny's face and blew the white, snapping sheet on Arthur's bed.

The bed was empty. Jenny grabbed hold of the sheets. They, too, were cold. Her chest pounded and her heart filled with a sense of dread. The French doors that opened on to the veranda swung wide in the breeze and banged against the inner wall of the room. The floor and whitewashed walls glowed, luminous with the whitish blue of moonlight reflected in the chamber.

Jenny leaned forward on the bed and stared out into the night. Suddenly, Arthur's great, raw-boned shadow crossed the doorway. He stood, nearly naked, his gown draped round his waist like a toga. His scarred muscles rippled in the chill breeze. His eyes, hollow gray rings with a pale fire in them, stared at the woman from a distance that seemed to make time and space meaningless. He stared at Jenny as though he knew her deepest heart, her darkest secrets. He beckoned to her.

"I knew you'd come," Arthur said, his voice as raw as the scars that marked his pale skin. "I knew you'd be here."

"Arthur?"

The blackout curtains lifted in the breeze like shadows from the grave. Suddenly, the silence fled with a rustle of wings. A great dark bird sailed through the window and flapped about the ceiling, then dropped to Arthur's shoulder and settled. Arthur swayed slightly, but remained on his feet. Within seconds, a legion of dark birds filled the night sky. Arthur took Jenny's trembling hand.

"Come," he urged quietly. Her heart thumped like a trip-hammer and she felt the blood rush to her head. She nearly swooned, consumed with dread. But an awful fascination accompanied the fear. The wounded king pulled her close to him.

Gently, he placed his bandaged arm around her waist and guided her out the door into the moonlight on the veranda. She gazed into the luminous night and believed that she must be dreaming. Far away, at the gate, the burning tip of a sentry's cigarette burned reassuringly in defiance of the blackout. But the moonlight on the green that swept out, away to the forested darkness, shimmered with an unreal, almost magical quality.

The ravens arrived in twos and threes and finally in flocks. Their fluttering filled the night air with the rustle of hundreds of dark wings. Finally, they blacked out the moon, until they began to drift in to land. The black birds settled on the green, and on the low stone fence, and on the paving stones of the veranda. Soon, they surrounded the couple. Jenny pressed herself tightly against Arthur, whose great, scarred body was cool as marble on the surface, but pulsed with warmth immediately beneath the skin.

"What is happening?" Jenny whispered. She dug her fingernails into the flesh of the king's back as if to prove he was real.

"Don't be frightened," Arthur answered quietly. "These are my guardians. My friends won't hurt you."

He gazed up at the sky and a bright circle of high cirrus cloud ringed the three-quarter moon. "There isn't much time, now," he murmured. "Time is fleeing with the moon."

As if in answer, a great raven took wing from the stone fence. Bigger than all the others, its wings spread until it assumed nearly the span of an eagle. It swooped round the king and his lady and crossed in front of the moon. It cawed loudly and soon all the other birds took to the air. They departed as quickly as they had appeared, flying as one in an ebony cloud that receded quickly over the darkened treetops of the forest beyond the hospital grounds.

As quickly as they'd gone, another noise filled the night sky. It was the drone of German bombers, their ragged unsynchronized engines forming a somber humming chorus that droned on toward London.

"If that's your answer, old man," Arthur said, "then I fight on alone."

Jenny buried her face in his chest. "Arthur, please tell me what is happening. I can't help it. I'm frightened."

He held her to him. Gently, he circled her waist with his strong arm and led her back into the room. With the single, good arm he lifted her on to his bed. Quietly, he closed the French doors and drew the blackout curtain. Then, he climbed on to the bed next to her.

"None of it matters, except that in this moment I am here with you," he whispered. He kissed her gently on the forehead, then on the lips, fully and with passion.

"Wait," she said, her tone hushed. She slipped from the bed and Arthur's grasp. In a single motion, she threw the lock to the door. In another motion, she dropped the white hospital coat from her shoulders. By the time she reached the bed, he could tell she had lost her fears. He kissed her bare shoulders and they found each other in the darkness.

Arthur's wound took weeks to mend, and Jenny visited him every day and brought him books. He asked for every age of history, and Yank brought his pulp adventures. The king nodded thanks and asked for technical manuals. One day a flight surgeon appeared, carrying orders signed by Richardson. Lieutenant King was pronounced fit to fly. Yank would come to collect King.

His last weekend before returning to Dragon Squadron was remarkably warm, almost a return to summer. Jenny and Arthur went to the country. The weather lured the cicadas and they created their own quiet symphony for the lovers. His appetite and strength returned, the king savored oranges from Spain and bananas that Jenny had snatched up at market after a convoy arrived.

Arthur admired the craftsmanship of the picnic basket. He repeatedly snapped and unsnapped the spring-lock. A bottle of Bass ale made him drowsy. He inhaled deeply and luxuriated in the fragrance of Jenny's hair as they lay on the rough army-issue blanket. Jenny traced a line with her fingers on Arthur's bare chest, following a ragged welt that bridged the distance between the lapels of his unbuttoned service jacket. The king smiled lazily and stretched, feeling constricted by the bandages that crossed his torso.

"How did you come by that?" she asked, pressing the scar softly but firmly. Arthur smiled.

"War wound," he replied. "One of many."

"What war? This happened a long time ago. We've only been at war with the Germans for a year."

"Well, as it happened, I was wounded a long time ago. It's unpleasant to think about it whilst I'm lying in a field of clover with my love."

"Where did you do your fighting, Arthur? I want to know. I want to know all about you."

"I fought in many places. It was my lot since I was a boy."

"India, then? The Hindu Kush? Or Africa?"

"We have a chap in the squadron, says he served in India. Seems terribly puffed up and proud about it.

You could say I've fought in the far reaches of the empire."

"You're so mysterious, Arthur King, the senior lieutenant who has no records, and who avoids questions about himself."

"Ah, but I have my friends to vouch for me," Arthur said playfully.

Jenny rolled on to her back and looked up at the sky. A cottony puff of cumulus rolled by, free of taint from fiery contrails or the smoke of burning engines.

"The Yank tells me you couldn't even fly an airplane just a few weeks ago."

"He told you that? What a lot of nonsense. I'm told that all foreigners have more imagination than is good for them."

Arthur hoisted himself up on his good elbow. He swept a wisp of hair from Jenny's forehead. He kissed the tress lightly before letting it fall through his fingers. Then he kissed Jenny's cheek. Then her lips.

Jenny kissed Arthur. Her lips lingered on his, luxuriated in them. Then, as if possessed by a thought, she pushed him back, playfully.

"Don't distract me, Lieutenant. I want to know more about you."

Arthur grinned. "Why should I cooperate when you tell me so little about yourself, Jenny? You can be mysterious."

"Am I?" she said. "I've always thought myself just plain Jenny Hamilton."

"There, you see. Certainly you don't believe that. I've seen no other woman physicians. Ever. You must be remarkable. Perhaps you're a witch, an enchantress."

Jenny laughed, as if caught passing a secret at school. She lay flat on the blanket, staring up the hill at a great oak. She made a little temple of her fingers and rested her chin on them.

"What do you want to know about me, Arthur?"

"Same as you, my dear Jenny. Anything," he said. "Everything."

"I'm twenty-eight, and I can't remember my mother. She died when I was little. So I was Daddy's girl. And at first, he wanted only boys. But early on, he realized I possessed the hands in the family."

She regarded her fine, strong white fingers. She wore no jewelry.

"These pretty hands made me the second woman in fifty years to go up to the Royal College of Surgeons. My father was the dean. He told me I had my mother's gift."

"The gift of healing."

She shook her head. "I think not. Few of my patients heal. I don't restore your comrades. I merely repair them. My father told me I have the hands of a pianist married to the logical mind of a medical practitioner. That and my brother's failure set me up in surgery."

"I don't understand."

She pushed herself up on an elbow and watched Arthur's gray eyes. "My brother failed his exams," she said. "He never wanted to be a doctor. He was a poet. So my father sent me up to the Royal College and banished William. One of us must succeed in the eyes of the world. In Father's eyes, anyway."

"Then you're not happy with your father's decision."

"Does anyone choose their role in life, Arthur King? Did you? I know what duty is, to king and country." She smiled sadly. "And to Daddy."

"You don't feel grateful to your father, then? Or love him?"

She grinned. "He made me what I am today," she said brightly. "Awash in the blood of lambs to slaughter. I sew 'em up, but I don't heal them."

Arthur picked a bottle of stout from the picnic basket. He regarded it for a moment, then emptied it in a gulp. He studied Jenny, and she smiled at him in return, her eyes an endless sea, green as the Irish coast.

"Thanks to a year of war, I've done more surgeries than most physicians twice my age, Lieutenant King. I worked very hard to learn this work, and I work even harder in the practice of it. But I'm no angel."

Arthur smiled. He stroked her cheek. For an instant, she trembled. "No," the king said. "There's much more to you. Aren't you the young lady who loves the old and lovely things? The one who taught me to dance. The one who knows 'Moonlight Serenade.'"

"Maybe there is another Jenny," she said quietly. "She gets lost sometimes in the war. And she gets lost from herself, too."

"That Jenny is one whom I love, and she's also a part of the Jenny who healed me. Who restoreth my soul. Who makes me to lie by the still waters."

She stared at him, taking all of him in. Partly, she watched in the manner of the careful student of anatomy. The other part of her drank Arthur's soul. Silently appraising him, she curled her lip and frowned.

"What is it?"

"You treated yourself, you know."

Arthur shook his head as if he didn't understand. Jenny continued, "I've never had a patient who called out for cobwebs, mud and holy water. It's entirely new to my experience."

"I must have been out of my senses."

"And in your delirium, you called yourself the king."

"Well, it's my name, isn't it?"

"No, no. Arthur. You called yourself a king. Not any king or some king. You referred to yourself in the imperial 'we,' as if you were born to the purple."

Arthur laughed. "Well, I am purple, aren't I? And

black and blue, as well. But feeling much better. Thanks to you."

"Don't patronize me," Jenny said. "All of you do, you know. All men. They think medicine is men's work. So they make jokes, and little pinches, and treat me as if I'm a child."

Arthur sat up painfully. He tried to gather her into his arms, but she resisted. "No," she said. "I don't want my heart broken, Arthur."

"Do you shrink from me because I'm a fighting man? We're all fighting now, those of able body."

Jenny turned on her side and spread the blanket with her fingers. She pulled a dandelion up by the roots and blew it so all the seedlings scattered on the wind. "That's so, Arthur. You're all fighting now. All the fine young men. I can't fall in love when you're all going to die."

"Have you lost a man? Is that it?"

"I lost my brother at Dunkirk."

"The poet?"

"William was my twin." She said the words in a flat tone, as though she had said it to herself often enough to drain emotion from the fact. "He was waiting for the evacuation boats. The Royal Air Force could not protect him from the Stuka dive bombers. That happened a lot."

She turned away. He heard the sob choke in her throat. Jenny spoke haltingly. "You see, Arthur, pilots are a sore point with me. I bind their wounds. But you're the first I haven't hated just a little."

"I'm sorry, Jenny." He touched her shoulder and she let his hand remain. The cloud had moved on and the breeze picked up.

She turned and looked the king full in his steel, gray eyes. "Who are you, Arthur? If I'm going to love you, and quite possibly lose you, I must know who you are."

He nodded his head gravely. "Your question is fair, Jenny. But it would be telling. I would betray confidence."

She turned away. "You don't trust anyone. Not even me."

"Trust," he said, tightening his grip on her shoulder ever so gently. "It's more than trust, lady. I love thee."

She shook her head. "Arthur, I've had strange dreams. Dreams of birds and flying and the night. Reason escapes me when I think of you."

She rolled on to her side and pulled him to her, nestling in the fold of his tunic. "You talk so strangely, Arthur. As if you're from somewhere far away."

"I come from near here," the king murmured. He gathered her into his good arm, encircling her. He kissed her forehead and inhaled her scent, the scent of thyme. "Abide with me," he whispered. "You're safe here, with me."

"Until they take you again."

"Yes, until I have to go and do what every man of this country must."

"Until all the good men are dead," she said darkly. "I'm sorry." She stroked his cheekbone, as if she were memorizing his face by touch.

"You'll tell me one day, won't you? You'll tell me your secret. Now that I've told you mine, it's only fair."

"Yes," he whispered. "I promise, I will tell thee, once my work is done."

"You are something more than a senior lieutenant in the RAF. That's true, isn't it?"

"It's a military matter."

"Sometimes I think our entire lives are secrets," she said. Jenny let it go. She traced the line of his jaw with her finger. He had left hospital without shaving and the stubble on his chin was rough. She ran her fingers through his cropped hair. "Are you going to save our land single-handed, or will you require help?"

Arthur grinned. "I've got the Yank, don't I?"

"He worships you. He needs a better opinion of himself."

"He needs confidence. With that, he'll come through."

"Can you help him?"

"Some things can't be taught."

"Can't they? No one ever taught you anything."

"Well, there was an old and particular bastard."

"That brings us back to it, then, doesn't it, Lieutenant? Where did the old and particular bastard come from?"

"He lived in a tree," Arthur said. "He taught me I could fly like a bird, if I applied myself."

"Take me seriously, Arthur."

He regarded the woman and winked. "I do take you," he said. "Seriously." He embraced her. She responded and their embrace deepened as he felt the smoothness of her back and she traced the line of scars on his.

"Yes. Take me," she said. And the king did.

Seriously, but gently, and with great ardor. Her cry of love cut through him like the surgeon's knife. And the movement of their love carried his soul aloft, airborne into the high, thin-air region of flight. He remained there, high and lofty and caught in the embrace of his new love until it was time to return to the war.

18

A t 5:42 A.M., on a cold, autumnal morning, General Kleist watched the sun rise from the gray sea on the coast at Calais. The pale orb radiated through some scud in the east, looking to the general like the face of death. Kleist spit the ersatz war coffee from his enamel mug and pitched the contents, making the steam rise from the ground. He walked over to the twin-engine fighter-bomber that a crew was busy at preparing for takeoff. The general tapped the wing of his aircraft and kicked the tires, with proprietary pride. He watched Mordred approach in the mist and he was filled with dread.

The armorers climbed down from the wing of the sleek, shark-nosed Messerschmitt 110. The men in the blue coveralls ran across the wet grass to retrieve the bomb trolleys. The general patted the nose of the aircraft as if it were a favorite mount.

"Today, we fly the Zerstörer."

"Destroyer," Mordred remarked. "What a lovely name."

"It's fast, but it turns like a pig," Kleist remarked professionally. "Still, it's a good reconnaissance aircraft and it's got four big guns in the nose. You will fly with me in the observer's seat. Mortal, or monster, or whatever you are, Morgan. It's your gun that protects our backside."

"I feel ready to fly it myself, all the way to England."

"Not yet. From me, you watch and learn for a little while still."

Mordred gave a mock salute. "I remain your faithful observer."

"Just so you keep the Hurricanes and Spitfires off my tail. You're learning fast. Maybe you can teach Tommy a lesson over Coventry."

"I wonder what the chapel looks like these days. Hard to imagine anything lasts a thousand years. But who knows? Your leader says his Reich will last a thousand years."

"Well, a thousand years. That's long enough." Kleist leaned against the aircraft. He felt nearly drained of will to live. "I'm glad I won't be here to see it," the general said.

The wind sock on the airfield twitched in the breeze. The early morning sun warmed the earth and broke up the pockets of fog that obscured the chalk cliffs of Dover. Mordred stared at the cliffs.

"Let's go," Kleist said. They mounted the aircraft, looking like two leather-clad knights ready for the joust.

At 6:01 A.M., the powerful twelve-cylinder Daimler Benz engines roared to life, shaking the slender fuselage and vibrating the black crosses on the wings. Methodically, Mordred checked the fit of the drum of 7.9-millimeter ammunition for the observer's gun. He finished strapping himself in, connected his radio leads and prepared for the rush in his stomach that occurred watching the ground sweep away from him on takeoff.

At 6:03, all checks completed, the ground crew pulled the chocks. Kleist waved and pushed the throttle forward. The fighter-bomber rolled down the field, gaining speed as Kleist steered the shark nose into the wind. The twin-boom tail lifted lightly as a sparrow. The French coast receded and Kleist whistled "Off to Bomb England" as the landing gear retracted.

Minutes later, Kleist announced, "England ahead."

"And France behind," Mordred said dryly. "It's good to know we're not lost, but aren't we flying awfully low? I hear the Channel is cold this time of year."

They flew just above the chop. Mordred could see the boil of the waves rushing by below him. "Why so low?" Mordred repeated, his voice rising in the intercom.

"The Brits have a little black magic box called radar. It searches out intruders. Too damned often, it finds 'em."

Mordred felt sweat streaming from beneath his leather helmet. His hands held on to the rubber grips of the machine gun. It might have been vibration of the gun, or his hands might have trembled. "Too low," he said, his voice trembling.

"If we stay low enough, we fool the radar," Kleist said. "Would you rather have a Spitfire on your tail?"

"No," Mordred replied, his voice somewhat shaky. "But I don't want to swim back to Calais, either."

Kleist flew the Zerstörer through the thick, heavy air that buffeted the aircraft at low altitude. The thought hit him suddenly. Morgan feared flying. It was the only time he relinquished control of the fever that wracked Kleist's brain. The general opened the throttle and flew on. For the first time in weeks, he felt a twinge of happiness.

The Zestörer zoomed low over the waves for ten long minutes. It zigged and zagged, and then the cliffs of Dover loomed ahead like a great white wall. Mordred looked down to see fishing boats in the Channel. They were so low, the knave prince could make out the fishermen's oilskin coats. They looked up at him, their vision aided by elongated tubes that Kleist called binoculars. Too many inventions, Mordred muttered. He hated to be watched.

The plane pitched up suddenly. Mordred felt a sickening lurch in the stomach as he watched the green-carpeted cliff tops recede behind him. "Sometimes I hate your fancy flying, Kleist!" he shouted.

"Get in the spirit," Kleist radioed back. "If you want to be king, you've got to command the air."

"Fly faster, Kleist. It's cold." Mordred shivered beneath layers of wool packed under his flight coveralls. He had flown in from another age, but no magic known to Mordred could ward off the cockpit's chill, or the fear of flying that made him sick in the pit of his stomach every time he climbed into one of the demon machines. Mordred worshiped the war planes for what they could do, and he hated them for what he feared they could do to him. In one instant, he felt the intense power of soaring on the devil's wind. In the next, he feared he would tumble off the end of the earth into the great nothingness. He feared hell less than he feared burning in the cockpit.

"We're still too low!" he cried out. Mordred sucked his breath in and hung on. Kleist flew with greater confidence.

At 6:33 A.M., the Zerstörer roared low over the Kentish countryside. Mordred could see the fields of hops sweeping wide and flat below him and colored the shade of a good pils. With the wind whistling in the open canopy, Mordred searched the horizon for fighters. His neck chafed beneath the silken scarf.

They passed over patchwork fields of oats and barley; Mordred felt his throat parched and he wished for ale. The plane crossed twice over twists and bends of the river Thames. For a while, Kleist followed the course of the flat, slow-moving gray water. He pulled away and swept southeast when he spotted bargemen watching the Messerschmitt from their river craft with their coast watchers' binoculars.

As Kleist and Mordred swooped away from the river, Mordred wondered if he would ever navigate the Thames through London. He imagined his own coronation. This bloody twentieth century offered opportunities for pillage undreamt of. But to be king. Really king. That would be something. Like the boy who once pretended to be king while cleaning out his father's stable, Mordred mused that being king might be a lot of fun. They would have to bring you apples instead of horse turds.

The wing tanks fell free and Mordred watched them quiver toward earth. Kleist navigated sometimes in view of the river, but always keeping low, sometimes nearly as low as the treetops that lined the shore.

"The trees are nearly gone," Mordred murmured.

That was it. The revelation came suddenly as he peered down at the autumnal fields. Someone had cut down the forests of ancient Britain. The entire island had been a great, leafy forested mass. It was the land the ancient Romans had tried and failed to subdue, if only for the density of its green trees where the outlaws and Pictish outlanders divided their booty.

Now, the Messerschmitt passed low over the gently rolling Saxon farm country. Pastoral and settled and peaceful looking, these lands existed a world away from the high-explosive thunderbolts the Luftwaffe hurled at London. This was a peaceful land, adorned with sheaves of wheat, and boys chasing geese and fallow apple orchards dotting the hills and farmers urging horses pulling loads of hay.

Mordred had rubbed shoulders with peasants in the stable. He hated low-born slaves. If he didn't kill them all, some of those working the fields below might live in order to serve his royal person. No, better, to worship him as vassals.

"Bring on the ale for Mordred, king of the Britons," he muttered.

At 6:46 A.M., the Messerschmitt banked away from the river and Mordred watched the oat-colored flat land of the farm country race by below. He saw a tank clanking along on the road, looking like a toy. It stood out in relief in the countryside where there was little evidence of war except for roadblocks at the crossings. These peasants could be beaten. Britons would be slaves. He choked back the bile in his throat as the plane buffeted on a wall of hard air.

Mordred had seen the sullen Gallic refugees of Occupied France, the high-stepping columns of victorious Huns, the armored carriers, massed cannon and fleets of bombers filling the sky with shadows. The Gallic folk were beaten. You could see it in their defeated eyes. Mordred wondered that the countryside of Britain seemed so pastoral, so little prepared for battle.

At 6:49 A.M., Kleist pointed the twin-engine bomber sharply north. They had avoided radar and the patrol sweeps of Fighter Command.

"On to Coventry," the general announced. "We'll first sweep past Stratford-on-Avon. Shakespeare hailed from there."

"Never heard of him."

"No matter. Our target lies due north. When I give the signal, turn on the camera, the yellow button I showed you."

The Zerstörer raced on. Now and then, a current of heavy air would buffet the plane, raising it up as if lifting it on an upturned palm. They crossed above another stream. "The river Avon," Kleist announced.

Arthur, Jenny and Bill Cooper ascended the stone steps, quietly entering the nave of the cathedral. As they stepped into the cool interior, Arthur looked up and shivered. The archways stood so high they looked like hands raised and joined in prayer to heaven itself. The boy's choir rose as one in sweet voice. As their Latin hymn blossomed and amplified in melodious crescendo, the early morning sun swept through the stained glass windows, illuminating the chapel with God's peaceful light.

"It's so grand," Arthur murmured. "Much bigger than in my day."

"I thought you'd not been to Coventry," Jenny whispered. "I wanted to bring you to hear the boys sing matins."

"I've only seen it in the pictures. It seemed so much smaller."

"Pictures? From a book?"

"Yes. Um, the *Daily Sketch*."

"The newspaper?" Jenny asked, her brow knitting in puzzlement.

Yank also cast a curious glance at Arthur. He wondered what day the pictorial newspaper had carried a drawing of this church, for that matter, any church. In 1940, editors filled the pages of the *Sketch* almost exclusively with the exploits of the RAF, along with pictures of aircraft in the battle, drawings of the air combats and photographs of the heroes. Yank popped a stick of gum in his mouth.

"Well, it's a mighty big church, Doc. I'll grant you that," Yank whispered to Jenny.

Gazing up at the high, vaulted ceiling, Yank whistled. His jaw worked methodically until he noticed Jenny's cold stare. Quickly, he removed his gum and stuck the wad under a pew.

Arthur gazed upward, taking in every detail of the grandiose, ancient stonework. The nave swept before them, wide as a Roman road and nearly as long. He felt a familiar tingle. His breath came quickly. He realized he was standing close to the spot where Mordred jumped through. But that had been another chapel. Much smaller. Nothing so grand as this. That encounter was in another century. Yet to Arthur, it felt like it passed only minutes before. Arthur felt dizzy as the organ music faded and the boys filed from the chapel. The king felt the motion of time swirling round him, as if he were caught in a vortex.

He seated himself in a pew, closed his eyes and held his forehead. Jenny kneeled next to him and touched him on his uninjured shoulder. "Arthur," she said. "You look faint."

"Please, lady. I'm in prayer," Arthur whispered, and he held his forehead all the more tightly.

Yank elbowed past him and seated himself next to the king. After he shuffled his feet for an awkward minute, he ceased movement and he too bowed his head as if in prayer. Jenny watched the fliers. She sat motionless. In a moment, she could see that the lips of both men were silently moving, and it was evident that they were, in truth, praying.

The bishop mounted the pulpit. The little man raised his palms toward the vaulted ceiling and spoke briefly of Christ's torment, his descent from the cross, then the Resurrection, and the life.

"Even now, as we find our island confronting the dark power of the enemy, we must be steadfast in the knowledge that we are carried along in the strong but tender hand of the Lord," the bishop intoned.

He raised his hand in supplication. "We pray, firm in faith that our protection lies in our trust in Him, the Prince of Peace, and that in his own time he will vanquish the gods of war. False gods. Only in our Lord's Prayer is the hope, the Way, and the truth and the life."

The candles flickered as a deacon made his way out, snuffing them gently, and allowing the full light of day to take their place.

The light splashed on to the flagstones of the ancient cathedral, reflecting back on the stained glass. Arthur looked up to see a window, filled with a riot of color edged in leaded glass. It carried the image of an armored king whose back was turned on the worshiper.

The king in the glass leaned on the hilt of a mighty, jeweled sword. The unknown king's head was bowed, as if in prayer. It was impossible to tell which fate the king awaited. He stood before a legion of warriors, crowded atop a hillock, but it could not be discerned from the pattern of the glass whether the multitude were followers cheering him on, or foes confronting him.

The white-haired deacon who snuffed the candles nodded gravely at the trio as he shuffled by. Then they were alone in the church.

"When was this mighty structure dedicated to God?" Arthur asked.

"The fourteenth century, Arthur," Jenny said. "Thirteen-something, I think." She fished in her bag for a guidebook.

"And what was here before? A chapel. Some smaller edifice?"

"I don't know, Arthur. Coventry is ancient. The entire center of the city is built from medieval timbers."

"Medieval?"

"Wood from the Middle Ages, dear. The city is more than a thousand years old. That's why I love it so. You must feel the same for your own old country."

"But it is a great city. What else is done here?"

"Don't you know, Arthur? Coventry is a great munitions factory. They build weapons here."

Arthur winced. "God save this age."

With an effort, he pushed himself up from the pew. He stared up at the stained glass window, filled with the image of the praying king. Arthur shook his head, as if shaking off a dream. Leaning on Merlin's stick, he walked into the center of the nave. Jenny watched him and was struck how, in a certain mistake of light, his pose resembled the king in the window. She shivered.

One little boy's voice pierced the silence of the church. The little soloist sang, his voice liquid as a songbird's:

"Deus in Excelsius."

His song was interrupted by the far-off wail of an air raid siren. Soon, sirens were rising in pitch across the roofs of the city. Arthur, first, then Yank and Jenny heard the low-toned growl of an approaching aircraft.

"Shelter!" the elderly deacon shouted. He scooped up the boy and vanished behind the vestibule. Arthur and Yank were moving steadily toward the huge, oaken cathedral doors. Jenny hurried after them.

Just as they reached the entryway, the Messerschmitt roared low over the spires of the cathedral. It flew so low, the people in the street below could make out the black-cross markings on the gray wings. Arthur identified the mark of the pentagram on the aircraft's fuselage.

As the plane nosed down, hedgehopping over the rooftops of the factories that surrounded the cathedral, Arthur shielded his eyes with his hand so as not to lose the aircraft in the sun. Some people ran for cover, scurrying behind taxis and vegetable carts. Others merely stared at the plane, their eyes nervously searching the skies for more raiders.

As the plane receded over the low, corrugated steel roofs of the munitions plants, Arthur saw a streamer fly free from the rear of the plane. It was scarlet, and descended gracefully as a lady's scarf dropped before the joust.

The plane flew a zigzag pattern, steering easily between a pair of barrage balloons. A few puffs of gray smoke from an antiaircraft battery popped ineffectually, hundreds of feet above the fast, low-flying aircraft.

"Mordred," Arthur said.

The plane wagged its wings and tail boom, as if in acknowledgment of a salute. It banked and disappeared into the sun.

19

The intelligence officer from Air Ministry was an elderly captain named Cornwell who had little tufts of white hair that spread like wings from beneath his service cap and a clipped, white mustache that looked like a smudge of milk. On the field table in the briefing shack at Hornchurch, Captain Cornwell unrolled the map of the greater London Air Defense Area.

The officers of Dragon Squadron hunched over the map. Squadron Leader Richardson pursed his lips and Tommy Stubbs chewed his nails. Gilbert Hawley examined his own fine manicure. All tapped their feet, waiting for the old captain to have his say. Nothing good ever came from ministry.

"It looks to Air Marshal Dowding that we're getting rather the worst of it," the intelligence officer said, pointing to bases on the map tagged with little pieces of red tape. "Jerry's pounding a lot of bases out of service. Pounding London, too."

"Too bad," Hawley said acidly. "When can we have a turn out of service? I should like a holiday."

Richardson scraped the ash cake from his briar with a pipe nail. "Look, Cornwell, airfield attacks have cut flying strength to the bone, but the attacks haven't increased significantly in recent days. That's good news."

"Still, there's the civilian dimension, Richardson. Got to consider it."

"What have bloody civilians got to do with getting us enough Spitfires and replacement pilots?" Tommy Stubbs demanded.

"Simply this," Cornwell said. "Jerry's set fire to London nine nights of twelve in the last month. If the home front collapses, we lose. There simply must be more cover over London. More sweeps. More kills. Churchill demands it."

"Can we demand more pilots?" Stubbs growled doggedly.

"Brother Stubbs is right," Hawley said. "Six, sometimes seven scrambles a day. Tell Air Ministry we're ready for miracles, but we're done working them."

"That sounds mutinous," Cornwell said crisply. He smoothed the creases of his finely tailored jacket replete with ribbons from 1918. "Air Ministry is more interested in your solutions to London defense. Certainly, we don't need complainers."

"Now just you hold on," Richardson said, snatching the sector map from the elderly captain. "We're flying full schedule with half the planes, and half the trained pilots. We're no malingerers." His eyes were puffed from lack of sleep and he swayed slightly as he spoke, with only the anger keeping him up.

Cornwell turned away. "Right, sir. But we still need more patrols."

They heard a racket outside. A metal firebucket fell

over and Arthur King burst in, with the Yank holding on to his coattails.

"Don't, Arthur!" Cooper said breathlessly. "There's a sign says 'Briefing in Progress.' You've got to knock. It's regulations."

Hawley barred Arthur's way, putting his hands on the king's shoulders. "Stand easy, King!" Hawley ordered. "You're not authorized."

"I couldn't stop him," Cooper said helplessly.

"Two cheers for trying," Stubbs said. "Now, get out, Yank. Before you're in trouble, too."

Cooper threw his arms up. At a cold nod from Richardson, he trooped out dejectedly. "Come to attention, King, before I see you under arrest," Richardson said, his tone quiet and serious.

Arthur drew his heels together and he saluted. "Sir, it was imperative that I see you. To tell you of the danger."

Richardson lit his pipe and smoke billowed. He always fiddled with the pipe when he found it difficult to keep his emotions in check. "What danger would that be, King?"

"The Huns are going to bomb Coventry."

"Really?" Captain Cornwell said, smiling with amused contempt. "Where did you glean this particular piece of intelligence, Lieutenant?"

"A Hun scout plane flew low over the city and dropped a streamer at matins this morning. It was a challenge."

Cornwell laughed dryly and shook his head. Stubbs frowned. Hawley glared at the king. More smoke issued from Richardson's pipe.

"A streamer," the squadron leader said. "Is that it? No bombs? No escorts? Nothing else to lend to this extraordinary deduction?"

"It was a scouting mission, sir," Arthur said. "I'm sure they mean to wreck the city. To sack it. We've got to alert the ground cannoneers and increase the patrols there."

The captain from Air Ministry tugged at the edge of his white mustache. "If we mounted a major sweep after every Jerry kite that launches a streamer, Goering would have us chasing our tails, wouldn't he?"

"They'll want to bomb Coventry because the city is ancient, sir, and because the cathedral is sacred. They want to destroy the sacred."

Cornwell shuffled his feet and chuckled as if he were embarrassed for Richardson. He'd heard all sorts of tales about fliers going bonkers in order to be relieved of flight status.

"Are all your pilots so pious, Richardson? Do they have visions? Scourge themselves, perhaps?"

"Only fools and gnostics scourge themselves," Arthur said, his cheeks coloring. "I'm telling you, this was a scouting mission in preparation for a raid. I've seen such things."

"Where?" Gilbert Hawley demanded abruptly. "Where in the name of heaven have you seen such things?"

Flustered, Arthur replied, "In previous conflicts. I know an advance preparation for a raid when I see it."

"What's this rot about previous conflicts?" Hawley sneered. "Be a little more specific, Lieutenant Arthur nobody from nowhere."

"Here now," Stubbs interjected. "Aren't we getting off the mark? Let's get King out of here and finish the meeting."

Hawley shouldered Stubbs aside. He glared at Arthur. "Wait a minute, Tommy," Hawley said, pointing at the king. "It's Lieutenant Arthur King who's barged in. Let's wring it out of him. What conflicts are you referring to, King? From where do you draw your vast wartime experience?"

"I've seen combat in various parts of the empire. With all respect, I'm not prepared to tell more than that to you, Flight Commander Hawley."

"Not good enough," Hawley shot back. "I've checked around on you. You've got no background at all, so far as I can tell."

Squadron Leader Richardson's face was a mask obscured by a cloud of smoke. "Go on, Hawley."

Encouraged, Hawley said, "Our mysterious stranger would have us believe he's some sort of war hero. But he's got no record."

"My records were lost."

"Ah, but that's not the tale you told the Yank. Yank's informed me you're down here on some dark errand from Air Ministry. Can that be correct, Captain Cornwell? You get around ministry. Do you know this man?"

Cornwell shook his head. "Can't say I do. Never seen him before."

Hawley nodded, gaining confidence. "What is the pet name of Air Marshal Dowding, King? You know it, don't you?"

Arthur stared directly at Hawley. He looked at the cold eyes of a man aiming a lance at him in tourney. "I don't know it," Arthur said quietly.

"It's 'Stuffy,' but not in here, King. Who designed the Spitfire, pray tell?"

"Mitchell," Arthur replied evenly. "Reginald Mitchell."

"Right," Hawley said tersely. "What was his principal honor?" Arthur faltered and shook his head.

"Any man who doesn't know Mitchell won the Schneider Cup for the sea plane trials doesn't know a Spitfire from a Stuka," Hawley said.

"What are you driving at, Hawley?" Richardson asked uneasily.

"I submit to you, sir, that this man is no pilot for the RAF. He should be under close watch."

"What's the charge? Not knowing who won the Schneider Cup?" Richardson asked.

"This man could be a Fifth Columnist. He fooled the Yank, but anyone could do that. Every time King shows up, our airfield is attacked. Isn't that right, Stubbs?"

"If that's true, he shot down one of his own," Stubbs said.

"They're a clever lot, these Fifth Column spies," Hawley said.

Stubbs chewed his mustache pensively. "I did see him reviewing squadron documents one night, when all the other lads were bending an elbow."

"Exactly," Hawley said. "Just what a Hun spy would do."

Arthur shook his head. He looked at the rough wooden planking that floored the briefing shack. "Please. You don't understand what you're saying," Arthur said. "You don't know what you're doing. You need to make plans for the defense of Coventry and you're wasting time accusing me falsely."

"What did you call the ack-ack, King? Cannoneers? What a quaint term, almost as though you studied English somewhere else," Hawley said.

The smoke cleared from Richardson's face. He knocked the pipe on a cork stub in his ashtray. The wing commander carefully repacked the pipe, tamped it and lit it. "What was the name of the service that preceded the Royal Air Force, King?" Richardson asked quietly.

Arthur stared at the floor. He had studied the technical details with such great efficiency, there had been no time to indulge his personal passion for history in the detail he had wished. "I don't know," he said quietly. "I can't remember."

"The Royal Flying Corps," Captain Cornwell said. "My branch."

"I don't know who you are, or what you are, King," Richardson said. "But you are evidently not what you purport to be. There will be an inquiry. Meanwhile, you are under arrest."

Richardson picked up his field telephone. He instructed the sergeant major to call the military police. "Immediately." Richardson put down the phone and stared at Arthur. The king returned his stare evenly, with dignity, like a Pendragon. They heard the boots clumping on the rough-hewn wooden planks that spanned the mud leading to the briefing shack. Nobody spoke. Hawley's close-set brown eyes gleamed triumphantly.

A corporal and two privates entered the shack. Hawley pointed at King and Richardson nodded. Arthur looked about him as if he were a man lost. He saw no friends. "Come along, sir. Please." Arthur shook his head. "Please, sir," the corporal insisted.

Arthur's shoulders slumped, and he shook his head. As he moved slowly toward the corporal, the low wail of a siren filled the air field and the sharp crack of ack-ack guns sounded. The roar of Messerschmitts drowned the sirens and antiaircraft guns. The bomb blast from the first attacking plane shattered the window and blew over the coal stove, knocking Captain Cornwell to the floor. He screamed in agony as coals spilled on to his shin and the hot, black iron of the stove scorched his shoe, filling the room with the odor of burnt leather and flesh.

Everyone's eardrums rang, along with the persistent ringing of the scramble bell. The tarpaper wall and pine lumber of the briefing room collapsed on Arthur and the fliers as the second, third and fourth bombs exploded. Outside the briefing shack, a hangar burned and the belted ammunition hanging from a Spitfire's wings cooked off like strings of firecrackers.

A second echelon of the shark-toothed Zestörer aircraft zoomed low over the field, strafing the airmen and fliers who scrambled behind trucks or jumped into slit trenches.

Arthur pulled himself from the wreckage of the briefing room, licking the salty taste of his own blood. He crawled first, then pulled himself up on Merlin's stick. He felt preternaturally alert, as if the airfield attack unfolded before him in the slow motion of a dance. He hobbled, hopping forward on his strong leg to where Yank Cooper stood ringing the scramble bell. A crudely painted sign tacked to the post said, "Ring the bell and run like hell!"

Arthur clapped Yank hard on the shoulder. The American looked dazed, as if he failed to recognize the king or his surroundings. An explosion buffeted the pair and sent a cloud of flame and black smoke issuing from a petrol lorry. Realizing he might be deaf from the bombs, Arthur slapped Yank.

"Run like hell!" the king commanded. Yank shook his head. Arthur shook Yank free from the bell rope.

"The Spitfires!" Arthur shouted. "Let's go." This time Yank nodded and loped along after the hobbling king.

Two undamaged aircraft waited at the end of the airfield, like trees that had been passed by a forest blaze. The smoking body of a pilot, a flying sergeant named Doakes, lay sprawled like a rag doll on the tarmac. Arthur scarcely stopped to snatch hold of the parachute that Doakes grasped in his dead hand. Arthur pulled it on awkwardly as he ran toward the Spitfire.

Arthur poked the chocks from beneath the wheel with Merlin's staff and climbed on to the wing. He dropped into the cockpit seat, pulled on the leather helmet that hung on the control column and connected the radio leads. He opened the throttle a half inch and plunged the priming pump. He switched the ignition on. As the airfield burned around him, the primer cartridge exploded like a rifle shot and the Merlin's twelve cylinders began firing evenly.

He pushed the throttle forward and nosed the aircraft on to the field. Merlin's staff rattled against his knees. He looked at the destruction rolling past. An ambulance truck blazed, and for an instant a vision of Jenny flashed before him. He pushed that thought back as he set the fuel mixture control to "Rich." The engine roared up to 3,000 rpms for takeoff. Arthur wished he could see the field ahead of him instead of the long snout of the engine cowling and the fan of the spinning propeller.

More than anything, he feared dropping the Spitfire's undercarriage into a bomb crater on the pocked field. The aircraft quivered, gaining speed. He opened the throttle and suddenly he was airborne.

As he retracted his undercarriage, he looked briefly down at the burning field. A Hurricane wobbling on to the taxiway was strafed and exploded, showering debris and blocking the way for the Hurricane's wingman. Arthur boosted the throttle forward to battle climb, ascending at a steep angle toward the sun that burnt a dull yellow through a low ceiling of ground haze. His neck sank back into the leather headrest. In his mirror, he saw a second Spitfire.

"Red Leader, this is Red Two," the radio crackled. It was Yank. "See any trade?"

"Red Two, let's get some altitude and see if we're still alive."

"Red Leader, affirmative."

Arthur maintained the battle climb. His injured shoulder throbbed. He reached heavily for the oxygen mask and covered his face with it, giving himself a lungful of half mixture. He'd never been more alert. Dancing by his peripheral vision, he saw a black spot streak through the patch of cumulus and still he climbed. Suddenly, he pushed the stick forward. His body lifted, weightless in the seat as he dropped over the top of the arc and dived.

He opened fire at a hundred yards, the cockpit filling with cordite fumes as the shark snout of the Messerschmitt lunged by. The pentagram pulsed like a slap as Arthur barely avoided collision. The enemy craft was climbing and Arthur was climbing inside of its tightly turning line of ascent. He tried for a deflection shot, but the tracers found only empty air.

The Messerschmitt twisted and dived. Arthur raced after it, streaking out of the cloud cover and finding the gray, flat windswept surface of the Channel opening below him.

"Red Leader, this is Red Two."

"Leave me be, Two. I'm flying!" Arthur shouted.

"Don't fly too far, Red King. We've only got half a tank. The riggers didn't finish fueling these kites."

The Messerschmitt was zigzagging above the waves, climbing and swooping and staying just beyond Arthur's gunsight, as if it were taunting him. He pushed to boost and closed the distance. His guns rattled, but the Me110 dropped beneath the tracers, just above the waves.

"Turn back, Red Leader! I can't cover you. I'm low on fuel."

"I'm going after the bastard, Red Two." Arthur flew on. He could see the waves rolling up against the French coast at Calais and the shark-skinned Messerschmitt skimming above them.

"Don't be stubborn, King! You'll get yourself killed."

"That's war, Red Two." Arthur fired his guns, but the tracers fell short. The Zerstörer hedgehopped above the sandy white beach, topped the cliffs and cleared the hedgerows behind the beaches.

"If we don't head home now, we'll ditch."

"Then go home, Two. I'll see you at base."

"I won't leave you, Red King."

"I'm giving you permission."

"Needle's near empty," the Yank said. The fuel needle dropped near the red mark on Yank's instrument panel. "Arthur, you've got to turn back!"

The radio fell silent and Arthur flew on like a hunting hawk. The Messerschmitt obsessed him, as if shooting it down would answer his quest. He knew his guns were nearly empty. Another three-second squirt and kill the bugger, just like Stubbs said. Then home for a pint of ale.

The Spitfire's nose shuddered. The blue flames jetting from the engine manifold vanished in a puff of black smoke. The Merlin engine sputtered. The high-pitched whine of the propeller dropped and the blades windmilled before Arthur, slowing to the velocity of a ceiling fan in the local pub. The nose of the aircraft pitched down. The king had run out of fuel.

Arthur lost sight of the Messerschmitt and, instead, looked down to see the low, slate roofs of an ancient French village rushing at him.

Yank switched his radio on to "transmit" for about ten seconds so that Sector could give him a fix. His IFF on, he acknowledged Sector's identification and began to drop speed and altitude as he cleared Folkestone.

"Red King Two, we have you twenty-five miles north of the river Styx," Sector's steady voice informed him. "Vector Six-Zero-Four. Your distance to Hornpipe, three-zero miles, give or take."

Yank recited Sector's fix for confirmation and acknowledged the thinly veiled code name for Hornchurch.

"Let's do it right the first time," Cooper said. "I'm flying on fumes."

"You're nearly home, Red King Two. Where is Red King Leader?"

"I don't know," Yank replied hollowly.

Yank descended to four thousand feet, dropping through a crummy mist. Even with the scud, he had no trouble spotting RAF Hornchurch by the stubborn spot fires still burning on the field in the gathering dusk.

His landing gear locked into place and the green light illuminated on his panel. He extended his flaps and dropped speed again, decelerating to 120 mph ASI. He felt the bile rise in his throat and the endless gray sky robbed him of hope. Yank looked down, searching anxiously for a decent patch of airstrip to avoid the ominous craters hammered in by the Messerschmitt 110s. He felt sick and lost without his wingman.

All Yank Cooper brought home were guns on full and tanks on empty.

The Spitfire's tires ballooned on to the field. Nose up. Engine running down. Firefighters and air crew rushed toward him, and he saw an ambulance waiting at the end of the strip. It was as if Yank had never left. Except that Arthur was gone.

The debriefing was rotten. In the quiet recess of the squadron leader's office, Richardson and Hawley and Stubbs circled Yank, staring at him silently. Cornwell, the intelligence officer from Air Ministry, pressed for the least single detail of Cooper's last sighting of King.

The bare bulb that cast a yellow glow on Richardson's desk reminded Yank of the gangster pictures when some copper tried to make Cagney sing like a canary. Yank just wished he had more to tell. Low on fuel, he turned back, he told them in a cold, dead voice.

"And I never saw Arthur King after that."

"You say it was the village near the coast?" Cornwell scribbled in a notepad.

"He was chasing an Me110," Yank said. "He was trying to get him."

"Or to join him," Gilbert Hawley said wickedly.

"Please, don't interrupt," the captain from Air Ministry pleaded.

Did Cooper recall if the steeple was a twin or a single? A twin. Did he spot any trade? Did he himself fire his guns? Did they get bounced? Did King transmit in German? Cooper stared at the elderly captain.

"No," Yank said coldly. "He didn't talk like a Hun. He's a Brit, like you."

Hawley looked down his long, patrician nose at Yank. Richardson smoked his pipe like the caterpillar in Alice. Tommy Stubbs stroked his mustache and grunted occasionally. Captain Cornwell snapped his notebook shut. When they released him, it was Stubbs who took him to his quarters. Not Hawley, his own flight leader.

"There, there," Stubbs said, clapping Cooper on the shoulder. "You did all you could, I suppose."

"Which was nothing."

"Rotten luck," Stubbs said. Stubbs shook his head absently and trudged back to Richardson's office, headquartered in the only undamaged structure on the airfield. He bumped into Captain Cornwell, making fresh scribbles in his pad as he left the squadron leader's office.

Lounging on the chair Yank had occupied, Gilbert Hawley smoothed his slick of oily Valentino hair and tamped a cigarette on his gold case. Richardson smoothed the stack of after-action reports piled on his desk and sighed. "That's that," he murmured.

"So, the book on Flight Lieutenant Arthur King is closed," Hawley said in his faintly malicious, nasal tone. "Gone back to his own kind with all the squadron secrets."

"There's hardly a squadron left to hold any secrets," Stubbs said. "If he's a Hun spy, he took nearly half of what's left in flying condition along with him."

"That's enough!" Richardson barked. "This is a lot of rot. There's nothing to confirm Gil's suspicions. King is just another missing flier. We've not an iota of proof he was Fifth Column."

"There's not an iota of proof he ever existed," Hawley said. "Except that he vanished with one of our aircraft, flying over the hill to Hun-land against orders."

"I suppose we'll never know the truth of it," Stubbs said.

"Better that way," Richardson said. "We've got enough to do here. Digging out from under."

"So, ring the bell, close the book and snuff the candle," Hawley said.

Richardson looked up, annoyed but curious. "Some drinking club rot, Gil?"

"My specialty at Oxford was pagan Britain, sir. It's what the ancients used to say when they rid themselves of some witch or warlock. Maybe with Arthur King gone, our luck will turn."

Richardson snorted. He hunted through the thicket of paperwork on his desk, looking for Flight Lieutenant King's file. Just as suddenly, he stopped, realizing that there had never been one.

20

When Yank entered the wreckage that housed
his quarters, he found Jenny sitting on
Arthur's camp bed. Her medical cape cloaked
her, like the camouflage of a bird in hiding. Yank's
quarters, like the rest of the barracks, were a ruin of
smoke and ash and scattered small personal posses-
sions. She held a half-charred copy of *"Aces,"* examining it as an archeologist might inspect ancient
rubbish, seeking a clue to a vanished civilization.

She looked up at Cooper, her fine-featured face
exhausted, a wisp of ginger hair crossing her forehead. "They say he's gone," she said bleakly.

"He's missing, Jenny. That could mean a lot of things."

"I know what missing means," she said. "My brother
was carried missing. But, of course, he was dead."

"Arthur could have parachuted," Cooper said.
"He's done it before. Hell, he's had more lucky
bailouts than most."

"But you didn't see him bail out."

"No."

"And you were the last to see him."

"Yes."

"I see." She said no more. She stared at the tattered pulp magazine. The cover showed a quaint World War I red triplane with black crosses, pursued by an Allied biplane. The cover story was titled "The Solo Kid."

"Look, there was no stopping him, Jenny."

"I suppose not."

"I couldn't make him turn back. I tried. Was I supposed to shoot at him? Make him run home to Mommy? I'm telling you, there was nothing more I could do."

"Evidently," she said. "Certainly you didn't."

"That's not fair, Jenny."

"You're so right, Flying Officer Cooper. It's not a fair war at all. I knew that. I just wanted to believe that with your great brotherhood of the air, you wouldn't let your friend fly off to die alone."

"You couldn't believe how stubborn he was, Jenny," Yank said helplessly. "He made his own bed."

"Yes, he did. And now you're home to yours."

"I don't have to take this."

"No, you're right. You're very tired, Bill. I'll leave."

Yank made a point of ignoring her as he rummaged about for his kit as darkness fell. Jenny rose and gathered the cape around her shoulders. A cold wind blew through the holes in the tarpaper shack. Jenny's hair blew wild and red about her shoulders as the sharp draft cut through and around the charred roof beams. A bomber's moon, three-quarters full, ascended, riding on an ocean of cloud like a ghostly ship.

Yank turned and Jenny was gone. A ray of moonlight fell on Arthur's commando dagger. The blade, embedded in a charred support timber, shimmered in the blue light, with the knife protruding from the wood like a sword in a stone.

21

Father Boniface pulled the bell rope, and it snagged. He yanked a bit harder, and still the rope resisted. Boniface clucked his tongue. To call the faithful to vespers, one needed a bell. Even a wandering Boche soul might need saving, and for that, the jackbooted wretch would need to hear the bells. Though he could count the number of Boche who had come to confession on the fingers of one hand. They preferred the cinema and the village's two cafes.

Boniface ascended the ancient wooden spiral that led up into the bell tower. He'd been the parish priest for Village D'Eauville since the Boche artillery claimed his left foot at Verdun in '16. Every morning and every evening since, the bells had been his to command. As his wooden foot clumped up the ancient steps, he sensed a shadow and he heard a noise like a sheet flapping on washing day. He ascended to the bell platform and saw the white silk billow through the steeple, wrapped round the bells.

"*Quelle étrange*," he murmured. Boniface felt utterly confused. France had already surrendered, even if Boniface had not. What was the meaning of the white cloth?

The priest grabbed at the silk. A portion tangled in the ancient iron bells ripped and slipped a few inches, and Boniface heard a grunt. He'd heard such grunts in the trenches: the panicked groans of men fearing sudden death. He heard the grunt again, joined by a foreign curse.

"Shit!"

For the first time, the wooden-footed priest saw the strings. They were meshed in the bells like tangled fishing line. He ran his shrapnel-scarred hand along them until the strings ran out off the ledge, and he looked down and saw the hanging man. In the fading light, Boniface leaned over the ledge and stared, transfixed by the man's steel gray eyes.

"Boche?" The priest had to ask. He still might kill for his country and confess his sin later.

"Briton!"

"Ah, Tommy!" The priest nodded and abruptly withdrew into the steeple. Carefully, Boniface tied a section of the torn parachute canopy around one of the bell ropes in a tight knot. He pulled at the knot with the same vigor he used to ring vespers. The knot held. He heard another grunt and another curse, and he hurried back to the ledge.

The hanging man was still there. Boniface leaned far over the ledge. The priest gave a British-style open-handed salute and disappeared again.

Arthur heard jackboots on the cobbles below. The sun sank behind the steeple and the wind whistled through the bell tower. The king twisted, his legs dangling in the harness. He heard the guttural shouts of the Huns some fifty feet beneath his wiggling toes.

The king looked down. Dusk swept the streets,

casting purple shadows across the village square. A black car pulled up alongside the soldiers. In their black helmets, the troops looked like Mordred's personal guard. A man in a black coat with a black flat-brimmed hat emerged from the car. The man didn't look like a soldier. Something about the bony-faced man made Arthur uneasy. He looked like death.

This was the first time the king saw the enemy at close quarters. They didn't look ten feet tall, and they didn't look like the Huns from his day. There was no blue paint streaked across wild, red-bearded faces. No war axes, or horned helmets or blond braids. These soldiers displayed no ritual scars. They looked unfriendly, though.

Unfriendly and dangerous because of their weapons. Unlike a sword or an axe, the weaponry of this age looked harmless waiting on a table to be cleaned, or mounted in the wing of an aircraft. In utility, the firearms looked like just another machine, resembled the horseless chariots, or radios, or the pull chain for the water closet.

A tug in the harness interrupted his meditation. He felt himself rising. The bells began ringing vespers. Soon his ears were ringing. The king prayed the Huns wouldn't raise their eyes to the sound of the bells.

As the harness inched upward, he felt his right shoe slip loose. The shock of a parachute opening often tore off all but the snuggest boot. His shoe hung precariously. He pointed his toes up and dug his heel down as if his foot were in a stirrup. Still, the shoe threatened to slip. The pain became excrutiating. His ears throbbed, his ankles ached. He chafed in the harness and his balls were constricted. The shoe dangled and bobbed with each ring of the bell and harness tug. It was agonizing.

Inside the steeple, Father Boniface whispered a prayer. He had tied the canopy like a sheet to the bell ropes, and with each ring of the bell, the canopy slipped over the top of the bell like a bucket of water raised from a well.

Arthur's good arm shot over the ledge, and his hand gripped the stones. His other arm throbbed painfully, but he hung on as if his fingers were talons. As he muscled his way onto the ledge, his shoe dropped. Before he cleared the ledge, the other shoe dropped. Each sole bounced off the old chapel escarpment. The soldiers' helmets bobbed as they looked up. Arthur swung his leg over the top of the ledge as he heard the words shouted, "*Englische Pilot!*"

The king peeped over the ledge and saw one plump Hun holding a shoe like a trophy. Other soldiers darted down the dark alleyway that adjoined the church. Arthur dropped to his knees in the bell tower. His heart pounded as he crouched in darkness, panting like an animal.

As the moon ascended over the village like a translucent globe, Arthur peered over the ledge to see the streets filling with trucks and soldiers. From one truck, a soldier jumped down, clutching a pair of large dogs tied with leather harnesses. The Hun presented the dog handler the shoe and the animals snuffled noisily. The hounds howled and the dog handler could barely restrain them. The man in the black coat strolled over to the dog handler and pointed down the alley beside the church. The dog handler nodded.

The priest touched Arthur on the shoulder, nearly making him jump out of his skin. The old man smiled and said, "*Cher ami. Merci beaucoup, notre champion de l'Anglais. Je suis Père Boniface.*"

Arthur shook his head. He always found Gallic incomprehensible. And their emissaries were rude. "*Allo, Tommy,*" the priest said. He seemed friendly enough. He was smiling. "*Vivre le grand Charles DeGaulle!*"

Arthur nodded. "*Gaul, oui.*" The priest put his finger to his lips. Silently, Boniface untied the suspension lines, then the folds of the canopy shrouds. When he was finished, he stuffed the canopy beneath his vestments so that they tied around him like a girdle. The priest smiled and held two fingers up in a "Victory" gesture, just like Churchill in the newsreels.

The old man disappeared down the spiral stairs of the church tower. Arthur peered over the ledge to the street below. It was full of soldiers. Like the streets of London, the village was blacked out, but the streets shimmered in the moonlight. Arthur held his breath when he saw the priest exit the chapel and begin walking into the village square.

A pair of old women crossed the street and crossed themselves. The priest nodded to them and urged them into church. Arthur listened, but could hear nothing. Arthur had not seen a man in the town except for the priest and soldiers. The king wondered if the conquering army had taken all the men of fighting age as hostages. At least that was the custom in his own time.

The priest was walking briskly when Arthur heard the man in the black coat shout "Halt!" The priest waited patiently while the bony-faced man approached. The priest gave a blessing, but the man in the long coat kept repeating the word "Documents." The priest shook his head as if he didn't understand, and finally, the black-coated Hun snatched the priest's vestment.

The parachute canopy dropped beneath the priest's robe. It glowed white in the moonlight. Still, the black-coated Hun failed to see it. He was busy berating the priest, who merely shrugged his shoulders and shook his head. The Hun gave the priest a push and the old man began to walk away, but with every step he took, the skirt of the canopy unraveled from beneath his robe.

The old man must have felt the fabric coming loose

because he stopped and crossed himself. He turned to see the man in the black coat pointing a small black pistol at him and smiling. Arthur watched the man in black blow the priest's brains out. The soldiers watched silently as the old man fell into the street. Arthur saw the priest's body sink, first going down on his knees as if kneeling in prayer, then falling forward on the paving stones.

"No!" Arthur whispered. The black Hun shouted orders to the squad sergeant. The squad picked up the priest and tossed the old man's body like refuse in the back of a troop carrier.

The Hun shouted more orders. The dog handler returned, his dogs now gnashing their teeth and baying. The man in the black coat snatched a shred of the parachute fabric that lay bloodied on the stones. The dog handler took it and held it under the snouts of the hounds. They bayed and began pulling the dog handler to the church.

Arthur pushed back from the ledge and ran down the wooden stairs of the church tower two at a time.

Even as the king descended the steps, the window-panes of the village began to vibrate. Even the windows in the chapel, anchored in their ancient bedrock, hummed. The dog handler's hounds momentarily forgot their errand. They halted and joined all the soldiers gazing up at the milky moon.

Soon, the din and roar over Village D'Eauville was deafening. The vibration mounted. Roof tiles fell into the narrow streets. A deaf shepherd gazed skyward. Women of the village held their ears. The moon turned dark as the wings of the bombers blacked it from the sky. None in the gathered company had ever seen so many airplanes.

22

Churchill chewed his eighth Havana of the day, and longed to light it. But at least on the platform above the "filter room" at Fighter Command HQ, he deferred to Dowding. From their vantage point above the operations floor, Churchill, Dowding and a select group of RAF officers that included Richardson watched the smartly tailored women of the Auxiliary Air Force move their magnetic pointers across the giant map. Behind Churchill hovered a gaunt man whose tweeds hung on him like a scarecrow. He sported a salt-and-pepper mustache and a confident grin.

Sir Stewart Menzies was, in fact, chief of British intelligence, and known as "C." The military men disliked and distrusted the gaunt Scot, but he held Churchill's ear so they deferred to him. He held Churchill in his thrall, because in the satchel he carried the secrets of Ultra, the code-breaking machine that deciphered all enemy communications.

In the filter room, the WAAF's calm urgency communicated an intensity unmatched by any croupier in a game of high stakes. The tiles on the map clicked quietly as the women received guidance through their earphones from the coastal radar stations.

Nightfall. Bombers approaching. The tiles and sticks moved ever quicker. "London again," Dowding said grimly.

"Perhaps," Churchill said. The old man waved his cigar. "Where might I light this, Air Marshal Dowding?"

Stuffy Dowding stiffened. He nodded curtly and said, "This way, Mr. Prime Minister." The entourage followed Dowding and Churchill off the platform into Dowding's Spartan office. Inside Dowding's inner sanctum, Squadron Leader Richardson leaned forward to light the prime minister's cigar, risking a cold scowl from Dowding. The prime minister remained oblivious to the air marshal's distaste for tobacco. He puffed until a small yellow cloud filled the room. Dowding grimaced. Finally, he spoke.

"Do you have any doubt that London is tonight's target, sir?"

"We defy augury," Churchill grumbled. "But sometimes, we know what lies ahead. The target for tonight is not London. It will be Coventry."

Squadron Leader Richardson looked up, startled as a deer in a clearing. He blurted out, "What, Coventry?"

Churchill regarded his cigar and surveyed the room. "Yes. London will be spared tonight. The East End can sleep while the Midlands suffers."

"By what means did we come by this information, sir?" Dowding asked. He stared mistrustfully at the gaunt Scot with the satchel.

"We are not prepared to discuss that," the man called "C" replied. "Suffice it to say, the information is reliable."

"That really is startling news, sir," Richardson interjected.

"How so?" Churchill asked.

"I've just rushed here from my aerodrome, where one of my men raised the subject of a raid on Coventry, sir. I don't mind telling you, we thought he was daft. Or treasonous."

Churchill glowered at Richardson. "Where is this man now?"

"Gone missing, sir. But he sounded quite sure it would be Coventry."

Now it was the intelligence chief's turn to look worried. "That knowledge is closely held. No one in the realm knows of it except the men in this room."

"Gone missing, you say?" Churchill said. "Who might this officer be?"

"Lieutenant Arthur King. He scrambled during the Hornchurch strike and we've not seen him since."

"Arthur King? That's got a ring to it," Churchill said. "I think I know the man."

"You know him?" Richardson asked, incredulous. "How, sir?"

"Met him at Beaverbrook's soiree. He seemed quite intelligent."

"Too damned intelligent if he knew about Autumn Sonata," Sir Stewart Menzies said grimly. "It seems an odd thing to guess at."

"What, if you please, is Autumn Sonata?" Air Marshal Dowding asked.

Churchill puffed his cigar thoughtfully. He placed it on the edge of Dowding's desk, allowing the fine, gray ash to burn toward the edge of the furniture like a dynamite fuse.

"It's Goering's code name for the attack on Coventry, and such an attack is most likely in progress even as we speak," Churchill said. "I imagine your WAAFs out there in the filter room are tracking Jerry's fleet even now."

"Sir, if the Hun mounts a major attack, Fighter

Command must be alerted immediately," Dowding said. "We must do what we can."

"It's too late," Churchill said. "We came by this news within the past hour. Of course, Fighter Command will be alerted, but no extraordinary measures can be taken."

"And why not, sir?" Dowding demanded.

The gaunt Scot who controlled British intelligence smiled, his thin lips drawn tight against his teeth. "It wouldn't do, you see. If we tip our hand that we were aware, we might compromise our source."

"What in bloody hell is the good of intelligence if one cannot make use of it?" Dowding said, his voice rising. "Are we to leave our people to their fate?"

"In this case," Menzies said, "I'm afraid it's unavoidable."

"We should have been better prepared," Churchill ruminated. "Coventry is a military target. No less than twenty-one aircraft and armaments factories near the city's center."

"And there's the cathedral," Richardson murmured. Suddenly, the wing commander spoke up. "Flight Lieutenant King said that the cathedral was the real target."

"Did he?" Menzies said, raising an eyebrow. "And why would that be?"

"He said the Huns wanted to destroy what is sacred. Just as we were about to press him on the point, Jerry struck our airfield and King vanished."

"A prophet of doom, then? An oracle gone up in smoke?" Menzies mused, his tone faintly amused. "Sounds like he's a bit barmy," the intelligence chief said. Then he added darkly, "Unless he's in contact with the enemy. We ought to round him up and let the boys at Five have a look at him."

"He seemed in all ways a right honorable Englishman," Churchill said. "The young man knew his history. There was no stopping his chatter with Beaverbrook about ancient armaments. A regular T. E. Lawrence. Well, Richardson, your oracular flier is right about one thing. The cathedral is sacred in terms of its place in England. But it's the armaments factories we must worry over."

Dowding broke in. "The city's virtually undefended, sir. It's not like London, with the balloons, heavy ack-ack and airfields circling the city. We've got to scramble as many of the lads as can be sent at this late hour."

Churchill had let his cigar go out on the desk. He looked at it with distaste. "It is indeed late in the day," the prime minister said. "But try your best. It's the least we can do for those poor people."

An aide knocked, entered and saluted. "We have hundreds of bandits on the screen, sir," he told Dowding. "The biggest raid we've ever seen."

Dowding looked at Churchill and held his tongue. The prime minister stared back at him stoically and lit a fresh cigar. The air chief marshal turned away.

"I wonder how King knew," Richardson murmured.

"Yes," Menzies agreed. "It must be looked into."

At a nod from Dowding, Richardson ran to inform staff in the filter room of the likely destination of the German bombers. As they reached the platform, they looked down at the map table to see the tiles depicting the German bomber groups clustered together and being pushed like an angry cloud toward Coventry.

The city lay exposed to the raiders, quite as naked as Lady Godiva, who once dared to ride her horse down the city's ancient streets.

*   *   *

As the shadows dropped into the crevices of the crabbed, narrow streets of Coventry's city center, Georgie Miller licked his lips. Blinkers, his cart pony, longed for a brushing and a carrot. The youth's cart clattered along and the empty milk cans jangled. As soon as Georgie returned them, the proprietor of Whitcomb's Sweet Shoppe would give him a rare Cadbury's milk bar.

Georgie worked from before dawn in one of Coventry's arms factories, forging barrels for Browning guns. Afternoons, he retrieved empty milk tins and bits of string and paper from Coventry's tightly packed lanes. The little bell tinkled and Georgie carried his tins into the shop down the way from the great cathedral. The shop consisted of three tables and bare shelves. No cocoa. No coffee. Little tea. Few biscuits. The army requisitioned sweets quicker than the guns stamped and forged nearby.

Whitcomb doled out Georgie's shillings hesitantly. Not because he was mean, but because like paper and string, petrol and cigarettes, money was woefully short.

"You didn't forget, sir?"

The shopkeeper tousled the youth's hair. Georgie had a forelock, like Blinkers. Some called Georgie a bit slow. "Here you are, Georgie," Whitcomb said, handing him the chocolate bar in the gold-colored foil.

As the curtain of evening descended on Conventry, the old man and the youth heard the bells. The sound jarred them, as by now it was an unfamiliar ring. For more than a year, the bells were silent, to be rung only in case of invasion. Whitcomb frowned. The boy looked at him anxiously.

The ringing was joined by a rising chorus of sirens. Soon, the factory whistles joined. In the darkened street, Blinkers whinnied. Without warning, the wooden floor shook beneath them. The walls moved and the shop shuddered as in an earthquake. They heard the first blast, followed by another and another.

The old man and the boy next heard the unsynchronized rumble of the Junkers engines, an orchestra of washing machines groaning. The sound of the engines drowned out the bells and sirens. Georgie's eardrums burst as the shock wave hurled him to the floor. The taped glass blasted in and the tin and plaster from the roof buried him.

People on the streets took to their feet and scattered. Looking up, they could see bomber fleets forming a dark cloud that blacked out the stars. The drone swelled. Soon, spot fires erupted across the city. The ancient timbers of Coventry's medieval structures ignited like cordwood and the flames rose to meet the shadow of the black crosses roaring over the city.

In the hundred acres of city center, the row houses, the shops and the factories burned like matches as the incendiaries dropped. Glass showered through the factory roofs like sharp, slicing crystal rain. With the fire blazing from house to house, the heat soon melted the glass and fused it.

The Heinkels, Dorniers and Junkers lumbered in, wave after wave, guided in on a radio beam that pointed like an invisible bony finger toward the heart of the city. As in London, many panicked people ran from the flames, or straight into them. Others stared in dumb shock up at the night sky that soon turned an angry red with the flame reflected against the moonlit clouds.

In the streets, a bus conductor's flesh melted on the bone of his blazing arm. Babies and mothers wailed. Some breathed on and groaned beneath the mountains of rubble. Others merely ceased breathing.

By morning, the combined forces of the Luftwaffe's Bombing Group Three dropped a million pounds of high-explosive bombs on Coventry. Altogether, the four hundred and forty-nine bombers massed over the medieval city dropped nearly a thousand canisters of incendiary in the greatest concentrated bombardment of Britain during the war.

The record of Coventry's long night lay buried in Merlin's pages, chapter the twentieth, but only Mordred possessed the knowledge foretold in the stolen text. Inside the bubble nose of the Heinkel, Mordred kneeled, suspended like a spider in the center of a great web of steel and glass. He watched a bomb line of incendiaries lifting feathers of flame up toward the clouds that glowed red with the reflected heat. A smile tightened his lips across the rows of sharpened, feral teeth.

A great column of smoke wrapped in cinders unfolded flowerlike from the blazing floor of Coventry. At fifteen thousand feet, Mordred felt the heat rising from the earth. Sweet streamed from beneath his leather helmet. He looked round the interior of the aircraft. The red glowing panel lights in the Heinkel illuminated it like some machine from the Underworld. In the blackness beyond the lurching bomber, Mordred sensed the hundreds of other lumbering aircraft. Despite the sickness he often felt while flying, he also sensed a growing awe of himself and the dark legion he controlled.

"There it is," he said. For an instant, a line of incendiaries illuminated the spires of the enormous structure at city's center. "My father's cathedral burns."

Indeed, as the Heinkel lumbered past at a stately hundred miles per hour with the bombs falling from its gaping belly, Mordred watched transfixed as the cathedral arches imploded, crumbling beneath the bombardment like a great collapsing coffin. Mordred's breathing quickened. His excitement mounted at the sight of thousands of fires joined together three miles beneath his feet. Soon, it seemed they were one blaze, a bonfire that beckoned all the other waves of bombers toward it.

"The cathedral goes, with everything else in Coventry. It burns," Mordred murmured. "But henceforth, it is Mordred who commands the air. I decide who suffers and who is spared."

A sudden lurch filled Mordred's chest with a wave of nausea. He grabbed the trigger grip of the nose gun, fired a long tracer burst and laughed at the bloodred heavens. The ring of hollow laughter filled Kleist with loathing and dread. He felt tempted to plunge the Heinkel earthward and bury the demon in the rubble, but a sudden sharp pain in his temple paralyzed his arm on the controls. He flew on among the hundreds of dark birds carried on the ill wind.

The converted ambulance still wore the paint of the Patent Steam Carpet Beating Co. The ancient Ford engine chugged and protested, but that didn't restrain Edith's heavy foot on the gas pedal. She hand-cranked the siren as if she were clearing the way for Churchill. A cat darted across Kings Cross Road and Edith nearly got one of its lives.

"Edith, slow down!" Jenny cried.

"We're on a mission of mercy," Edith insisted as she mashed the gears.

"If we have a wreck, there's no mission. Blood's no good once it's spilled."

"Yes, Doctor," Edith said as she resumed cranking the siren.

Jenny and Edith wore the soup pan helmets of air wardens. They carried a crate of rare blood types collected for the RAF hospital. A newly licensed ambulance driver, Edith grabbed every chance at the wheel with the eagerness of a destroyer captain. Edith rounded a corner, tilting the Ford on two wheels, terrifying the old woman who fed the birds on the steps of Coventry Cathedral. Edith's siren wailed so it hurt Jenny's ears.

Jenny craned her neck to determine the old woman's fate. It was then that she looked up at the dusky sky and saw the curtain of approaching bombers cutting through the mist and emerging from the clouds like locusts.

For the first time, she heard their low moaning above the ambulance siren's wail. And for the first time, she heard the city sirens that warned too late of the imminent raid. Jenny pulled into the cab like a turtle into its shell as the first bombs whistled to earth.

The shock wave from a hundred-kilogram bomb pitched the ancient ambulance into a street lamp and bashed Edith's forehead against the wind visor. The siren stopped abruptly. Edith bled from the scalp and looked dolefully at Jenny. "What's happened?"

Other bombs soon struck, erupting in the puzzle of streets surrounding the cathedral. They fell, *crump, crump, crump* and quickly became too many to count. The ordnance rumbled like cannon fire, shaking the street beneath them. The ambulance vibrated like a box rattled by a child to discover its contents.

Jenny pulled Edith from the wheel. She grabbed the gas mask in Edith's canvas bag. Edith, shivering from shock, allowed herself to be handled. Jenny tugged Edith's helmet free. She pulled the mask over Edith's head and donned her own. Even with the mask on, Jenny felt the heat. She saw the fine hairs on the back of her hands singed away. She climbed down, ran round the bonnet and pulled Edith from the cab. She scanned the street vainly, searching for a shelter.

"The Tube," Edith mumbled. "The Underground."

"There's none, dear," Jenny said. "We're not in London."

Jenny pulled Edith along and watched the sky glow red on the rooftops from the incendiaries. The shouts and screams of civilians filled her ears as they fluttered by like moths, waving their arms like great wings as they ran.

The groan of the bombers high overhead in shadowed sky formed a ghastly, low-throated counterpoint to the rumble of falling timbers and roar of the great blaze building up in the center of Coventry.

The eye sockets on Jenny's mask fogged over. Her breathing quickened and she felt panic rising in her chest. She held Edith as if she protected a child. With an effort, she urged her onward. Moving was better than standing still. A row of houses tumbled like building blocks into the street behind them, and Jenny pulled Edith, running now.

They turned into the lane adjoining the cathedral and faced a solid wall of flame. She turned round and ran the other direction. With the tumbled rubble of the street facing them and the fire behind them, Jenny pulled Edith into an alley, where they nearly tripped on the carcass of a pony. A splintered door hung ajar and Jenny tumbled through it like Alice.

They found the old man and the youth huddled beneath one of the heavy wooden tables of Whitcomb's Sweet Shoppe. As the thousand bits of shattered glass shook on the linoleum floor, Georgie Miller called to Jenny and Edith.

"There's no gas," he said, coughing. "Just dust." He nearly choked on his words. "But that's bad enough, isn't it?"

Jenny pulled free of her mask and gently removed

Edith's. The first sob escaped from Edith like a gasp. She hyperventilated. Georgie nodded at her as he carefully unpeeled the gold foil from the Cadbury Milk Bar. With a surgeon's care, he divided the chocolate into four parts. Edith took her square of chocolate and wept, her tears smearing the blood and rouge.

Mr. Whitcomb took his Cadbury like a communion wafer. Jenny bit hungrily into the chocolate. Amid the explosive rumble and snick of the flames outside, candy had never tasted so sweet. As the bombs fell like raindrops, the youth took to folding the gold wrapper into ever smaller triangles, until it was the size of a small gold nugget. Then he would unfold the paper and repeat the process. Outside, the whistle, crump and shaking of the bomb blasts persisted until it seemed the world had never been any other way.

"Where's our side? Where's our lads?" Edith cried out plaintively. "Make them stop!"

Jenny hugged Edith to her, as if she were comforting a child. And the nurse nestled in Jenny's arms. The terrible droning would fade, and just as the roaring ceased, a new wave arrived. Jenny shuddered and Edith hugged her tighter yet. Unlike the huddled masses of Londoners crowded into their massive, well-laid-out Underground shelters, Coventry's quarter-million souls faced their long night of the Blitz without warning.

The suddenness of the Luftwaffe's arrival created terror that mounted as the echelons of aircraft streamed in over the city, groaning like a monstrous Gregorian chant. The Heinkels and Junkers descended on Coventry first in the dozens, and finally in the hundreds. They were what the fliers would come to call a bomber stream, a river of steel and fire flowing over a city like hot lava.

The bombers followed a radio direction beam transmitted by the Luftflotte Three operations staff operating far away on the Pas de Calais. Ten thousand feet below the fur-lined boots of Kleist and Mordred, the subjects of their experiment experienced a punishment that the German propaganda machine would refer to in days to come as "Coventration."

In the third hour of the bombardment, the skies of Coventry were white-hot with flames that licked the night sky. Old Mr. Whitcomb's heart seized up on him in the shaking and the heat. Jenny watched helplessly, and Edith began to go mad.

A direct hit between the cathedral and the shop collapsed half the roof of the sweet shop. The tin ceiling crumpled like a chocolate wrapper, nearly trapping them. The heat from the flames outside shimmered off the tin, making the huddled space within the wreckage unbearably hot. Edith screamed and wouldn't stop. Jenny slapped her until she fell silent, her lips a blood-caked smudge beneath two saucers that stared without seeing.

Georgie Miller spotted a shard of glass protruding from Mr. Whitcomb's neck.

"Surely, he'll die, miss," Georgie said. "Can't you do something? You said you were a doctor."

As he spoke, Jenny tore a strip of her blouse. Next, she plucked the shard of glass from the old man's neck. She fleetingly remembered Arthur removing the steel so skillfully from his shoulder. She placed the strip of blouse on the old man's carotid artery and pressed.

"Put your hands on his neck and press hard," she said to the youth. "You'll have to take over while I get some things."

"Where are you going, Jenny?" Edith asked. Her voice quivered on the edge of hysteria.

"I need my kit from the ambulance."

"Don't leave," Edith whispered. Jenny was already up and crawling over the wreckage of the counter. "We'll die if you leave!"

"Then come along, dear. But don't scream. I can't stand it."

"I can't," Edith wailed. "We'll die out there, too."

"I must get my things," Jenny said as she slid over a tabletop and looked out into the ruin of the street. The spot fires tranformed night into day.

"Don't leave us!" Edith cried. And Jenny was gone.

An inferno surrounded her, like Elijah's pillar of flame, reaching up to the sky where the black cemetery crosses of the Luftwaffe reigned. Jenny felt the oxygen being pulled from her lungs. She saw a fire truck, its hoses leading to it burnt like lines of gunpowder. She staggered a few steps further and spotted the ambulance. It rested on its rims, the tires a gooey puddle. The street lamp, too, had melted.

The old truck glowed like a coal in a fire. Jenny knelt in the street and sobbed. A rumble behind her made her turn. The block with the shop and Edith in it had collapsed into a tomb of brick.

The RAF Fighter Command flew one hundred and twenty-five sorties against the Luftwaffe raiders. Among these, only seven spotted Kleist's dark squadrons pouring their rain of steel and death. The Blitz had been complete. Two RAF planes engaged the raiding force as it rumbled through the skies of night. None of the raiders were shot down.

The reports to Fighter Command at Bentley Priory were spotty. The full magnitude of the catastrophe was not known until the next day. Churchill received the call from the king at Buckingham Palace. The prime minister was in full agreement. They must go to Coventry.

23

Kleist shuffled the after-action reports handed him by Captain Vilner, the monkish, bespectacled officer for fleet operations. On seeing the general, Vilner was shaken by Kleist's appearance. The color of life had fled Kleist's face. The news from the raid all looked good, but the general looked ghastly, as if he were afflicted by a life-draining illness. Mordred scowled at the captain and the aide scurried out of the operations tent to gather more reports from the returning bomber crews.

The paperwork flowed nearly as swiftly as the planes returning from England. The twin-engine bombers roared in from the Channel, shaking the tent and bumping onto the airfields, their way lit by smudge pots that made the field look like witches gathered on All Hallow's Eve.

In the tent, by the light of a hurricane lamp, Kleist scanned his bomb tallies intently, noting the ordnance delivered on Coventry. The only pleasure left to him lay in performing functions that he realized Mordred did not fully comprehend. He added up the figures in neat columns. Nearly a half million kilos delivered on target. A military success for Operation Autumn Sonata that even Berlin would have to acknowledge. But for Kleist the victory was hollow. The demon sat nearby, as ever, grinning like a wolf.

Mordred put his boots on an empty ammunition crate and reclined in a canvas chair. Mordred smoked a cigar. His face was streaked with cordite and grease beneath his leather helmet. He looked the complete twentieth-century warrior. He poured a cognac, knocked back the amber liquid and wiped his lips. He watched Kleist scribble notes and he chuckled. "Much smoother than mead."

"What's that?" Kleist asked absently. When he pursued his routines, he felt relatively free from the iron grip of Mordred's power over his mind.

"I was saying, Herr General, that in my time, we burned the cities and drank to victory. No writing. No paper. That's fool's work. Only priests scribble away at scroll work."

"Records must be kept," Kleist said as he continued to scratch his signature at the bottom of each report.

"Why?"

Kleist looked at him quizzically. "So the world will know what we accomplished."

"They'll know well enough from the fires of the cities we burnt," Mordred said. "They'll sing songs about it at court, one day."

Vilner hurried into the tent nervously. "Reichsmarshall Goering is coming! His staff car is driving up from the airfield."

Hearing Goering's powerful staff car roar up, Kleist rose from his field desk. Annoyed at the interruption to his self-adulation, Mordred pulled himself to his feet just as Goering swept into the tent, his sky blue cloak wrapped about his shoulders as if he were afraid to be seen. Vilner called attention. Kleist dismissed the captain with a wave of his hand and Mordred slouched in an imitation of military courtesy. Vilner fled gratefully.

"Herr Reichsmarshall." Kleist saluted. "We are honored."

Goering's pendulous jowls shook and he glared at Kleist. "Have you heard the news, General Kleist? The Führer has canceled Operation Sea Lion! There will be no invasion of England this autumn."

"I don't understand."

"It can only mean he has lost faith in the Luftwaffe, and lost confidence in me, personally." Goering swept his bloodshot eyes around the tent and fixed them resentfully on Kleist. "I hold you responsible, General."

"How so, Herr Reichsmarshall? I've followed your every order."

"Every order put forward by your assistant," Goering sputtered. "But the damnable English still resist our forces. Your bombers have failed."

"That's strong language, Reichsmarshall. It sounds like Berlin talking. Try and remember we fly the missions while others dine at Horcher's."

Goering stomped his foot. His beet red face seemed to swell as he shouted, "Don't you dare be insolent with me! I'll have you shot!"

Kleist's head nearly exploded with pain. He glanced at Mordred, whose eyes bathed him in their steady serpent's gaze. "Shot, Reichsmarshall?" Kleist said miserably. "You would be doing me a favor."

The Luftwaffe chieftain rubbed his own forehead as if he were defending against a sudden onset of migraine. The big man leaned heavily against Kleist's desk. His voice faded, sinking to nearly a whisper. "I promised the Führer a great victory. I promised him they would sue for peace."

A faint grin curved the edges of Mordred's moist lips. He licked the points of his teeth and said, "Reichsmarshall, you can bring your leader glorious tidings."

"What is Colonel Morgan speaking of?"

"We smashed the munitions plants of Coventry tonight," Mordred said, his tone of voice pleasant, barely concealing his jubilance. "There has never been such a rain of death. On Britain, or anywhere. A proud moment for you."

"Is this true?" Goering demanded. He rushed to Kleist's field table and seized the map of England. "Show me. I need facts and figures. His appetite for information is endless."

Mordred smoothed the map for the Reichsmarshall. "General Kleist can show you his scratchings. I'll tell you how it looked. I saw the city glow like a stove, Reichsmarshall. With their factories crippled, they must yield. Best of all, we destroyed the cathedral. Surely London will plead mercy."

Goering grunted, then seated himself on the ammunition box as if settling on a throne. He rested his pendulous chins on a clenched fist in porcine imitation of Rodin's *Thinker*. Finally, he shook his head. He took a bottle from his cloak, shook a handful of pills from it and chewed.

"I have made such prophecies about the English before. When they should give way to intelligence and surrender, they spit in your eye."

"They will yield," Mordred said, his voice growing husky. "I promise it, Reichsmarshall."

The Reichsmarshall's bloodshot blue eyes stared deep into Mordred's glittering, emerald eyes. "If you deliver on that promise, I'll get you a field marshal's baton, but don't make a fool of me. I want to hear that cry for mercy from the BBC."

"Coventry is the beginning of the end for the English," Mordred said. "News from Britain in the days ahead will be startling."

"Yes, yes," Goering said, nodding anxiously. "I will hold you to that." The second most powerful man in the Third Reich gathered his cloak about his ample shoulders. Greedily, he scooped up Kleist's reports.

"I'll take these with me to Berlin," Goering said. He flashed his cape and swept from the room like an opera cavalier. Kleist and Mordred remained at attention until they heard the Reichsmarshall's Duesenberg rumble away into the night.

"He is an idiot," Kleist said.

"Yes. And for a little while, he has the power of a prince," Mordred said. "But that will soon change."

Kleist's head hung from his shrunken shoulders. He realized he was dying by the minute. He glared at Mordred, gathering all the strength left to him. "What is it that you want? What do you want that you need my life to get?"

Mordred smiled, his teeth spiny and pointed as a snake's. "I've told you, General. The king of England's head on a pike." He turned away. Quietly, he added, "And there is yet one more king I must settle with. Forever."

Kleist stared at the floor of the tent. He felt an impulse to grab the hurricane lamp and smash it. He saw the tent on fire and smelled his own flesh burning. It was as if he had voiced the thought, for he looked at Mordred's terrible emerald eyes and realized he had no idea that was not known to the demon.

"I have helped you, creature," Kleist said. "Everything you commanded, I have done. What is left for me?"

Mordred grinned. "There is one more thing you

must do. Fulfill my commands and you can go to the grave in peace. Defy me, and your imagination could not describe the torment you will know."

"All I ask is a soldier's death, and my soul."

Captain Vilner's moonlike face popped into the tent, looking more fearful than a little while earlier when he announced Goering's arrival. "Another visitor," he said. "The SS is coming," Vilner amplified, his voice trembling. "He wants you and Colonel Morgan, outside, on the road."

Mordred's eyes flashed. "Is he the one we sent for?"

Kleist nodded somberly. "Most likely."

"Then we'll parley."

The pair emerged from the tent to watch the starlight bathing the rolling Norman countryside. The village in the valley below looked peaceful. On the hill behind them, the stones of Chateau D'Eauville glowed like a skull. The open black Mercedes purred like a panther as it rolled up to meet them on the gravel road. One man drove alone.

The nocturnal visitor's equine face was marked by almond-shaped eyes, the heritage of some outrider for Attila, and a pale scar that ran the length of his prominent cheekbone. The silver death's head on the SS man's black-and-silver peaked cap flashed in the moonlight. In lieu of a salute, the visitor nodded almost imperceptibly.

"I am Obergruppenführer Reinhard Heydrich. Which one of you is Morgan, the one whose fame grows in Berlin with every fresh attack on London?"

Mordred bowed. "I am Morgan, though I have many names."

Heydrich nodded. "You had an offer, I believe, transmitted by Enigma code to Reichsführer Heinrich Himmler, commander in chief of the SS and bodyguard to the Führer himself."

"And am I favored with a response?"

The almond eyes twinkled. "I speak for the Reichsführer. What is the offer?"

"The British king and the warlord Churchill, dead as last night's fire, and credit to you."

"By what means is this to be achieved?"

"Pinpoint aerial attack. No survivors. No loose threads."

"And if the plot fails?"

"It dies with me and no blame is attached to you, or your masters."

"I have few masters on this earth," Heydrich said.

"Nor I, Heydrich. Nor I." Their eyes met in an instant of nocturnal recognition. Even Kleist in his weakened state could see the two were kin, brothers under the skin. They knew one another across the currents of time.

"And for this favor, Oberst Morgan? What does the colonel want from the SS?"

"I am related distantly to the British crown. It's a blood tie that is important to my family, who have a claim to some ancient lands denied them. After we invade, I crave a position."

"What position?"

"Regent. Lord Protector. There are princesses, I believe. Two of them."

Heydrich's thin lips tightened into a saurian imitation of a smile. "You don't ask for much, Oberst Morgan. A German colonel on the throne of England, and the little princesses in the Tower?"

"I can give much. The king. The kingdom. The island, ready for the taking. A people confused and helpless without a king, or a war leader."

"And you believe the English would submit to you, ahead of all other warriors of the Reich?"

"I possess a talisman they will recognize. A proof of my kinship. They will know it, and in their moment of loss and dread, they will fear me."

"What is this talisman?"

"A sword in a stone."

The SS man's eyes widened. "This artifact is known to the Reichsführer. He has searched for it."

"He has searched for it, but it is possessed by me. It belongs in my family, and we belong at court in London."

Heydrich turned so his fair skin glowed pale in the moonlight. His profile shared with Mordred the aspect of the predator gazing down from on high, surveying the prey. He turned and stared at Kleist.

"We are jealous, General Kleist," Heydrich said. "How is it that we lost this man to the Luftwaffe? He thinks like an SS man."

"He does, indeed," Kleist said hollowly. "Colonel Morgan is one of you by nature." Mordred smiled and bowed. Heydrich rested his razor chin on his fine violinist's hand and stared up at the night sky, lost in thought and the moon. Finally, he spoke.

"SS foreign intelligence, the SD, is well connected to the Court of Saint James." Heydrich spoke in a confidential, almost chatty tone. "Our source in the palace is most reliable. King George and the war minister Churchill will go to Coventry tomorrow by motor convoy."

"Then, they will die together on the road."

Heydrich nodded. He lit a cigarette and the end glowed red. "Goering promised you a field marshal's baton, Oberst Morgan. If you succeed in this, Reichsführer Himmler will improve that offer considerably."

Mordred stepped back, surprised. "Your ears are keen and sharp."

"We are everywhere."

Mordred nodded, impressed. "I see that now. I feel as though I am meeting my own kind."

As the first pink streaks of dawn crossed the eastern sky, a flare lit up the fading night above the village. "What is that?" Heydrich demanded.

"A flare," Kleist said. "Fliers use them when they ditch in the Channel."

The magnesium illuminated the sky over the village. The flare's streamers dripped to earth like the light from a star in the east. In the distance, a chatter of machine guns chirped from the village.

From the tower, Arthur watched the streets glow white from the flare as if the power of a million stars reflected from the cobblestones. Arthur wounded two soldiers with short bursts from the machine pistol as they ran across the square. He fired a long burst to finish them. The Schmeisser jumped jerkily in Arthur's grip. It handled as easily as a mace.

The Gestapo man in the black leather jacket marshaled his dwindling force behind the truck parked in front of the cafe. His squad of a dozen men had been halved. He peered up and saw only darkness in the steeple.

As he watched the square below, Arthur prayed for forgiveness for the blood already shed.

Unarmed, he had run down the steeple steps, attempting to escape into the village. He rushed by the sacristy as the soldiers burst through the chapel doors. The king reached for the nearest weapon at hand and speared the first trooper with a candleholder. That soldier stumbled back out of the chapel and died on the church steps.

The next soldier charged him with rifle and bayonet. Arthur swung the priest's censer and split the man's skull. The sick sweet aroma of incense mixed with blood filled the chapel.

The brained soldier fell to his knees in front of the confessional and died.

The king grabbed the brained soldier's rifle and swung it like a club, killing another pair of troopers. He scooped up the Schmeisser machine pistol and the rifle and retreated up the spiral stairs into the recess of the bell tower. The survivors fled.

Now, the remaining troops besieged the chapel. But they lived each minute of the terrible dawn in mortal fear of what the man in the bell tower might do. At the moment, he was praying.

The light from the flare dwindled. Across the eastern sky, the gray dawn spread and the moon evaporated into the purple horizon.

The Gestapo man feared the English maniac would kill them all.

"I want reinforcements from the castle," the Gestapo man said, his words escaping his lips in nervous, frosty puffs. "Get me the radio, Sergeant."

"The radio is smashed," the sergeant replied. "The English devil dog got it."

"Telephone, then. We need more men."

"The telephone is in the post office across the square. The flier's got a clear line of fire. Do you want to go and make the call, Sturmbannführer?"

As the sergeant spoke, he tied a pressure bandage on a trooper's leg. The soldier grabbed hold of the sergeant, his eyes fixed on the sergeant's Iron Cross. "Easy, lad," the sergeant counseled. "Don't look at the blood."

Panic crept into the Gestapo man's voice. "We must have reinforcements. We are pinned down."

"We need more troops, many more," the sergeant said with a professional's detachment. "I've never seen one man kill four with his bare hands. The man in that church is a human panther."

"You hold down the position, Sergeant. I'll drive to the castle and get help."

"That might not be wise, Sturmbannführer," the sergeant said. "I understand the SS shoots a man for running."

"Are you calling me a coward?"

"Of course not," the sergeant said genially. "But we need your leadership. Send the wounded boy with a motorcycle runner. That'll make 'em get a move on back at headquarters."

The soldier with the leg wound whimpered, but he dared not speak. He so wanted his life that he knew he must not ask for it.

"Send the gimped bastard, then," the Gestapo man growled resentfully. He glowered into the wounded boy's face. "You'd better bring help. I won't forget your lucky escape."

"*Jawohl, Sturmbannführer.*"

The sergeant signaled to a corporal. "Get Schindler in the sidecar. I don't want him dead from hemorrhage before you bring relief."

The corporal helped the sergeant roll Schindler into the sidecar. The corporal kicked the starter and the motorcycle rumbled away, leaving the Gestapo man and the few soldiers to face the terror in the tower.

Arthur watched the motorcycle roll down the dark street. As he watched the truck and troops in the square below, the king wished he could fly away, that he had turned his Spitfire round when the fuel gauge hit the red mark.

"What now, Merlin?"

A black raven circled the tower and cawed. The king sensed movement behind him and swung the machine pistol. He stopped short, seeing the priest leaning against the parapet of the bell tower.

The priest's silver hair was cropped close like his beard, his features cragged as the face of a cliff, his skin brown and the texture of tanned hides. His medallion, the druid's mark, oddly resembled the RAF roundel. The old man's sad, starlit eyes filled Arthur's soul. It was Merlin, in body and soul.

24

The corporal on the motorcycle gunned his engine while the portcullis cranked up. The motorcyclist had to listen to Private Schindler's groaning in the sidecar while the black Mercedes carrying Heydrich, Mordred and Kleist rumbled ahead of him into the castle keep. As soon as he cleared the gate and roared into the inner bailey, the dispatch rider lifted the bleeding Schindler and carried him toward the Luftflotte Three headquarters' entrance.

"Corporal," Heydrich called out from the staff car, "how was that man wounded?"

"He was shot at the village, sir. He needs blood urgently." The corporal grunted. The dispatch rider saw the SS man's silver collar tabs and shivered. Even in the dim light he recognized Heydrich's scarred face from the newsreels, and stammered, "The Gestapo chief in the village urgently requests reinforcement."

"Partisans!" Heydrich declared. "I'll alert my bodyguard troops. We'll deal with it personally." The SS man gripped Mordred by the arm. "You will let nothing interfere with your mission." The pair's eyes met and they understood one another.

Mordred leaped out of the vehicle. Kleist climbed out after him and made a mighty effort to remain on his feet. As Heydrich's staff car raced through the castle gate, Mordred grabbed the dispatch rider, who buckled under the weight of the wounded private.

"What's happened down there?" Mordred demanded. "Was it partisans?"

"No, Oberst," the corporal said. "Herr Heydrich would not wait for an answer. An English pilot hiding in the church slaughtered six of our comrades. He has nearly killed this one, Herr Oberst."

Private Schindler fainted. Mordred pushed the wounded man away from the corporal so that he fell to the ground. "Six men killed by one? How?"

"Stabbed or bludgeoned most of them," the rider said, casting a fearful sidelong glance at Schindler. "The Englishman's a tiger.

"Really?" Mordred said, his voice increasingly agitated. "Tell me everything you saw."

The corporal stooped to tend to the unconscious Schindler, but Mordred pushed him away. The corporal shuddered at the sight of Mordred's glowing eyes.

"The Englishman ran a man through with a candle-holder. He brained another with a censer," the corporal said haltingly. "He had unnatural strength. He threw the bodies of Leni and Johannes out of the church like sacks of grain."

Mordred stared down at the wounded private. "He's come here to find me," Mordred said quietly. "I must find him first." Mordred scowled at the corporal. "Get out of here."

"Herr Oberst?"

Mordred kicked the corporal hard in the shin. He pulled a Luger automatic from his flight jacket and jammed the barrel up next to the corporal's ear. "Leave us," Mordred said. The corporal's eyes welled with terror, and he stumbled away backward across the courtyard.

Mordred prodded the unconscious private with his boot. "This one's dead. Now that's seven. Are common pilots in the habit of impaling their victims with holy relics? Do they kill squads of soldiers like horse-flies?"

Mordred's eyes were everywhere, like a creature possessed by devils. "It's him, all right," Mordred muttered. "We must go to the village," Mordred said, his voice dropping to a whisper. "Or I shall never see my throne."

Mordred marched to an alarm horn and pulled the lever. The high-pitched blast alerted the garrison. Within seconds, the battle-hardened troops of the Hermann Goering Division were streaming out the passageways of the castle.

Mordred jumped into the motorcycle sidecar and pointed at the saddle, ordering Kleist to mount. "So, Father," Mordred said quietly, "we meet again in mortal combat on holy ground."

"Your village phantom must be a real dragon, if you are more worried about him than orders from Heydrich," Kleist observed as he climbed onto the motorcycle and pushed the starter. For the first time in weeks, a shadow of a smile crossed his lips.

With sudden strength, Kleist shouted a few hoarse orders to the paratroopers. Moments later, the general was leading a truck convoy toward the village to slay the dragon in the tower.

*   *   *

In the steeple, Merlin gazed at Arthur with a pro-found solemnity. Then his starlit eyes surveyed the besieged village. In the distance, the wizard and the king heard the rumble of approaching engines. In the first glow of dawn, they saw the gray trucks on the road leading to the town square.

"I fear that will be Mordred," Merlin said.

"I could sense his nearness. He carries with him the smell of death."

"Any news of the book or blade, Arthur?"

"It's a long time since I've learned pleasant news. I've none to give."

Merlin sighed and the trucks rumbled through the crooked streets. As they stopped, each blocked an alley or lane. The paratroopers, with their bullet-shaped helmets and camouflage smocks, dropped heavily from the troop carriers. Like Arthur, they carried machine pistols. Unlike the king, they possessed abundant stocks of ammunition strapped to their chests.

Arthur stared down at the soldiers as they deployed with machinelike efficiency. For the first time, Arthur noticed a curious scaffold in the square. Twin perpendicular beams reached to the sky from a base formed by a table the size of a man. Suspended between the beams hung a blue steel blade.

"That device, Merlin. Is it some sort of siege machine?"

"For very personal sieges," the ancient remarked dryly. "It's an improvement on the chopping block. They call it a guillotine."

"There's no end of improvements in this age."

"It's much like your own time, Arthur. Chaotic and cruel, but bright with promise."

"I've seen the cruelty. I've yet to see the promise."

Merlin's deep-lined face didn't lack for compassion, but the wise man's penetrating gaze contained an austere severity. "Mordred and his kind seek to steal that promise and shape it to their own twisted purpose."

"What drives him? He could have known comfort at court."

"So long as he swore fealty to you. But Mordred did not want that. He doesn't seek comfort."

"What, then?"

"Your birthright. He seeks to rule, Arthur. In that way, you both want the same thing. But in this century, he will find many more of his own kind. And their rule is a dark dominion."

Merlin cocked his head, as if listening to faraway music. "Your season here is ending. With the moon in shadow, or the end of your own days, I cannot foretell which it will be. I lack the book."

"What is the book's power?"

"The pages of the twentieth volume tell the tale of my most distant travels. So, it gives foreknowledge to the one that holds it. This was the furthest I'd come, so I do not know the way ahead."

Arthur peered over the ledge. "Well, then, neither does Mordred. From this point, we make our own future. That is as it should be."

"But you are alone and surrounded, Arthur. Where are your comrades? Where is the one called Yank?"

"The others think me mad or a traitor," the king said hesitantly. "The Yank, I sent away."

"So you couldn't even lead Bill Cooper into the fray? You remain a solitary champion, Arthur. It's your pride. And your fall. You never could accept help, save from me. But there are times when magic won't work and victory must be won in the realm of the real."

Arthur watched the paratroopers setting up crew-served weapons, heavy machine guns, each pointed at the church. A team of sappers unreeled wire attached to a box with a handle on it. Arthur lifted the

Schmeisser and aimed at the soldiers with the wire spools, but they scrambled behind the trucks before he could spit more death from the gun.

Arthur looked up from the gunsight. "Once, Merlin, I felt unstoppable and without need of counsel, except for yours. Now, I feel doubt."

A trace of a smile crossed the old man's lips and his strange eyes brightened. "I never heard you express doubt. That's fresh."

"I don't want to die now, Merlin. There are things I've still to do." Arthur lowered the gun and grimaced. "I've met a woman, of this time."

"Is she bright with promise?"

"Oh, bright. Bright as the morning. She's a healer named Jenny. She's soft, but strong. And she's like you, Merlin. She's wise."

"Such women exist. Sometimes they can complete a man."

"I don't want to lose her."

"I understand," Merlin said. "All whole men dread such loss on the eve of battle."

A motorcycle pulled up behind one of the trucks. Two men clambered out of the cycle and sidecar. The one who climbed out of the sidecar doffed his leather helmet and stared up at the church.

"Mordred," Arthur whispered.

"I'll not be with you long," Merlin said. "It took most of my power to bring you here, and the rest was used up to bring myself. Like any real work, magic can be terribly wearying."

Suddenly, Merlin slumped. The movement startled Arthur. In all their times together, the king considered Merlin sturdy as an oak, supple as a yew bow. The ancient reached for his stick, which rested beneath the edge of the parapet. He grasped it, and immediately, his fingers closed with renewed vigor. Color returned to his cheeks. "That's better."

"Are you well, old man?"

The wizard nodded. "Now, I am restored. I'll have to take the staff. I've been too long without it."

Arthur stared at his mentor, the warrior, priest and magician. He felt a sense of pending loss. "Is there anything you can tell me, Merlin?"

The brushy brows above Merlin's hawklike eyes twitched. Arthur lost himself for an instant in the starlit flecks that flickered in the constellation of Merlin's eyes. The eyes changed again, taking on the appearance of an owl's, the wisdom, the tenderness of the patriarch bird.

"O, king," the priest said almost tenderly, "the answer to the riddle of this age and all others lies in your heart. If you survive the day, you will know more. If you lose the day, it will not matter."

"Old man," Arthur said in anguish, "what good was the quest if I've come only to die in Gaul at the hands of my hellspawned son?"

"Every journey has its purpose. You lost the sword Excalibur in a careless moment," Merlin said. "The same way you lost your kingdom. Forget your precious, regal self and consider forgiveness."

"Forgive the unspeakably cruel enemy?"

"Consider it. And if you should make it home to where Camelot calls, meditate on the strength of kindness over regal exercise of power." The old man's face became animated, and his hand grasped Arthur's wrist like the talon of some great bird.

"Bright promise is what I raised you for, Arthur Pendragon." The old man's voice deepened as if coming from within an ancient oak. "All my strength and power is dedicated so that you may live." Merlin sighed. "Win the day, Arthur, and give all of time a measure of hope."

The wizard embraced the king and Arthur felt the old man's love surrounding him, and he felt lifted, elevated as if he might himself levitate and fly free above the village.

A small truck with a quartet of trumpets mounted on it rolled into the square. An amplifier's screech pierced the king's ears. The static whine sounded to the king like so many souls burning in hell. Next, he heard a familiar voice that boomed from the horns atop the sound truck, mixing with the amplified static. The voice became clear.

"Father! You didn't think I'd forget you up there?"

Mordred's taunt echoed off the village walls. Arthur turned and Merlin was gone. He heard the flutter of raven wings and looked to see a bird winging west that held a large twig in its long claws.

"I hear you, Mordred," Arthur called out. "There's no need to throw your voice from a demon box. I know it's you."

"Of course it's me," Mordred retorted. "What else would lure you to Norman territory? Love of the French?"

"I came for love of my land. You can help her, too. Open your heart and listen."

"What silly song am I supposed to hear in my hollow heart, Father?"

"First, my apology for not acknowledging you."

The loudspeaker on the truck fell silent. Only the scratch of static crackled and snapped, reverberating off the ancient stones and slate roofs. The loudspeaker crackled with hot, heavy breath popping in the microphone.

"What did you say?" Mordred demanded.

"It dawns on me clear as the new day, Mordred. I wronged you."

"Have you been struck by lightning, Father?"

"Perhaps. Through the night watch, I have meditated on why you should hate me so. And it came to me with the light."

"And the light told you that you should love me, King Arthur? Your sworn and dread enemy?"

The king hesitated. He spoke carefully. "I realized that I was cold. I pushed you away when I should have drawn you near. I am sorry. I apologize to you, my son."

Arthur heard what might have been a sigh escape from the demon box. The king leaned over the parapet and held the young man's eyes in his own, steady gaze. Suddenly, Mordred's eyes hardened, green as emeralds. He regained himself.

"So near to death, you shame yourself, Arthur," his voice boomed hollowly across the square. "A cheap *ruse de guerre.*"

"There is no trick, Mordred. I would make peace."

"Sound strategy with your back to the wall," Mordred retorted. "Do you also intend to make peace with my friends?" He gestured to the troops.

"I cannot surrender to Huns, my son. They come to destroy our kingdom."

"My kingdom, Arthur. Lay down your weapons and we'll see about peace."

"I cannot do that. But if battle is joined, let me fight the Huns. Stand aside. Let there be no more blood shed between us."

Mordred shouted a command. A bolt snapped on a machine pistol. Then another, and another. A squad of paratroopers cleared the way and Arthur spotted a lean, commanding figure in black livery. The man in black had a long scar marking his pale, cold features and he, too, carried a machine pistol.

Heydrich herded a group of a dozen local women before him. Two women held infants in their arms. Another led a ragged girl by the hand. One old woman wept and the SS chieftain slapped her. The others walked on in silence. They entered the square, looking back, fearfully, at the man in black and the cold-eyed squad of ebony-clad soldiers guarding him.

The women sensed what lay ahead and their faces were filled with terror. Heydrich put his boot in the back of the old woman, shoving her forward. He waved the machine pistol and the women trembled. The group shuffled onto the church steps and stopped, still as a single animal facing a hunter. Now, the ragged little girl began to cry.

"What do you know about dynamite, Father?" Mordred's voice boomed. "They use it now for breaking sieges. It makes things go boom and vanish."

"More slaughter, Mordred?"

"You decide, Father. You can surrender, or I shall send your little church to hell, with the women and babes in the bargain. It's not on as grand a scale, but it would be something like the way I laid waste to Coventry last night. That was a nice church, too."

Arthur's shoulders slumped. He leaned over the parapet and dropped the machine pistol. It bounced and clattered on the stones. "You should take confession, Mordred. Your soul is forfeit."

Mordred laughed. "The devil will take my confession."

Arthur brushed dust from the RAF pilot wings on his breast pocket and straightened his blue Irvin jacket. As he descended the stairs, he heard the women below him, weeping. Arthur walked past the women huddled between the pews, and whispered his penance. He felt his heart pounding strong in his chest. His thoughts were of Jenny. As he stepped into the square, the blue steel blade of the guillotine flashed in the morning sun.

25

The ground fog steamed up from the earth in the gray morning light. Yank sat Indian-style atop the dirt revetment used to shield the Spitfires from airfield attacks. He stared ahead, oblivious to the men working feverishly to repair the bomb-cratered runways. His trousers were soaked with dew but Yank didn't care. He tossed the knife mechanically. By turns, it would spin on the flat of the blade, or it would stick in the grass. Cooper would pick himself up and retrieve the knife, then return to the exact spot and repeat the process.

Jenny approached him as he pulled the commando blade from the wet ground. He saw her coming, but paid her no mind. He wiped the blade on his trousers and returned to the place flattened by the seat of his pants. He threw the knife and it landed on the flat of the blade. Yank shook his head, disgusted by his lack of aim. Jenny watched him in silence.

Her medical cape was in tatters and her face was filthy, streaked with dust and dried blood. She looked like a refugee from the "March of Time" newsreels. She kneeled on the ground beside Cooper as he raised the dagger.

"It was the only place I could think to come," she said bleakly. "Arthur hasn't returned." She made the question a statement uttered in a tone devoid of hope.

"You look like hell, Doc." Yank turned to her. "Get caught without your umbrella?"

"Yes, at Coventry. That's a dangerous game to play with a knife."

He tossed the knife and it landed, point in the ground. Yank grinned strangely. "You throw the sticker in the ground, call mumblety-peg and win."

"If you lose?"

"Throw it again. It can go on forever."

"Like war."

"You said it. Huns burned our field again. Who else got it? London?"

"I told you. It was Coventry."

Yank started. He turned and stared hard at Jenny. "Arthur said it would be Coventry."

"Once a pilot's gone missing, that's the end, isn't it?"

"Mostly," Yank replied. He walked over and picked up the knife and stared at the blade. His lips moved as he read the word engraved on the blade above the maker's mark from Sheffield. "Excalibur," he murmured. He watched Jenny's breath form a little cloud in the wet cold of morning.

"Jenny, how did he know about Coventry?"

She looked at him, but seemed to look through him, her green eyes faraway and distracted. "They killed Edith."

"Oh, no."

"She begged me not to leave her while I ran out for my medical bag," Jenny said softly. "But I did leave. And the bomb fell and she was gone." Yank reached to touch her and she pulled away. "Isn't that the way, though, Bill? We're never able to save the ones we love. They die, get sick, get killed. They leave us and there's nothing to do."

"We can't save anyone, Jenny. It's a crazy world."

"I came here looking for Arthur," she said. "Or to find some feeling of him." The words began to tumble from her in a breathless rush. "I had a hope he might not be dead. I know that's not so, now. At least you've got his knife. I don't have anything. It's as if he never existed."

Jenny's shoulders slumped. A sigh, then a great, heaving sob escaped from her. The hot tears streamed in rivulets down the streaks that marked her face. Yank dropped the knife and took her in his arms, and she folded herself into them. He held her tightly.

"Where do they go?" she cried. "Where do they go when they leave us behind? How can they do it, Bill? It's so cruel. If they knew what we felt, they could never leave us."

He held her tighter and hugged her, as if she were a small child. He didn't know what else to do. "Let go, Jenny. Let it go. I'm sorry."

"No," she said through sobs. "Don't apologize. You couldn't save Arthur any more than I could protect Edith."

"I needed ten minutes' fuel." He dabbed at her face, the dirt smudging hopelessly with the tears so that she looked nearly like a singer in blackface.

"No, stop. You're making it worse." She reached into the pocket of her cape and produced a silk handkerchief. "I'll use this."

"No, don't," he said, grabbing her wrist. "It's too

nice. C'mon. I'll walk you to the mess, or what's left of it. We'll get you cleaned up."

Yank replaced the knife in his boot. They climbed down from the revetment and walked past salvage crews and grunting airmen who poured hot asphalt slurry into the bomb craters. A work gang pushed a wrecked Spitfire off the field. Halfway to the mess, they heard an aircraft buzzing overhead. Looking like a memory of the last war, the old Hawker Hart biplane bumped noisily onto the field. Yank hadn't seen it since he'd taken Arthur airborne in it for his flying lesson.

"That's probably the last flyable aircraft at RAF Hornchurch," Yank said bitterly. "I taught Arthur to fly in that jalopy."

"He wasn't a pilot already?"

"Not until he started shooting down Huns."

"I don't understand."

"Neither do I. Doc, gimme your kerchief." Jenny looked at the kerchief. She looked up to see Yank smiling. She gave it to him and Yank held it to his nose and sniffed its scent.

"Lavender. It's nice." He nodded toward the mess. "There's a phone that might still work. Stubbs'll get you transport back to the hospital." Yank stuffed the handkerchief in the pocket of his leather jacket. "I may need it," he said. He marched off toward the biplane.

"Bill!" Jenny called out. "Where are you going?"

"Pas de Calais, or straight to hell, whichever comes first," he shouted. Now he was running. He turned and shouted, "If I find Arthur, I'll send you a post-card."

Yank bounded onto the bottom wing of the Hart. An airman was handing a box of spare parts down from the rear seat to the ferry pilot. Yank grabbed the airman by the shoulders and tumbled him onto the ground. He dropped into the bucket seat of the open cockpit and pulled on the leather helmet and goggles that hung draped from the stick.

Yank took the stick of the idling aircraft and pushed the throttle forward. He felt the big tires begin to roll bumpily down the field. The Hart, old as it was, contained an enormous engine and could make nearly 200 mph with a tailwind. Yank leaned his head out the open cockpit. He saw the blurred faces of the running airmen rush by, and the wind brushed raw across his face. The Hart took a flying leap and bumped into the air, and suddenly the biplane's double wings were lifting him high, a kite rising above the field.

He looked down once to see Jenny waving. Her red hair blew freely round her shoulders in the wash of the Hart's propeller. Frantically, she waved a blue scarf.

Yank pulled on the stick and banked the biplane toward Folkestone and the Channel. He grabbed the silk kerchief from his pocket and raised it high above his head, where it snapped in the windstream like a lady's favor.

Cooper dropped the biplane so it barely skipped above the Channel boil. He flew low so the visual clutter from the dark water and waves might hide the silvery crate from roving Luftwaffe hunter-killers. The dense, salty air burned his lungs and the cold slashed at his neck between the kerchief and his collar. The engine torqued the fuselage to starboard so he held the stick hard to port to keep the nose pointed straight ahead. It was exhausting open-cockpit work that returned to him in a rush of memory.

*   *   *

On toward sunset in upstate New York that autumn evening in 1930, Bill Cooper's heart pounded with a ten-year-old's terror and exaltation. His dad smelled of shaving soap and Old Overcoat rye. Big Bill gave the boy a stick of Beeman's and hoisted him by his denim overalls like he was another sack of mail. The DeHavilland's cargo hold was dark and smelled of creamy letters and excelsior stuffing in packages. Big Bill handed the boy the Indian blankets. They smelled warm and coarse.

"You want to lay still so you don't shift the load, Billy," the lanky flier in the leather jacket told the boy. "Your ears get to hurtin', you chew on that gum extra hard."

The boy nodded.

"There's a Coke-Cola waitin' at the Brockerhoff after we clear the Bellefonte Gap," Big Bill said.

The flier buckled the leather straps that secured the cargo hatch. In the twilight, the boy watched a blur of windblown weeds through the porthole as the DeHavilland gained takeoff speed. The mail sacks cushioned him as the baby buggy wheels bounced off the field.

The U.S. Post Office DH-4 flew banked slowly as it headed west into the sun setting behind the Alleghenies. The temperature dropped as they gained altitude and lost the last light. The steady explosion of the engine vibrated the craft. The boy huddled in the mackinaw coat and pulled the Indian blanket around him. This would be the longest trip ever. All the way to Cleveland, with overnight for the refuel in Bellefonte, Pennsylvania.

Little Bill flew for the first time when he was five, in a Curtiss Jenny. Big Bill bought the Jenny as surplus for a hundred dollars. He sold the plane to quit barnstorming after the government hired him for the airmail service. The steady work allowed him to buy a little house in Hartford instead of moving all the time.

The fights ended when Mama left. She left after Big Bill told her he'd never quit flying. Billy's sister, Meg, did the washing and kept the house ready for Big Bill's frequent arrivals and departures. He'd hit the door exhausted, and sometimes he drank too much Old Overcoat. Billy remembered the whiskey smell. He was too little to remember much of Mama.

The two Bills were happiest around airplanes. The boy would sit on a wooden bench in the hangar shop and watch his father work on the engine like a garage mechanic. The castor oil smell in the hangar laquered over the Old Overcoat on Big Bill's breath.

Upstairs at home, little Bill would stare at the medals on the purple cloth and Big Bill pronounced the name of each one with care, including the Croix de Guerre pinned on him and Eddie Rickenbacker by Marshal Foch. Foche pronounced like Boche, the French word for Huns. Little Bill wanted to be a knight of the air and kill Huns.

The snow swept in across the Alleghenies like a cloud of sugar. The thunderheads rolled in and collided, hiding the jagged peaks and erasing the stars that winked in the inky night. Bill watched the condensation gather in rivulets on the porthole. Then there was a white nothingness, and the DH-4's engine hiccuped. The rickety plane rose hundreds of feet and would drop suddenly, pitching like the deck of a ship in a storm.

Finally, the rickety marriage of sticks and fabric was swept into a downdraft. The plane plunged from whiteness, into blackness again, then further into the whiteness that was the side of a mountain rushing at them. Bill closed his eyes and clenched his fists, his teeth, his entire body. Then the plane swooped up. The DH-4's buffeting shook little Bill like a leaf, terrifying the boy, but he never believed for an instant his dad would crash.

In a plane, his dad could do anything.

The two Bills dined at the Brockerhoff. Turkey and trimmings, mashed potatoes, gravy. Fresh cranberries and Coca-Cola, on the house. Mail fliers never paid. They put Bellefonte on the map. The next morning, rested and fueled, the two Bills prepared the DH-4 for the next lap. The children of Bellefonte's primary school turned out to watch the takeoff, each consumed with silent envy as they watched little Bill help his dad.

Somebody snitched. Because when they got to Cleveland, the Post Office fired Big Bill Cooper.

The Cleveland postmaster wanted to fine Bill Senior two hundred and thirty-five dollars for the boy's weight as mail freight, but they let it go. They just called him a rummy and told him they'd mail him his pay.

Big Bill Cooper never got another steady flying job after that. Sober, he was a natural mechanic. Drunk, he was no use at the hangar or anywhere else. He stayed drunk until the social worker put little Bill and his sister Meg into the home.

Bill Junior flew solo at fifteen, about the time the old man took the cure for the first time. First Bill Junior ran errands at the airfield. He swept up and did odd jobs in return for flying lessons, but there wasn't that much he didn't already know.

The airlines had taken over the airmail, and the only barnstorming was out in Hollywood, where Howard Hughes hired only the best fliers from the Great War. So Bill Junior flew freight and dreamed of flying a Gee-Bee in the nationals. He hadn't seen Meg for three years when he got the telegram.

Consumption got Big Bill before the Overcoat did.

Then the Germans got Poland, and England got into the war with the French, just like Big Bill's war. Bill Cooper, Jr., crossed the border to Canada to find the RAF recruiting post. They called every American who turned up a "Yank" and wanted to know if they had previous flying experience.

The engine torque kept Yank's mind focused on just holding the stick straight. To bank left, he just let the stick go to center a bit and it sideslipped. He watched the waves rolling up on the talcum powder beaches of the Normandy coast. The hedgerows flashed by beneath him like the ties of railroad tracks on a speeding train.

He saw a farmer standing atop a haywagon give the "V" for victory sign and Cooper wagged his wings, feeling for an instant like a flying ace from the Great War. He blushed, suddenly, realizing he had yet to shoot down a single enemy plane.

"Not so great, yet," he murmured. "Even Arthur's got kills."

Cooper checked his gauges and his heart skipped a beat, with the fuel needle resting near the "empty" mark. He banged on the glass and the needle bounced back to the half-full mark. Yank grunted in relief and edged the throttle forward, pushing the old biplane bomber along at treetop level.

The Stuka dive bomber dropped out of the sun. The Stuka pilot, spotting the silver biplane with the RAF roundels on its wings laughed out loud at the easy pickings. The dive bombers rarely attacked another aircraft. Their sharply angled wings and clawlike undercarriage made them resemble nothing so much as a hunting hawk. But the Stuka's mission was precision bombing, not aerial combat. Yank heard the piercing shriek from the Stuka's dive whistles and looked up at the last instant. A dark projectile hurtled by.

The bomb hit the ground, sending a curl of flame and smoke up from the trees as Cooper's aircraft rushed forward. He let the stick go and the plane swung hard left, nearly in a compass circle. As the Hawker biplane spun around, the Stuka dived into the path of Yank's twin Browning guns. Bill Cooper fired a long, continuous burst and the Stuka exploded.

"Christ!" Bill shouted.

The kill had happened so quickly that everything changed before Yank realized. He was thundering through the air, alert and suddenly unafraid. He looked ahead to the forbidding turrets of Chateau D'Eauville with the neatly parked Messerschmitts and Heinkels parked behind a ring of ack-ack guns. Yank let the stick swing left a bit, turning the bomber away from the castle and airfield. Dead ahead, he spotted the twin steeples of the village D'Eauville. He opened the throttle and climbed to get a better look.

26

Arthur gazed up at the twin spires of the guillotine that rose to the sky and formed a small truss to seat the blade. He watched the steel wedge slowly rise to meet the truss. Two sentries wearing black helmets with lightning flash insignias hoisted the cutting edge a notch at a time, using a cranked pulley. A shirtless giant supervised, with his muscular arms folded and his face concealed behind the black executioner's hood.

"So, they still have need of your kind," Arthur remarked to the hooded man. "How little things change." The headsman stood silently, his unblinking eyes taking measure of the sunburnt thickness of the king's neck.

Across the square, the sun crossed between the twin steeples of the church. Arthur heard the songbirds and breathed deeply. With his wrists manacled and his enemies surrounding him, he took a moment to look at the sky, a dreamlike blue adorned with puffs of cumulus like a woman's sleeve. He imagined that he saw Jenny, half hidden by the veil of clouds.

In that instant of clarity, he felt so close to the woman healer. His quest to save the kingdom seemed abstract and general. He realized that in loving Jenny, he loved life itself. Life was the kingdom, and the realization of love was the quest. His heart was at peace in the knowledge of his love, even if warfare raged on earth. In the cold, pale faces of his guards he saw only death. He felt pity for them, that they existed only to serve the executioner. He knew, though, that death could not triumph, because life sprang anew in every moment of living.

Arthur was held fast by two black-liveried varlets. Their hair was the color of straw and their eyes were pale ash from a dead fire. They wore garish red armbands with a runic cross. The silver braid on their caps told Arthur they were palace guards. In his free hand, one of the guards held the large iron ring with the key to Arthur's shackles.

With each step to the scaffold, Arthur's power of observation became more acute. The sleeve ribbon on one of his guards bore the words "Adolf Hitler" embroidered in silver filigree. Arthur spoke the word or two he knew of Hun-speak. The words dropped awkwardly off his tongue. The guards ignored him.

"Is Hitler your chief?" he repeated. He then saw his son make his way through the throng of stone-faced soldiery in the square and run up to the scaffold, leading a pair of guards who labored under the weight of a stuffed pig.

Mordred bounded up the steps, leading two soldiers who hoisted the swine with the apple stuffed in its mouth. The soldiers lugged the shoat up onto the scaffold and shoved it onto the guillotine's bed.

"This is a test," Mordred said gleefully. Arthur saw

the swine's head placed into the guillotine's collar piece. Mordred shouted a command and the blade dropped with a hiss and the swine's head separated from the shoulder and dropped neatly into a basket by the scaffold.

Mordred removed the spiced apple from the severed head and tossed it in the air, catching it like a ball. He smiled at Arthur. "Hello, Father," he said, holding the apple toward the king. "Want an apple? No?"

"You give orders to these black-liveried varlets like you were a proper Hun officer, Mordred. You've become one of them."

"Oh, no. I'm a Briton, just like you. But there are differences that divide us. Soon, your head will grace a pike and mine will wear the crown."

"Britain will never surrender to you, Mordred."

"I won't ask them politely. I have powerful allies. As you can see, the throne is mine to seize. You can't stop me this time, foolish Father."

"You could never really reign, son. You were always taken in by your swinish friends. It's your diseased mind that makes you a usurper. Even on the throne, you could not rule. You lack purpose."

"Don't be tiresome, Father. One more lecture and I think I'm going to stuff this apple in your mouth. Then I'm going to crush your lands."

"Our people are not so easily crushed. They have suffered your bombs, and burning, and then braced for more. They can take it."

"Really? We'll see about that after we kill their leaders." Mordred's eyes narrowed. "Check, then mate. After I send you to hell, your precious Britain will kneel for King Mordred."

"I doubt you will live to see that day, son."

"Still posturing, King Arthur? Even with your neck on the block? I only regret your head won't be loosened by Excalibur. That would be rich."

"Where is my sword?"

"Well hidden, until it suits my purpose to unsheath it."

Heydrich mounted the scaffold. He put his hand on Mordred's shoulder. Arthur recognized a word or two of Hun-speak, and he heard the officer whisper a word he recognized from the blond raiders of Tintagel: *"Schnell!"*

"What's the hurry, you Hun bastard?" Arthur said.

The halves of Heydrich's divided face twisted into a smile and he spoke a passable English. "Why do you speak, Tommy? You're already dead."

The SS chieftain gave the king a pat on the cheek and winked. Then the king spat in his face. Heydrich drew back, his Janus features contorted with rage. Mordred lunged forward to strike Arthur, but Heydrich grabbed his hand.

"In a few moments, you will be dead, Tommy," Heydrich said cooly. "But before you die, I want you to know that your beloved King George and Winston Churchill will also be dead before the day is ended. And so, the sun will set on the British Empire. Take that knowledge to the scaffold."

Arthur struggled against his manacles, but the SS guards held him fast.

"Well," Mordred said, "I haven't time for dead fliers. We have to get back to Coventry. Date with royalty, you know."

"Get him on the block," Heydrich ordered, and the SS men began lifting the king awkwardly onto the base of the guillotine.

"We won't see each other again, Father," Mordred gloated. "When they cut your head off, I hear the soul flies into limbo."

The SS men rammed Arthur against the base of the guillotine, and one hoisted his legs onto the bed. The king struggled, with the guards lifting him up on his back. Vainly, his eyes scanned the sky for a trace of a raven. The steel ring that held the guard's keys flashed before him and he grabbed for it. As he reached for the ring, he saw a flash of silver against a cloud.

Flying fifty feet off the deck, the blood raced in Yank's head and his heart still pounded from the Stuka duel. Flying above the road to the village, he could see the gray shoebox contours of German troop trucks. He flew past an outlying village with its small churchyard and cemetery, separated from the highway and vineyards by hedgerows. He planned to circle the village when he spotted the wreckage of Arthur's Spitfire in a field just outside the town.

Yank believe Arthur most likely would be taken prisoner in the village, or might have been spirited to the airfield by the castle. With the castle so heavily fortified, he opted to reconnoiter the village first. Suddenly, it dawned on him that he was flying by the seat of his pants, just like his dad. "There ain't no plan!" he shouted into the wind. "This is it!"

The single road leading to D'Eauville was wide enough to accommodate a pair of wagons to market. With the oddly angled rooftops of the village looming ahead, Yank banked his wings twenty degrees to drop between the cornices. He zoomed past roofs of medieval thatch. A pair of cranes bounded up, their wings spreading in front of Yank's propeller, nearly forcing the Hawker to plunge nose first into the ground. The great birds flapped crazily skyward, some of their feathers fluttering past Yank's goggles.

Yank opened the throttle, with the leaded panes of village inns and shops flashing by him like the windows of a speeding train. Yank cracked his gum and pulled the stick back, rising sharply. The Hawker Hart nosed up, nearly perpendicular above the village square.

He executed a graceful Immelmann loop, lifting the biplane in a slow elliptical half-circle above the square. He heard scattered rifle shots and then the chatter of machine guns. With the Hawker nose to earth, Yank saw the cobblestones rushing at him. He let go a short burst from his machine guns, scattering Goering Division soldiers like chickens in a barnyard.

As he hurtled toward earth, his hand gripping the stick, he saw a big man on the guillotine, struggling with his captors.

"Arthur King!" Yank shouted into the propeller wash and engine roar.

Arthur kicked one guard from the scaffold and struggled with the other. The king felt the struggling guard's holster rub against his leg. He felt the guard grabbing for his pistol. Arthur grabbed the man's other wrist. He pushed the hand that clenched the key ring down hard on the guillotine platform. He felt the pistol clear the holster.

The king saw the hooded, gleaming torso of the executioner lumbering at them. He felt the pistol clawing his back. The king rammed the guard in the groin with his knee and the pistol fired. Gunpowder filled Arthur's nostrils as he watched blood spurt from the headsman's chest. Felled by the wild shot, the headsman tumbled onto the guillotine release.

Arthur held the guard's arm high and gave a last push as he heard the powerful wedge of steel slice the air. The SS man's face turned white and his eyes popped wide as he stared at his gushing stump of an arm and passed out.

The king dropped from the scaffold, scooping up the key ring from the severed hand of the SS man. Arthur crouched, hearing the roar of the silver plane.

The king watched small bombs fall from the biplane wings and he tensed for the explosion. Instead, great clouds of powder burst on the cobblestones. Arthur heard the Huns shout "Gas!" but it looked like millers' flour to the king.

He watched the panicked Germans pulling on their gas masks and he wondered which mask concealed Mordred. Still, more flour projectiles hurtled into the square. As the powdery clouds rose flowerlike in the square, the king's eyes widened with amazement. At the far end of the square, he saw the silver biplane drop between the buildings that lined the entry road and bump forward onto the cobblestones, its propeller feathering and its guns firing.

The Hawker swung heavily around, and Arthur saw the Yank waving his gloved hand to urge him on. "Arthur! For Christ's sakes!"

The bullets began to fly from behind the clouds of flour dust and a ricochet hit Arthur's boot, knocking him off his feet. He stumbled and kept going. He heard the Hawker revving and the silver plane began to roll forward as more shots streaked through the air. Arthur ran raggedly as the ground fire intensified.

Yank's biplane gained speed and Arthur sprinted, his legs pumping like pistons. Arthur saw Yank steer the plane with one hand and reach with his other to grab for the king's out-thrust manacles. Yank grabbed and missed, the biplane lurched ahead as the bullets whizzed by.

"Try, Arthur!" Yank shouted. Arthur dropped his manacles around the boarding stirrup. Yank opened the throttle and the tail dragger gained speed in fitful bursts, dragging Arthur as it accelerated. One final push and the biplane bounced into the air, with the king hanging from the stirrup by his chains.

As the king was hauled airborne, he dangled, his feet windmilling. The biplane wobbled and fought to gain altitude and the king looked down on the receding rooftops of the village. With the wind howling past his ears, he looked up at the silver fuselage of the Hawker and felt the blood nearly drained from his hands, which clutched the key ring.

Hanging from the stirrup, Arthur felt each lurch of the plane like a man drawn and quartered. He heard the engine groan and the fuselage shudder. Oil streamed in brown, greasy streaks onto the silver fuselage and he saw streamers of black smoke and snicks of flame from the manifold. He looked down to see treetops rush beneath his feet like a green-gold carpet.

The engine stopped and the wind howled. "Arthur, let go!" Yank shouted above the whistle of empty air singing through the wires and struts.

The king pulled up with all his might, bringing his chest even with the manacles and the chain slipped free of the stirrup. His body whirled through the air and smashed into a tall hedgerow. The king's body rebounded from the hedge onto a clump of moss that knocked the wind from him. He looked round to see that he was lying among the dead.

He lay awhile in the ancient churchyard. On his back among the mouldering stones and iron saints, the blue stars swam before him, blinking through the brighter blue of the cold autumn sky. Dimly, his ears registered the thump of an explosion, like distant thunder. Then his nostrils filled with the stench of smoke and aviation fuel and he lost consciousness.

"Yank?" he murmured finally. "Have I killed you?" Bill Cooper walked up and leaned on a headstone. He peered down into Arthur's face and grinned.

"You didn't kill me, brother," Yank said, his face blackened with grease. "But if you don't get on your feet, the Huns're gonna kill us."

Gently, Yank loosened the key ring from Arthur's

grip and unlocked the manacles. The Yank then gripped Arthur by the wrist and pulled the king to his feet. They both looked up and saw a small German plane bank and roar by the churchyard. "Search plane," Yank said, ducking behind a gravestone. "I think he saw us."

Arthur took a tentative step and felt his knees crack, then crumple. Yank grabbed him and pulled one of Arthur's arms over his shoulder. "C'mon, Arthur, we've got to move. I saw trucks back on the road. Blitz troops."

Arthur nodded. His left ankle was sprained. The right leg was stiff. The king limped, hanging on to the Yank. The churchyard's iron gate hung rusty on its hinges. Yank pushed it, and it creaked open. The search plane buzzed angrily, barely clearing the roof of the small country chapel. Arthur and Yank backed against the lichen-covered wall and they rushed round the corner.

A German lunged at them with a rifle and bayonet.

Arthur dived for the soldier's knees in a tackling motion. The blue steel blade flashed by Yank Cooper's face, nicking him as he jumped out of the way. As the SS man tumbled forward, he kicked free of the king's arms and regained his feet. Snarling like an animal, the German rushed at Arthur and stopped suddenly, blood spewing from his lips.

The German dropped his rifle and reached for the commando dagger that Yank had hurled. He pulled at the knife buried deep in his chest. His fingers failed to close around the haft before his knees hit the ground. He looked at Yank with the unasked question that marks the eyes of the dying.

"Mumblety-peg," Yank murmured in amazement.

Arthur reached down and pulled the dagger from the German's chest. He closed the SS man's eyes with a smoothing motion of his hand. He wiped the blood from the dagger clean on his trouser leg. He ran his fingers across the letters on the blade of the knife and murmured, "Excalibur."

In the distance, they heard shouts. Cooper climbed the stone fence that circled the churchyard and chapel. He turned back to Arthur and said in a low tone, "Infantry. They're closing in."

Yank clambered down from the fence. "Arthur," he said simply, "it doesn't look good. Out there, I see one old plow horse hitched to a hay wagon and about a hundred Hun troops. We're gonna need more than a rifle and a couple of toad stickers."

Arthur picked up the dead guard's rifle, examined it briefly, then pointed it at the slain SS man. "What was this one guarding, do you suppose? He was separate from all the others."

The guard's helmet had fallen from his head, displaying the same shock of ash blond hair as Arthur's captors in the square. Yank tugged at the man's sleeve and examined the embroidered lettering on the cuffband. The Yank whistled. "Hitler's personal bodyguards."

The shouts of the infantry sounded closer. They were nearly in the yard.

"Let us go in the chapel," Arthur said. "We've done our best. We must pray and prepare to meet our Lord."

"And take out as many of the bastards as we can."

Arthur nodded and pulled open the sturdy oaken door of the chapel. Yank picked up the slain guard's rifle from where the king set it down and followed Arthur. The pair stepped into the stone cellar coolness of the little church. The chapel had fallen into disrepair. The stained glass windows had been blasted by bombs or artillery, allowing sunlight refracted in bright colors of red and blue to stream into the sanctuary.

The sunlight splashed brightly onto a black stone and anvil, holding fast a black sword: a large, two-handed sword, magnificent in its forging even beneath the coating of paint that had been poured on in a crude attempt to disguise it. Arthur's breath left him, and the word, like magic, escaped from his lips.

"Excalibur."

The king moved forward, as if in a dream. The sword and anvil were coated with black paint. The grinning death's head symbol of the SS had been stenciled in white onto the base of the stone, and in gothic lettering the words, *"Eigentum der Oberkommando SS."*

Arthur took the commando dagger and scratched at the base of the stone. Yank looked out the window and chambered a round into the bolt-action Mauser. "Just like Gary Cooper in *Sergeant York*," he muttered. "Here goes nothing."

Yank saw a motorcycle ramming the iron gate and rumbling into the churchyard. Still, Arthur scratched away at the base of the stone. Yank fired a round, killing the machine gunner in the sidecar. The motorcycle tumbled, the wheel spinning. He chambered another round and shot the cyclist. Arthur scratched furiously at the iron engraving, then ran his fingers across the letters.

Yank fired a third and fourth round.

Arthur uttered the words to himself. "Whomsoever shall pull this sword from this stone shall rightwise be crowned king of England."

"They're coming through the gate, Arthur!"

The king placed his boot on the black stone. He grasped the haft of the sword and tugged. It held fast beneath the black paint. Arthur pulled again, and still failed to prize the blade from the stone and anvil.

"I could use a little help, Arthur!" Yank shouted.

"Once. Twice. Thrice," the king cried. He gave it a third heave and the blade, almost imperceptibly, moved. "I am rightwise king of England," Arthur shouted.

"And I'm the pope!" Yank yelled. "Fix bayonets, Arthur. They're coming in."

The king pulled the paint-crusted haft free of the stone and the polished blue steel of Excalibur flashed as he swung it over his head. Yank turned his head briefly, hearing the long blade's wind song as it cut the air.

A squad of paratroopers burst through the chapel door and Arthur cried, "Excalibur!" The king bounded forward and the royal blade flashed like a shimmering scythe.

Yank stared, horrified, as he heard the cries of the dying and watched blood soar like a scarlet banner. None of the Nazi troops got off a shot before they fell, scattered, in parts across the entryway.

Bill Cooper looked at Arthur and gasped. He saw before him a large man wielding a bloody sword. He saw a light in Arthur's eyes that made him look as if he had dropped to earth from another time, an earlier and savage time. The king's chest heaved as he surveyed the cleaved bodies of Excalibur's toll.

"I would not do murder in the Lord's house, but we were offered no choice," Arthur said, panting. "There remains the Lord and Excalibur's will to be done," Arthur said, each word escaping his lips in a desperate breath.

"Who the hell are you?" Yank felt his knees buckle as he asked.

"Arthur, king of England."

"I'm dreaming," Cooper said. "You look like the man in the book."

"No, Bill, you're not," Arthur said. "Come help me save England." Arthur was already climbing through the shattered glass.

Yank stumbled after Arthur through the wrecked

window. He watched the king clamber up the stone
fence, holding the sword as if it were part of him.
Arthur peered over the stones, seeing the cordon of
infantry waiting, a hundred yards distant. They were
waiting for the all-clear from the storm troops in the
chapel, the signal that would never come.

The old farm horse also waited. Arthur snatched
an apple from the tree he balanced on and bit down
on it, holding it in his teeth. He clambered over the
stones and dropped to his knees. Yank rolled off the
fence and landed in a heap beside him. The horse
snorted. Arthur whispered in its ear and gave it the
apple. The horse snuffled.

A sergeant shouted a command and the infantry
rose up, as one, in a line of march, with their
weapons at the ready. Warily, they began advancing
toward the church.

Arthur swung Excalibur so it cut the dappled
steed's reins loose from the hay wagon. He motioned
for Yank to mount the nag. "Can't do it, Arthur,"
Yank whispered desperately. "I never rode a horse."

"And I never flew a plane," Arthur replied fiercely.
"Climb up on the wagon and slide over its arse if you
want to get home with me." Gingerly, Yank complied
while Arthur whispered an endearment in the beast's
ear.

Arthur gently poked Excalibur's blade into the
earth. He mounted the wagon steed, sliding easily
over its flanks in front of Yank.

"Hold on with your legs and put your arms round
my waist, Bill."

The king leaned down and pulled the sword from
the ground. He placed the shortened reins between
his teeth. With one hand, he lifted Excalibur to shoulder height, then joined the other hand to grasp the
sword and hold it above his head.

He gave the steed the sharp edge of his heels and

leaned forward. The nag walked, then trotted. Then, with another dig of the heels, miraculously, it began to run.

Sergeant Dieter Vogel had never before seen a man on a charging horse swinging a sword. It was the last sight he ever saw.

Some of the others watched the sword-wielding horseman vanish into the woods. Others watched the two halves of Sergeant Vogel fall neatly into the field. Not one soldier fired a shot.

The Norman steed carried Arthur and Bill into the woods at a trot, obeying the king's heels. Horse and rider seemed confident of each other. For all its years, the beast had pulled a hay wagon, answering the coax of the carrot or stick. It was a big steed, and strong, if a bit swaybacked and long in the tooth. But with the dig of the rider's heel, the horse sensed some fire in its blood carried down the line since the charge at Agincourt. It was a horse of sufficient size, strength and heart to carry an armored knight. Or two tattered fliers and one large sword.

Arthur dropped the reins and eased himself, painfully, to the ground. He reached into the tatters of his Irvin jacket and produced a fresh apple, which the stallion snagged with a knowing crunch of its great yellow teeth.

"Move forward on the beast's back," Arthur said. "You're going to take the reins."

Yank stared at the king. Since the church, he'd had no chance to appraise the wild man with the sword, a different Arthur than the one he knew. This Arthur seemed more himself, more natural. With their enemies on their heels, he was almost relaxed. Yank could not feel at ease on the horse.

"If you think I can make this nag go, you must be crazy, Arthur."

"We've come this far, Bill. Do you mean to tell me we'll die in France because you can't make this beast giddy-up?"

Bill turned to Arthur and met his gaze, eye-to-eye. "I want to know about the sword in the stone."

"There's no time, Bill. The king's in mortal danger."

"The sword, Arthur." Bill's breath caught. "Oh, my God. Arthur King. King Arthur. The sword. Oh, no." The Yank held his head as if it ached mightily. "My dad used to see snakes crawling the walls when he was tanked." Yank's chest heaved. "But I'm not tanked. I must be battle happy."

Arthur patted Yank's knee. "Don't think it to death, lad. The world's gone mad, hasn't it? Let's do our part to save our small share of it."

The Yank knit his brow and frowned in concentration. Quietly, he said, "Just tell me the sword was a trick, Arthur."

The king nodded patiently. "Bill, I don't know whether a machine that flies is magic, but it's strange to me. Right now we need a plane. That means you've got to make the horse go."

"Where are you going to be?"

"Right behind you." The king hefted his sword and swung it so it cleaved the air. "I wield Excalibur. You fly the horse."

Arthur whispered to the horse and it back-stepped to a fallen log. The king walked up the log as if it were a footstool and mounted behind Yank. Yank took the reins in both hands. The king, holding Excalibur over his head, clicked his tongue. "Squeeze the animal with your heels, Bill."

Bill obeyed, and so did the horse. Suddenly, the ground vibrated. The leaves shook in the trees. A gale twisted the branches and it felt as though the earth

were going to open beneath them. The horse whinnied as they heard the roar of hundreds of bomber
engines firing. Arthur clicked his teeth, and the steed
moved deeper into the woods toward the rumble of
the engines.

27

The BSA motorcycles, piloted by the smart-looking Grenadier Guards, wheeled into the forecourt at Buckingham Palace. The long, black 1938 Rolls Royce rolled in behind them, its smoked-glass windows concealing the bulldog face and long H. Uppmann cigar. It was a clear, "blitzy" day, with an open sky for bombers, but protocol demanded the appropriate array of vehicles and ceremony. In this case, as if for a funeral.

The old man, feeling dark and dyspeptic, crunched the tip of the Havana cigar heavily into the ashtray. He rolled down the bullet-proof glass window for a peek at Queen Victoria's memorial as the armored touring car prepared to roll through the palace gates. It looked the same as the morning he'd been summoned to court to accept the post of prime minister.

Churchill concluded that the king often felt uneasy in his presence, despite their friendship and common interest. Had the king ever forgotten Churchill's letter urging Parliament to oppose abdication for Edward, now duke of Windsor? Still, Churchill and the king found common cause for Britain, for the empire, for their island people. This day's pilgrimage to Coventry was one of those things that must be done in service of the English.

The prime minister donned his top hat and arranged the dress of his pinstripe trousers with the grace of a man of large girth. He accepted salutes from the guards with alacrity as he mounted the steps and entered the domain of His Majesty. His shoes tapped on the palace marble like the ticking of a clock.

The king accepted the prime minister's salutation, but his handsome, regular features remained possessed by a sadness depicted in one of his portraits from life. He was a tall and noble-figured man. Unlike Churchill, he never coveted leadership. He had wished to live his days out as prince. Now, he shared the reins of empire in wartime with the commoner, the bulldog spirit known simply to every Briton as Winston. Today, they grieved in common for the ancient city and its people, stunned in the flames and rubble of the Luftwaffe's assault.

"It has gone hard for the people of Coventry, then?" the king ventured.

"If anything, harder than for London, Your Majesty. Coventry, we now know, was utterly unprepared for the Blitz. We are doing what we can to feed and clothe the survivors. All who survived know of someone who did not."

"The children?"

"Some remain in the city. Hardest for them, I should say. Hardest for the motherless ones. Then, also, there is a shortage of water and shelter and an abundance of burst sewage and gas lines. We must work quickly to ward off disease."

The king winced. But finally, he had come to respect Churchill's blunt eloquence in service to the truth. "We must go."

"Indeed, Your Majesty. If the English are there and suffer, we must show our faces to them, and let them know we share their pain."

"We can do no less," the king agreed. "The cathedral?"

"The walls still stand. It's a hallmark of the Nazis' blasphemy, Your Majesty. The rest of the cathedral is rubble."

The king nodded sadly. The tall monarch and the House of Commons man left the king's chambers in lockstep, their pinstripes and tails whispering behind them. As they descended the steps to their separate vehicles, the Guards snapped their rifles to port arms.

The skies over London were silent. The barrage balloons hovered near the palace like storm clouds. The Guards escort slammed the doors on the leaders' cars. The motorcycle escorts' engines gunned to life, and the men at Britain's helm set their compass for the road to Coventry.

The Stuka pilot adjusted his goggles as the big Junkers engine roared up to takeoff rpms. The tail gunner moved his MG-15 machine gun up and down in its cradle and locked the cockpit glass in open position. The pilot gave the dive bomber enough throttle to roll forward on the grass field. Even taxiing for takeoff, the Stuka was a fearsome-looking bird of prey. The sharply angled wings resembled a vulture's. The talon-shaped landing gear made the Stuka dive bomber the symbol of blitzkrieg.

The Stuka's engine hit the high revs and the plane rumbled across the expanse of autumnal, grassy field that bordered the stand of poplar trees on the hill.

Arthur took note of the blowing wind sock as he peered over Yank's shoulder. In the distance, he could see the French castle with its Nazi pennants blowing in the wind. He also saw the Yank's fists trembling slightly as they clutched the reins. "Easy, Bill. Riding is much easier than flying."

"I've never flown a nag," Yank said, his breathing shallow and rapid. He was pale and Arthur could see him fight to control his hands.

The Stuka began to gather speed, rolling forward on the grass. Yank caught his breath as he saw the cockpit glass slide backward, allowing the wind to blow in the pilot's face. "He's gaining speed. We're gonna lose him."

"Go now," Arthur said. He gathered a great gust of air into his lungs and shouted "Forward, Battle!" The steed was moving before Yank could dig his heels in. The dappled swayback galloped down the hill.

"My balls!" Yank shouted as the steed gained speed and its backbone rose up like a wave hitting Yank's manhood. The steed raced across the airfield, its hooves striking sparks on stones and slicing great flying clods of earth.

"Balls!" Arthur shouted gloriously.

The Stuka gunner's eyes widened as the gray steed charged the plane. He shouted into the radio, but the pilot was giving full attention to takeoff preparations. The pilot leaned forward, pushing the throttle toward takeoff speed, until he sensed motion at his side. He turned to see the horse and riders galloping along nearly even with the aircraft's wingtip. He saw two ragged RAF fliers, one swinging a great, two-handed sword over his head.

The sight so startled the Stuka pilot, he let go of the throttle and the JU87 dropped speed. The flier pushed the stick hard to starboard and the dive bomber fishtailed. Arthur hopped from the steed

onto the wide wing surface of the Stuka as the aircraft slowed to a stop, its engine groaning in protest
from the aborted takeoff.

Arthur snagged a radio aerial on the wing with
Excalibur's hilt just as the pilot got his hand back on
the throttle. The bomber jerked along the taxiway
and Arthur pulled his body even with the aerial. The
king was lying prone, spread over the wing's black
cross marking. The pilot reached into his jacket for a
pistol and fired three wild shots.

Yank rode surprisingly well, trotting a few yards off
alongside the careening aircraft, frustrating the tail
gunner's efforts to swing his barrel around. Yank saw
one of the pilot's pistol shots knock Arthur from his
footing, back flat onto the wing. Strangely, the king
seemed unhurt. He kept crawling toward the pilot,
never losing his grip on the long, fearsome sword.

Arthur grabbed the radio aerial, rose on one knee
and thrust the four-foot blade of Excalibur fero-
ciously, stabbing the pilot in the neck. Blood spurted
from the flier's artery and Excalibur's steel cut short
the pilot's death cry.

The plane swung heavily around as Arthur reached
and grabbed hold of the cockpit. He lifted Excalibur
and dropped the blue blade onto the pilot in a chopping motion, cleaving him mercifully from shoulder
to breastbone. The pilot slumped, pushing the throttle so the powerful Jumo engine screamed.

The machine gunner leaped to the ground, sprain-
ing his ankle and nearly getting swiped by the errant
aircraft's swerving tail. He limped, screaming, toward
the control tower. Arthur dropped Excalibur into the
gunner's seat and pulled back the throttle. The king
unhooked the pilot's body from the harness and lifted
him from the cockpit. He waved to Yank, whose
mouth hung open, wide as a hooked trout, as he
managed the reins.

"Come on, Bill! Come on!" The horse reared up on its hind legs and whinnied as if it had conquered the legions of darkness. Yank fell, roughly, on his back.

"Ouch!" he yelled.

Arthur held on to the cockpit's glass bonnet and reached down from the trailing edge of the wing. The aircraft was turning slowly, like a ship without a rudder. Yank got up and grabbed Arthur's hand. The king pulled Bill roughly onto the wing.

"You fly, Bill," Arthur shouted above the engine's roar. "You know how."

Yank nodded and climbed into the cockpit, glad to be off the horse and oblivious to the blood spattered on the instrument panel. He made a rapid assessment of the controls and gauges and opened the throttle. Seconds later, they roared airborne. From the gunner's seat, Arthur peered out from the open cockpit and watched the autumn gold fields of France fall away beneath him. His prayer was answered. They were winging their way home to England.

"Twenty minutes to Hornchurch!" Yank shouted into the wind.

As the Stuka circled the airfield and pointed its vulture's nose toward the Channel, the horse in the field whinnied and stomped its hooves. For a few seconds, it capered like a colt. Then at a leisurely gait, it trotted back toward the woods, sad that the man with the apple had vanished. In the charge down the hill, and the encounter with the great roaring, winged creature, the horse knew it had faced a dragon. And in that mad dash, the beast had known glory.

Yank hedgehopped, flying barely above the low scrub, hedgerows and small orchards that terraced the coastal farms leading down to the beaches of Normandy. They flew so low over the bluffs that the

German ack-ack crews gave them friendly waves. Arthur waved back.

"We've got to stay low, and we've gotta evade any planes from RAF Coastal Command," Yank shouted into the dive bomber's intercom microphone.

Arthur heard Yank's disembodied voice in the earphones that hung from the seat next to the protruding hilt of Excalibur, wedged between the seat and the ammunition boxes. He picked up the earphones and put them on. Arthur fiddled with the buttons on the microphone, spit into the mouthpiece and tossed it to the floor in frustration. He had a hard enough time with English wizardry, let alone trying to master the finer points of Hun radios. He turned around and shouted, "Hurry it up, Yank!"

"We won't get anywhere if we're shark meat," Yank radioed back, his voice surging with a new-found authority. Hours before, he had shot one of these planes down. Now he was flying one. "Just like Lindy," he said.

Yank kept the dive bomber as low over the Channel froth as he could without ditching. He looked up and spotted large echelons of black-winged bombers, droning toward London at three o'clock high. Hundreds of small black crosses, the Messerschmitt escorts, tended the dark cloud of destruction.

"It's Mordred!" Arthur shouted into the wind.

"We can still beat 'em home. We're flying faster and more direct," Yank yelled. "Maybe they'll draw fire from Fighter Command."

Arthur picked up the headset again and fiddled with it. He pushed a button and got a squawk. He grinned and held the microphone key down.

"That's a good idea, Yank," the king said. "We'll get fresh horses, then ride on to Coventry."

"No nags this time, Arthur," Yank replied dryly. "My butt's still sore. We've gotta get Spitfires."

"Roger, Bill," Arthur said. "No nags."

Arthur looked up through the machine gun sight to see the green wedge shape of a Hawker Hurricane diving at them. The king gripped the machine gun reflexively. Then he realized they were being attacked by a British plane. He saw the flashes erupt from the Hurricane's wings and heard the bullets tear into the Stuka's fuselage.

Mordred flew toward England, perched like a gargoyle in the command formation's lead bomber, a powerful twin-engine Junkers 88 that could handle like a fighter in the right hands. From their cockpit aerie, Mordred and Kleist observed the panorama of Luftwaffe might, lumbering forward in the sky like a legion of black crows.

Above the bomber fleet, the loosely grouped Messerschmitt fighters spread out across the sky like an escort of hunting hawks. There were two hundred bombers in the sky, plus a hundred and fifty fighter escorts. The sheer size of the formation would draw out the RAF. Beleaguered aerodromes surrounding greater London would exhaust their reserves flying to meet the bombers.

"I have kept my part of the bargain," Kleist said quietly. His gaunt hands hung on the control yoke. His hollow eyes gazed at Mordred. "I want my soldier's death."

"There's no peace for you until my reign is declared. I'll keep you as long as I need you, Kleist. That's my bargain."

Kleist leaned sideways in his cockpit seat. His words in the earphones had a hollow, metallic ring beneath the incessant vibration and jounce of the bomber's flight. "Did you ever win a battle, personally, monster? Did you ever vanquish your foe in combat? Or are you just a parasite?"

Mordred glared and Kleist's brain felt the fury of his anger. The aircraft wobbled and Mordred relented. The bomber righted itself.

"I am going to win this war, General," Mordred said. As he spoke, his words escaped in puffs of steam in the cold cockpit, giving him a dragonlike air.

He continued, "Your war will be won neither by Goering, nor Himmler nor the one they call Führer." He panted in his reverie and licked at the ends of his sharpened teeth. "The victory will be mine, and he will elevate me. I'll rise high as Lucifer, mark me." Mordred made a sweeping gesture with his leather flying glove. It could have been a trick of the light in the cockpit, but to Kleist, the demon's eyes seemed to take on a green glow.

"I will carry this day, and the next, and the next," Mordred vowed. "My mother, Morgan, sent me forth in darkness to rule the humans." He pointed his gloved finger at the fleet of bombers surrounding their wingtips. "These aircraft, like you, Kleist, are mere instruments of my will, tools of my imagination."

"You are a monster," Kleist said weakly.

"A monster that owns you, as surely as your leader owns the Hun folk. It's an age for monsters. You exist to do my bidding. Soon, all the people below will serve me, as you do."

The bomber swarm droned on at a steady hum. Stray cirrus clouds obscured the aerial legion so it took on a dreamlike appearance as the chalky cliffs of England loomed before them. Kleist banked the bomber on course for the Thames Estuary. The formation moved with him.

"Entire cities that opposed our will no longer exist," the general mused. "Guernica. That one was for practice. Soon there were others. Warsaw. Rotterdam. Piles of stones and cities filled with souls that I erased. It must have been evil, but it seemed good at the time. Was it me who conjured you, monster?"

Mordred laughed. "So like a human. Weak. Tonight, by the light of the moon, this island will be mine, and the world will tremble." A low laugh that mimicked the low growl of a wolf escaped from his throat in a puff of steam.

"What is your real name?"

"Mordred. The sorrow of Britain."

Kleist shivered. "You're quite mad."

"If I win, what does it matter?" Mordred sat up in the cockpit seat, watching the bomber formation clear the cliffs at Dover. "Home again," the black prince said. "Home for good."

The bombardier fired a clearing burst from the nose gun, then a longer stream of bullets, sending tracer fire arcing toward the first, outnumbered Spitfires flying up to attack the formation.

The .303 machine gun bullets sprayed the Stuka's fuselage and spattered the starboard wing surface, sending a shudder through the fuselage. Yank tried to climb, but the Hurricane's burst shot up a control cable and the Stuka's flaps balked. The Hurricane zoomed past the Stuka and climbed sharply, turning to come from behind on a second pass.

"Another good hit and we've had it!" Yank shouted.

Arthur attempted to sight in on the Hurricane, but his hands froze on the firing button. He saw the red-and-blue RAF roundels cross his sight and he clutched. Suddenly, an Me109 dropped in from the sun, firing a burst at the Hurricane. The 109 scored a hit and the Hurricane wobbled its wings and cleared out, leaving a telltale streak of glycol. Yank muscled the controls and kept the Stuka nosed toward the English coast. The Messerschmitt zoomed past the Stuka, and Arthur could see the pilot wave. Beneath his goggles, a cigar jutted from the pilot's teeth. Its fuselage was marked with the comic figure of a pistol-waving mouse.

"Saved by a Hun who thinks he's Mickey Mouse," Yank yelled.

"Who was that?" Arthur asked.

"Mickey Mouse, or the Hun?"

The Messerschmitt sped after the black smoke trail of the Hurricane. Arthur turned round to watch, tensing in anticipation of the German pilot's kill when he saw the Hurricane pilot's chute pop open over Dover. He rejoiced silently. Yank urged the dive bomber over the coast and Arthur saw English earth beneath him with sheaves of oats ready for harvest. The Junkers engine sputtered and the king saw oil spitting by on the glass. He craned his neck, but all he could see was the bullet-riddled bomber's wing.

"Five minutes to Hornchurch," Yank yelled. "I'm going to keep this crate up, if I've got to carry it."

"Will the lads be glad to see us, do you think?"

"We're gonna have to put down short of the aerodrome, or they'll blow us to hell and ask questions later."

"Have faith, Bill." The king gripped Excalibur, as if the hilt were a control column that could lift the aircraft. He pulled the hilt toward him, and strangely, the Stuka gained altitude. Arthur blinked. He pushed the hilt forward slowly and the dive bomber nosed down a bit. He pulled back quickly and the aircraft climbed. Through the bright sun slashing through the cockpit glass, Arthur saw the raven. "Thanks, Merlin. I'll take any magic you've got."

He gripped the sword and laughed. The plane flew on and the black wings of the raven fluttered from the king's sight. The Stuka wobbled again, and Arthur lifted the sword. He rose and turned in the cockpit seat. The windstream blasted in his face, and he lifted the sword heavily with both hands, so that he carried it as if he rode a war horse in full charge.

Yank turned to see Arthur holding the sword in the air and, seemingly, holding the damaged aircraft aloft. "Sweet Jesus," Yank said. "He is the king."

"Find a firm field to land this crate, Bill Cooper! We're home to win the day for Arthur and England!" As he shouted, a bullet cracked the cockpit glass and another must have struck the engine, because a streamer of black smoke streaked past Arthur.

"It's gonna have to be this field, Arthur. I think we took a round under the bonnet." The black smoke became a cloud and the engine sputtered and choked. "Ground fire!"

With the large, three-bladed propeller windmilling in front of him, Yank nosed the Stuka down, dropping Arthur and Excalibur heavily into the rear compartment. The Stuka rumbled into the open field, landing roughly with its prop feathered and black smoke streaming from the manifold exhaust.

"Jump, Arthur! She's gonna go!"

The king leaped from the gunner's seat, gripping Excalibur. His feet hit the damp ground and he rolled. Arthur looked up into the barrel of an Enfield rifle, leveled at him by a grizzled Home Guardsman. The guardsman stood on the flat of the blade of Excalibur.

"*Hand der hoch,* you Hun bastard," the rifleman said. "Get your hands up. Now!"

The king reluctantly let go of his sword. Bill Cooper also was surrounded by guardsmen, including a vicar who wore a stiff collar and soup pan helmet. He brandished a Webley revolver.

"Hey, we're on your side!" Yank protested as a guardsman with a pitchfork poked his ribs. "Lookit my wings! We're RAF, see!"

"You don't speak English," the guardsman said, and he poked Yank again.

"Hey! That hurts. I'm American. Okay?"

The vicar looked at Yank with interest, tugging at his breast pocket to examine the RAF wings. He turned and stared with sharper interest at the two-handed sword held fast by the rifleman's muddy shoe.

"And who might you be?" the vicar asked. "A knight of the round table?"

"Indeed, sir," Arthur said. "And we've got to be on our way."

"Imagine them teaching Jerry to talk like that," the rifleman said, keeping the Enfield trained on Arthur. "He sounds like a storybook."

The vicar holstered his Webley revolver. "An American pilot and an Englishman of courtly manners carrying a sword," the vicar said, rubbing his chin. "And they land in our vicarage in a Stuka. Next you know, Rudolf Hess himself will drop in."

"They're flying a blinking Nazi bomber and wearing English blues. They must be infiltrators," said the guardsman with the pitchfork. "We should string 'em from a lamppost."

"That's not only rude, Lester, it's unintelligent," the vicar said. "We certainly can't sort this out by ourselves. Perhaps the staff at the aerodrome will know better what to do with them."

"What aerodrome?" Yank said.

"Hornchurch, down the lane and over the hill."

"There. They are spies!" the rifleman said. "They want information."

As the debate deepened, they heard the roar and hum of the bomber fleet headed toward London. Yank and Arthur stared at each other. They heard a rumble of vehicles on the road. It was a phalanx of motorcycles, escorting a pair of Rolls Royce sedans at high speed. Yank looked at Arthur and drew his breath in. "The king," Arthur whispered. "And Churchill."

"Take us to Hornchurch, Your Reverence," Yank said. "And may they hang us as Nazi spies if we aren't tellin' the truth."

"I rather think they'd merely send you on to Scotland," the vicar said, chuckling. "That's punishment enough for ten spies. On your feet."

The vicar's squad marched Yank and Arthur to an ancient Ford truck. The guard with the pitchfork put it down and tried to pick up Excalibur. He could not lift it. Arthur turned and smiled. "Only I can wield that sword, good sir. Either let me heft it, or let it lay in the field until Britain needs it."

The vicar looked at Arthur strangely. "Are you saying only you can lift that blade?"

"Arthur doesn't lie," Yank said solemnly.

The vicar walked over to the puzzled guardsman and attempted to lift the blade. It proved too heavy for him as well. He looked at Arthur. "We're all old men in the Home Guard, you know," he said apologetically. "Perhaps we're too weak. You may drag the sword along with your hands."

Arthur stared at the vicar with an intensity that made the churchman shiver. "Bind my hands quickly, then, and take us to Hornchurch. Britain is in peril most grave."

The guardsmen tied Arthur's hands behind his back with their belts. So the king dragged Excalibur through the field to the old lorry. As the vicar ground the gears and turned the wheel toward RAF Hornchurch, the German bombers droned on, covering the sky like a dark cloud.

28

In her twenty-seven years, Jenny Hamilton never wandered. In her few quiet hours, she might spend time with a book or a painting that she loved, or stroll in Hyde Park in the spring rain. But she inherited a keen sense of place and time from her surgeon father. Until Arthur, she had never missed rounds. She had never missed an appointment, until this autumnal day with the cold wind blowing. So it was that she walked in a dreamlike fog of her own making that enwrapped her as she sat huddled in her cape on the airfield at Hornchurch. The last attack on the aerodrome muddied her face, her coat and sturdy shoes. She didn't care. Nothing mattered.

Carried on the rolls of Coventry's missing, she wandered.

After the Yank had flown off in the biplane, she found herself in Yank and Arthur's ramshackle quarters. She lay down on Arthur's iron camp bed, holding fast to his coarse military blanket, holding his man smell close. But a feeling of abandonment overcame her. She walked out to the edge of the airfield, and there she sat atop the blast revetment and watched the sky, like a sea widow waiting for a captain who would never return.

She watched the starlings scatter, singing their empty, chittery songs. And she scanned the trees and heavy clouds for sight of a silver plane, or a night black raven. Hope eventually left her, and gradually she drew ever deeper into herself. When the sirens screeched anew and the drone of the aircraft engines roared ever closer, it was as if she had turned deaf. Nothing could move her. Jenny sat as still as a druid.

The shark-toothed Zerstörer attack bombers roared in fast and low over the stricken aerodrome, buzzing the tarmac like monstrous dragonflies. Jenny watched the attack unfold as if it were a film that slipped the loop at the cinema and slowly melted on the screen. The dirt and lumber flew high in the air as the bombs skipped across the airfield and exploded the aerodrome's remaining undamaged buildings. She felt a wave of heat shimmer across her face, but it was nothing compared to the blast furnace of Coventry.

All Jenny could do was watch, her fine surgeon's fingers clinging to the muddy dirt of the revetment. Unlike Coventry, there was no impulse to run to the rescue; she believed there was no one she could save. The bombs fell, the bullets flew and Jenny felt only a great emptiness. When the fire engines rolled out to spray enfeebled streams of water on the few remaining aircraft and hangars, Jenny lay still, like a child daydreaming.

Like all the British, she had heard the stories of the Nazis and their poison gas. She now wished the gas would come so that all the immediate horror would end. As a doctor, she realized there would be a few minutes of horrible pain, the gasping and choking. A seizing up of the lungs, a closing off of blood to the brain, then she could go on to join her dear ones.

She wanted to be with her brother, and with Edith. But most of all, she wanted to join Arthur, the scarred man in the moonlight. Why in war, she wondered, did no one ever get what they wanted, except the evil ones?

The attack had passed, and still she lay on the mound of earth, not tempted to move. It seemed as if the attack had happened years in the distant past. Finally, the starlings returned. More bombers droned in the distance.

Jenny barely noticed the old farm truck lurch onto the field, so overloaded its ancient springs groaned. She shook her head ruefully at the sight of the pitchforks and pikes and ancient shotguns the guardsmen carried. Little sticks to hold back the Luftwaffe.

She saw the Yank and gasped. Her heart raced. The guardsmen pushed the American down from the truck. His hands were tied as if he'd been taken prisoner. Then she saw the broad, familiar shoulders of the man she knew, the large man with his hands bound behind his back and an enormous two-handed sword clasped between those bound hands.

She was on her feet, racing the wind.

Jenny ran so her feet barely touched ground, with the wind whistling in her ears and her copper hair streaming behind her like a lady's favor. Two words flew from her lips repeatedly like a telegrapher's message she shouted at the top of her lungs:

"Arthur King! Arthur King! Arthur King!"

Surrounded by the guard, Arthur leaned his weight against the sword hilt, the blade sticking in the ground. His exhausted, bound form cut a figure that was ragged, dirty, bearded and imperious. The king's gray eyes took in the ruin of the airfield surrounding him, and he looked up in the sky, listening to the fading drone of the bombers. He looked across the field and his eyes found the running woman.

"Jenny," he whispered.

She burst through the ring of guards like a rugby player and fell on Arthur, knocking him flat on his back, clear of the huge, two-handed sword, which stuck in the damp earth like a cross of steel. She smothered his face with muddy kisses. She grabbed the tatters of his Irvin jacket and shook him as if he were an enormous child.

"Arthur, don't you ever leave me!" She sobbed and pummeled him, then grabbed and kissed him, again and again. Firm, hard, fast, needful kisses. "Never," she panted. "Never, ever leave me. Never, I say. You swear! Swear to me."

She lay atop him, panting, crying and kissing him all at once. Arthur, still bound, could do nothing but groan the words, "I swear, my love."

The guard with the pitchfork put his arm around Yank's shoulder and he untied Bill Cooper's bonds. "I don't know about you, lad, but judging from the lady, it does look as though that one must be local," the guardsman said.

"His people have lived here a long time," Yank murmured. He looked at the king and shook his head. "It's very strange. But real."

The vicar untied the belt that bound the king's hands. Jenny buried herself in Arthur's arms. "Then you can vouch for him, my dear?" the vicar asked gently. "We feared that these two were spies."

"He's Arthur King," Jenny said, hugging Arthur fiercely. Her eyes flashed at the vicar. "He's my forever love."

Arthur King gazed at her green eyes, his gray steel eyes clouding. Gently, he folded her in his arms and trembled. "Never leave me," he commanded quietly. "Please."

Squadron Leader Richardson hobbled up to the group, leaning on a cane. His head was bandaged and dried blood caked over his ear. Hawley and Stubbs followed, looking ragged and exhausted. It appeared they were all who were left of Dragon Squadron. "We're evacuating the field," Richardson said. "You two will be carried by ambulance and interrogated at Air Ministry."

"Debriefed, you mean, sir," Yank said.

"Interrogated," Hawley rejoined. "As possible infiltrators."

Hawley folded his arms and his eyes gleamed triumphantly as he smiled at Arthur and Yank. Stubbs looked about uneasily, his eyes shifting across the ruin of the field. An ambulance approached, escorted by military policemen in a motorcycle and sidecar. The MPs dismounted, jangling loose ancient pairs of handcuffs. Richardson waved them over with his cane.

"Here they are, Sergeant," Richardson called out. "These two. Put them in irons."

The MP sergeant approached Arthur warily. "No struggling now, sir," the sergeant said. "You're in enough trouble."

Arthur turned to Richardson. "You're making a blunder."

"Of course you are!" Jenny piped. "Arthur and Bill are no traitors. They're loyal as the king."

Hawley sniffed. "Loyal to whom? The Fifth Column, perhaps?"

"Doctor Hamilton," Richardson said, "we're going to need more than your good word to sort out the doings of the mysterious Lieutenant King. And the American stole one of my aircraft."

"I'd steal one now, if I could," Yank said urgently. "If we don't scramble, the Huns are going to kill the king!"

"And Winston, too, I suppose?" Hawley chuckled. "I always took you for a fool, Cooper, or a knave."

Arthur cleared his throat. He inclined his large head toward the sergeant with the shackles. "If you try to put me in irons, Sergeant, I'll break your collarbone." The sergeant's eyes widened and he took a step back. Arthur turned to Richardson.

"Unless you help me, your king will die today, just as Flying Officer Cooper said."

"They're both mad as hatters," Hawley said.

"I know nothing of hats, but I've returned to Britain with knowledge that will save our island kingdom, or end it."

"You're raving, King," Richardson said sadly.

"Am I? Ask the guardsmen to tell where they found me," Arthur said evenly. He nodded toward the vicar. "Describe the aircraft I captured."

"The American landed with this officer in a Stuka," the vicar said. "We thought they were Huns."

"Help us," Arthur pleaded, taking Richardson's arm. "Get on the radio. Alert the antiaircraft. Call the other squadrons. Tell them to get fighters patrolling the approaches to Coventry. If you don't, the king and his minister will die."

Tommy Stubbs sank to his knees and murmured sorrowfully, "Even if Arthur weren't daft, we've not got a wireless to relay a warning. Not even a phone. Jerry got it all the last swipe. There is no Dragon Squadron." A siren blared. Airmen working to clear the field ran for the trenches, and the Home Guard poked their rifles in confusion at each other. "There's nothing left to blow," Stubbs declared. "Bloody Huns want to make the rubble bounce."

Hawley slapped Stubbs on the back. "Stubbs! It's no raid siren. Look!" Hawley pointed toward the wreckage of the aerodrome gate. A motorcycle escort, sirens blaring, rolled past the fallen gate. The motorcycles, with their smart-looking Guards regiment cyclists, ran flying squad for a large Rolls Royce.

"Churchill!" Arthur said.

The motorcycles roared up and the door of the coach swung open. Stepping into the daylight, blinking like a mole, was Lord Beaverbrook. Richardson hobbled over and saluted the armaments minister. Jenny held fast to Arthur as the others milled about. "This airfield is due for resupply," Beaverbrook declared grandly. He took off his bowler hat, looked around and sighed. "It looks as if Hornchurch is a bit frayed at the edges."

"RAF Hornchurch is no longer operational," Richardson said wearily.

"Oh, yes it is," Beaverbrook said. The aircraft minister dabbed at his broad, pink forehead with a silk handkerchief. He looked up. "There. There's your squadron, coming in on a wing and prayer."

Everyone looked to the skies and heard the faint hum. Then, shining in the sky they appeared, faint at first like silvery slivers. The crowd on the field could see the Spitfires take shape, descending like a quartet of winged daggers. They touched onto the field delicately, their propellers feathering. On the ground, the silver planes became ungainly as geese. They bumped along as if their riders were unsure of their steeds.

"Factory new," Lord Beaverbrook said. "Haven't even got paint on 'em, but they'll fight. They just need pilots. Real pilots. Cadets flew 'em down. Fine lads. Didn't crash 'em, anyway."

Four raw youths in reservists jackets climbed down from the cockpits, looking eager, uncertain and unfinished. Their flight leader ran up and saluted Richardson. The squadron leader's hand dropped uncertainly from the edge of his field dressing. The squadron's armorer shouted orders and the air crews ran forward to arm the Spitfires. The airfield's remaining truck rolled out to top off the tanks.

"Our orders are to deliver the aircraft, sir!" the reserve cadet shouted breathlessly. His cheeks blazed red, and he had no need to shave. "We're at your disposal. Sir!"

Richardson smiled a gaunt, sad smile. "I've two pilots left to scramble for sorties over London, and God save the king."

"You can't do that, sir," Yank said. "You can't send those kids up, sir. It's slaughter."

"You're hardly the one to give military advice," Hawley sniped. "You and your pal King are prisoners. Sergeant, put these men in irons." Again, the MP sergeant looked doubtfully at Arthur, then at Richardson.

"Do your duty, Sergeant," Richardson said. Beaverbrook glanced over at Arthur and Jenny. With the woman clinging to him, Arthur once again leaned against the hilt of Excalibur.

Lord Beaverbrook asked, "What's their offense, Richardson?"

Richardson stammered, "I don't rightly know, sir. But they're in custody until I find out."

"Only cowardice or treachery would ground a combat pilot," the minister said.

"Oh, no, Your Lordship!" Jenny Hamilton cried out. "They captured an enemy plane in France. They're heroes."

Beaverbrook saw Arthur, and a smile of recognition dawned across the old man's face. The aircraft lord saw the large, two-handed sword with its crude coating of paint and his eyes fixed on it as if he'd found the crown jewels lying in a field. He moved toward Excalibur as if pulled by a magnet. Lord Beaverbrook stared at the sword, then at Arthur, thunderstruck.

"Where did you find this?"

The king grasped the hilt with easy familiarity. "It's been in my family for generations," he said. "It is mine."

Beaverbrook touched the crosspiece of the sword, his fingers dabbing at it as if he were afraid they might burn. He looked in Arthur's gray eyes with the intensity of an old man who had been searching for something lost in childhood and finally found.

"Is it possible? May I hold the sword, sir?"

Arthur looked deep into Beaverbrook's eyes, and finally he assented. "If you are able," he said quietly. Arthur loosened his grip on the hilt and it slipped into the minister's grasp. The sword immediately fell to the ground, heavy as a lodestone. Beaverbrook, still holding the hilt, looked up at Arthur in wonder.

"Who are you?"

"King, sir. The name is Lieutenant Arthur King."

"Yes," the minister said. "I can see that. You're the one who has come in the hour of greatest need, the one annointed to save the kingdom."

"If I am able."

Lord Beaverbrook looked with longing at the sword and let go. He regained his feet and put his hand on Richardson's shoulder. He pointed at Arthur. "Send him to defend the skies over London. He's the hope of Britain."

"Coventry, sir," Arthur said. "The target for today is Coventry."

"Nonsense," Richardson said. "Coventry's in ruins. They're burning London again, even as we speak."

Beaverbrook squinted, "Why do you say Coventry, King?"

"Because Churchill will be there," Arthur said.

"And the king will be there. The attack on London is only a feint. They want the checkmate."

Beaverbrook gripped Richardson's arm. "He's right! Churchill and the king are traveling to comfort the survivors of Coventry as we speak. I go there to meet them."

"You'll never make that date, Your Lordship," Yank said, "unless me and Arthur get the squadron airborne."

Beaverbrook looked at the sword. He looked up into Arthur's gray eyes. "Tell me something, King. What's the engine that gives the Spitfire so much power?"

Arthur grinned. "That's simple. It's a Merlin."

Beaverbrook nodded gravely. "Squadron Leader, you must let these officers take Dragon Squadron to defend king and Coventry."

"With all due respect, Your Lordship, that's a military decision."

"I speak for England. Would you lose the king and Winston for want of four silver planes?"

Richardson shifted his feet uneasily. He sighed. "All right, then. Hawley flies lead. Dragon Squadron goes to fly cover. Can the king be warned?"

"Too late," Beaverbrook said. "They're already halfway there."

Arthur looked at Beaverbrook. "Thank you," he whispered. "My sword."

"I'll guard it personally. I've waited all my life just to look at it. I knew that it existed."

"We've gotta go," Yank insisted.

At a nod from Richardson, Yank, Hawley and Stubbs ran to the waiting silver aircraft. Arthur hugged Jenny and tore free from her, running raggedly to join the flight. The pain in both legs seemed to spur him on as he climbed onto the shining wing and dropped into the shiny new cockpit.

He was adjusting his safety straps and connecting

the radio lead to his flying helmet when he felt a hand grip his arm and squeeze it like a melon. He looked up to see what the armorer wanted and instead looked deep into Jenny's wild, green eyes.

"You must live, Arthur. Because I can't live without you."

"There are so many things I want to tell you." The words caught in his throat.

"On my life, you must live," she said, shaking him severely. The Merlin engine vibrated the fuselage and tears streamed from Jenny's face. The twelve cylinders roared, the rpms mounted steadily and a blue-jacketed airman climbed aboard and caught Jenny like a stowaway, carrying her quickly off the wing.

"They're like that, you know, sir," the sergeant called out, barely keeping hold of the struggling Jenny. The sergeant shouted, "My old woman's the same, sir! Every time my leave is done."

The king saw the first plane of Dragon Squadron rolling to takeoff position. He pulled the cockpit bubble closed and pushed the throttle forward. He looked up to the sky and saw the faint black crosses of German bombers flying in somber V-shaped echelons toward targets in Britain.

The baby-faced cryptographer at the Government Code and Cipher School outside London offered the flimsy paper to Sir Stewart Menzies. The young man's hand trembled as the intelligence chief snatched the flimsy.

"Well, what is it?" Menzies demanded. "What does Ultra say?"

"The message is quite clear, 'C.' Top Secret, classification Enigma. Jerry plans to kill Winston."

"Where and when, boy?" Menzies said, his ruddy Scottish cheeks coloring.

"Doesn't say, sir. Just that it's today. And it's a Luftwaffe job."

The man called "C" rushed from the basement in search of intelligence about his prime minister's whereabouts.

The king's convoy sped toward Coventry, spreading terror among the chickens and geese that scattered from the road. As the motorcade roared through the villages, the pub patrons emerged from the dark warmth of their cozy autumn quarters to watch the parade of cycles and Rolls Royce coaches race by. Realizing it must be Winston, they gave the "V" salute.

In the skies above England, the exhausted pilots of the Royal Air Force rallied their scattered formations of Spitfires and Hurricanes to duel with the might of the Luftwaffe over London. As Churchill's gallant few flew to duel with the Hun, a crack squadron of Junker 88 attack bombers flew past the great dome of Saint Paul's Cathedral. The London fire companies labored to save the cathedral from the flames and smoke that threatened to engulf it and Mordred broke off from the main formation and flew toward Coventry and destiny.

Spotting a line of barges chugging along on the flat, gray surface of the Thames, Kleist's squadron banked sharply away from the city and flew north, carrying their load of special incendiary bombs each marked with the sign of the pentagram.

29

Gilbert Hawley led the formation, with Yank flying as his number two. Arthur flew wingman to Tommy Stubbs. Thanks to Stubbs' four kills at Dunkirk, Dragon Squadron had adopted the "finger-four" formation. The pilots flew in two loosely grouped pairs like the Luftwaffe instead of the RAF's arrow-shaped "vic" pattern. The finger-four gave each pilot free range to scan a vast expanse of sky. Like four talons, the Spitfires of Hornchurch spread in a diagonal slash across a quarter mile of cold, empty air. The pilots each watched the gray clouds above, the ground below and a ceiling of darkening rain-filled mist that closed above them at ten thousand feet.

"Blue Leader to Blue Three," Hawley radioed to Stubbs. "Prepare for battle climb. Want to get above this crud."

"There's no time! We've got minutes, not hours,"

Arthur cried out in the clear, too excited to give a call sign.

"Identify yourself or stay off the air, Blue Four," Hawley scolded. "And stay off the air anyway, unless you're attacked."

"Blue Leader, Three here. Must agree on chucking the battle climb," Stubbs radioed back. "It's minutes we simply haven't got."

"You're not running this show, Blue Three."

"Quite right, Blue Leader. But who's going to get the blame if we're late to the party?"

"Roger," Hawley said tersely. "We'll fly low and Blue Four can take it up the arse as Tail-End Charlie."

"You're all heart, Blue Leader," Yank volunteered.

"Further unauthorized transmission will result in court-martial," Hawley declared.

"Bugger off." Nobody gave a call sign.

The cockpit radio crackled like dry leaves and the voice at Sector transmitted like silk. "Chalice, this is Camelot calling. Hold for a vector, over."

Hawley responded, "Camelot, this is Chalice Leader. Anytime you're ready, over."

"Chalice, this is Camelot. Transmit for fix." Hawley left his radio on transmit for about ten seconds, allowing the direction-finding stations to triangulate on his location and assign the vector.

"Camelot to Chalice Leader. We have you forty miles southwest of the patrol line. We identify zero bogeys or bandits. No trade at all."

"Roger, Camelot. Thanks, anyway. Proceeding to patrol line."

They climbed to eight thousand feet, just below the cloud cover, and set the throttles for cruise at about 280 mph true. Each man scanned the skies above and the mist-veiled rolling contours of the earth below, looking for a sight of bandit aircraft, or a convoy moving on a black thread of highway.

"Any trade, Blue Two?" Hawley demanded.

"Negative," Yank answered.

"Blue Three?"

"Not a biscuit," Stubbs replied.

"Blue Four?"

"Blue Four finds nothing," Arthur responded.

"And I doubt that you will, Blue Four," Hawley said. "We should be covering the palace instead of playing hares and hounds out here."

"Ours is not to reason why, Blue Leader," Tommy Stubbs said.

"Bugger off, Three. Blue Leader, out."

The darkening sky hung before them like a canvas sail on a Channel dorry. Arthur searched to infinity ahead, above and behind. The needles of the new aircraft twitched and jumped, dancing with the tautness of factory-new machinery. Oil pressure. Fuel pressure. Artificial horizon. Compass swinging by degrees of turn. The throttle responded with a stiffness, and yet it felt as familiar now in the king's hand as a glove. He had learned the machinery of this age as surely as he knew his own sword hand.

As the silver Spitfire sped forward at five miles a minute, old questions gnawed the edge of the king's spirit. All the purpose of the new machinery confounded him. Instead of awe at invention, the king felt only frustration and disappointment. So much of the Machine Age was dedicated to the improvement of armaments. The equipment of this new Dark Age was faster, more powerful, more deadly. But better? What was the use of a machine designed for toasting bread if one were to be bombed to hell before breakfast?

Much of the new age machinery only killed its human prey more efficiently than the arrows and slings of his day, Arthur concluded. Racing to a point on the horizon in order to slay his own flesh and blood, the realization of his mission made the king's heart turn cold. What could man learn if the perfection of utility was harnessed primarily for ever more effective destruction?

He pondered the weight of the deed before him: to slay his own son in order to save the future. Arthur had slain many men in battle, but never exulted in bloodshed. He saw it as duty. The king felt a turning in his stomach unrelated to the pressures and pulls of a bucking, unpressurized cockpit. He hooked on his oxygen mask and took a squirt of the pure mixture in order to clear his head, but it did his heart no good as he tried to remember the childhood of the man he must meet in mortal combat.

He remembered the dark tower in Eire. He remembered the dark lady.

Little more than a child himself, Arthur the boy king had held the infant Mordred in his arms in bewilderment. Disturbed and distracted, he handed the infant away to a hooded midwife. All Arthur could see was the glint he perceived in the baby's darkling eye, and tiny fingerlets that were already sharp like needle points. Then, the creature's mother, the witch Morgan Le Fay, swept down the spiral stones of her dark retreat and laughed in the young king's face.

The witch mother banished Arthur from her emerald kingdom by the sea. The rawboned youth had served her dark purpose. The cruel woman had a son sired by a mortal. With the young Arthur's services no longer required, he could return to his adventures and destiny. Yet even at court in Camelot, he remained tied to unwholesome memories spawned by the changeling's birth.

Mother, father and bastard offspring had all been

forever distant after their enchanted interlude. As Arthur grew to maturity, he feared they formed an unholy trinity, separate but tied together in a union created without love.

Life became ever more complicated when Mordred was delivered to the king's court, a disjointed youth wearing a jester's livery. Mordred's mischief, his cruelty to animals, children and ladies at court made the young king mad with frustration. Finally, he banished the lad to work in the stables. Mordred remained there, tended by the servants until the day he quit the castle. The servants found the char girl's twisted body buried beneath the straw, Mordred's farewell to the king.

Mordred remained outcast and outlaw until the day he rode at the head of an army of Hun mercenaries and Pictish rebels, leading unholy revolt against Camelot's proud towers.

The Spitfire buffeted in the dense, cold air.

"Blue Four, close it up," Stubbs called out. "You're wandering."

"Roger, Blue Three," Arthur responded. "Closing up."

"You're onto something, Blue Four," Stubbs said suddenly. "If the target is what you say, this all could be the entire game."

"Roger, Blue Three," Arthur said. "You've been a friend. Thanks."

Arthur glowed at the trust given him by Stubbs. He knew that the mission mattered. He knew that it all mattered. Stubbs had listened and believed. And Yank believed him. Believed in him. Not one, but three knights on the quest. The king realized suddenly that he held the kingdom as near at hand as the little band of brothers gathered round him. He felt as determined as if the control column in the Spitfire's cockpit were Excalibur itself, guiding his destiny.

Arthur scanned the darkening sky with greater intensity.

Somewhere out there was Mordred. Left unchecked, he could bring on the darkness as surely as the black sky that threatened to unleash its fury. The machines, the silver Spitfires, like steeds in battle, must be harnessed to fight today's good fight. A good world would have to wait.

The convoy carrying Churchill and King George VI halted at the crossroads while the escort captain reconnoitered. The road signs had been removed to confound German invaders. But as happened often, they had succeeded in muddling the way for decent Englishmen. The Rolls Royce sedans pulled off the road and parked beneath a pair of spreading oaks. The guardsmen jumped from their cycles and surrounded the vehicles, their tommy guns bristling and heavy from the weight of the big drum magazines that held nearly a hundred rounds.

Churchill emerged from the second sedan, chewing away at his cigar like a bulldog on a postman. He tugged at the brim of his top hat and stumped up purposefully to the officer of guards. The captain raised a pair of binoculars and scanned the barley fields in the distance. They were pockmarked with the hollowed forms of rusting autos planted across the countryside to frustrate Nazi gliders.

"The Home Guard has called in a Jerry paratroop scare from the coast watchers, sir. They do it often. We shan't be delayed more than a few minutes."

"Well, Captain. Clear the road. We've got a rendezvous."

Churchill grinned and returned the salute of a corporal armed with a tommy gun. Churchill looked with interest at the Thompson gun. "May I try it, Corporal?" Churchill asked.

The corporal surrendered his weapon to the prime minister. Churchill brandished it gleefully as a boy with a new toy. With submachine gun in hand and cigar jutting from his teeth, he looked like a cherubic Al Capone.

"Goebbels calls me a gangster, you know," Churchill said with a wink. He pointed the gun out toward the open field and sighted on one of the rusted hulks. He looked about ready to pull the trigger, then thought better of it. Churchill nodded toward the second sedan. "The king and I take weekly target practice at the palace, you know."

"Jolly good, sir," the corporal said, nodding.

"We have to be ready to fight the Huns anywhere, you know," the prime minister said, tapping the drum magazine. "If need be, we'll face them on the landing grounds and the beaches. We shall fight them in the streets, and in the hills."

"Yes, sir."

"We shall never surrender."

"No, sir. Of course not, sir. I shouldn't have got my feet wet at Dunkirk to let Jerry take his pint in me own pub, sir."

"That's right," the prime minister said, clapping the soldier on the shoulder. Churchill handed the corporal his tommy gun and opened his waistcoat, revealing the gold watch chain and the dark, massive Webley revolver. The captain trotted up to the pair, saluting the prime minister.

"The road to Coventry is clear, sir."

Churchill nodded. "Let's get on with it." He stumped back to his sedan and the soldiers mounted their motorcycles, kick-starting their engines and roaring down the country road toward the ruins of Coventry.

*   *   *

At seven thousand feet, the clouds closed in around the JU88s. Mordred clutched the trigger grip of the machine gun that protruded from the cockpit. They flew inside an envelope of endlessly unfolding gray mist. The fog unsettled Mordred, reminding him of his journey through time.

"We can't see," he said, his lips pulled tight across his teeth. He panted like a cat in an automobile, and he repeated, "We can't see."

Kleist curled his lips, his smile ghastly. "I can see."

"You're an oracle, then," Mordred said, his voice tinged with panic. "When will we find our way through the clouds?"

"The radio beam from fleet HQ in Le Havre will guide us to the target. When I drop below two thousand feet, we will fall from the sky like hunting hawks. King George and Churchill will be the rabbits on the road."

"That leaves only Arthur to reckon with."

Kleist adjusted the chinstrap on his leather helmet. He took account of the altitude and showed a cold, detached skill in his flying. He had none of the panic of the fog-bound sailor. The bomber roared on in the cloud bank, beads of mist gathering on the cockpit glass. Kleist's eyes burned with a cold intensity. He kept his eye on the screen between his knees, moving the control yoke a few degrees to keep the luminous line from the radio beacon centered in the screen. He pushed the yoke forward, and the Junkers bomber nosed forward into a bumpy, gradual descent.

The mist vanished, and the sweep of the English countryside rolled out beneath them. In the distance, piercing the wreckage like the mast of a great ship stood the ruined cathedral. The bombs that burnt Coventry had hollowed it out so that only a mountain of stones remained. But somehow the walls, latticed by the magnificent windows, still stood. The walls stood defiant, holy and somehow undefeated.

The sight chilled Mordred. The bomber banked back toward the southern highway that led to the city.

The cloud enveloped Dragon Squadron and Arthur's hand instinctively closed on the stick. He could fly, but flying blind? Beads of sweat made his neck moist and the salt stung at his eyes. His breathing in the oxygen regulator gurgled like water in an ocean cave.

"Blue Flight, this is Leader. We're going to get out of this. Ceiling should break around three thousand."

The Spitfires dropped down at a twenty-degree angle and shed altitude rapidly. The altimeter needle pushed through the five-thousand-foot mark and Arthur watched his hand tremble on the stick as they plunged through the wet, gray shroud. "Merlin," he whispered. "God save us."

"Steady, Blue Four." Yank sensed the king's fright. "You've got plenty of sky. Just hold your position and dive."

They plunged through the three thousand mark and the cloud smothered them like a blanket. At twenty-five hundred feet, Arthur still flew blind.

"This must end," Hawley cried out in alarm. Arthur's altimeter indicated nineteen hundred feet.

An enormous explosion buffeted Arthur's aircraft, and the mist turned yellow with the light of a great fire. The shock wave flipped Arthur's Spitfire and the king pitched below the cloud ceiling. Flying inverted, the king glimpsed the huge black cross of the JU88 racing by beneath him. He pushed his firing button. It answered with a hollow click. The German bomber sped on.

Arthur held the stick hard to starboard and the

Spitfire spun over. He opened the throttle wide and gave chase. A stream of tracers arced toward the Junkers bomber. He dropped a few degrees and pushed the firing button again. Another click; the guns were jammed.

"Blue Two, Three, Four! Any Blue pilot!" It was Hawley.

"Stubbs bought it," Yank responded. "Bandit, twelve low!"

The Junkers thundered on, steady as death. It flew barely above treetops. The three remaining Dragon planes pushed their throttles through the gate to close the half-mile gap. Hawley and Yank fired too early, their tracers falling short. The pilot jinked to the right, dropped a few feet, then pulled left. Like a scorpion's stinger, the Junkers' gunner returned a stream of tracer to fend off the pursuers.

The Spitfires raced past a trestle bridge. Arthur spotted the twin blurs of shining black metal. He saw the escort motorcycles, like outriders guarding the king. He watched in horror, the convoy moving rapidly off the bridge as he glanced far ahead, to see the Junkers bomber turning. It looked like a boar, rearing to charge the hunters.

Yank and Hawley's planes overflew the Junkers and pulled up high to swing round in an Immelmann, but they were coming round too slowly to impede the bomber or find the shot. Their tracers singed the barley field, firing wide of the convoy and whizzing by Arthur's silver wing.

The door to the Rolls Royce coach swung open and the corporal tumbled Churchill onto the ground by the lapels of his morning coat. The prime minister skinned his knee on the gravel as he scrambled in the dirt. The guardsman swung his Thompson gun skyward and fired, the gun bucking wildly and nearly jumping from his right hand as he jostled Churchill with his left. They stumbled together down the dirt embankment beneath the trestle bridge as the silvery Spitfires roared overhead, their guns blazing.

Beneath the bridge, Churchill huddled next to King George and the Guards captain. All three men clutched their revolvers as the guardsmen fanned out, aiming their tommy guns at the sky. Some huddled in the reeds by the wide stream that curled beneath the trestle bridge. A pair of silver planes flashed overhead, reflecting a beam of sunlight through the cloud.

"Ours, or theirs?" the king demanded.

"At least one's a Hun," Churchill grunted.

They heard the drone of several aircraft, banking and turning. The prime minister gripped his revolver, and his eyes swept the sky like a searchlight battery in London. Instinctively, he stepped in front of the king. In a reflex motion, he reached for a cigar. His hand patted nervously at his dusty coat, realizing he'd dropped his leather cigar case in the road.

"You missed!" Mordred shrieked. His hollow voice bounced off the faceted glass of the cockpit, an enraged echo. Kleist felt the top of his head coming off from the blast of Mordred's mental wrath.

Kleist turned and glowered at his tormentor. He felt the sweat streaming down his forehead.

"Win your own battles," he said, grinning crookedly. "I'll see you in hell."

The German flier pushed the control yoke forward and the bomber plunged like a boulder from a cliff. Mordred pulled the copilot's controls and the aircraft yawed violently.

*   *   *

The three aircraft hurtled at Arthur like runaway siege engines in line abreast. The silver wings of Yank and Hawley's Spitfires glinted in relief against the wingtips of the dark, green German bomber. The Junkers' faceted bubble nose assumed the visage of the dark knight's faceplate in full charge. The bomber roared straight on until Arthur found Mordred's terrified eyes opened wide to the sockets and his mouth forming the scream that precedes collision.

Arthur blinked and the bomber dropped, plunging just beneath him. The silver Spitfire wings flashed by in his peripheral vision. The king heard the groan of metal on metal and felt his wingtips shudder, brushed by the other planes. The Spitfire pitched up, vertically. Arthur pushed the throttle full out, but he felt the airframe stall. In his cockpit's rearview mirror, he saw the bomber arching like an arrow toward the bridge, and a contrail of smoke trailing from one of the Spitfires.

The king's propeller feathered and the plane slowly twisted and fell backward. Arthur pushed back the canopy and fell into the air, clawing for a ripcord that wasn't there. He'd brought no parachute.

The king hit the black water feet first, and the mud fastened his left boot to the river bottom like an anchor. As the water pushed through his nose and pumped into his lungs, he tore free from the boot. As he rose through the bone-chilling dark water, he saw the air bubbles escape from his clothing, and he saw the fishes. And he saw the lady in the reeds. He shivered, and she vanished. It was not his time. The surface shimmered above him and beckoned. His legs scissored and he floated toward the light, away from Avalon and the Lady of the Lake.

The king propelled himself up through the depths

of the moving water until he saw the surface shining before him, drawing him up even as his lungs threatened to burst. The sun broke through the cloud cover, its rays drenching the water. Arthur saw the light flattening on the surface of the water like a great, round table. He pulled toward it with strong strokes.

Arthur burst through the surface of the stream, coughing. He paddled to the bank and pulled himself up into the reeds. Through the rushes, he saw the wreckage of the German bomber, smoking in the field. A little ways beyond, he saw a battered Spitfire fuselage, the shiny new plane crumpled like tin foil. Smoke issued from the engine cowling and the silvery plane exploded in flame, issuing a fireball above the barley field.

The king moved crabwise along the muddy bank of the stream and watched the figure of a man emerging from the twisted wreckage of the Junkers bomber. It was Mordred. Arthur pulled a smooth stone from the mud and began to stumble into the open field.

Mordred crawled out of the cockpit, dropping past the contorted body of Anton Kleist, whose arm hung lifelessly over the pentagram mark beneath the cockpit. Blood trickled down Kleist's scalp, forming rivulets on a face that was finally at peace. Mordred swayed on his feet and watched the dripping, muddy figure of the king approach him. Mordred's face twisted into the unwholesome grin of his youth.

"Have we arrived at the end of the game, Father?"

"You must yield, Mordred," the king ordered quietly. He held the stone in his hand but made no move with it. "You've done all the harm you can do, in this time or any other. Yield, and I'll see mercy done."

Mordred dropped to his knees. He placed his hands together in mock prayer. "Oh, thank you, Father. Mercy, please. Now I'm bound for the dungeons of antiquity. Your kindness knows no bounds."

Mordred's eyes flashed, glittering, ancient and full of hatred. "If only I'd cut off your head, the crown would be mine."

Arthur held the stone high, ready to fling it down. Then, he relented. "We must leave this time together, Mordred. It belongs to the people who live in it to work out their destiny. Surrender Merlin's book to me, and we will work out the justice of mercy together."

Mordred rose from his knees. He pointed at the smooth stone the king held in his hand.

"Were you going to bash my brains in before your change of heart, Father?" Mordred pulled a Luger pistol from his flight jacket. He jacked a 9-millimeter round into the chamber and aimed it at the king's chest.

"Swords and stones, Father. You're so old-fashioned."

"Mordred!" Arthur cried out.

Mordred fired twice, the steel-jacketed bullets blasting the king into the muddy earth of the open field. Mordred looked down at the king's body and grinned.

"At last, Father," he murmured. "Our journey together is ended as it must." He looked up at the cold, gray sky and heard a starling's song. Then he heard a whistling in the air.

"Excalibur!" a voice cried out.

Mordred's eyes opened wide in surprise. He gasped and staggered forward, clutching the thrown dagger that had plunged deep into his throat. With a jerk, Mordred pulled the knife free from his neck. He gurgled and looked down in horror to see King Arthur getting up from the ground.

"Father," he rasped.

"It wasn't me, Mordred." The king rose groggily, reaching out.

Holding the blade in his hands, Mordred dropped

to his knees, holding the dagger before him like a crucifix. "Good-bye, Father," the knave prince gasped. As he fell forward into the field, his form vanished like a fighter plane's exhaust contrail. The empty flight suit lay in the rich barley dirt, covering the scattered pages of Merlin's book.

Yank stepped out from his hiding place behind the bomber wreckage. He whistled long and low. He picked up the commando dagger and shook his head.

"His will be done," Arthur murmured. He gathered together the leatherbound parchment and stuffed it into his flight jacket.

Yank bent down to wipe the blade on his pants leg but found no trace of blood on it. He murmured the inscription, "Excalibur," as he ran his hand along the flat of the blade. Yank stared at Arthur. "What was that thing? The Hun who shot you? And how come you're not shot? Are you real?"

Arthur nodded his head. "Real enough, Bill. Bullets tear my flesh like any mortal's. But my armor still works." He unbuttoned the shirt collar and opened his soaked Irvin jacket to reveal the forged steel collarpiece from his ancient breastplate. The gorget retrieved from Beaverbrook's library displayed the dragon emblem of House Pendragon, and two rough dents where the bullets struck.

"Where did the Hun go?"

"Back where he belongs, somewhere in the abyss."

The guardsmen marched out into the field, their tommy guns at the ready. They closed a circle around Arthur and Yank, like the Hun infantry at the chapel in France. Gilbert Hawley walked with them, marching alongside the Guards captain.

"There they there," Hawley called out. "Those two are all right. They're RAF from my flight. They put paid to the bomber that was aiming for His Majesty."

The Guards captain nodded and called across the

barley field, "Hallo! You there by the wreckage. Any Huns about?"

Yank shook his head and called back, "Not anymore."

Gilbert Hawley nodded appreciatively. His lips tightened in a thin-lipped trace of an upper-crust smile. He called out, "Well, then. I suppose we're done."

"What about the king and Churchill?" Arthur shouted, trying to rise to his feet. He felt dizzy, and sat down again.

"Gone on to Coventry," Hawley said, walking up to the pair and extending his hand. "Got to tell the rabble that Britons never shall be slaves."

Yank lifted the king from the ground and Hawley hurried forward to support Arthur's other arm. The king rested himself between the two fliers, and they all began to walk toward the bridge.

30

The three fliers stared as the enlisted men lowered the flag-draped coffin and carried it into the hangar. The Union Jack hugged the casket, tight as a sheet on a military cot. The trio wore suitable dress, long greatcoats and stiff-brimmed officers' caps. The sealed remains of Flight Lieutenant Tommy Stubbs came to rest on a pair of saw horses while the hard-pressed air crew of RAF Hornchurch worked feverishly to restore the aerodrome and refit the planes. Sparks from welding torches flared in the recess of the dimly lit hangar. Trucks rolled by outside, bringing fresh spares, ammunition, tinned biscuits and tea. Airmen moved by in hurried knots, carrying wrenches and determination to get on with it.

Hawley passed his silver monogrammed flask, first to Yank, then to Arthur. Wing Commander Richardson, freshly promoted, hobbled up on his cane. Hawley pocketed the flask and saluted.

Richardson returned the salute and the quartet stood, their heads bowed for a silent moment.

"A good man," Hawley said tersely. "He had no taste in clothing, food or liquor." Hawley's words caught in his throat and he turned away.

"Stubbs was not the last good man we'll lose," Richardson said. "But he's as good as we'll see die for king and country."

"But not in vain," Arthur said. "The king lives, and the country will hang on through the present darkness."

"Not through many more days like today, I hope," Hawley said quietly.

The men of Dragon Squadron saluted Stubbs in his casket. Hawley nodded at Arthur. "You'll be flying my number two, King. The Yank gets Tommy's flight."

Yank stuffed his hands in his pockets and shuffled his feet. "Thanks, Gil."

"Don't thank me. You've earned Tommy's place. At the table, and in the air."

Richardson took Arthur by the arm. Quietly, he said, "You're to come with me, King." The wing commander guided him from the hangar, out onto the moonlit airfield where airmen worked by the light of hurricane lamps.

"We shall be in bad shape if Jerry strikes again," Richardson said, hobbling with the cane and holding Arthur's arm to steady him. "We need aircraft, men, everything. Another attack and we're through."

"They won't come tonight," Arthur said, glancing up at the sky. The moon moved behind the clouds like a ship crossing the Channel. "You'll have a breathing space, time to regroup. And the RAF will win as surely as darkness must give way to light."

"You sound so certain, King," Richardson said, stopping to stare at Arthur. "You're close to His Majesty, aren't you?"

"We are distant relations. Very distant."

"Well, use your influence at court to move his minister from my airfield. Lord Beaverbrook's been there since this afternoon, still as a stone. I can't move him."

"And Jenny?" Arthur gripped the wing commander's arm. "What's become of the healer, Jenny Hamilton?"

"I can't get rid of her, either. Beaverbrook won't budge until he speaks with you. You've got to help get my airfield cleared. I can't have a runway blocked by a lord. Or a lady, for that matter."

The moon broke through the clouds, showering the airfield with its luminous, blue light. Arthur spotted the shadowy form of Beaverbrook's Rolls Royce.

"I have to get the field repaired, so I'll leave you here, King," Richardson said. "See to it."

Arthur looked up to see the clouds rolling rapidly across the sky, a fleet of silver ghost ships, each with sail unfurled, revealing a facet or trace of the full moon's radiance. The king stepped round the coach. He saw the stooped figure of the aircraft minister kneeling by the shimmering blade of Excalibur.

Before Arthur could speak, Jenny ran to him and they embraced, his greatcoat tangled in her hospital cape. "You!" She kissed his neck, his face, and traced her fingers across his temples. She grabbed his visored cap and threw it and kissed his scarred forehead. "You!" she repeated.

The king groaned. "Have I hurt you?" she demanded as she hugged him ever closer. "No, I couldn't. I could never hurt you, Arthur. I'm going to take care of you. I'm going to heal all your wounds."

"Jenny," he whispered. "You already have."

"I'll mend you, Arthur. And when you're well, I'll love you without rest or mercy. You're mine, Arthur King. Forever."

A shadow passed over them. Arthur looked up to see the gaunt visage of Merlin framed in the moonlight, his silvered head illuminated by the passing clouds. The ancient wore an RAF staff officer's uniform and leaned on his gnarled staff as if it were a gentleman's walking stick.

"It's time, Arthur. Camelot calls." He offered his hand, and Arthur handed him the book from within the fold of his coat. "Good," Merlin murmured. "Time and tide arrive to speed you home. The moon will not wait."

"Take you where, Arthur?" Jenny said, her voice rising in alarm. "Not away, not again."

Yank stepped into the circle of light formed by the clouds unfolding round the moon. A cold breeze kicked up, blowing bits of paper and trash that transformed into a flight of ravens on the wing.

Yank put his hands gently on Jenny's shoulders. "He can't stay here, Jenny. This isn't his time. He's got to go be King Arthur."

The king felt strength flowing from him as the ring of clouds round the moon whirled, becoming a silver vortex. "Who are these people, Arthur?" Jenny cried. "What madness is this?"

Lord Beaverbrook stepped into the circle of light. The moon was so bright it bounced off his bald pate. He also stood by Jenny and touched her gently. "He can't live his life in this time. He has to prepare the way for it."

Jenny broke free from the old man and the Yank. She looked up at the strange, silver-haired man who held the gnarled stick and the leatherbound manuscript.

"What is happening?" she shouted at Merlin into the howl of the wind. "Go away! Leave my Arthur alone. You can't help him. He has to be with me."

"Camelot calls him," Merlin intoned gravely. "He

must return to the time when he was king to finish
the quest. His work here is done. He must fly home,
or there will be no Arthur and no England."

Jenny took Arthur by the shoulders, and she too
could feel the strength ebbing from him. Trembling,
she ran her fingers across his face, which was rapidly
going cold as stone in an abbey. "What are they saying?" she pleaded. "Who are you?"

"I'm Arthur King," he said, smiling. He lifted his
hand to touch his fingers to her face. "Never leave
me, Jenny."

She fell on him sobbing. She looked round, and all
the men who faced her—Merlin, the minister and the
Yank—seemed her mortal enemies. "You can't have
him!" she cried. "I must be with him."

The king touched his fingers to her copper hair.
"My time is one of ignorance and tyranny and death.
I couldn't bring you to it."

She held the king by his greatcoat. "Don't be a fool,
Arthur. What is this time? What is any time but all of
those things? You can't live without my love. You can't
survive without it. Neither can I live without you."

The king's eyes glimmered. He looked up at
Merlin, who hovered above him in the moonlight like
a specter. "Please," he whispered. "Please, Merlin. I
must have my queen."

Jenny looked at the ancient as if she'd been shot
through with lightning. Merlin put his stick on the
ground. He placed his hands on her shoulders and his
silvered eyes stared deep into her soul. She stood
numbly gazing at the sorcerer's eyes, which held her
like the power of the moon.

"Can you do it?" the ancient asked. "Follow him
anywhere? Brave any danger? Can you live in a world
lit only by fire?"

She nodded with certainty. Merlin spoke in a low
tone to Yank. "Carry him to the sword. Quickly."

Bill Cooper nodded. He motioned to Beaverbrook. "Help me, Your Lordship, sir."

As Jenny kneeled, spellbound before the ancient, Yank and the aircraft minister lifted Arthur and pulled him to the place where Excalibur lay. A sky full of ravens circled the moon now. "He must grip the sword," Merlin said.

As the ancient spoke, his spell on Jenny was broken and she rose and began to walk across the heath toward him. As the king's fingers closed on the hilt of the dragon sword, he hesitated, seeing her move toward him stately as a queen. She held her hand out to him and he pulled her alongside. He held her in tight embrace and gripped the haft of Excalibur. The moonlight burst full through the clouds, illuminating the blade in a shower of silver light and the pair was gone.

Merlin turned and smiled at the men staring at the empty space where the lovers had been an instant before. "That was magic," Merlin said. "Sometimes it works."

Yank looked up at the ancient, his face forming a painting of a lost boy. "We'll never see them again? Ever?"

"You're a knight, now, Sir Bill," Merlin said, tapping Cooper lightly on the shoulders with his staff. "You must rely on yourself, as you have learned to do. But if you want to see them, you must go to the cathedral."

The aircraft minister rose from his knees. He looked about in confusion. He looked at the ancient, staring at him with his starlit eyes. He stepped toward Merlin, reaching, as if to take hold of his staff.

"Merlin!" the old man cried, but he grasped empty air, and looked up to see the large, black wings of a great raven ascending toward the moon.

*   *   *

The attacks on London relented. Hitler postponed his cross-Channel invasion of Britain, at first for the rest of the year. Then forever. The RAF got its breathing space, and Bill Cooper got a twenty-four- hour pass. There was snow in the air, and Christmas was coming. The countryside held the aroma of chestnuts and old pages from Dickens. The bombing fell off, then relented.

Yank steered the BSA motorcycle through the twisted streets of Coventry, speeding past the marketplace, the bridges and the squares. There was rubble everywhere still in the city center. But there was also the straightforward, plodding activity of renewal. He eased the throttle on the motorcycle, parked it next to a twisted street lamp and pressed his chewing gum under the seat for luck.

He dismounted and walked toward the ruin of the cathedral, looking up at the points and facings of the hollowed, bombed walls of the church. What remained was nearly as awesome as what had stood before. The steep walls, sharp in relief against the cold, gray sky, stood defiant as Britain.

Bill Cooper walked through the remains of the crumbled entryway and scanned the quarter-mile of rubble from the nave to the apse. The Germans had blasted every arch and brought down the ceiling. In a stark fit of destructive power, the cathedral was laid naked to the sky. Still, it was magnificent in its desolation.

Yank walked the length of the center aisle, watching an ordnance team tap away at an unexploded bomb whose fins with the pentragram symbol painted on them pointed up from the rubble. Yank heard the screw turn on the fuse, and the metal chink of the arming pin fall on the stones. A loud sigh from the EOD men, and they all lit a cigarette. Two matches for three men. No bad luck.

Yank walked past the tumbled mounds of stone and stared up at the stained glass window that reached to the sky. In the design, he saw the finely detailed faces of a king and queen. It was Arthur and Jenny. They gazed at one another across time in the fullness of love with hope for the future. The king and the queen shared the perfect rose. Yank whistled long and low.

The Yank executed a perfect about-face, stuffed his hands in his trousers and marched out of the cathedral whistling "Moonlight Serenade."

The Best in Science Fiction and Fantasy

A FISHERMAN OF THE INLAND SEA by Ursula K. Le Guin. The National Book Award-winning author's first new collection in thirteen years has all the majesty and appeal of her major works. Here we have starships that sail, literally, on wings of song... musical instruments to be played at funerals only...*ansibles* for faster-than-light communication...orbiting arks designed to save a doomed humanity. Astonishing in their diversity and power, Le Guin's new stories exhibit both the artistry of a major writer at the height of her powers, and the humanity of a mature artist confronting the world with her gift of wonder still intact.
Hardcover, 0-06-105200-0 — $19.99

L OVE IN VEIN: TWENTY ORIGINAL TALES OF VAMPIRIC EROTICA, edited by Poppy Z. Brite. An all-original anthology that celebrates the unspeakable intimacies of vampirism, edited by the hottest new dark fantasy writer in contemporary literature. *LOVE IN VEIN* goes beyond our deepest fears and delves into our darkest hungers—the ones even our lovers are forbidden to share. This erotic vampire tribute is not for everyone. But then, neither is the night....
Trade paperback, 0-06-105312-0 — $11.99

A NTI-ICE by Stephen Baxter. From the bestselling author of the award-winning *RAFT* comes a hard-hitting SF thriller that highlights Baxter's unique blend of time travel and interstellar combat. *ANTI-ICE* gets back to SF fundamentals in a tale of discovery and challenge, and a race to success.
0-06-105421-6 — $5.50

Today . . .

HarperPrism

An Imprint of HarperPaperbacks

SMALL GODS by Terry Pratchett. International bestseller Terry Pratchett brings magic to life in his latest romp through Discworld, a land where the unexpected always happens—usually to the nicest people, like Brutha, former melon farmer, now The Chosen One. His only question: Why? **0-06-109217-7 — $4.99**

MAGIC: THE GATHERING™—ARENA by William R. Forstchen. Based on the wildly bestselling trading-card game, the first novel in the *MAGIC: THE GATHERING™* novel series features wizards and warriors clashing in deadly battles. The book also includes an offer for two free, unique MAGIC cards. **0-06-105424-0 — $4.99**

SEAROAD:Chronicles of Klatsand by Ursula K. Le Guin. Here is the culmination of Le Guin's lifelong fascination with small island cultures. In a sense, the Klatsand of these stories is a modern day successor to her bestselling *ALWAYS COMING HOME.* A world apart from our own, but part of it as well. **0-06-105400-3 — $4.99**

CALIBAN'S HOUR by Tad Williams. The bestselling author of *TO GREEN ANGEL TOWER* brings to life a rich and incandescent fantasy tale of passion, betrayal, and death. The beast Caliban has been searching for decades for Miranda, the woman he loved—the woman who was taken from him by her father Prospero. Now that Caliban has found her, he has an hour to tell his tale of unrequited love and dark vengeance. And when the hour is over, Miranda must die.... Tad Williams has reached a new level of magic and emotion with this breathtaking tapestry in which yearning and passion are entwined. **Hardcover, 0-06-105204-3 — $14.99**

and Tomorrow

PR-002